HOUSE of the RISING SUN

Also by Richard Cox

Rift
The God Particle
Thomas World
The Boys of Summer

HOUSE of the RISING SUN

A NOVEL

⊣ RICHARD COX ⊢

Night Shade Books + NEW YORK

Night Shade books may be purchased in bulk at special discounts for sales promotion, corporate gifts, fund-raising, or educational purposes. Special editions can also be created to specifications. For details, contact the Special Sales Department, Night Shade Books, 307 West 36th Street, 11th Floor, New York, NY 10018, or info@skyhorsepublishing.com.

Night Shade Books® is a registered trademark of Skyhorse Publishing, Inc.®, a Delaware corporation.

Visit our website at www.nightshadebooks.com.

10 9 8 7 6 5 4 3 2 1

Library of Congress Cataloging-in-Publication Data is available on file.

ISBN: 978-1-949102-43-7

Cover design by Claudia Noble

Printed in the United States of America

For Richard and Janie Cox

AUTHOR'S NOTE

This novel was already written and had been through several rounds of editing before the virus that causes COVID-19 began to propagate across the globe. As I write this in March 2020, 657,960 cases have been reported worldwide resulting in 30,434 deaths. By the time the book is published, the number of people impacted by the pandemic will have increased by an amount that is tragic and difficult to contemplate.

While the story you're about to read has nothing to do with a virus, there are scenes and themes in the story that resemble the reality we currently face and may still be facing when you read it. But don't expect the characters in these pages to be aware of those similarities: The book was too far into the publication process to begin another rewrite that could capture the context of the pandemic. Also, the events described were meant to take place in 2020, so I have removed references to the current calendar year to avoid confusion.

The major set pieces in this novel tend toward disaster and chaos and confusion, but more importantly the story explores the reactions of ordinary, flawed people to a reality turned upside down. I hope it provides a bit of escape during this surreal time. I hope you and those close to you are safe and healthy.

-RC, 03.28.2020

ACKNOWLEDGMENTS

When I turned eighteen, my dad wanted to buy me a special gift to mark the occasion. Every autumn since I was ten he'd taken me bird hunting, so the gift he had in mind was a shotgun I could call my own.

By then I had been writing short stories for seven years, first in longhand and later on an ancient electric typewriter that produced a hum so powerful I could feel it in my fingertips. The typewriter was a hand-me-down from my grandmother, who for years had written articles for the *Olney Enterprise*. I was a shy kid and never spoke to my parents about writing stories. It did not seem like the kind of industrious work they wanted for their firstborn son: sitting at a desk all day, imagining other worlds.

But even if my parents didn't seem like fans of the liberal arts, they were hardly restrictive when it came to the interests of their children. Not once during my years at home did they forbid me from reading anything, even when I graduated to adult fiction at age twelve.

Still, I was stunned when my dad asked if I would prefer a new typewriter to the shotgun. I couldn't believe he'd noticed all the time I spent writing, and it was even more difficult to picture my salt-of-the-earth father standing in an aisle at Sears, mulling over which typewriter to buy. I accepted the gift and used it to write one bad story after another, applying the fierce determination I inherited from him toward a goal that seemed so distant and farfetched it might as well have been fantasy.

Today I understand my parents were more into the arts than I believed at the time. Every Sunday morning my dad played classical music at thunderous volume on his B&O turntable, and my mom enjoyed the albums of Willie Nelson and Waylon Jennings until she wore the magnetic tape to shreds. As a teenager I pretended to loathe any song my parents loved, especially the "oldies," but there was one exception: "House of the Rising Sun" as performed by The Animals. This favorite of my dad's became one of mine as well, and I wanted to someday write a novel with the same title. I couldn't say what this story would be about, and I wasn't sure how I would ever fit a novel to a pre-determined title, but once the idea planted itself it wouldn't go away.

My dad likes to tell whoever will listen that writing a book seems impossible. He believes my aptitude for it is nothing that could have come from him. But the difference between being an aspiring author and a published one is largely a matter of effort, and I would never have sold one novel (let alone five) without emulating the work ethic I learned at home.

* * *

Just like my others, this novel would not have been published if it weren't for the support and guidance of my friend and agent, Matt Bialer. Oren Eades provided shrewd editorial insight and the project is much better for it. Christine Herman's notes on an early draft proved invaluable.

Also, a special thank you to my wife, Kimberly, for her patience while I worked on this story for what seemed like forever ("Just get to the DC already!"). I'm proud to be your husband. And to Dillan and Milou, my two precious daughters, for sleeping late on weekends. It's a privilege every day to be your father. Also thanks to everyone who read this story while it was still a manuscript.

And anyone who purchases the book or checks it out from the library.

You guys rock.

HOUSE of the RISING SUN

HOUSE of the
RISING SUN

Interviewer: Are you ready for what's coming?

Blaise Bailey Finnegan III: Ready as I'll ever be.

RISING SUN, FALLING STARS ├

ONE

It must have been a malfunction, a breaker failing to interrupt the powerful current of his self-loathing, that had produced such a dark and unnatural state. Even now, as he washed down the last of the Xanax with a deep swallow of Jack Daniels, Seth could not ignore the relentless and magnetic pull of survival. It seemed to originate from all bearings, but most noticeably from the direction of the car door, which he imagined was speaking to him. *Open me*, the door seemed to whisper. *Don't be selfish.*

But as powerful as it was, the instinct to survive was being overridden by an even mightier force: compulsion. For as long as he could remember, Seth had been ruled by the desire to satisfy whatever cravings were most insistent at any moment in time, no matter the cost to himself or those he loved. It was probably ironic how the same compulsion that had driven him into this dark place would now stop him from saving himself, but Seth was not the kind of thinker who could place his actions into a broader context. He was beholden, simply, uncritically, to his impulses.

Seth had always been ashamed of this weakness and had long waited for the moment when his moral debt would be called in. Even as a child he carried dread around with him the way other children carried blankets or pillows. He sucked his thumb during the day and at night curled under the covers, resigned to nightmares as eventual as the rising sun. The problem wasn't that he committed shameful acts. The problem was he couldn't stop committing them.

In high school people were amused by the gambling. The Texas 5-A state football playoffs began with 64 teams, and during his freshman year Seth decided to track the bracket on a rectangle of white poster board. His construction was meticulous. He drew it with drafting tools. And once he'd inscribed all the school names in their proper places, Seth showed it to one of his buddies.

Who remarked, innocently enough, *Hey, we could use that to bet with.*

To that point he'd never been a popular kid, but when word got out about the bracket it seemed like everyone knew Seth's name. Coaches played, teachers played, and what seemed like half the student body. The success of this gambling operation even impressed his father, which was more rewarding than newfound fame at school. Smaller and less accomplished than his older brother, not pretty like his little sister, Seth felt unspecial and largely ignored. The rare smile on his father's face was an endorsement Seth never expected but was ecstatic to have earned...even if that smile was now a distant memory.

Had there been any way out of this despair, any lever to pull, he would have done it. Every night he prayed and begged for forgiveness. Every day he imagined a miraculous, last-minute reprieve from his suffering, from the burden of his debt. He pictured this absolution as a lightning bolt from the sky, as divine intervention, but his prayers went unanswered. Seth was down to his last chip. He'd placed it on the table.

And now he waited, terrified, for the dealer to collect his bet.

* * *

Over the years Seth had become an expert at masking the electronic trail of his gambling exploits. After Natalie climbed into bed, he pretended to pay bills and review their investment portfolio, but his real business was to research players and coaches and stadiums, to manage bets and record final scores. He tracked the family's actual revenues and expenditures in a secret clone of their Quicken account, and at the end of every research session he surgically erased all evidence of these maneuvers from his Internet browsing history. Despite this vigilance, Seth lived in fear of being exposed, and when it finally happened the scene was worse than he ever imagined.

Was it already five days? Almost a week since Natalie sent the boys to bed and sat down with a bottle of wine to watch *The Hunger Games*? In predictable fashion, Seth had misinterpreted her intentions, especially when she opened a second bottle and disappeared in the direction of the bedroom. Eventually he followed her, expecting Natalie to be waiting for him under the covers, but the only visible light in that end of the house was shining in their office. He found her half-empty bottle of wine standing next to the glowing white rectangle of the computer, and whether she had forgotten to close her email or intentionally left it for him to find, Seth didn't know. The important thing was life as he understood it was over.

> Natalie,
> You've got to tell him what happened. I know this isn't easy but the longer you let it fester the worse you're going to feel. By now I'm sure he can tell something is bothering you.
> Let me know how it goes.
> -T

For a moment Seth stood there, unmoving, as if the reality of this message had sewn him to the floor. The idea of Natalie cheating on him after all the sacrifices he'd made for her and the boys was impossible to accept. Still, *You've got to confront him* and *Just tell him what happened* left little room for doubt about her behavior. Possibly worse than those damning phrases was the way her lover had signed his message. A single initial conveyed familiarity. Confidence. Intimacy.

Seth ground his teeth with such force he could hear them screeching. His pulse throbbed in his eyes. How could Natalie do this to him? He loved every atom in that woman's body! He loved her hiccuppy laugh and her cobalt blue eyes and the way she cried in front of the closet when she couldn't find anything to wear. He had sacrificed everything for her. Everything!

According to the message header, the sender was some jerk named Thomas Phillips. And it was obvious Natalie had attempted to hide her correspondence with him, because there were no other messages from Thomas in her inbox. Eventually Seth reopened the offending email and scrolled farther down, where he discovered a note from Natalie that had prompted Thomas' response. Sent two days earlier, it read:

> Thomas,
> Seth is "away on business" again, so I drank a bottle of white wine and finally got the nerve to call JJ. Figured Seth would be there with her, but no one answered, and there wasn't even a greeting on her voicemail. I just can't believe he would hide money from me to spend on her! It makes me so angry I can't see straight!
> Nat

Seth read this message three times before he finally accepted what the text seemed to imply: Natalie believed *he* was cheating, that he'd been with a woman named JJ two days prior. But two days before this he'd been in New Orleans, trying desperately to assemble a winning streak at the craps table. He'd gotten so drunk that night he couldn't remember how he made it back to his suite.

And JJ wasn't a woman. He was a bookie, and Seth owed him more than two hundred thousand dollars.

The automatic response was to lash out at Natalie, to accuse her of retaliating against infidelity that had never happened. But just because he wasn't sleeping with someone else didn't mean she was wrong about him. Only instead of falling into the arms of another woman, Seth had betrayed his wife by gambling away an inconceivable amount of money. Any day now Seth was going to open his door and find one of Jimmy's strong-armed friends standing there, or else the bank would show up and lock the doors to their house. He'd gambled away his family's security like so many poker chips and there was nothing more he could do to get it back.

Even if he confessed his shameful addiction, and even if Natalie somehow forgave him, the next step would be to extricate the family from financial ruin. But how? Austerity wouldn't help, not when much of the debt was owed was to a man unburdened by collection laws, so Natalie would suggest they borrow money from his father. The elder Black had retired a millionaire three times over, incurred few expenditures, and carried no liens of any kind.

But even this live-saving option was unavailable. Partly because his father was a stingy bastard, but mainly because Seth had already taken what he should have asked for long ago.

The first time he borrowed from his father's retirement account, Seth swore he would put the money back. The old man kept his passwords handy on a sticky note glued to the monitor, and one afternoon last summer, while his father napped in front of the television, Seth crept into his office and logged into the computer. In minutes he had liquidated enough stock to replenish the twins' college savings accounts and stake himself for another run. With that money he planned to win enough to pay back his father's unknowing investment and quit gambling forever.

But that's not what happened. What happened was he lost the borrowed money and was forced to take more. By now the evidence was impossible to hide, and eventually his father would discover he had unwittingly loaned his second son $704,525. Combined with his debt to Jimmy and the various credit cards that were maxed to their limits, Seth's total burden had grown to more than a million dollars.

He understood how impossible his actions would seem to someone who wasn't him. There was no possible way to convey the darkness he'd carried for as long as he could remember, or that the only way he knew to neutralize his pain was to risk the love and security of those he loved most in all the world.

He was a broken human being. Worthless. He didn't deserve Natalie's forgiveness, and anyway she didn't deserve to be asked for it.

* * *

It seemed obvious insurance wouldn't pay if you took your own life, but in the fine print of his policy he discovered a surprise: the suicide clause. As long as Seth didn't kill himself during the first two years of coverage, the policy paid no matter how he died. By now he was well past the time limit, and the benefit would be nearly $600,000. Even if this wasn't enough to cover all his debts, it was enough to pay Jimmy and satisfy their mortgage. And he didn't think his father would come after Natalie once Seth was gone. The old man could be a real jerk, but he was a lot friendlier if you weren't his middle child.

Still, what if some hotshot adjuster trying to make bonus found a way to deny Seth's claim? If he wanted to truly insulate his wife, Seth required insurance against his insurance, and that's where Thomas Phillips entered the picture. Surely a jackass brazen enough to fuck another man's wife would be compelled by guilt to shield her from the claws of a small-time mobster.

Eventually the only step left in his grand plan was the suicide itself. And because he was too frightened to use a gun, or jump from a great height, Seth was left with poison. But an overdose of prescription pills might leave him brain damaged but alive. And after watching a YouTube video of a criminal investment banker writhing in agony on a court-room floor, the idea of death by cyanide went out the window as well.

That left him carbon monoxide, which was easy to arrange once he learned how to disable his Acura's catalytic converter. You could learn all sorts of interesting things on YouTube if you knew where to look.

So here Seth was, on a sunny Friday morning, hands resting on his soft beer gut, thumbing through pictures of Ben and Brandon and Natalie on his phone, ears listening to the low rumble of his damaged engine exhaust. He'd chosen to die in a Dallas Cowboys T-shirt and a pair of khaki cargo shorts, and every so often he took another drink of whiskey. Drugging himself was the only way he would get through this, and even then he wasn't sure he would make it. He wanted to drive to the daycare and see his boys in person, hug them again, hold them tight and promise nothing bad would ever happen to them. He wanted to kiss Natalie one more time.

Over and over Seth had watched the video of Michael Marin swal-lowing capsules of cyanide when his guilty verdict was announced. Drowning in debt, Marin had been caught trying to burn down his own house to generate an insurance payout, and courtroom cameras happened to capture his response. Sometimes Seth watched the video one frame at a time to better scrutinize a face that was flush with the reality of impending doom. Marin had contemplated darkness while monotone voices orchestrated the minutiae of a prison sentence that would never be carried out, and the look in his eyes still haunted Seth. It was the gaze of a man who had stepped into the infinity of nothing, who was forced to endure moment after horrifying moment as poison strangled cells by the billions. In all, seven long minutes elapsed before

Marin's body finally succumbed to the cyanide, and Seth had a pretty good idea what had been going through the guy's mind:

Nothing in death could be worse than a wasted life.

Two hundred and fifty miles to the south, as the morning sun climbed into a cloudless sky, Thomas Phillips was on his way to meet actress Skylar Stover at Dallas/Fort Worth International Airport. Yet so far this exercise had been plagued by problems. His iPhone refused to download new messages (The mail server at imap.gmail.com is not responding), and all the way to the airport on crowded freeways he found himself trapped behind morons who intentionally clogged the leftmost lanes to enforce impractical speed limits.

The real source of his anxiety, though, was the actress herself. Skylar Stover was a worldwide celebrity attached to his second picture who wanted to discuss possible changes to the script and her character in particular. Thomas should have been floored by her interest, by her willingness to stop in Dallas on her way to L.A., since by any reasonable measure she was one of the most alluring women in Hollywood and honestly the entire planet of women. If her turn as a disaffected college student in the acclaimed *Life . . . Unexpected* hadn't won over every human male on the earth, her blonde hair extensions and ample cleavage in the action thriller *Darkest Energy* surely had. In fact, when his agent first told him about the requested meeting, Thomas assumed he was joking.

The project in question was *The Pulse,* a post-apocalyptic story so brutal it had frightened him even as he wrote it. But now that the film had been greenlit (primarily because Skylar was attached to it) her power over the project vastly exceeded his own. Which wasn't the worst outcome Thomas could imagine. Skylar had studied philosophy at Yale. She was one of a few actors who could bounce between independent films and glossy comic-book thrillers and somehow remain both credible and bankable. Depending on the project, she was paid scale or eight figures, and her compact, buxom figure was the standard by which other women were judged. Thomas was nervous as hell to meet her.

All morning he'd been deliberating on how to demonstrate respect for Skylar without appearing too earnest. Thomas had been paid a staggering $6 million for the screenplay, which compelled the trades to label him "Scribe of the Moment," but no amount of money or favorable press could overcome Skylar's towering influence in the film industry. Which meant the only way to keep her fingerprints off the script would be to earn her respect, and the way to do that, Thomas felt sure, was to impress her with his wit and charm and intelligence. Easier said than done.

Eventually his phone connected to Gmail, and a few minutes later he was standing in a special terminal designated for chartered flights, feeling out of place. Several women had gathered in front of an elevator door and kept looking at Thomas as if they should know who he was. He resisted the urge to look at his phone again and tried to imagine the scene of their meeting. He would shake hands with Skylar. Introduce himself. And then what? Thank her for agreeing to star in the film? He didn't want to come across as a fan. This was his idea, after all. His story. And still he didn't understand why she had bothered to come all this way to talk to him in person. The only reason that seemed to make any sense was that she wanted to take the plot in a different direction, that she planned to hire another writer. She was here to break the news to him gently. That had to be it. Anything else could have been handled through email.

Then the elevator doors opened and chattering flight attendants parted like a Biblical sea. Skylar looked smaller than he had imagined. Thinner. Her eyes were a bug's eyes, black and round, at least until she flipped a pair of sunglasses over her forehead and used them to pin back her thick, blonde hair. By the time she reached Thomas, he could see her actual eyes were human-sized and an electric shade of green.

"Thomas!" she said and threw her arms around him. Her hair was shoulder length and smelled vaguely of coconut. Her skin was soft. Her arms were toned but feminine. Everything about her was feminine.

"It's so good to finally meet you," said Skylar. "*Thomas World* was awesome. And I have some ideas for this new project I hope you'll really like. If you're open to that sort of thing, I mean."

Their encounter had begun so differently from what Thomas expected that his only answer was a burst of nervous laughter. He realized he was smiling at her. And not a confident smile, either, but an earnest, goofy grin that would send exactly the opposite message he hoped to convey.

"I'm glad to meet *you*, Skylar. I honestly couldn't believe it when you agreed to do the film. Your talent and screen presence will—"

"Don't do that. Don't blow that industry sunshine up my ass. And please don't call me Skylar, either."

"No?"

"Call me 'Sky.' Everyone does."

"Sky?"

"That's me."

It was strange how the world worked. Two years ago, Thomas had agreed to end a marriage that had never been a real marriage in the first place. He spent his days toiling in a cubicle and his nights alone, agonizing over past relationships and what had gone wrong with them. Naturally Thomas assumed the problems were his, because everything he touched turned to shit—including his own screenwriting career. But then one evening, while he sat drunk in front of his computer, a story idea so basic and absurd occurred to him that he couldn't help but open Final Draft and start banging away. Six hours later he'd written twenty-five pages and felt energized in a way he hadn't known in years. He slept until noon, got up to write again, and by midnight had completed *Thomas World*, the story of a man so unhappy with life that he built an improved reality inside his computer. On first read, Thomas realized he'd written a screenplay transparently about himself, had saddled the protagonist with his own problems and burdened him with the dreams he had chased for years. It was the sort of amateur exercise that should never have been exposed to the outside world, but instead of burying the document in an archive folder, he got drunk again and emailed it to his agent. The next morning, as Thomas suffered under the hot glare of a hangover, his agent called to say how much he loved the script. He loved it so much he got four producers to feel the same way, each who tried to outbid the other until the property sold for an even three million dollars. Eighteen months later the completed film was branded the "thinking person's thriller" about "an ordinary man in extraordinary circumstances," and went on to become the second-highest grossing movie of the year. His agent had leveraged the equity of that success to sell *The Pulse*, and now Skylar Stover wanted him to call her Sky, and the whole scene felt unstable. Like any minute he would wake up and find himself in front of the computer, having awakened from a two-year dream.

"Well," Thomas finally said. "Now we need to figure out where to pick up your luggage. Then we'll get out of this airport and find some breakfast. Hungry?"

Sky was repositioning a backpack on her shoulders.

"Starving. But I have to run to the ladies' room first. And anyway I have this form that tells me where to go for the luggage. So if you can wait a short minute, I'll just run in here and do my thing, and then we'll get my bags. And then some B. Man, I am *starving*. I never eat on planes unless it's overseas, but now I wish I had nibbled on one of those bagels. *Not* smart."

Sky disappeared into the bathroom along with her electric magnetism. If this was how she behaved with everyone, it was no wonder she was so goddamned famous. Even a blind person would be drawn to her.

To clear his head, Thomas pulled out his iPhone, reflexively clicked on Apple News, and scrolled through the list of stories.

Markets panic as Trump tweets gibberish again
Scientists concerned about supernova after neutrino detectors go haywire
Juan de Fuca could trigger "deadly tsunami"

Being connected to every facet of his electronic life had turned him into the same kind of over-dependent technology snob he'd poked fun at in *Thomas World*. Before smartphones, he could go hours, sometimes an entire weekend, without watching the news or reading email. Now even five minutes seemed too long to wait.

He switched to mail and saw this:

Dick McClaren   9:56 AM
Get BIGGER with PROMO

Overfat, M.D.   9:44 AM
Lose more weight with this ONE weird trick

Seth Black   9:39 AM
Time to pay up, wife-fucker

Thomas swiped the first two messages away and his thumb was on the third when he realized something was terribly wrong. Seth Black could be no one but Natalie Black's husband. And "wife-fucker," well, that made no sense at all.

Six weeks ago, Thomas had spoken to Natalie for the first time since high school, an encounter occasioned by their twenty-year reunion. Over the course of a surreal, drunken weekend, Natalie had unloaded a burden she clearly had been carrying far too long. Thomas listened to the story of Seth's infidelity and offered as much support as he could, even via email in the weeks after the reunion. But there was little anyone could do until Natalie confronted the situation directly, which thus far she had been reluctant to do.

The accusation of adultery was mystifying and a little frightening. He nervously opened the message and saw this:

Dear Mr Phillips,
I don't even know where to start. Thanks a lot for fucking my wife. Even if she came onto you, you didn't have to accept. She's a married woman.

Thomas looked up to find bustling passengers and bored flight attendants and a smiling pilot who tipped his hat to Thomas as he rolled by with a pet suitcase. He didn't want to look at the phone again. Any moment Skylar would step out of the bathroom and Natalie's angry husband was the last thing he wanted on his mind.

Anyway, I need to ask you a favor and I expect you to honor it considering what you . . .

"All ready?" asked Sky, who had materialized next to him.

"Uh, sure. Let's go get your bags."

"Everything okay? You're looking at your phone like it just bit you."

Thomas shoved the phone into his pocket. It was obvious now he should never have corresponded with Natalie after the reunion. Even when your intentions were pure, it was always a bad idea to insert yourself into someone else's marriage.

"Sorry," he said. "Personal thing."

Sky giggled and hooked her arm through his.

"I know this visit is totally last minute. Don't feel like you have to babysit me. We've got all weekend to talk shop, right?"

Thomas looked over at Sky and was again struck by her eyes. He'd believed them at first to be green, but now he could see blue in them as well, which produced a color not unlike tropical ocean water. Under other circumstances he would not have been able to stop thinking about eyes like that. Skylar was by far the most beautiful woman he'd ever seen in person, and she was looking at him as if he were the best thing that had happened to her in weeks.

"We do have all weekend," he said. "By the time we're done, the screenplay will have Oscar written all over it."

"I can't fucking *wait*, Tommy. Can I call you Tommy?"

"Not if you expect me to answer."

"We'll see about that. This is going to be a weekend to remember, Tommy. Mark my words."

Thomas did mark them, so to speak, and often thought of them later. How prophetic they had seemed, even as she uttered them.

After all, those words were the kind of scene-ending dialogue he might have written himself.

* * *

In a nearby office they found Sky's luggage, an expensive-looking black suitcase and a smaller pink bag embroidered with the Hello Kitty logo.

Thomas knew he wouldn't be able to stop thinking about Seth's email until he read the rest of it.

"Let me go get the car," he said as they approached the exit. "I'll pull up to the door and—"

"I'm not fragile cargo," Sky replied. "I can walk, at least if you slow down a little. What's the rush?"

"Sorry. If you want to wait here, I can just get the—"

"I'll walk with you."

"But people are going to recognize you."

"It's happened before, you know."

"Right. Okay."

She smiled and kissed him on the cheek. Thomas stood there feeling ridiculous.

"So let's go!" Sky told him.

She pulled the sunglasses over her eyes and they strode toward the door. At first no one noticed them, but outside the terminal, on the sidewalk, a teenaged girl was waiting at the shuttle stop. Her jaw fell visibly open as the two of them approached.

"Oh my God! You're Skylar Stover!"

Sky smiled and lifted her sunglasses. "I am! What's your name?"

"*My* name? I'm Dillan Johnson. But you're Skylar Stover! Holy shit, will you take a selfie with me?"

A nearby elderly couple, also waiting for a shuttle, pretended not to notice.

"Of course I will." Sky stood her suitcase on the sidewalk and put her arm around the girl. "You're going to be a hit on Instagram."

The girl's response was an unintelligible screech.

Eventually Thomas realized there was time during this transaction to retrieve his phone. He switched on the display, where Seth's email still waited.

. . .I expect you to honor it considering what you did. I did some Googling and figured out your a rich screenwriter. Whoopdy fuckin do! Guess what I am? A million dollars in debt! Most of it is to my dad but $213 grand is to a bookie in Dallas. Which happens to be where you live, lucky me. My insurance policy should take care of all this but just in case they screw me over I want you to . . .

"Tommy?"

Sky was tugging on his arm.

"You ready?"

The look in her eyes was not impatience, as he might have imagined, but excitement. By now there was no way to take her manner with him as anything but flirtatious, which Thomas found in equal parts flattering and impossible to believe.

Still, his mind kept going back to Seth's email, back to gambling debts and a bookie and an insurance policy. How did you redeem a large insurance policy other than—

Skylar tugged on the sleeve of his shirt.

"Which way is your car?"

"It's, um, this way. Follow me."

He directed her across the street and into the amber darkness of a parking garage.

"Is everything okay?" Sky asked.

"I think so. My car is down here at the end. But I'm going to check something real quick if you don't mind."

"No worries. Just don't leave me in the dust. I'm doing my best to keep up."

As they walked toward his car, Thomas looked down at his phone and found the message again.

. . .I want you to pay off this bookie. His name is Jimmy Jameson. His contact info is below. It's a lot of money for me but it's nothing for a rich Hollywood guy like you. Consider it payment for fucking my wife.

Here's another thing: You should probably come here and take care of Natalie and my boys. They're gonna need help after I'm gone. Why not get married? You can be one big happy family! Move Nat to L.A. so she can be a celebrity. It's what she's always wanted. I could never satisfy her champagyne taste.

You must know where we live but in case you don't have the address I put it below too.

Have a nice fucking life. I'm ending mine now.

All at once Thomas couldn't feel his hands. The phone slipped from his grasp and clattered to the concrete floor of the garage. When he picked it up, he saw the screen had shattered, glass forking into jagged shapes as if split by lightning.

"Shit."

"Oh, no," said Skylar. "Don't tell me your phone went to meet its maker."

They reached his car, a '68 Ford Mustang Shelby convertible, cherry red, painstakingly restored. He'd brought it to impress Skylar. He felt like an idiot.

"It's not the phone," Thomas muttered, and tossed her bags into the rear seat. When he opened the passenger door and scooted Sky inside, she'd finally had enough.

"Thomas!"

A few seconds later he was behind the wheel. The engine roared like a jet.

"We have to go. I need to think. Fuck."

He backed out of the parking spot and steered quickly for the exit.

"Will you please tell me what the hell is going on?"

"Natalie's husband just sent me an email. Sounds like he's going to kill himself."

* * *

Compared to the low ceiling of the parking garage, the sky looked enormous, blue and empty except for the rising sun. While Thomas squinted through a spider web of cracks to find Natalie's number, Skylar fidgeted in the seat next to him.

"Who's Natalie?"

"This woman I know from high school."

"And you think her husband is going to kill himself."

"That's what he said in an email he just sent."

"He emailed that? To you?"

Finally, Thomas had Natalie's name in front of him. He put the call through and waited for the phone to ring. By now he was on the airport access road, six lanes wide, built like a freeway. Traffic was steady but not bumper-to-bumper. He wished he hadn't left the top down, because wind noise overpowered the phone speaker.

Voice mail answered.

"Natalie. You need to call your husband. Like right now. He just sent me an email. It sounded like a suicide note. Someone needs to check on him right away. It's ten o'clock on Friday morning."

All at once Natalie's problems came into clearer focus. If what Seth said was true, his extended time away from home and any missing money was not related to a mistress named JJ but a gambling problem and a bookie named Jimmy Jameson. Seth was overwhelmed by debt and not thinking clearly. Thomas hoped Natalie was already on the phone with him.

Sky was waiting to hear more, but since Thomas wasn't sure where to begin he looked back at Seth's email again. He noticed there was an auto signature at the bottom. There was a cell number in the signature.

"Dude," Sky finally said. "I don't want to butt into your personal business, but if some guy is threatening suicide, you need to call the police. Like 9-1-1. Voice mail isn't enough."

"What if I call the guy directly?"

"You have his number?"

"It's at the bottom of this email."

"Then, yes! Call him now!"

The telephone number was a hyperlink, but if Thomas were honest with himself, he was hoping no one would answer. He wanted Seth to have already thought better of his plan and aborted.

The phone rang. Then rang again. And again. And again. And—

"Hello?" asked a raspy, broken voice. "Who is this?"

"Seth?"

"Whoever you are, your timing is improbable."

"Seth, it's Thomas.

A long stretch of silence passed while Thomas piloted the car and glanced at Skylar, whose aqua eyes were wide and concerned. He had never imagined his encounter with her would begin like this.

"Dude," Seth said in a weak voice, "I told you everything you need to know. Can't you just let me be done with it?"

"Don't do it!" shouted Thomas, surprised at the sudden empathy he felt for this man he'd never met. "I can help you. You don't need to do this."

"Help me with what?"

"With money! With whatever you need."

"If this is about money," Skylar offered loudly, "I'll help, too."

"Who is that?" grunted Seth. He sounded lethargic, like he'd woken from a deep sleep.

"We just want to help you. You don't need insurance. You don't—"

"It doesn't matter. Even if you paid every last dime of my debt, I still have to live with what I've done. And I can't. I won't. It's too late."

"It's never too late, Seth. Let me help you."

"Just come here when it's over. Please."

"Seth."

"Promise me, man. Promise me you'll come here and take care of my family. Please."

Seth was crying. His voice was hoarse, and he coughed as if his lungs were failing him.

"Please, man. Promise me."

"I promise, Seth. Just stop and I'll do whatever you want."

Now there was no answer.

"Seth?"

Thomas pressed the phone to his ear, trying to dampen the sound of the wind, but it was no use. Eventually he looked at the display again and saw it was dark. He swiped and tapped the screen, but nothing happened.

"Thomas, look out!"

He glanced up and saw he was about to rear-end a white Ford sedan that was either slowing down or stopped. He quickly checked his mirrors and veered into an adjacent lane. Jammed his hand on the horn.

"What the hell is wrong with you?" he yelled involuntarily. "This is a highway!"

"Thomas, again!"

He looked back at the road and saw they were rapidly gaining on a black pickup truck rolling on four enormous tires. Thomas changed lanes, sliding just past the truck and the noise of its monster tread.

"What the hell is going on?" he yelled.

"I don't know, but something is weird. All the cars are slowing down. Look over there. It's the same thing on both sides of the road."

Skylar was right. Everyone was slowing down, but no one seemed to be using their brakes. Well, wait. In the far-right lane, about fifty yards ahead of them, a small car came to a screeching stop and Thomas heard the dull thunk of bumper-to-bumper contact.

"He totally hit that truck!" Sky yelled. "Why is everyone stopping?"

Thomas had slowed down and was switching lanes almost continuously as vehicles around him came to rest. When he looked briefly at Skylar, he saw something in the sky above her, something so odd and unexpected that he could hardly make sense of it.

People were beginning to climb out of their vehicles. Others stood in the road, gawking at the sky. Thomas moved toward the inner shoulder, trying to divine a clear path, but other drivers were having the same idea. Ahead, a woman stood beside a giant Lexus SUV and gestured to him.

"Skylar," he said. "Look in the sky on your right."

Thomas was rapidly approaching the woman on the shoulder. She was tall and thin, wearing a yellow sundress and flip flops. Maybe thirty-five years old.

"What is that?" Sky asked.

"Looks like a star, doesn't it?"

"Yeah...except you don't usually see stars during the day."

They reached the woman in the sundress. She approached the driver's side door. Her face was drained of color.

"Excuse me, sir. Do you know what's happened?"

"I'm not sure. But I would guess it had something to do with that."

Thomas gestured toward the new point of light in the sky, which was twenty or so degrees above the horizon, brilliant and white. It was bigger and brighter than any nighttime star but much smaller than the sun, which was almost directly above it. In different circumstances, like if he had been on his back porch, looking at it over the lake, the new star might have been the most amazing thing Thomas had ever seen. Instead, Natalie's husband was trying to kill himself and the airport freeway was a war zone and the whole world seemed to have lost its mind. No vehicle was operational except his and people were noticing. Especially because, aside from the rumble of his engine exhaust, the airport was quiet. Eerily quiet. Nothing else mechanical was running.

Nothing.

The woman's face was slack, her mouth wide open. She seemed to be holding back tears. Next to him, Skylar whispered words he couldn't hear.

Something was terribly wrong about the silence. It was never quiet on this road, ever, not even in the middle of the night, because D/FW was one of the busiest airports in the world. The sound of jet engines and traffic was so ubiquitous you never even noticed it.

Until it wasn't there at all.

"I'm sorry," he said to the woman. "We have to go."

Thomas inched his car forward. The woman's eyes widened.

"Wait! Can you help me? I'm stuck here."

Thomas kept driving, watching the stalled cars carefully. He picked up speed. Changed lanes often.

"Don't you think we should have helped that woman?" Sky asked.

"Help her do what?"

"I don't know. Get home. Something."

"We only have so much room. We can't take them all."

Thomas realized why his car worked and the others didn't. Honestly, he'd known it all along.

In his new screenplay, the one Skylar was here to discuss, he'd written about an apocalyptic event known as an electromagnetic pulse. The eponymous pulse in his story was the byproduct of a massive solar flare and had rendered useless every electronic device on Earth. The way this happened was technical in nature, but easy enough to summarize: Transistors and microchips and power transformers were fried by intense electromagnetic radiation, and anything that relied on them was rendered useless. Like for instance the entire power grid and just about every vehicle built since the 1970s.

His acquisition of the vintage Mustang, therefore, was no accident. He loved to drive it, but the reason Thomas had even considered a classic vehicle was because research for *The Pulse* had frightened him. In a world without power, without daily deliveries of food into large cities, chaos would erupt almost immediately, and a working car could mean the difference between life and death.

He'd never expected such an event to occur, at least not of the magnitude he'd written about in *The Pulse*, and maybe this was not that. Maybe the new object in the sky had generated a temporary disruption that would soon be over. But if the event was not temporary and the effect was anything like what he feared, it was imperative to push them as far away from the airport as possible.

But it was already too late. Thomas had driven maybe a hundred more yards when he heard it, the whining roar of a plane in uncontrolled descent. He looked in the direction of the sound just in time to see a sprawling, bubbling cloud of orange and black. The impact was maybe a half mile away. The shock wave arrived a moment later, louder than anything Thomas had ever heard, the sound so deep it hummed in his bones. Heat swirled around the car, a searing wind choked with the heavy smell of fuel.

Sky was crying. Screaming. People were climbing back into their cars. They were running away from the blast. Thomas drove as fast as he safely could, watching the fireball recede into the distance, but he knew they weren't safe yet. How many planes circled the airport at any one time, waiting to land? Five? Ten? Fifty?

"Oh my God, Thomas. Oh my God. Is this because your car is old? Is that why it's still running?"

"Should we stop?" he asked her. "Pick up someone? I could fit a couple of people in the back seat."

"I don't know! Maybe? I don't know!"

Thomas reached into her lap and used his free hand to grab hers.

"Skylar, I'll get us out of here. It'll be okay. Trust me. I'll get us to a safe—"

Before he could finish, another plane hit, just as close, somewhere behind them. The reflection of the fireball covered the entire surface of his rearview mirror. The heat was a hand that pushed them roughly forward. The air itself seemed to be on fire, shimmering and bubbling in front of him. Thomas kept driving. He tried to keep his eyes on the road, ignore the fireball, but it was impossible not to look at it.

The plane had landed on the highway in roughly the same spot where he'd spoken to the woman with the SUV. The woman who was dead now.

Skylar was still screaming.

"Don't stop! I'm sorry but if we stop we might die!"

Thomas drove faster. People were fleeing on foot. They veered into the grassy median and were running north, away from the airport. They were children, mothers, teenagers in football jerseys. Thomas saw a man in an expensive-looking suit slip and fall headfirst, spilling the contents of his briefcase into the grass. Incredibly, the man stopped to gather scattering sheets of paper as people streamed around him. Thomas felt an instinctive need to pull over and help someone, like maybe the elderly couple that was struggling to make progress in the crowded median. But he couldn't stop now. The car would be swarmed by helpless people trying to flee the airport. If he stopped here, they'd never get going again.

A few seconds later, another plane hit, farther away. Then another one, closer again, a massive explosion that dwarfed all previous impacts.

"Oh my God, Thomas! Oh my God!"

"I think that one hit the terminal. Imagine all the planes parked there, the fuel trucks..."

"Can we get to your house? Is that where you're headed?"

"Yes. I think we can make it there. As long as the roads aren't blocked."

"Thomas," Sky finally said. "This...this is just like your screenplay, isn't it? Your car is still running because there aren't any computers in it."

He nodded. "The pulse must have come from that thing in the sky. I'm not sure but I think it might be a supernova. I read about them during my research, but they don't happen very often. Everyone assumed if an EMP got us it would be a solar flare or a nuclear strike."

"So that means everything is off? Power. Cars. Phones. The Internet."

"Hopefully not. Maybe it's not as bad as we think."

Another plane hit then, this one to their southeast, a couple of miles away. Within seconds, a giant plume of smoke rose above the tree line, and now the entire southern sky behind them was apocalyptic. The horizon itself seemed consumed by fire.

"It looks pretty bad, Thomas."

THREE

It had occurred to Natalie Black only recently that she'd wasted too much of her life relying on men. And it was no secret why. Her father, a strong, old-world patriarch, had ensured the women in his life never wanted for anything, so when lung cancer took him before Natalie could finish college, she felt as if she was left floating in space, untethered from reality. At that point she'd been dating Dan only three months. He was a gorgeous, wealthy kid with confidence to burn, and it wasn't long before she pressured him into a short engagement and an even shorter, disastrous marriage.

The experience with Dan had opened her eyes to a different kind of man, one who might not be handsome on the outside, or even confident, but who would direct his energy toward loving her deeply. It was this niche Seth had leveraged to win her heart, and for many years she had enjoyed stability that reminded her of her father. When the twins were born, and Seth found a way to let her stay home full-time, Natalie realized she was finally living the life she'd always dreamed of as a little girl.

But that long run of peace was over. By the time Natalie summoned the nerve to snoop through Seth's phone, she realized it had been over for some time, and once again a man she trusted had played her for the fool.

She wasn't proud of her actions with the phone, but at least she finally had proof of his infidelity. Because surely if "JJ" were one of his male friends there would have been other natural details of the relationship, like text messages or posts on Facebook, or maybe Seth could have said something to her about it. Instead, he had never breathed a word about anyone named JJ, even though this person (this woman) had been calling him repeatedly for days.

All this was made more annoying by how jealous Seth had recently become about Colin Scott, her manager at the nonprofit. He was convinced Natalie was attracted to Colin, that rather than perform any actual volunteer work she spent all day flirting with him. And while Seth's suspicions were mostly unfounded (her tiny crush on Colin lasted all of two seconds and was completely harmless), the fund-raising golf tournament complicated her defense.

Colin, after all, was in charge of tournament staffing, and the role he'd given her each year was to pass out free drinks to generous donors of the Deckard Foundation. What the job actually entailed was permitting loudmouthed, poorly dressed idiots to flirt with her and gawk at her boobs.

Natalie had never relished her role as "cart girl" and had always made herself look as plain as possible. Last year she'd worn a baggy white T-shirt and khaki shorts and giant black sunglasses that covered most of her face. But this morning she was dressed in a sleeveless pink top and cute plaid skirt and had put on extra mascara. She was tired of feeling unloved and unwanted at home, and if her sexy golf outfit attracted a few extra glances and better tips than normal, wasn't that something she deserved? A little attention?

She had expected Seth, before he left for work, to notice her outfit and maybe accuse her of dressing up for Colin. In fact she'd been hoping for a confrontation that might lead to some truth about JJ. Instead Seth had barely glanced at her, which wasn't a surprise. When her husband was in town, he was either ecstatically happy or dark and sullen and she could never find the courage to mount an offensive against these extremes. Increasingly, though, he'd been traveling for work, and on those days he barely spoke to her at all . . .probably because he was with JJ doing kinky things in a faraway hotel room.

Natalie was on her way to the eleventh hole when her cell phone buzzed. She reached into her purse and glanced at the display and was surprised to see Thomas had called her. She'd given him her number on the last day of the reunion, before she drove home, but in the intervening weeks he'd never bothered to use it. Why would he? She was married, and he was a single, wealthy screenwriter surely interested in younger, hotter women than her.

"Natalie. You need to—"

The message was interrupted then, like it went to dead air, and when Natalie looked down at the screen she saw the phone had turned itself off. When she tried to switch it back on, nothing happened. This made no sense because she'd charged the battery all night specifically so it wouldn't run out during the tournament.

Eventually Natalie reached the eleventh tee and set her phone aside. She was already stepping out of the cart and ready to reach for the beer cooler when she noticed none of the golfers were looking her way. Instead they were all standing near the cart path, facing the same direction, looking at something above the trees. Natalie followed their gaze and saw a star in the morning sky, very bright, sitting below the sun. She'd never seen anything like it and immediately began to worry.

"What is that?" she asked.

An older man turned to face her. He was wearing a red Oklahoma University ball cap and an ancient white golf shirt that was too large for him. He smiled a creepy smile and involuntarily glanced at her boobs.

"I dunno. Maybe a spaceship."

"It ain't a spaceship," said another of the men, who didn't turn around.

"I just saw it," Natalie said. "How long has it been up there?"

"Not long. Twenty or thirty seconds. We were just getting ready to tee off when Blake thought he saw a blue flash in the sky. We figured he was full of shit until we seen that light up there. I'd say it's getting brighter by the minute. Like it's getting closer."

"I can't get my phone to work," she said loudly, hoping one of the others would notice her. "I wonder if that thing messed up the satellites or whatever?"

Finally, another guy pulled a cell phone out of his back pocket and looked at her. He was tall and bookish and wore glasses with thick brown frames.

"Cell phones don't talk to satellites," he said. "They talk to towers. Either way, mine doesn't seem to be working, either."

"Is that bad?"

"I don't know how it would be good. What cell phone company are you with?"

"AT&T."

"I'm on Verizon. So it's not just one. Definitely not good."

Natalie's vague sense of worry was becoming more like dread. Her two sons were in drop-in daycare this morning because school was out. It figured that something terrible would happen on the one day she wasn't home and her boys were in an unfamiliar place.

"You think I should drive to the clubhouse and see what's going on?" she asked. "Maybe it's on the news? I'd like to make sure everything is okay."

"It's definitely not a spaceship," said another golfer in his 40s, who looked bored with the whole thing. "No need to panic."

The younger guy in the glasses was a little more sympathetic.

"Drive up there if you need to," he said. "It's only two holes away and then you won't have to worry."

"Thanks. I'll be back soon if it's no big deal."

"Sounds great. I'm Blake, by the way."

"I'm Natalie."

She climbed back into the cart and was about to leave when the old man walked up to her, smiling again.

"Can we get some beers before you go? If we're gonna be invaded I want a nice buzz while it goes down."

A minute or so later she had finally turned around and was puttering toward the clubhouse. She couldn't imagine a slower vehicle in the world than this drink cart. The clubhouse sat atop a small hill, and as Natalie approached she could see a crowd had gathered outside. Several golf carts were parked there, and ten or twelve people were standing in a rough circle talking. Most of them were looking in the direction of the light in the sky.

In the crowd Natalie found Colin, who smiled when he saw her.

"Can you believe this?" he said in a casual voice, as if cell phone-killing spacecraft appeared on the regular.

"Does anyone know what happened?"

"I don't think so. But everybody is pretty freaked out."

"Does your phone work?" Natalie asked him. "Mine doesn't and I'm worried about my sons."

"Nothing works."

"What do you mean nothing?"

"I was inside on the computer when the power went out. I thought maybe it was a tripped breaker, but then Jeff came running to tell me about that."

He gestured to the point of light, which indeed seemed brighter than a few minutes ago. Just looking at it made Natalie uneasy.

"Anyway," Colin continued, "I came out here and saw that light and figured it must have killed the power. Someone else said they saw a blue flash in the sky. And now the phones won't work. Even the land lines don't work. It's like anything that needs juice is out of commission."

"Colin, I should probably go get my kids. If the power's out at the daycare, they're probably worried sick."

He nodded. "I don't know if we should keep playing or cancel the tournament or what. Hell, I couldn't cancel even if I wanted because the P.A. system is off. I'm sure people will eventually figure out something's wrong and—"

The sound of a golf cart approaching made them both look up. It was Blake, the young guy from before.

"Seems silly to play golf when something like this is going on," he said. "Any word?"

"Colin here told me the power inside the club house doesn't work, phone lines don't work, nothing does."

"What do you mean nothing?"

She was about to elaborate when they were interrupted by a yelling voice on the other side of the clubhouse.

"My car won't start!"

Natalie turned around, they all did, to find a kid of about twenty approaching the crowd. His golf cap was facing backward and he was out of breath.

"What?" someone else asked.

"I was trying to go home to check on my kid. The door wouldn't open with the key fob thing, so I used my actual key to unlock the door. But the car wouldn't start."

"Did it try to turn over?" someone asked him.

"No. I pushed the button and nothing."

Natalie's head swam with fear. Here she was at a golf course, more than five miles from her children and even farther from home, and how was she supposed to get to them if her car wouldn't start?

Well, wait. If the golf carts were still working, conceivably she could take one of those. They weren't fast but they were better than walking. Only how to arrange it? Ask for permission or just take off? One way or another she would get her children and take them home where they could wait this out in safety.

And what about Seth? His office was more than ten miles from their house. If his car wouldn't start, how would he ever make it home? What would she do in the meantime?

The crowd had dispersed, but Colin was still nearby, speaking to one of the other golfers. Natalie wanted to ask for permission, but what if he said no?

"Holy shit!" someone yelled. "Will you look at that!"

A man was pointing toward the sky. At first Natalie didn't know what he meant. But then she saw it—an airplane flying too low. Way too low. It was huge and silver and about to disappear below the horizon of treetops.

A moment later she saw a brief flash of yellow and orange, followed by a deep booming sound, so deep she felt it in her bones. Black smoke roiled upward in a cloud. Natalie put her hand over her mouth to stop herself from crying out.

"Holy shit!" someone else said, and the crowd, or what was left of it, streamed around the club house to get a better look. "It's them fuckin' terrorists! Fuckin' jihadis!"

Natalie saw her chance. She hurried to the drink cart and climbed in. It lurched forward as she mashed the pedal to the floor. She made a quick turn and angled toward the parking lot, not even bothering to stop at her car. There was nothing from it she wanted. The only thing she really needed was a head start.

"Natalie!" someone called. "Wait!"

She would have ignored the voice, but the cart was too slow to outrun anyone.

She turned around and saw Blake. The guy with the glasses.

"Where are you going?"

"I was trying to get my children and take them home. What do you expect me to do? Walk?"

"I don't want you to walk," Blake said, jogging toward her. "But I don't think you should drive that golf cart—"

She brought the cart to a complete stop, resigned to defeat.

"All I wanted was to pick up my boys."

"That's great. Take the cart. I just don't think you should drive it by yourself."

"Really? I did it all morning."

"What I'm saying is maybe you could use a passenger. If all the cars have stopped working, and everyone is stranded in the street, don't you think someone might try to steal the cart?"

Natalie blinked tears out of her eyes. She hadn't thought of that.

"So how about I make you a deal? I'll ride along to pick up your kids and back to your house, you know, to protect you from would-be golf cart jackers."

"And then?"

"And then you let me take the cart so I can get home. Assuming there's any gas left."

Natalie knew there was no reason to trust the guy. Blake could easily push her out of the cart as soon as they left the golf course. But it was also true she'd probably never make it to the daycare on her own. In a crazy situation like this, who knew what people would do?

"All right," she said. "You've got a deal."

Finally, they drove away from the club house, Natalie behind the wheel and Blake brandishing a couple of golf clubs from his bag. In a minute they were out of the parking lot and into the street. The cart seemed even slower on a normal road than it had on the golf course. How would she ever make it to her children in this? What would she do if they ran out of gas?

Natalie had never been so terrified in all her life. And here she was again, relying on a man.

FOUR

The first images were yellowish and streaky and binary; on and off, on and off. He felt as though he were swimming up from a great depth, the world sharpening as he approached the surface. A giant spoked wheel rose before him like a dark sun, and the air smelled of sulfur. Was he dying? Already dead?

But eventually Seth realized the dark sun was a steering wheel, and rotten fumes of engine exhaust were the source of the terrible smell. He was still very much alive and about to be sick to his stomach.

Seth reached for the door and got it open just in time. A hot slug of vomit poured out of him and splashed onto the floor. Eventually he rolled out of the car, hands slipping in the mess, knees and elbows colliding like bowling pins. For a moment he just lay there, face pressed into the smooth concrete. His head felt dense, heavy with fatigue. His brain throbbed painfully, but the agony of failure might have been worse.

Not only was he still alive, but the screenwriter had called to intervene. By now Thomas had notified Natalie, and she was probably rushing home, ready to blurt humiliating words of encouragement, explaining why he had every reason to live even though he no longer wanted to.

Seth climbed to his feet and shut the door. He couldn't remember the end of the phone call. Had Seth disconnected or had Thomas? And now he realized something even more ominous—the engine had stopped. There was no way he was out of gas, not after starting with a full tank, so did that mean someone had killed the ignition? And if so, why leave Seth in the car?

He couldn't know if Thomas had alerted Natalie. If she had rushed home or called the police to generate a quicker response. But anyone who bothered to shut off the car would surely have removed him from the garage or at the very least opened the door to let in fresh air.

Maybe no one had come at all. Maybe he'd broken something when he disabled the catalytic converter. Maybe only seconds or minutes had passed since his phone call with Thomas.

If that was true, Natalie might still be on her way. And if Seth didn't want to be around when his wife arrived, he required a faster way to get the job done.

He stumbled to the door and lurched inside. All the lights were off, which seemed to confirm no one had come to stop him. The master bedroom was the first door on his right. In the bathroom he spotted Natalie's bottle of Ambien and leered at the scores of pills he discovered. Surely, if he ate the whole bottle and washed it down with the rest of the whiskey, he'd go to sleep and never wake up. All he wanted was to sleep, to be released from his guilt. He stumbled back to the garage, bouncing through the doorway and choking on an invisible cloud of exhaust. He found the whiskey bottle in the car. Was there enough time? The last thing he wanted was for Natalie to show up while he was waiting for the overdose to take effect. Maybe he could drive away. He pushed the ignition button. Nothing happened. He pushed the button again with the same empty result.

Something was wrong with the car. How much time did he have? He grabbed his phone and pushed the button to activate it.

Nothing happened.

Seth stared at the phone. Pushed the button again.

Nothing happened.

How impotent it felt to be rejected by a button! Pushing a button was surely the simplest act a human could perform and expect an action in return. To be refused by a button was to understand your place in the grand hierarchy, which was beneath the world of objects, which was all the way down, all the way to the bottom.

For a moment Seth sat there, pressing the button over and over, staring at the dark display. Finally he stepped out of the car and looked at the pathetic mess on the floor. He couldn't even kill himself without screwing up. All he wanted was to be gone from this world and even that was outside his reach.

Seth grabbed the whiskey and marched back into the house. He slammed the bottle on the counter and set the Ambien next to it. He looked at the clock on the microwave, but where there should have been bluish green digits, there was only darkness. For that matter, the oven clock was also out.

"*Oh my God you have got to be kidding me!*" he screamed at the dead clocks, at the empty kitchen.

He trudged into the bedroom and looked at the alarm clock. This, too, was dark. He went into the study and found the computer still and quiet as a mouse. Clearly the power was out. But how? It was impossible to imagine an event that could shut off the electricity and shut off his car and fry his phone. So maybe he had died after all. Maybe death was a world robbed of power. Maybe the afterlife was what you made of such a world.

Seth staggered toward the living room and looked out the front windows. A small crowd was gathered around a car stopped in the middle of the street. The hood of the car had been raised, but no one was working on it. Instead, everyone was looking into the eastern sky. One of them was pointing at the sky.

What could it be? Had aliens landed? He couldn't imagine anything else able to generate such a widespread outage. For some reason all he could think of was aliens.

Instead of going out front, where someone might invite him to talk, Seth headed for the back door. He stepped outside, into the lawn, where he could get a clear view of the eastern sky. And that's when he saw it.

There was a star up there, or what looked like a star, burning brightly. As far as Seth knew, the only heavenly objects visible during the day were the Sun and the Moon, so this new star had violated the normal order of things. It hovered below the sun, maybe fifteen degrees, and though it didn't look like much, it was unquestionably the author of a major event. The star's appearance and the power failures could not be a coincidence. Something had happened, something serious.

Seth looked around the sky, wondering if more of these objects were up there, and to the west he discovered a black plume of smoke billowing upward. The smoke was several miles away. The dark cloud rose to such a great height it looked almost like a tornado.

Eventually Seth stopped looking at the sky and walked back through the house again. When he reached the garage, the smell of exhaust was like a wall, and without thinking he pushed the button to open the overhead door. But nothing happened because the power was out. He went to the car and sat down and pushed the ignition button.

Still nothing.

No power in the house, no power in his phone, no power in his car.

The strangeness of all this pointed to aliens, but the object in the sky looked like a star. Only how could a star suck the energy out of everything? Without power, there was no television, no Internet, no way to research the answer. And since his car wouldn't start, he couldn't even drive somewhere to find out.

For the first time he wondered just how widespread the event was. Was the power out across the city? The state? What if Thomas hadn't disconnected their call? What if he was staring at his own phone, wondering what happened? What if he was never able to call Natalie? If that was true, Seth's suicide attempt became non-existent, in a way, at least until the power returned. Because right now the only other people who knew about it were more than two hundred miles away.

And what if the power stayed off for a while? A catastrophic event from the heavens didn't seem like the sort of thing that would be easily reversed. A world of crisis, where electricity didn't flow and cars didn't run, was the kind of world where Seth might thrive. The idea of supporting and protecting his family instead of forever failing them was intoxicating. Enchanting.

It seemed impossible after all his praying and wishing that a bolt from the heavens had finally arrived. Yet here he was, standing in the garage where he had tried to kill himself, and possibly the only reason he hadn't succeeded was because of an event that with no exaggeration could be described as apocalyptic.

With a mounting sense of optimism, he grabbed a bucket from the kitchen, filled it with soap and water, and returned to the garage. He used a mechanical release to free the overhead door from its electric-powered chain and raised it to clear out the foul-smelling air. His hot water heater and stove were both powered by gas, which meant even if the electricity didn't come back on today, or tomorrow, they would be able to bathe and prepare food. And speaking of food, maybe he could stop by the grocery store and pick up some essentials, especially dry goods, because an event like this was sure to bring out the hoarders.

When everything was clean, he wrote a note to Natalie explaining where he'd gone. Normally he would be at work at this time of day, so he invented a story about coming home sick (which wasn't much of a stretch when you thought about it). He'd retrieve Ben and Brandon from daycare and then hit the store, and if Natalie wasn't home by then they would set out looking for her.

As long as the power stayed off, nothing was going to be easy. But anything was easier than living another day as a fraud. As a failure to his family.

Maybe this was the apocalypse. Maybe it was the end of everything.

Or maybe, possibly, the heavens had handed him a new beginning.

FIVE

S kylar couldn't stop watching the side mirror, couldn't stop turning around to look at the disaster behind them. The smoke was black and dense and rose above the horizon like a mountain range. It made her think of that terrible morning in 2001 when the Manhattan skyline had turned apocalyptic, how she'd been sure the whole world was coming to an end. But the world hadn't ended after 9/11. It had instead become gripped by fear and tribalism and absurdity. Divisive cable media coverage widened narrow political differences into canyons impossible to traverse, and for what? To sell bad products and even worse ideas? To separate unassuming people from their hard-won dollars?

How frivolous it all seemed now that there was an actual problem to face. Now that the world had been served an apocalypse that was not self-inflicted.

There was also this: If Thomas hadn't offered to pick her up, if she'd hired a car service, Skylar would never have made it out of the airport. For that matter her decision to land in Dallas had been last minute. Her original flight had been direct to Los Angeles, and if she hadn't changed her mind, that plane would have fallen out of the sky somewhere over the American heartland.

She wondered if her parents were okay. And her brother. And Roark. Why couldn't she be facing the apocalypse with Roark instead of a man she'd met only a half hour before?

For the past ten minutes Thomas had been making steady progress on the expressway, dodging cars and declining to make eye contact with hordes of people walking in the median. Now Skylar noticed new movement in the side mirror. It was another operational vehicle, an old red pickup. When she turned around, she could see it was slowly gaining on them, slaloming between stationary cars.

"Hey," she said. "There's a—"

"Truck, I know. Get down."

"Why?"

"Please."

Skylar was not accustomed to taking orders, especially from someone she barely knew, but the commanding tone in Thomas' voice was undeniable. She bent over awkwardly, as if she were looking for something in the floorboard.

"This is stupid."

"We don't know these guys."

"But they're going to see me doing this. I'm not invisible."

"Yeah, but down there you're just some random girl and not Skylar Stover."

Guys who weren't famous always wanted to handle her like fragile material. They seemed to forget she lived with her fame every day. Of course she loathed the paparazzi, always being stared at, always hearing whispers when she bought groceries or coffee or maybe a book. Who wanted to be asked during dinner to take selfies and sign autographs? What actress was pleased to see her stricken face on the cover of *Us Weekly* and *OK?* But in the end, all the attention seemed like a fair trade for the benefits afforded by celebrity. And if a drooling fan ever got too close, four years of cardio kickboxing might come in handy.

She assumed Thomas would have understood all this, since his first screenplay had put him on the map in Hollywood, but then again writers were a different breed than actors.

"Hey!" a man yelled over the growl of an engine, his voice colored by a deep drawl. "Nice car, boy!"

Thomas didn't say anything she could hear.

"Where y'all headed? And what's she doing down there?"

"Lost a contact lens," Thomas yelled.

"Y'all need help?"

"Nah, we're good!"

A few seconds passed, and Skylar expected to hear the pickup recede into the distance, but it didn't. That's when she realized why Thomas was being so cautious: Even though they were traveling on a highway in the middle of the city, without an obvious or even implied police presence, the two of them were on their own if there was trouble. She was also forced to concede that certain people would be more likely to harass them if they knew she was a famous actress.

"Ain't this a trip?" the fellow in the pickup yelled. "Whole world's fucked up!"

"You got that right," Thomas replied.

"Well, good luck to ya. You got a runnin' car. I'm sure we'll see you around!"

"Maybe so," Thomas yelled back.

Finally, the pickup seemed to pull away.

"Can I come up for air yet?"

* * *

By the time they left the turnpike, the pickup was long gone. Skylar hid behind sunglasses while Thomas steered them between stalled cars on surface streets. He didn't bother to stop at intersections because none of the traffic lights were working, and anyway no one was coming. Since the truck, they hadn't seen another working vehicle or any sign of electricity.

People were everywhere. They streamed on sidewalks and stood in parking lots and sat in their cars with the doors open, as if their engines would come back to life if they waited long enough. Skylar wondered what they were all thinking. How many people even knew what a pulse was?

That made her remember the suicidal husband. Had the pulse interrupted his plans? Would they ever know without going to check on him? How could they *not* check on him? Either to help Seth or the family he would leave behind?

She almost said something to Thomas about it, but the dark and determined look on his face convinced her to wait.

Eventually they arrived at an intersection that was completely blocked by stalled cars. A blue Chevy SUV had plowed into the back of a black Infiniti SUV, and several cars had swerved to dodge the accident. These evasive maneuvers had filled all available lanes and even some imaginary lanes. Thomas shifted the transmission into reverse, intending to bypass the intersection through an adjacent parking lot, and when he did, a nearby young woman and her daughter approached the car.

"Excuse me, sir," said the woman. Her blonde hair was tied behind her head and Skylar could tell she had been crying. The little girl's eyes looked vacant, as if she had opted out of reality.

"Yes, ma'am?" said Thomas, his smiled visibly strained.

"Why is your car running when others aren't?"

Skylar noticed other pedestrians drifting toward them. In the distance, over the tops of buildings and trees, black smoke continued to roil into the sky. She tried not to look at the new star, but it was impossible to ignore.

"I'm not sure," Thomas said. He put the transmission back into gear and began to roll forward. "At this point we're just trying to get home."

"Where are you headed? Can you give us a ride? I only live a few blocks that way."

The woman was pointing in the direction Thomas had been headed. The desperate look on her face and the vacant look in the little girl's eyes made Skylar want to reach out and hug both of them.

"Ma'am, I—"

Skylar grabbed his hand and raised her sunglasses.

"Thomas, please."

He stared at her for a moment, considering his answer, and then turned back to the woman.

"Get in. Do it fast."

Skylar opened the door and used a lever beneath the seat to scoot it forward. The woman lifted her daughter into the back and climbed in behind her.

Other people were approaching. Skylar fell into her seat and shut the door.

"Excuse me," a woman cried out. "Excuse me! Can you take, me, too? Please?"

Thomas hit the accelerator and the car shot forward.

"Asshole!" the woman yelled.

"We can't take everyone," Thomas muttered.

"Thank you," the woman said from the back seat. "Thank you so much."

* * *

"It's up on the right," the woman said after they'd been driving for a moment. "We're in Grayhawk on Bruschetta Drive. Do you know where that is?"

"No. Just tell me when to turn."

The friendly and accommodating Thomas Skylar had met at the airport was noticeably absent since the pulse. But honestly she had no idea who Thomas was or what he was really like. Everything she knew about him she'd gleaned from the trades, from his scripts, from a feature in *Entertainment Weekly*. He'd become a Hollywood darling after the success of *Thomas World*, which was one of those cross-cultural juggernauts that pulled viewers from nearly every demographic. On its surface the film was science fiction, following a man whose life turns out to exist in a computer-simulated world of his own creation, but at heart it was a love story. And the film had come armed with a built-in marketing gimmick, because Thomas the protagonist was essentially the screenwriter Thomas. This blending of worlds caused fans of the movie to wonder just how much of its story was true, eventually spawning a subreddit dedicated to tracking down Sophia, the unrequited love from his college years, as well as his ex-wife, Gloria. After the divorce, Thomas had fallen into depression, only to rise from the ashes of his failed life by selling his story to a major Hollywood producer. And when his next project sold for twice that of the first, he became the industry's hottest screenwriter.

Considering the struggles Thomas had overcome, she expected him to demonstrate a little more empathy for the less fortunate around them. Instead, the appearance of the new star had turned him surly and selfish.

"What's your name, honey?" Skylar said, turning to face the little girl.

After a moment of eye contact, the girl wiped tears from her cheeks and turned away.

"Come on, darling," said the mom. "It's okay."

"Hey," Skylar said to her, "did you ever see the show 'Jeffrey's Special Friends' on Nickelodeon?"

The girl was still ignoring her, or pretending to, but recognition flickered in her guarded eyes.

"Do you remember Milou? The girl who made friends with the tiny people in her dollhouse?"

Now the little girl looked up again. Skylar pushed her sunglasses back and smiled.

"So, do you recognize me?"

The girl flashed a brilliant smile.

"Oh my gosh! You're Milou! What are you doing here?"

"Well, honey, I'm an actress. Milou is a character I used to play. I came to Dallas to talk to Thomas, this guy next to me. He writes movies."

Skylar had learned about Thomas' new project three months earlier. By the time she called her agent, she'd already been placed on the short list of possible leads, and after some negotiation and two weeks of waiting became attached to the project. That was when she requested an in-person meeting with the screenwriter. It was an unusual request and she expected Thomas to understand this.

For a short while, after her first breakout film, Skylar had relished the luxury of being universally desired, and this had led her to date a variety of actors. Intellectually she was drawn to gaunt men who didn't shave much and who looked for projects outside the Hollywood bubble. With these guys she never wanted for attention or intellectual stimulation, but there was a hollowness to her attraction for them, a missing sense of security and sexual satiety that she fulfilled by dating another kind of man—less thoughtful, more clean-shaven, perfectly-groomed stars of thrillers and action-oriented pictures who considered the term "art film" an oxymoron. And when she finally found someone who embodied both archetypes, she impulse-married him after two months of dating. Skylar and Roark had been mocked by celebrity magazines and cable entertainment programs and late-night talk show hosts (*Us Weekly* had bestowed them with the portmanteau "Skylark") but she hadn't minded because she knew exactly what she was doing. She was a twenty-seven-year-old woman sitting on $75 million in career earnings. Her life bore no resemblance to reality the way most humans understood it, and this made her feel obligated to behave in absurd ways. Like run off to Milan where she married Roark in a ten-minute ceremony. Like celebrating their nuptials with ring finger tattoos followed by cinematic sex in a dark alley amidst the pouring rain. It was no surprise the marriage survived only two years, but Skylar was caught off guard by how depressed she'd been over the divorce. Which was why, when news of *The Pulse* had come along (just three months after Roark retrieved the last of his things from the house in Beverly Hills) she jumped at the chance to star in the film.

Skylar had flown to Dallas to discover which qualities the real Thomas shared with Thomas the screenwriter. Thomas the screenwriter adored women, and he believed in the power of romantic love even in a social media world where relationships were often untraditional. But now her plan was pointless. Now, the world felt like it was ending and her reason for coming here seemed ridiculous.

Except it was also the only reason she was alive.

"You're Skylar Stover," the girl's mother said in a small voice. "My name is Chanda. I'm sorry I didn't recognize you before. I was so freaked out about the car and having to walk home that I didn't really look at you."

Skylar smiled awkwardly. She looked at the little girl again.

"I still don't know *your* name."

"It's Amanda. Well, Louise if you include my middle name."

"Pleased to meet you, Amanda Louise. I'm Skylar Inez."

"Inez is your middle name?"

"Yes, ma'am. I have one just like you."

When Amanda smiled again, Skylar's heart ached. What would happen to this girl and her mom after Thomas dropped them off?

"Where should I turn?" he asked.

"Up here on Grayhawk. Make a right and a right and then a left. I'll show you."

Amanda was still smiling broadly and sneaking furtive glances at Skylar, but Chanda looked like she might throw up.

"So what are we supposed to do? I mean when we get home? What are y'all going to do?"

"I just flew in from New York," Skylar said. "I landed twenty minutes before this happened. We barely got out of the airport."

"I can't believe it," Chanda said. "I was in my car when it stopped working. Just stopped. I thought it was something with the alternator again, 'cause I only had that worked on three weeks ago. But then I looked around and saw all the cars were stopped. Pretty soon people were getting out and walking around, looking confused, and that's when we saw the light in the sky. We all knew it came from that, but no one knew what it was. Some guy said aliens. He said a spaceship could look just like that, a point of light, and maybe they're launching an attack, killing all our cars and power so we can't fight back."

"I don't think it's a spaceship," Thomas said. "But it might be a star that exploded. I've never seen one before, but I think that's what it would look like. And no matter what it is, it's going to be a big problem if the power doesn't come back on soon. Which street do I turn on?"

"Right here on Swan Lake. Then your second left. Now just a few houses up. Yeah, right there. This is it."

"Great," Thomas said. "Let's get you going."

He stepped out of the car and helped the woman and her daughter onto the sidewalk.

"Thank you so much," Chanda said. "I can't thank you two enough."

"We were happy to give you a ride," Skylar told her.

Thomas took Chanda by the shoulder and pulled her aside. He spoke in a quiet voice.

"I want you to know it's possible the power might not come back for a while, and you should prepare in case it doesn't. Go to the grocery store right away and buy whatever food you can, like rice and beans and stuff that will last a while. Beef jerky. Canned vegetables. You realize if cars and trucks don't work, it means no more deliveries to grocery stores. Without those deliveries, the city will run out of food very quickly."

"You're scaring me."

"And before you leave for the store, fill your tubs and sinks and all your bowls with water. Without electricity the pressure will die in a couple of days and your faucets will stop working."

"Are you joking? How do you know this?"

"Do you have a bicycle?"

"My daughter does. I think mine works but the chain needs oil."

"When you go to the store, buy oil for the chain. Do you have cash?"

"Why do you act like this is the end of the world? Why don't you think the power will come back?"

"Maybe I'm wrong," Thomas said to her. "But what would you do if the power didn't come back on for a month? A year?"

"Oh, my God," Chanda said. She reached instinctively for her daughter and Skylar could see she was near tears again. "You don't honestly think that could happen?"

"There's no way to know for sure, but it's better to be safe. How much cash do you have?"

"I don't know. Like ten bucks?"

Thomas reached into his pocket and retrieved a money clip. He peeled off two hundred-dollar bills and handed them to her.

"Use this to help. But don't hoard it. Spend it all today. When people figure out the power isn't coming back on, they'll stop accepting cash. They'll want something else, like to trade."

"How do you know all this? Who are you?"

"Just a guy who writes movies, honest. But I've also done a lot of research about something called an electromagnetic pulse. It can come from a solar flare or a nuclear weapon or even a supernova, and it can knock out the power and kill every electronic device. If that's what this is, things will become very different. Do you have a gun?"

Chanda looked at him for a long moment without answering.

"I think you're overreacting. This isn't a third world country."

Thomas glanced at Amanda, then back at her mother.

"Maybe not. But that could change really fast. Stock up on food and water, just in case."

Chanda looked both frightened and defiant, and Skylar wondered what she would do in the mother's shoes. Without context, the things Thomas had said seemed outlandish. But Skylar had read his script, and she couldn't see any reason why the real world would fare better after an EMP than his fictional one.

"Thanks for the ride," Chanda finally said. "I'll think about what you told me. But I hope to God you're wrong. Honestly, I hope you're full of shit."

* * *

Once their passengers were gone, Skylar had nothing to do but look around, and all she saw was dread. Hordes of people were crowded on sidewalks, clustered in groups, looking at the new star, looking toward the airport, streaming into and out of convenience stores and banks and churches. Others were on bicycles, and she even spotted two off-road motorbikes. But almost everyone she saw, no matter who they were or what they were doing, stared lustily at Thomas' Mustang. And to Skylar it seemed like a feral sort of envy.

Again she thought of her mother and father in New York. They'd both grown up poor and knew the meaning of hardship, but today they lived in an expensive apartment on the Upper West Side. Her father worked in the Empire State Building, on the 53rd floor, and her mother's office was a short walk from their apartment. Both would have been at work when the new star appeared, but what were they doing now? With no elevator, on bum knees, how would her father ever make it to the street?

Her brother, Sean, lived in Echo Park, and he was one of the smartest men Skylar knew. But there were twenty million people in southern California, and the only agriculture Skylar had ever seen near the city were vineyards and fruit orchards. What were twenty million people going to eat when there were no trucks to bring them food?

What about Sallie and Jessie, her two precious Chihuahuas?

Even though she was a girl and couldn't always help it, Skylar took great pride in not crying in front of other people. Especially men. So she looked away from Thomas, toward the street, and through her tears saw a woman pushing a stroller. The woman's face was stricken white. Skylar made eye contact with her and then quickly looked away, into the side mirror. She saw movement in the side mirror. It was a policeman waving his arms.

When she leaned closer, hoping to get a better look, she finally realized the officer was waving at them.

"Thomas, there's a—"

"Cop, I know. We're not stopping. Don't turn around."

"What? Why?"

"Because he probably wants my car and I'm not giving it to him."

"But he's a police officer, for heaven's sake. Maybe—"

Thomas had slowed to navigate an intersection choked with stalled cars, but now he was through it and accelerating again.

"You want to risk it? You want to walk two more miles to my house?"

Skylar thought again of her family, stranded, and shut her mouth.

"I'm sorry," he said. "If this really is a pulse, no one will be able to help us if something goes wrong. There are seven million people in this city. For the police, having one working car would be like shooting a rifle at a spaceship. It's not going to make a difference. But for you and me, it makes all the difference in the world."

"You really think no one is coming? You really think the government doesn't have a plan for this? I just can't believe today of all days is the end of the world."

"Until we know for sure, we should proceed like we're on our own. Don't you think?"

"I'm worried about my family," Skylar said, and gave in to the tears. "Especially my parents. They live in Manhattan. What are they going to do?"

Thomas reached over and lightly squeezed her shoulder.

"I'm sure they're okay. At least right now they are. And maybe you're right. Maybe the government is already on its way to fix all this."

It annoyed her that Thomas wouldn't address the improbable nature of what was happening. Not just this awful disaster, but specifically how similar it was to the screenplay he'd written. *The Pulse*, after all, was the story of a global catastrophe ignited by the same kind of technology-melting apocalypse the new star had induced. Thomas had written about planes falling out of the sky, about fires that swept across cities, about people caught in unfortunate places like elevators and Swiss gondolas that were trapped halfway between the ground and their distant destinations. That Skylar had flown here to discuss an apocalyptic story which was now in the process of unfolding was inconceivable. It was frightening. And Thomas hadn't said a word about it.

Eventually they left the crowds of wandering people behind and crossed a lake on a four-lane bridge. After another stretch of mostly empty road, they turned onto a narrow and lonely-looking street that wandered into Thomas' neighborhood. From there it was a short drive to his house, a large, French country home that stood on the shore of the lake and looked like it had been built yesterday.

Thomas unloaded her luggage and carried it toward the house. Inside she found European sofas that sat near the ground, a mixture of dark and light woods, enormous plate glass windows that opened to a grand view of the lake. As if any of it mattered.

"It's great that we're here now, but I'm still scared to death. I'm afraid I'm never going to see my family again."

He reached for her then, and Skylar let herself be held. She barely knew this man, but she also understood they were in this together. She was overwhelmed, near panic, and somehow Thomas seemed so unflappable about it all.

"I hope you're wrong," Skylar confessed. "Just like that woman said. I hope you're full of shit. Because in your screenplay almost everyone dies."

Thomas let go of her and put his hands on her shoulders.

"Listen to me. I don't know what's going to happen. No one does. But we have a better chance than most."

"Why is that? Because of your car?"

"Not just that. Let me show you something."

Thomas led her deeper into the house until they were standing in front of a sturdy steel door. He retrieved a key from his pocket and inserted it into the dead bolt lock.

"This is a safe room. The walls are eight inches of reinforced concrete. It's built to withstand an EF-5 tornado and even a catastrophic fire. Hence the name."

Thomas threw the door open. With no windows, the room was dark, but he grabbed a couple of flashlights and handed one to her. He switched his on and waited for her to do the same.

What she saw took her breath away. Shelves had been mounted, from floor to ceiling, along all four walls. The room was as large as a typical bedroom.

Food covered every available surface. Rice and beans and cereal and oatmeal. Dried milk and jars of pickles and mayonnaise. Industrial sized cans of vegetables. Canned meats and sauces. Gallon jugs of water were stacked in crates, along with hundreds of individual bottles. Cases of beer and liquor covered an entire corner. Flour and sugar and spices and salts. Packages of corn chips and potato chips and an entire platoon of nuts—cashews, peanuts, mixed nuts, Spanish nuts, pecans, almonds, pistachios.

"Good lord, Thomas. This is so much food."

"After I wrote that film," he said, "after researching the ways to prepare for an EMP, I decided to build this room. Primarily to amuse myself. I never imagined I would have to use it."

She knew he wanted her to be impressed with his astonishing provisions, and of course she was. But seeing such careful preparation also made her feel uncomfortable. Conspiratorial. It seemed impossible that anyone could know about an EMP before it happened, but a part of her still wondered if he had.

"It's kind of you to share your food with me. But I can't stop thinking about how similar all this is to your screenplay. That's why I came here, to talk about *The Pulse*, and then a fucking pulse happens right after I land. That doesn't seem a little strange to you?"

"It's an incredible coincidence," he said. "But so what? How does it change anything?"

Skylar didn't know. But she also didn't see how it could be an accident. In *Thomas World*, the entire story had taken place inside a simulated world created by the eponymous protagonist, and the success of this film had furnished real-life Thomas with the kind of money and fame few screenwriters ever achieved. *Wired* even published a story about the topic called *Art Creates Life: How Thomas Phillips transformed fantasy into reality*, in which the author postulated how the film's success—and the ripple effects created by that success, including the author's own *Wired* story— were all part of a larger, artificial reality designed by some extra-dimensional Thomas. Even late-night comedians pounced on the idea, like Trevor Noah, who on "The Daily Show" quipped, *Hey Thomas, if this world is yours, that means Donald Trump is your fault. Thanks a lot, asshole!*

"Maybe it's not even happening," she said. "Just like in your first film."

"Maybe it isn't. But what then? We just sit around and wait for the game to end?"

Skylar stared at him. She picked at her cuticles.

"If you saw the film," Thomas said, "you know it doesn't matter if any of this is real. The only thing that matters is what we do with the reality we're faced with."

"Like just sit here and eat peanut butter and wait for everyone else to die?"

"If you want to live, I don't see what other choice we have."

"That's not good enough," she replied. "We have to share your food. We have to help other people. We have to do something."

"If anyone else around here finds out about my safe room," said Thomas, "they will march over here with guns and take it from us. We won't be able to stop them. There will be too many."

Skylar remembered the starving mob in his screenplay and knew Thomas was right. If they were going to help someone, it had to be on the sly. And a limited number of people.

"I think we should check on Seth," she finally said. "You promised him you would."

"Skylar—"

"I know you don't want to leave this fortress of solitude. But if Seth is dead, we really should help the wife and kids."

"That's a nice idea," Thomas agreed. "Except Natalie and her family don't live around here."

"Where do they live?"

"In Tulsa."

"Like Oklahoma?"

"Which is four hours away. At least it was."

"Holy shit," Skylar said. "I didn't expect that."

"I know I made a promise, but that was before all this. That was basically about money. Now, trying to save their lives could mean losing our own."

"So all you want to do is hunker down? Live off your rations until everyone dies and then repopulate the world?"

"I didn't say that. But it's a long drive into empty countryside where anything might happen. We might not make it there. We might not make it back."

"Maybe not," she said in a quiet voice. "But what's the point of surviving all this if survival is the only point?"

SIX

Natalie tried to focus on the road, but she kept looking up at the new star. It had risen higher into the sky and seemed to be following her. She turned away and imagined the faces of her boys, the moment she would have them safely in her arms.

"I just can't believe it," Blake said. "It's like something in a science fiction movie."

"You don't have children, do you?"

"No, why?"

"How about a girlfriend?"

"Nah. I moved here from Austin a few months ago but my girlfriend didn't come along."

"Aren't you worried about her?"

"I suppose, but we broke up and she's far away and I don't know what I can do about it, anyway."

"You could worry about her like an empathetic human being!"

"Eh, they'll get the power back on pretty soon. And even if they don't, what's the immediate danger?"

They were on the 71st Street bridge, crossing the Arkansas River. Steering the drink cart between numerous stalled cars made it feel like they were moving faster than they really were. Many of the vehicles were still occupied, as if their drivers expected someone to come along and rescue them.

Natalie was struck then by an insight so obvious that it was shameful to have only just thought of it. Everything that had happened this morning—the immobilized cars, the power blackout, the dead cell phones—was almost identical to the central premise of Thomas' new screenplay. He'd told her about it at the reunion, about how much the concept had frightened him while writing it. In his movie the event had been caused by the sun, but the effect was essentially the same.

Cool dread seeped upward from her toes, as if she were being lowered into a dark lagoon. Because in the story Thomas had written, everything that died stayed dead. It was the computer chips inside things that were fried, and they couldn't be easily replaced because the machines that manufactured such chips required chips themselves. Natalie hadn't understood the interest in a movie like that, since the lives of each character became immediately worse after the pulse and kept on getting worse. What followed was a gradual descent of American culture into a savage state just this side of the stone age.

"I can't believe you're not more worried about this!" she said and gestured toward the column of black smoke on their right. "On top of everything else, a freaking plane crashed."

"Look, I realize this is a messed-up situation, but I don't see how it helps to panic."

"Who's panicking? I just want to make sure my children are safe."

"Why wouldn't they be?"

"Because this is happening and I'm not there!"

"I'm saying unless a plane went down on top of the daycare, they're fine. They probably don't realize anything is wrong except the power is out."

"People at the daycare might be doing what I'm doing. Going home to get their children. Then mine are left all alone."

"You think anyone would abandon a group of children at daycare?"

Natalie swerved around a glut of stalled traffic at the Riverside intersection. There were at least ten cars crowded next to each other, filling all available lanes in both directions, as if an accident had occurred. People were looking at the road or at the sky or both. Someone yelled "Hey, lady!" but Natalie drove on without looking to see who it was.

"You're being an ass," she said to Blake.

"And you're being hysterical."

"I am not hysterical!"

They rode in silence for a while. At a Burger King she saw a line of stalled cars in the drive-through lane. Thirty or forty people stood in the parking lot of Quik Trip. There were people on sidewalks and loitering in the street with strange looks on their faces, confused or expectant or frightened. No one seemed to know what to do.

Beyond the Lewis intersection, 71st Street was almost empty, but it was also the beginning of a long, uphill climb. The drink cart's motor began to protest and they slowed down dramatically.

"Shit," she said to Blake, to the awful world at large. "We're not gonna make it."

"Sure we will. Golf carts don't go very fast, but they have plenty of torque."

"For such a smart guy you can be pretty dumb about life."

The cart continued to climb the hill steadily, as Blake had predicted. Despite his annoying comments, Natalie was glad he had come along. She was afraid the only reason some other man hadn't approached her was because she wasn't alone.

And once she secured her children, what then? How long would it take Seth to walk home from work? Hours, surely. Maybe he'd stay at the office, expecting the power to be restored sooner instead of later. Or maybe he would abandon his family the way Natalie had often feared.

Her mouth tasted like pennies. For a moment she thought she might faint. Blake seemed to notice and squeezed her shoulder.

"You okay?"

"No," Natalie said, suddenly overcome with tears.

"Want me to drive?"

"Would you?"

They stopped and switched places, but afterward Natalie wished they hadn't. Without the road and its obstacles to distract her, she retreated into her mind where there was nothing to do but worry. Her heart beat too fast. Her limbs felt heavy. Her thoughts degraded into static, audible static, the sound a radio made when it was tuned into nothing. It was a painful sound she endured all the way to the daycare, and even then it didn't really end.

* * *

Blake waited with the drink cart while Natalie went inside to retrieve her sons. The daycare was housed in a newish brick building made to look on the outside like a residence. Even with plenty of windows, the entryway was uncomfortably dark. A frail woman of about sixty rounded a corner and intercepted Natalie on her way to the classroom.

"May I help you, ma'am?"

"I'm here to pick up my sons. Ben and Brandon Black. They're in the second-grade drop-in class."

"Of course," the woman said. "And your name is...?"

"Natalie Black. I'll just head back to the classroom and get them."

But the frail woman, who couldn't have weighed one hundred pounds, stepped into her path.

"Mrs. Black, may I ask you to wait a moment while I go talk to the teacher? It's been quite a morning and we're trying to be as careful as we can with the students."

"I'm here to pick up my children. It *has* been quite a morning, and I'd like to take them home if you don't mind."

"Please," the woman said. "Wait here just one moment. I'll be back with Miss Lopez shortly."

Natalie's nerves were bare wires and she was close to faltering. But losing her cool now, when she was so close to seeing her sons, would only make things worse.

"Of course," she said. Her teeth chattered and her hands shook so badly she was forced to knot them behind her back. "I'll just wait here."

The old woman disappeared around the corner. Natalie's insides were gelatin and her toes tingled with electricity. Adrenaline had dominated her bloodstream since the new star appeared, and she was tired, irritable, vulnerable. She was not prepared to see Miss Lopez appear without Ben and Brandon at her side.

"Mrs. Black," said the teacher, who was a little younger than Natalie and beautiful. She'd always been jealous of women with olive skin and brown hair, of their effortless sexuality. "I'm sure this is confusing, but—"

"Where are my sons?"

"Their father arrived about ten minutes ago to take them home."

"That's impossible. My husband works downtown. There's no way he could have made it here so quickly."

"With the power out, we don't have access to the pickup list. But he presented proper I.D. He said he walked here to get them."

"But his office is more than ten miles away."

"In any case," the teacher said, "they left only a few minutes ago. I'm sure you could catch them if you hurry. I bet they would be glad to see you're okay. This has been quite a morning."

"You can say that again."

"Do you happen to know what's going on, Mrs. Black? Only a few parents have come by to pick up their children and no one seems to know anything. But I saw that vehicle you drove here and wondered if maybe you might know something more?"

"I don't know anything. I was working at a charity golf tournament when that thing appeared in the sky. I was driving a cart full of refreshments. When I realized no cars were working, I took the cart. For some reason it runs. It just doesn't go very fast."

"You're very fortunate to have access to some kind of vehicle. I'm not sure what to do with all these children. A few of them have parents who both work downtown. It might take them all day to arrive, if at all."

Natalie realized the teacher was as frightened as she was.

"I'm sorry if I was rude," Natalie said. "I know you're in a tough spot with all these children. I wish I could help you, but I have to get home. Please understand."

Miss Lopez's eyes sparkled with tears.

"I'm just so frightened. Nothing like this has ever happened before. At least not here."

"I hope whatever it is gets fixed soon. Because if it doesn't, I'm not sure what's going to happen."

"Nothing good," said Miss Lopez as she wiped tears out of her eyes.

* * *

Blake was rooting through the storage compartment of the drink cart when Natalie approached. He found a couple of candy bars and offered her one.

"They aren't here," she said, ignoring him. "The school says Seth came to get them. My husband."

"Well, that's good, right? They're safe?"

Natalie climbed behind the steering wheel and mashed on the accelerator. Blake jumped in as the cart lurched into gear.

"So it's not a good thing?"

"I don't see how the man who showed up could be my husband. She said he walked. How on earth could he have walked here from downtown faster than we drove from the golf course?"

"Yeah, that is strange."

Natalie steered the cart onto Yale and turned left, headed toward her house. There was a large crowd gathered at another Quik Trip, half of them looking at the sky, the other half milling around and talking to each other. When she considered the same scene unfolding at every convenience store in Tulsa, in the entire country, she tasted pennies again. Heard static in her brain again. If she didn't find her boys soon, Natalie was afraid she would break down completely.

The road here was only two lanes wide, and she was forced to carefully maneuver around numerous cars and trucks. Already it had become familiar for the roads to look this way, like vehicle graveyards, and she was beginning to wonder if that's how they would always look.

"Someone came over from Quik Trip while you were inside," Blake said.

"What did they want?"

"The golf cart."

"Are you serious?"

"The guy offered me three hundred and twenty dollars cash, everything he had on him."

"No shit. What did you say?"

"I told him it wasn't mine to give."

"Good answer," Natalie said. "Although he probably figured out we borrowed it."

"Is that what we did?"

The road turned left and then right as they climbed a steep hill. The engine groaned. But as soon as they started down the other side, she cried out. Her husband and two sons were now within sight, just ahead and descending the hill.

The three of them had already turned to look, having heard the cart's engine. Even through her tears she could make out their surprise.

"Mom!" Brandon cried. He shook free of his father and ran toward the cart. Ben, always the more cautious twin, maintained a tight grip on Seth's hand.

"Where did you get this thing?" Brandon asked her, gawking at the drink cart like it was a spaceship.

"From the golf course. Are you okay?"

"Sure. Did you think I was hurt?"

Now Seth and Ben approached. Her husband was smiling broadly, but Natalie could tell right away something was wrong with him. His face was pale and tinted green.

"I went to get the boys," she said. "How on earth did you beat me there?"

Seth reached awkwardly forward and embraced her. She couldn't remember the last time he'd done that, at least not of his own volition. Up close she could smell something strange on him, like rotten eggs or nausea.

"I got sick to my stomach at work," Seth said. "I went home early, so I was there when the power went out. Took me a while to realize it was *that*."

He gestured toward the point of light in the sky.

"Since you were at the golf tournament, I figured I should get the boys. Man, I'm so glad you're safe."

Seth smiled again and then glanced at Blake.

"Sorry," Natalie said. "Seth, this is Blake. He was nearby when it happened. He offered to come along in case someone tried to take the cart from me."

"That was very nice of you, Blake," said Seth as if it hadn't been nice at all.

"And I promised I'd let him take the cart after we made it home."

"Ah. I see. How far away do you live, Blake?"

"A couple of miles north. Near 41st and Harvard."

"The cart must be running low on gas. Do you know how to siphon?"

"I could if I had to. Not sure where I'm going to get the fuel, though, unless I steal it from an abandoned car. And I would need a hose."

"You might find one at the Food Pyramid on 81st. We'll drive past it on the way to our house. I was going to stop, anyway, and buy some groceries if they're open."

"Can't hurt to look. But I don't have much cash on me, and I have a feeling they may not take my debit card."

"That's a good point about cards," Seth said. "Babe, do you have any cash?"

"I think I have twenty dollars, but...um...."

"What?"

"I have money from the golf course! From the tournament. I bet there's a couple hundred dollars in that pouch."

"Well done, babe!" Seth said. "You're a life saver."

"But the money isn't ours. Neither is the cart for that matter."

"We'll pay it back. When everything is working again, we'll give the money back with interest. But right now we need food. The store could already be a madhouse. Remember what happened last year before the blizzard?"

Natalie saw his point.

"So let's see if we can all squeeze in," he said, "and take a ride to the store."

* * *

They pulled into the parking lot about five minutes later. A small cluster of cars sat near the entrance. Some people were heading into the store, and one emerged carrying plastic sacks of groceries. A couple of store employees had gathered near the doors, talking and looking up at the sky.

"Seems as though they're selling food," Seth said. "That's a good sign."

Something was different about her husband. He looked and smelled as if he'd recently been sick, but he wasn't behaving like someone who didn't feel well. Instead, there was an unmistakable strength in his voice, a timbre of confidence she hadn't detected for a long time. By no means did this display erase Seth's betrayals, and sometime soon she would be forced to confront him, but right now was not the time. Right now she found herself willing to be led by him...a development nearly as surprising as the new star in the sky.

Natalie steered the drink cart into an open parking spot and stopped.

"I can take this key out," she said, turning the ignition to OFF. "You think that will stop someone from stealing it?"

"Unless they're willing to hotwire the thing in broad daylight," Blake said as he stood up and stretched. "I think we'll be okay for a few minutes."

"Okay, then," Seth said. "Let's roll."

Natalie watched her husband grab a hand from each of his sons and glance over his shoulder at her. Together the family strode toward the Food Pyramid with Blake in tow. Once again Natalie felt a jolt of unexpected attraction for her husband, this man who was suddenly, unquestionably in charge.

The automatic doors had been propped open, and the first thing Natalie noticed when they walked inside was how dark the store was. The checkout area was lit by rectangles of sunlight thrown by the open front doors, and candles marked the end of each aisle. But the store as a whole was darker than she would have imagined. Before today Natalie had never noticed there wasn't a single window in the entire building.

A security guard nodded to Seth as the five of them approached. Only one register was open, and the line behind it was so long it snaked into one of the candlelit aisles. At the register stood a small crowd of store employees, including a man who was writing something on a pad of paper.

Blake stood behind them and finally spoke as Seth grabbed a shopping cart.

"Like I said, I don't have much cash. Can I use some of what came from the golf course? Since we're borrowing it?"

"Get what you need," Seth said. "We'll meet you back here in a few minutes and give you enough to cover your groceries. Within reason, of course."

Additional candles had been placed halfway down each aisle, and Natalie could see the bread shelves were more than half empty. Seth scooped up eight or ten loaves, some white, some wheat.

"Natalie," he said. "Why don't you walk over to Produce and grab a few bags of potatoes and anything else that won't spoil right away? I'll get some sacks of rice and beans and we can meet back up in a minute."

"What about milk?"

"We have no way to keep it cold. If I can find it, I'll grab some dried milk. And pasta. Stuff like that. Whatever we can store without refrigeration."

In the vegetable aisle, Natalie couldn't find any sacks of potatoes. The entire Russet display had been ravaged. In a dark corner, though, she discovered Red Pontiacs and Yukon Golds in loose piles and filled a couple of plastic sacks with them. She grabbed carrots and onions. Some tomatoes and apples and a few pieces of squash. She didn't even like squash, but it looked like something that wouldn't go bad for a while.

Several other women were standing nearby, each collecting vegetables with shaking hands in near darkness. Natalie wondered what they must be thinking. She remembered the recent blizzard and how the Food Pyramid had quickly been depleted of bread and milk and eggs. As if, when you were snowed in, the only appropriate response was to cook mountains of French toast. In that situation it had been funny, watching overprotective mothers round up grocery staples as if twenty inches of snow really meant Armageddon.

Today it was not funny. Without TV or cell phones, there was no way to find out what had happened to the power, and what, if any, response was coming. Everyone was in the dark, literally and figuratively.

When she could carry no more plastic sacks of produce, Natalie walked back toward the store proper, looking for her family.

"Dad, I want Coke. I *hate* Pepsi!"

Natalie smiled. Only Brandon could find a way to complain about the end of the world.

"What difference does it make?" Seth replied. "The Pepsi is on sale. We need to get as many cans as we can."

"I don't want a lot of cans of Pepsi! I want less cans of Coke!"

"Brandon," Natalie said as she approached with her vegetables. "Do you want Pepsi or do you want to drink water?"

"I want *Coke!*"

"So you'd rather drink water, is that what you're saying?"

"No."

"Well, it's Pepsi or water. Your choice."

"Fine. Make it Pepsi. Even though I hate it."

She dropped her load of produce into the shopping cart, which was nearly full already. Potato chips, rice, beans, peanuts, cereal, two boxes of dried milk. They could have been preparing for a wagon trip to the frontier, except there was no wagon and no place to go.

"Is this enough?" she asked Seth. "Can we get in line now?"

"I think that ought to do it. This will get us by for a week or two, and surely by then there will be a relief plan in motion."

"You think?"

"There are too many smart people and too much money at stake to let everything go to shit."

Natalie appreciated Seth's confidence, but she couldn't stop thinking about what Thomas had written.

They found Blake beside a cooler at the front of the store. A couple of teenaged girls were standing nearby, handing out Styrofoam bowls of free ice cream. Before Natalie could stop them, each of her sons stepped forward and accepted a bowl. The Food Pyramid girls smiled and held out more bowls. For some reason Natalie felt like screaming at them. How could they stand there with retail smiles on their faces, doling out treats, at a time like this?

But instead of screaming, she looked over at Blake and tried to smile.

"Did you get enough food?"

"I don't know how much is enough. But this ought to last me a week or so."

Seth positioned himself at the end of the register line and motioned Blake to fall in behind him.

"This is gonna take forever," Seth said.

At the front of the line, an elderly gentleman fidgeted as his cart of groceries was processed. For each item, the checker, a middle-aged woman with leathery skin and disheveled brown hair, called out the name of the product and its size. Next to her stood a lanky kid of about twenty, dressed in a black sweater and orange knit beanie, consulting a thick stack of printed pages.

"Prego spaghetti sauce, roasted garlic and herb, twenty-four ounces."

The kid flipped through his list, a stack of pages so thick it must have numbered in the thousands, and finally called out a price, which he wrote down on a pad of ruled paper.

"Ronzoni Healthy Harvest whole wheat pasta, thin spaghetti. Twelve ounces."

The kid went flipping again. He flipped and flipped.

Finally, he looked up and said, "No record."

And that's when a third store employee, a burly, balding fellow wearing a white oxford shirt and blue pants, stepped in.

"Max, we need a price check!"

A reedy, tanned kid with long, sandy blonde hair skipped off in the direction of the pasta aisle.

The elderly man, purchaser of the spaghetti, looked perturbed. The conveyor belt was crowded with groceries and he'd unloaded only half of what was in his cart.

Natalie counted ten people in line ahead of them.

"We're gonna be here forever," Brandon moaned.

They stood there waiting for the sandy-haired kid, who finally returned with a price. The checker processed two more items before running across another one that wasn't on the list.

"Max, we need a price check!"

Ben groaned.

When all the man's groceries were finished, he pulled a checkbook from his back pocket and requested a pen. The checker glared at him and said something Natalie couldn't hear.

"Are you kidding? I always pay by check at this store! A check is the same as cash! Always has been!"

At that point another store employee walked over, thin and officious-looking. His moustache looked like gray wire and his beady eyes made Natalie wonder if he molested children in his spare time. He murmured something the elderly man didn't like.

"I don't care what the situation is! You should treat customers with respect, power or no power. I spend six hundred bucks a month in this store and always pay by check. Why should today be any different?"

The officious store employee murmured something else, and once again the elderly man took offense.

"I don't give a crap about your computer system! I—"

The store employee said something else.

"There's a bank branch not thirty feet away! Right over there by the deli counter. That's where my money is. Go ask them."

But when it became clear the officious employee would not relent, the elderly man grabbed his checkbook and marched toward the exit.

"You'll be hearing from my attorney about this! I won't stand to be humiliated!"

When the man walked out of the store, he left a full cart of processed groceries standing there alone. Natalie felt a collective shudder move through the line of customers. A woman raised her hand and gestured at the officious employee until she had his attention.

"Um, are you accepting credit or debit cards?"

"I'm sorry, ma'am, but due to the unusual nature of this situation, we will accept only cash. We announced this a few minutes ago and there's a sign posted by the door."

"We didn't see your damned sign," another shopper yelled. He was severely overweight and dressed in a black knit shirt with a car logo on it. "No one uses cash anymore!"

"I understand," said the store employee. "But with the power and computer networks out, there's no way to know if these non-cash methods of payment are valid."

"Who are you to decide who gets to eat and who doesn't?"

"I'm the manager of this store."

"So you're going to deny honest, hardworking folks the food they need just so you can follow your stupid rules?"

"I'm sure the power will be back on shortly, sir. In the meantime it's my job to protect the financial integrity of this store. You would do the same if you were in my place."

"You just turned away an old man!" a woman yelled.

"I'm sorry," said the store manager. "I can't pick and choose who to apply the rules to."

"So none of us who don't have cash is gonna be able to buy food today?" someone else asked.

"I'm sorry for the inconvenience. Truly. But until the power is restored, we can only accept cash. U.S. currency."

"And what do we do in the meantime?" someone yelled. "We can't exactly go to the ATM and get money!"

The store manager nodded. "I'm sure the banks keep hardcopy ledgers. It may take some time, but eventually you'll be able to withdraw your funds."

Natalie glanced at the desk for Bank of Oklahoma. As far as she could tell there was no one on duty. Was the staff on lunch break, or had they simply gone home?

"This is bullshit!" someone else yelled. "Be reasonable, man. We just want to buy food from you. That's all. Be a human being, for Christ's sake."

"I'm very sorry."

"Right," the overweight man said as he pushed his cart of groceries into a display case and walked toward the door. "I bet you wouldn't feel so sorry if I came back here with a gun."

Over the next couple of minutes, at least half the people waiting in line left the store without their groceries.

Even so, it was more than an hour before Natalie and her family finally made it to the register.

SEVEN

So they were really going to do this. They were going to leave behind the relative security of his house, abandon things like food supplies and the generator and the water pump, in order to make a trip of more than two hundred miles to check on a family connected to Thomas by nothing more than an ancient high school crush. It was terrible what Seth had done, or tried to do, but the awful truth was that after the pulse, a single suicide was but a drop in an ocean of death.

The only way to survive an extinction-level event was to make decisions others would not. You had to be ruthless even if you were anything but. Still, the look on Skylar's face when she proposed the trip left no room for negotiation. If Thomas had refused, her opinion of him would have never recovered. And he wanted her to like him. Partly because of who she was and partly because they might be stuck together for a very long time.

Now he was loading a cooler of food and drinks into the back seat of his Mustang. He'd already placed four plastic containers of gasoline in the trunk and tossed a Rand McNally North American street atlas onto the dash. The atlas was dated 1997. Its cover was falling off.

He kept thinking about Seth's email and the address included at the bottom. 7702 S. Braden. Or 7720 S. Brandon. Or maybe some combination of the two. He couldn't be sure and now there was no way to check. There was a Tulsa city map in the atlas, but it was too small to resolve residential streets and basically useless.

"You stocked up on everything except maps?" asked Skylar, who stood nearby, overseeing the operation.

"The atlas seemed good enough at the time. I didn't think I'd be going anywhere for a while. And certainly nowhere specific."

When he opened the garage door (manually, with an emergency release) the two of them walked outside to look at the southern sky. The smoke was a black and billowing mountain range on the horizon. He could smell the acrid odor of fire and even this far away there was a curtain of haze in the air. He wondered when he would wake up and realize all this was a terrible nightmare.

Finally, Thomas started the car and pulled into the driveway. Skylar had suggested driving with the top closed, but he wanted as much visibility as possible. He wondered if someone would hear the engine and walk outside to look, but no one did. Eventually Skylar climbed into the car and shut the door.

"This route looks the most direct," he said, pointing at the atlas. "121 to 75, which goes straight north."

He flipped pages from Texas to Oklahoma.

"But we'll want to avoid towns as much as possible, so we should maybe take this turnpike."

"Sounds good to me," Skylar said.

They worked their way out of the neighborhood, toward State Route 121, navigating the same intersections as before. An increasing number of the stalled cars were abandoned, and the sidewalks were becoming crowded, as if people had given up on immediate rescue and were migrating toward permanent destinations. On the freeway they found rivers of more stranded drivers walking on shoulders and the median. Vehicle carcasses dotted the highway like slain buffalo. Thomas navigated them with care, gradually picking up speed. On the other side of the road, a couple of small motorcycles sped by in the opposite direction. People in the median craned their necks to watch. Others stared at Thomas and his own working vehicle. Once again Skylar had hidden herself behind sunglasses.

"I feel like I'm living in your screenplay," she said. "This is exactly how you described it. It's fucking weird."

During every minute since the new star appeared, as it became more and more likely a real-life pulse had occurred, Thomas ignored any relationship the event bore to his screenplay . . .partly because he'd been consumed with getting them home safely, but also because conflating such a horrific event with his own work felt wildly self-indulgent. Still, it was impossible not to see a connection between today's events and the plot of *Thomas World*, in which his fictional doppelgänger had written a story that became reality. Even spookier was the presence of Skylar herself, an actress who was here to discuss *The Pulse*, who landed minutes before a real pulse paralyzed the world.

But weird as that all was, how much did it matter right now? Whatever had caused the pulse seemed less important than how they chose to react to it.

"Pretty strange," he eventually said.

Ahead, a highway interchanged loomed. According to a big green sign, the entrance to Highway 75 was gained by driving onto a high, curving access ramp. But from here it looked like cars were stalled directly in front of the ramp's entrance.

"I don't think we're going to make it," Skylar said.

"Sure we will. See that gap on the left?"

There had been an accident between a white BMW SUV and a silver Honda Accord. From what Thomas could tell, the BMW had abruptly veered away from the ramp and collided with the Accord. Both cars appeared empty.

"I don't think you're going to make it," said Skylar.

"Yes, there's plenty of—"

"No, there isn't!"

"Jesus Christ, would you please—"

He interrupted himself by slamming on the brakes. A man, muscled arms raised, had emerged from behind the BMW and stepped directly into their path. His eyes were wild and panicked.

"Help!" he yelled. "Can you help us?"

"What's the problem?" Thomas replied.

"We were on our way to Durant," the man said, "when our car broke down."

He gestured to his wife, a petite blonde who emerged slowly from behind the SUV.

"We tried to call Triple-A but our phones don't work, either. What the hell is going on?"

"I'm not sure," Thomas said, and gestured toward the new star. "But it probably has to do with that."

"We live in Frisco," the man said. "We have no way of getting back. It's hot and my wife is pregnant and we need to get home. Will you take us?"

The man was moving slowly toward them and continued to block their path. His wife wasn't following, though, and didn't look very pregnant.

"I'm sorry," Thomas said. "We have an emergency. Frisco is the other way and we don't have time to go back."

"No one else has come along! You can't leave us stranded here!"

"Everyone is in the same boat," Thomas said, and made a sweeping gesture toward the road. "None of these cars are working."

"Yours is! Why is yours working?"

"I don't know. Maybe because it's old?"

"You're going to help us," the man said. His voice was so distraught it was nearly a moan. "Or I'm not letting you pass."

"So you want me to run you over?"

"Kevin!" the wife said. "Get out of their way!"

"He won't run me over. It would leave a big dent in his fancy car."

"You're right," Thomas agreed. He reached beneath the seat and retrieved a handgun he'd stowed for this very reason. "I'll shoot you instead."

At the sight of the gun, Kevin's face drained of color and his hands shot back into the air.

"Kevin!" the wife yelled. "For the love of god get out of their way!"

"All I want is a ride for my wife and you'd rather shoot me?"

"All we want is to be left alone," Thomas replied.

Kevin stood there for a moment longer, his hands still in the air, and then moved aside.

"Farther," Thomas said, and motioned with the gun. "Give us plenty of room to pass."

Kevin obliged, and when he was a safe distance away, his wife rushed to his side and put her arms around him.

"You're horrible!" Kevin yelled as they slid past. Despite Skylar's prediction, they squeezed through the opening with several inches to spare.

"Just an awful human being! You should be ashamed of yourself!"

Thomas ignored this and pushed his car forward, climbing the long, curving entrance ramp toward Highway 75 and beyond.

* * *

The new road was many lanes wide and offered more room to steer between stalled vehicles, which meant Thomas could drive faster. Some of the cars were still occupied, but by now most people seemed to have given up hope of immediate rescue. The Mustang's engine could surely be heard approaching from far away, and everyone watched them closely as they drove past. Thomas couldn't bring himself to make eye contact with anyone.

On the right, a single tower of black smoke leaned crookedly forward. Beyond it, even farther away, he thought he could see the faint outline of another plume of smoke. Looking into the rearview mirror was so awful he had given up doing it.

"So tell me about Natalie," Skylar eventually said.

"We were friends in high school."

"But not since?"

"Before our reunion, I hadn't spoken to her in twenty years."

"Wow. So why the hell would Seth send his suicide note to you?"

"At the reunion, Natalie got drunk and told me how Seth was cheating on her, how her marriages kept failing, how she was afraid she would never be happy."

"Did you two date in high school?"

"No. Just friends. She would tell me about whatever guy she was with and all the things he was doing wrong."

"Did you want to date her?"

"Every guy wanted to date Natalie Perkins."

"So, at the reunion, you turned the tables on her."

"What do you mean?"

"Come on. You're rich and handsome and wrote a movie everyone saw. She spills her guts to you about her terrible relationship, only this time you've got all the leverage. That had to feel good."

They came upon a place in the road where all four lanes were occupied, and Thomas was forced to slow down and drive onto the inside shoulder. When he did, a couple of men yelled at them from the other side of the concrete median. They were wearing purple TCU T-shirts.

"Hey man, can we have a ride?"

"Sorry," Thomas said. "We have an emergency."

"So do we!" said the other guy. "We're stuck out here!"

Thomas moved beyond the traffic pileup and accelerated again.

"Hey, man!" said the first guy. "What the hell?"

He kept driving and tried to forget the conversation he'd been having with Skylar. Because of course she was right about the reunion. The entire reason Thomas had bothered to attend was to close the door on childhood insecurity. He'd been a quiet student in high school, a kid who got lost exploring the terrain of his own mind, and the few people who knew him didn't seem very impressed. Even as kind as Natalie had been, Thomas knew she'd never imagined him as a romantic interest. Which was why the selfish and immature side of him, mostly eradicated but never quite gone, wanted her and all of them to see how wrong they'd been, how he'd risen far above whatever uninspired goals the rest of them had hoped to achieve.

But the reality of the reunion had been different than he expected. The petty grievances and imagined rejections from his teenage years, he came to understand, had mainly been the product of his pubescent imagination. Everyone he spoke to was friendly and appeared to remember him fondly, even if they knew little about him. *You were so quiet,* more than one classmate explained. *No one ever knew what you were thinking.*

And then there was Natalie, object of his teenage fascination, who turned out to be less textured and interesting than he remembered. At the bar, late on Friday night, she had drunkenly revealed a callous and myopic point of view on almost every topic, complaining to him about universal health care and gun control and social justice warriors. She believed the world was on a hopeless downward spiral, or so she said, but on Saturday night she revealed the real source of her frustration: her husband.

Would it matter to Natalie if his behavior had been driven by a gambling addiction instead of infidelity? And what if Seth was still alive? Would he come clean with her? Would she even want to be rescued?

"So did it?" asked Skylar.

"Did it what?"

"Did it feel good to show up at the reunion as Mr. Hollywood so Natalie could see the mistake she made not marrying you?"

"Maybe. I don't know."

"For such a talented screenwriter you don't tell a very good story. Why don't you want to talk about this?"

"Because it makes me feel guilty. I did have a huge crush on her in high school, but at the reunion I could see she was a lot . . .smaller than I remembered. She hadn't matured much and her grasp of the world was limited. It made me wonder what I'd ever seen in her."

"It sounds like you challenged yourself and kept moving forward and maybe she didn't."

"When I lived in that town I always felt like an outcast, like everyone was better than me. All I wanted was to be accepted by the social elite, by any clique at all, but I never was. Except Natalie. No matter what anyone else said or did, she was always kind to me."

"So you feel sorry for her?"

"I just think she could have been so much more. She was certainly smart enough. But there's something about the culture in these sweltering Texas towns that stops a lot of people from ever trying to become who they really want to be. Like they see no point in it. Like there's no hope left in the world."

Skylar looked away from him and gestured at the road, at the countryside where in the distance a plume of black smoke rose toward the sky.

"Maybe they knew something we didn't," she said.

* * *

Twenty miles outside of Sherman they came upon a family that had made camp in the grassy median. A heavyset woman approached the shoulder and began waving her hands. When Thomas didn't slow down, a teenaged boy and a younger girl also jumped to their feet and waved. There was a third child, a baby in a car seat, that someone had protected from the sun with a small white towel. The woman made exaggerated pointing gestures at the ground, and as they grew closer Thomas could see a man lying in the median. He could not find feet or legs, only a great, white abdomen that sloped out of the grass. The man's faded blue polo had been hiked to his armpits, presumably to administer CPR or some other emergency procedure.

"Are you going to stop?" Skylar asked him.

"And do what?"

"Take him to a hospital. He could have had a heart attack."

"Skylar—"

Before he could continue, the woman stepped into the road. Thomas swerved to avoid her. The cooler of drinks bounced around in the back seat.

"Jesus Christ!" Thomas yelled.

"*My husband is dying!*" the woman yelled back. "Please come back!"

"Thomas!" Skylar said.

"*FUCK YOUUU!*" the woman screamed at them, her voice already fading as they sped away.

"Come on, dude," Skylar said. "We can't just leave some poor sap dying on the side of the highway."

"Imagine a hospital right now," Thomas said. "Everyone on life support? Dead. Anyone in surgery? Also dead. If you have a heart attack and need a zap with the paddles? Too bad. No power. Hospitals are chaos. They're death traps."

"Hospitals have emergency power."

"Emergency power that relies on electronic controls. It's all off, Skylar. You know this."

"But I still can't believe it. I can't believe a man can lie there next to the highway, all alone, like this is the goddamned Middle Ages. My parents are going to die in Manhattan. My brother is going to starve to death in L.A. I'm never going to see them again, am I? This is how it is forever. Isn't it?"

Thomas wanted to make Skylar feel better, but to say anything optimistic would be a lie. He reached instead for her hand, but she jerked it away.

"Not right now," she said and looked away from him. "I need to be alone for a while if you don't mind."

By the time they reached Sherman, the density of stalled cars had increased again, but there weren't as many stranded drivers on the highway because the median had narrowed. Near the middle of town they saw a couple of pickups and an old VW bus moving on surface streets. A few people called out, but no one accosted them as the panicked wife had. Soon they were through Sherman and a little while later they found a similar scene in Denison.

A few minutes later they reached the Red River bridge and crossed into Oklahoma without incident.

THE ASCENSION OF ┼
AIDEN CHRISTOPHER
(IN HIS OWN WORDS)

EIGHT

S ometimes I think about all the terrible places you could have been when the power went out, like elevators and underground highway tunnels and window washing in downtown Manhattan. Being in a commercial airliner was surely one of the worst, since those huge, computerized jets had no chance to land safely once they lost power and communications. Even so, the people in the air met their end quickly. Think about astronauts in the space station. They could have had enough oxygen to last for days. They could be alive *now* for all I know, looking down on our huge, blue planet, waiting for the lonely moment when their oxygen finally runs out, all the while unable to know how things are going down here. Imagine having desperate, end-of-days sex in zero gravity. What a hoot.

I was in Dallas when all this happened, in the upstairs VIP area of a club called Cinnamon, recovering from a night of debauchery with a buddy and some dancer friends of his. The reason I came to Dallas in the first place was for a golf tournament, but after it was over I decided to hang around a few extra days. Ever since I lost my job I don't keep what you would call a regular schedule. Still, waking up drunk in a strip club on an average Friday morning is pretty nuts . . .unless, that is, you're on the town with Jimmy Jameson.

Jimmy runs what he calls a small-time sports gambling Web site, but the cash he pulls from this venture seems remarkable to me. On Thursday night, before the power went out, we were still on our first drink when a muscular friend of his walked in the door carrying one of those vinyl zipper bags people use for bank deposits. The contents of the bag comprised the previous week's proceeds from the gambling enterprise. I didn't want to pry into his business, so I didn't ask how much money it was, but Jimmy's the kind of guy who always knows what you really want.

"So this week's total came to just over ninety thousand," he said. "During football season it might be two or three times more. Then there are the weeks where I get fucked and have to cough up fifty or sixty thousand. You don't want to be around me when that happens."

Last year, when I was still employed, I made almost fifty thousand dollars and felt like I was doing all right . . .at least before I paid taxes and health insurance and tucked a few bucks into my hapless 401(k). That probably sounds like a lot of money to some people, but in the twelve hours we spent at Cinnamon between Thursday night and Friday morning, Jimmy shelled out nearly half of my gross annual salary. In cash. If you think there's no chance to fuck a stripper in the club, twenty thousand dollars will do it for you. And then some.

By law the club shuts down at two in the morning, but Jimmy is what you call a special customer. He shelled out five grand for use of the VIP room, two-thousand-a-piece to four separate girls, three grand to the manager on duty, a grand to our server, and the rest went to booze. Around midnight the party began to slow down, and I was lying on a sofa next to this dancer named Keri, languidly making out with her. That's when Jimmy produced two bubble packs of green pills that turned out to be X. Apparently he pays some pharmacist to cook them up. I'd never rolled before, so I didn't know what to expect, but half an hour later Keri pushed me into one of the private dance rooms, yanked down my pants, and swallowed me like I've never been swallowed. Keri is one of the sexiest women I've ever laid eyes on, she has the best set of natural tits you can imagine, and that night every square inch of her skin had been rubbed smooth with lotion and sprinkled with body glitter. We are talking the wildest porn dream you can imagine turned into reality by a woman who normally wouldn't have looked twice at me. But throw a couple grand in her purse and ply her with vodka and MDMA, and suddenly you're a rock star and she is your groupie. Even if I wasn't the one who paid for it.

The next thing I remember is waking up on the couch with a raging headache and a mouth so dry it felt like my throat was permanently sealed shut. At first I couldn't figure out where I was. Then I remembered Keri and her amazing skin, the hair that smelled like coconut, and assumed she had vacated the premises now that her paid work was done. I was so hungover I could barely summon the strength to hold my head in my hands. Naturally, I started in on the typical morning routine of self-hatred, wondering how I could have blown half my severance pay on a singles cruise where I didn't meet anyone, or how the $80,000 in my 401(k) had cashed out to $41,000 after taxes and penalties. I spent fifteen years saving that money one paycheck at a time and in six months had blazed through more than half of it. All while not finding the time for a single job interview.

So there I was, head in my hands, wallowing in hangover depression, when I heard someone approaching. I looked up and saw Keri standing there with a Bloody Mary in one hand and a joint in the other. She had changed into a pink spandex T-shirt and a black tennis skirt and did not look like a woman who had matched me drink for drink all night long.

"You look like you could use some breakfast," she said. "I've got just the thing to fix you up."

I couldn't understand why she was still in the club or why she was bothering to dote on me. Most of the women I meet can't get away fast enough. I wondered if she'd been slipped a morning bonus.

"Where's Jimmy?" I croaked.

"He left around four. Krystal drove him home. I think he drank a whole bottle of Jameson."

This information confused me, so instead of saying anything else I took the drink from her and knocked back a couple of swallows. It tasted strongly of lemon. I love the taste of lemon and in seconds the glue in my head began to loosen.

"Do you smoke?" she asked, pushing the joint toward me.

"Not very often."

"The Bloody Mary will help, but weed is the real hangover cure. Smoke this and you'll glide right out of here."

For a moment I just stared at her. Finally, I said, "You're a lifesaver, Keri."

"You remember my name?"

"Sure. You spelled it for me, remember?"

"In here I normally go by Kat. I don't like giving out my real name, for obvious reasons, but I know Jimmy is cool and you seemed like a nice guy."

"You were pretty cool yourself," I said. "I had a really great time last night."

"So did I," she said, smiling, her eyes shrinking to slits.

I wasn't sure what to say next. The club was empty and dimly lit and we seemed to be the only two people there. I didn't know what arrangement Jimmy had made with her or how long she was expected to keep me company.

"So if Jimmy is gone, I guess I should call a cab? I'm sure you want to get home."

Her smile vanished.

"A cab?"

"I don't want to be presumptuous and expect you to—"

"After going on half the night about wasting your savings, now you want to call a cab instead of asking me to drive you?"

I didn't remember whining to her about money. I couldn't believe I had whined to her about money.

"You're right. Sorry. I would love for you to drive me."

"Me, too," she said. "But not to Jimmy's. Not yet. Maybe you don't remember, but you owe me one, mister."

Again I had the feeling I was asleep, like this whole scene was some kind of high-concept wet dream. Exactly how much cash, I wondered, had Jimmy given her?

"By the way," she said and winked at me. "I don't even drive to work."

"What? Then how will we—"

"Lyft," she said. "It's so much safer with a job like this."

Imagine how futuristic that will sound to the people who survive all this: Arranging rideshare through an app on your smartphone!

Anyway, I smiled and was reaching for her hand when the lights went out. There were no windows in the building and we were thrown into the blackest possible darkness.

"Shit," she said. "I don't like this."

By now you know the drill. I reached for my phone, to use it as a flashlight, and it wouldn't turn on. Neither would Keri's. Panic quickly ensued and I took her hand in mine.

"You brought me that joint, right? You must have a lighter."

"I do!" she said.

After she found it in her purse, I took the lighter and produced a flame.

"I'll hold this and you lead us out of here."

A few minutes later we reached the rear exit and pushed the door open. By then our pupils must have been huge because we could barely open our eyes. Even so, I knew something was wrong. Really wrong. Cinnamon is just off the George Bush Turnpike, where the roar of traffic is constant, but instead of cars and trucks going by we didn't hear anything except the distant sound of people shouting and dogs barking. The quiet was so formidable it was like someone had unplugged us from reality.

"What the fuck?" said Keri.

That was when I happened to look up and see the new star in the sky. I didn't think much of it at first. About three seconds later, we heard the first of many massive explosions to the south. We didn't know yet what had happened. To us it looked like the beginning of a war.

The way Keri screamed then was something I'll never forget. I thought she would rip her vocal cords to shreds. I thought she might go into cardiac arrest. But she didn't.

All the really bad stuff came later.

* * *

I was still holding Keri, staring at rising clouds of smoke, when the back door of the club opened and the night manager stumbled out. He saw us standing there and approached quickly.

"Hey, buddy," he said. "I think you've—"

Then he stopped and looked around, as if he'd walked straight into a wall of silence.

"What the fuck?"

I don't know if the guy was still drunk or high from the night before, but he kept turning around, clockwise, saying "What the fuck? What the fuck?" until he nearly fell over. This was so unexpected and ridiculous-looking that in spite of everything I started to laugh.

"Holy shit!" the guy said. "What happened? Do y'all know what happened?"

"It was already like this when we came outside," Keri said.

The manager didn't seem to hear. Instead he ran toward a lonesome red Buick in the adjacent parking lot and climbed into it.

Keri and I watched as he sat in his car, unmoving for a period of seconds, before he climbed out again.

"It won't start!"

"Look around, man. There aren't any cars running anywhere."

"What are y'all going to do?" the manager asked.

It was a fair question. Whatever was happening was major and awful and I was a couple of hundred miles from home. I had no particular place to go, other than Jimmy's, which was several miles north. And I didn't remember how to get there.

"Do you live nearby?" I asked Keri.

"Not too far," she said. "Down the turnpike that way."

"I don't want to be presumptuous, but—"

"You can come. Although it'll take forever to walk there."

"I guess I better head home myself," said the manager. "My wife is with the kid and she's probably worried sick."

Neither of us knew what time it was, and Keri didn't know in miles how far away she lived. I would say the walk took about three hours. It might have been faster if not for pedestrians everywhere, streaming out of their cars, out of stores and office buildings, out of their houses. You don't know the look of real fear until you've seen it in the eyes of ten thousand people wondering if the country is being attacked, or if the world is about to end.

Eventually we got thirsty and stopped at a convenience store. The parking lot was crowded with people cursing and crying and looking up at the sky. A couple of unfriendly-looking dudes in Dallas Cowboys jerseys gawked at Keri as we walked by, and without my firearm I felt naked. Normally I conceal-carry, but I came to Dallas on a plane and I was too lazy to pack my piece the right way. Boy, did I regret that.

Before we went into the store, I told Keri to locate her bill of smallest denomination and hide the rest. She was carrying two grand of Jimmy's money, in hundreds, but luckily found a couple of twenties in her roll. We were fortunate to have cash because the guy who ran the place was taking nothing else as payment. When she bent over the counter to pay for the water, I imagined what the two of us might do while we waited for the power to come back on.

Keri's apartment was more like a loft, and from the outside it looked surprisingly upscale. Later I discovered she'd been making around three grand a week at Cinnamon. So you can understand my surprise when, as we walked in the front door, she stumbled over a stack of pizza boxes and nearly went sprawling across the floor. None of the window shades were open, and the only visible light was a bright rectangle thrown by the open door, but even so I could see dirty dishes and clutter everywhere.

"Did you throw a party?"

Keri thought I was joking and punched me on the arm.

"Oh, you," she said, and kicked aside an empty PBR case that was blocking the way to the kitchen.

While she stumbled around, opening window blinds, throwing more light into a living room where war had seemingly been waged, the lust that been building inside me winked out like a match tossed into the toilet. If this was how Keri kept her house, what did that say about her personal hygiene?

Eventually she stumbled into her kitchen, which might have been home to entire bacterial civilizations, and found an enormous bottle of lemon-flavored vodka.

"I don't want to think about what's happening," she said, her eyes wild and frightened. "Not yet, anyways. Let's take a couple of shots and go upstairs."

I know what you're thinking: Why weren't we trying to find out what had happened? How could we be so cavalier about a possible military attack or worse? Liberal elites might call our behavior a lack of intellectual curiosity, but the way I look at it, even though it was an awful situation, it was also out of our control. No one knew what was happening.

I swallowed a couple of ounces of vodka and followed her upstairs. As I watched her magical ass, eye level in front of me, I imagined a queen bed with a pink comforter, Keri bent over, tennis skirt yanked down past her thighs. Instead, at the top of the stairs, disorder was so profound I cried out in surprise.

"I know," she said. "I need to straighten up. You don't have to make a thing of it."

Even now I'm not sure I can trust my memory of her bedroom. The only area of the floor not covered in clothes or junk was a path that connected the stairs to the bed and the bed to the bathroom. Every other square inch of carpet, every available surface in the room, in fact, was buried under an avalanche of discarded shirts and pants and jackets and bras that averaged something like twenty inches in depth. The only explanation for this mess was she never bothered to do laundry, that she wore each item one time and then cast it aside like trash.

When she led me to the bed, ready to turn my pornographic dreams into reality, I resisted.

"I still feel like shit," I explained. "Maybe we should bring that vodka upstairs."

"Good idea. Be right back."

While she was gone I closed my eyes and pretended I was back at Cinnamon, which had looked pristine compared to this. Then Keri returned with the vodka and a handful of what looked like dead weeds.

"Let's eat some of these, too," she said. "I want to stop thinking about the world out there for a little while, don't you?"

See what I mean? It's not like we weren't aware. We just didn't care to worry.

"What are these? Mushrooms?"

"Yes, and they're awesome. What do you say?"

"Sounds great," I said, and washed down half a handful with more of the lemon vodka.

"You sound great," Keri said and pulled me to the bed.

* * *

Later we drifted downstairs, our blood riding high on vodka and psilocybin, and I began to see the clutter of Keri's loft as representative of a larger, more acute disorder of the world at large. We made our way outside and marveled at the new star, twinkling even in the light of the day. We lay in the front grass and watched the setting sun turn the sky violent with color. I was fairly sure I could hear smoke floating above us, billions of collisions between water and gas molecules producing a terrible, high-pitched screech that rattled my teeth.

"I'm not so sure this is a war," Keri said.

"Me either. You think there would be troops or planes or something."

"Maybe it's aliens," said Keri in an ominous and musical voice.

But I wasn't sure about aliens, either. Instead, I was starting to wonder if it was God who had turned off the power and killed all the cars. Maybe He was trying to flush us down the toilet like He did in the days of Noah.

"I'm hungry," Keri said. "Let's go get something to eat."

"What's nearby?"

"Down the road there's a KFC and a Whataburger and some restaurant. Saltgrass, I think?"

By now I know these restaurants are a quick walk of less than ten minutes from Keri's loft, but that evening we seemed to wander toward them for hours. I kept expecting to see squares of light and color, KFC red, Whataburger orange, even though cognitively I knew the electricity was out. People were on the sidewalks and in the roads and a few of them spoke to us, but I don't remember what they said. The smell of smoke was powerful. I felt like I was on the set of a post-apocalyptic movie filming the scene where survivors mill about with no clear understanding of what has happened or what's coming next. Everyone seemed to be waiting to be told what to do.

Eventually we reached the intersection where the restaurants stood. The door to the Whataburger had been propped open and a line of people stretched around the building. There was no line at the adjacent KFC, so that's the direction we headed. It never occurred to us to wonder why there was a giant line at one restaurant and not the other, at least not until someone waiting for a Whataburger called to us.

"Where the hell you going, man? Ain't no chicken at KFC."

"How do you know that?" I asked, stepping protectively in front of Keri.

"*Look* at the place, homey."

I looked again and noticed the front door of KFC was not propped open. It was missing altogether.

"What happened?"

"The manager was a dick. He wouldn't serve nobody and people didn't like it. I heard someone shot him."

"*Shot* him?" asked Keri. She threaded her arm through mine and pulled me close.

"That's what I heard. Then some dudes stormed the place and took all the food. But turned out it was frozen."

"They took a bunch of frozen chicken?" I said. This seemed unlikely, but then again the door to KFC was definitely not present. And no one was waiting in line.

"What about Whataburger?" I asked.

"They say he's giving it away. The manager. Cooking all the frozen food on a propane grill. But as you can see the line ain't moving so fast."

I looked across the street at Saltgrass, where a shorter line snaked out the door and into the parking lot.

"Why aren't you waiting over there?"

"Gotta have cash over there. I ain't got no cash. Who carries cash anymore?"

I looked at Keri.

"Let's try it," she said.

As we walked away, the fellow in the Whataburger line called out.

"You got cash, man?"

"A little."

"How about sharing a little green with the man that gave you the 4-1-1?"

"Sorry," I said. "We don't have much."

"Oh yeah? Or maybe you're full of shit."

"Be cool, man," I said. "Be cool."

* * *

Keri and I waited for a while in the Saltgrass line, but eventually a broad-shouldered fellow marched outside and announced the food had run out. There were a lot of groans and a few lazy threats, but the crowd seemed to understand the supply wasn't endless. Half the line shuffled over to Whataburger, and as I watched them, I noticed the 4-1-1 guy had barely moved. We decided to walk farther down the road to see what else we could find. By then my mind had returned to its normal, human size and I spotted two more restaurants ahead: Ruby Tuesday and Red Lobster. But when we reached them, we could see they were both dark and apparently deserted.

"I'm really hungry now," Keri said.

"Me, too. You don't have anything at home?"

"All I can remember is chicken nuggets and edamame in the freezer. But there's an H-E-B a little farther up if we want to buy groceries."

"Maybe we should do that. I was just thinking that even if we find a restaurant with food, what will we do for breakfast in the morning?"

"I was thinking the same thing."

It was another ten or so minutes to the H-E-B, where we found a sizeable group of people, mostly men, loitering in the parking lot.

"Don't bother unless you got cash," said a fellow as we approached the front door. He was short and slight, but the look on his face was angry and formidable, like a miniature dog posturing in front of a Doberman. He leered at Keri for a moment and then looked back at me. "You got cash?"

"We have a little cash."

"Ain't much food left, anyway," said another nearby fellow. He ran fingers through yellow hair and looked up at the sky. By now it was almost dark, and the new star was near the horizon. It was brighter than anything I had ever seen in the night sky, even the moon.

"That's why we should go in there and take what we want," said the first guy. "We deserve to eat like anybody."

"It ain't time to start robbing stores," said the fellow with the yellow hair. "It's only been one day."

"That's right! It's been a whole day and we ain't heard shit from no cops or the government. Nothing. It's like we ain't even in America, man. Like we're some kind of third world country."

The guy was still muttering as we approached the store. The front windows were almost dark. What light there was seemed to be chemical in nature, and inside I could see they had set up propane lanterns and candles.

A security guard greeted us immediately.

"This store only accepts cash," he barked.

"We have cash," I said.

"Let's see it."

"Pardon me?"

"Look, buddy," he said. "We got people coming in here pretending to buy so they can walk out of here with shit in their pockets. Show me some cash or I'll show you the way out."

I nodded at Keri and she produced a twenty from the waistband of her leggings. There were a couple of hundreds in her shoe. We'd left the rest back at her apartment.

"Fine," he said. "We don't have much food left, anyway."

He wasn't kidding. I had never seen a grocery store with shelves so barren. If you didn't know otherwise, you might have thought the building was being remodeled. The only ready-to-eat items we found were a loaf of blueberry breakfast bread and a package of Fritos shaped like corkscrews. Scattered around the store were other items less easy to prepare, like baking mixes, spices, and canned goods in the variety of beets and turnip greens. The only produce left were vegetables of little nutritional value: radishes, shallots, limes.

I had expected the store, like the restaurants, to be packed with desperate customers. But the only other shopper we saw was a hollow-eyed old woman who wouldn't make eye contact and seemed to be whispering to herself.

"I feel like a ghost," Keri said at one point. "Like I've come back from the dead to haunt this place. It's fucking creepy."

"I can't believe all the food is gone."

Laugh all you want at our ignorance. But we were accustomed to being assaulted by information, all day, every day. Remember how your phone would light up every five seconds when a news alert came through? You had Facebook reminding you of the past and Instagram barking about someone's story and "Guess What Donald Trump Just Said? Tonight at 6!" It didn't seem like a real disaster without the non-stop news coverage.

There was one checkout line open and it was manned by a sleepy-looking kid of about sixteen. He was tall and wiry and his earlobes were punctured with iron rivets.

"Where is everyone?" Keri asked him.

"We're out of food," said the kid. "After that woman leaves I think we're going to close."

"Was it a lot busier before?" I asked.

The kid looked at me like I hadn't spoken English.

"Did you sleep all day? Don't you know what's happened?"

Keri and I looked at each other.

"We know something terrible is going on," I said. "But still we didn't expect the store to be so empty."

The kid laughed.

"Dude," he said. "It's the end of the freaking world."

"What?" said Keri.

"The supernova. It killed everything. How do you not know this?"

"We're not idiots," I growled. "We can see things aren't running. But surely the government will fix it soon."

The kid looked at me with an expression of such pained tolerance that I was tempted to punch him in the face.

"Let me explain what an EMP is," he said. "Then I'm going home to my mom."

* * *

At the end of his speech, the checker informed us the store was out of bags and piled our meager groceries into a cardboard box that had previously contained jars of Miracle Whip. Then we headed for the door, tearing immediately into the bag of Frito twists.

The darkness outside was overpowering. Suffocating. By now the new star (the supernova?) had fallen below the horizon, and the other stars were so bright they didn't seem real. But they didn't cast much light on our path.

We should never have been caught so far away from Keri's apartment after dark. Partly because the walk would take forever, but mostly because of all the people who were still outside, people we could barely see in the pitch-black darkness.

"Aiden," Keri said. "Do you think that guy is right?"

"I don't know. He sounded pretty smart."

"I'm scared. This is way worse than a war."

After we crossed the H-E-B parking lot, when we reached the sidewalk, a man stepped out of the bushes and blocked our path. His gaze focused somewhere between Keri and me, rather than directly at either of us, and his fists were balled at his sides. It was the yellow-haired guy we'd seen before.

"We need your food," he said.

I stepped in front of Keri just as the guy lifted his shirt to reveal a handgun that was jammed into the front of his pants.

"We gave you a chance to loan us money and you didn't. So hand over the food."

Normally I'm not aware of my beating heart, but in that moment it seemed ready to burst out of my chest. Keri put her arms around me and pressed her face into my back. She whimpered and sniffled but, admirably, didn't break down or scream.

As frightened as I was, the natural thing would have been to hand over the box and back away. But something had hardened in me after listening to the grocery clerk's explanation of the EMP. If what he said was true, everyone in Dallas who hadn't previously prepared an evacuation plan was probably going to die. At first this seemed impossible, but the more I thought about it, the more I could see how mass starvation might happen. The H-E-B had been emptied in less than twelve hours. If no supplies arrived in the next few days, let alone weeks, pandemonium would be the natural result.

At that moment, though, as we were being mugged for our wretched haul of groceries, potential mass starvation was no match for my clear and present hunger. The last meal I could remember was a slice of pepperoni pizza someone had delivered to Cinnamon around two in the morning. We had wasted the afternoon sleeping and failed to take proactive steps after the power had gone out. I was in no mood to give our food to some asshole with yellow hair, gun or no gun.

"I thought you were the nice one," I said.

"Fuck you," was his answer. His eyes peeked left, toward the bushes, and then he looked back at us. "Give me the food."

"Where'd your buddy go?" I asked. "The one putting you up to this?"

Yellow Hair glanced left again and then put his free hand on the butt of the gun.

"You're honestly going to commit a crime for some funny Fritos and weird bread?" I said.

Finally, the bushes rustled, and the short guy climbed out.

"You have cash and we don't," he said. "You can get food somewheres else. All we have is you."

"Look—"

Now he reached behind his back and retrieved his own large handgun. Pointed it at my forehead.

"I'm done talking to you. Give us the fucking food."

I held out the box. My heart was beating in my brain. Yellow Hair stepped forward and took the groceries from me.

"That's better," said the short guy. "And now, honey, why don't you step out from behind your little bitch bodyguard?"

"Dude," I said.

He stepped forward and pressed the gun barrel into my forehead. It was hard and warm and suddenly my bladder seemed too full. My mouth was electric. I imagined an explosion in front of my face. Being split open by the bullet. The moment when sensory input would cease. When I would cease.

It was the most electrifying moment of my miserable life. I could die right then, and who the fuck cared? Like what was the big deal? Die and go to Heaven and everything comes up aces, right?

"Come here, honeypot."

"Leave her alone," I growled.

"Shut your fucking mouth," said the short guy as he pressed the barrel harder against my head. "Or I'll shut it for you."

Keri was crying. She stepped out from behind me.

"Look at that," the short guy said. He moved closer and touched her cheek with his other hand, the one that wasn't holding a gun to my head. "We could have some fun, you and me."

"Chuck," said Yellow Hair. "Stealing food is one thing, but this . . . don't do this."

"Why the hell not? No one's coming. No one can even see us. We can do whatever we want."

"The power's been out one day, man. It comes back tomorrow and you are in deep shit."

"Thing is, I don't think the power is coming back anytime soon. I think this is how it is for a while."

Maybe it was Keri's whimpering that did it, or maybe Yellow Hair's sage advice, but eventually the short guy stepped away from Keri and me. Already I felt adrenaline draining away and mourned its passing.

"Fine," the short guy said. "But maybe we'll see you later. Maybe there's another chapter to our story."

And with that, he grabbed Yellow Hair, turned around, and disappeared.

* * *

I don't know how long it took to find our way back to Keri's apartment. The intense darkness had a way of distorting the passage of time. Keri saw potential assailants everywhere she looked, even when no one was there. The sidewalks and streets weren't as crowded as before, but people were still out, and they emerged from the darkness like swimmers surfacing from ocean depths. Eventually we reached her loft and collapsed onto the sofa.

Keri nuzzled her head into my neck and cried violently. When I whispered that everything would be okay, her answer was to moan the words *No no no, no it won't.* For a while this was all we did, and I was thankful for the darkness, which obscured the chaos of her living room.

I kept thinking about the warm steel of the gun barrel against my forehead. My first reaction had been fear, but then something else had risen inside me, a complicated feeling best summarized as a brazen sense of superiority. As if I had realized for the first time that death was an event like anything else. It was eventually going to happen no matter what, and when it finally did, I wouldn't know until I was floating on a cloud somewhere, being fed grapes by naked angels.

To be clear, I'm not saying I *wanted* to die. I simply realized there was no reason to be afraid. To know this was to be different than everyone else. Better. Smarter. Awake.

As my mind adjusted to the new reality, I realized I was hungry again. Really hungry.

"Keri," I said. "Let's see what we can find in your kitchen."

When there was no answer, I realized she had fallen asleep. I slid away carefully, assuming the motion would wake her, but she barely moved.

Now all I had to do was find my way to the kitchen.

Normally, when the lights are out, you expect to use faint shapes or shadows to guide you. But that night I could barely see my hand in front of my face. Navigating such black terrain in a stranger's house meant inching forward with my hands splayed out in front of me while hunger pangs echoed off the walls. I felt observed, as if someone was watching me on an infrared camera, amused by my blindness.

Eventually I reached the kitchen, where I was nearly knocked over by the humid and rancid odor that poured out of the refrigerator. When I felt around, the shelves were almost empty, but I did find one Tupperware container that had been carelessly covered with aluminum foil. Whatever was inside this plastic bowl was the source of the rancid smell. There were condiments in the door and a jar of what my probing fingers decided were sliced jalapenos. I popped a couple of them into my mouth and was immediately sorry: They were so overwhelmingly hot I thought my face would melt.

After I wiped my watering eyes, I reached into the freezer and found the chicken nuggets and edamame, which were a few degrees cooler than room temperature. I unfolded the bag of edamame and sucked the seeds out of a couple of those, hoping to dampen the fire in my mouth, but this had little effect on the burning sensation or my hunger. Next, I nibbled on a chicken nugget, which was soggy and vaguely cool in a way that made me want to gag. I choked it down, anyway, along with a couple of others. This left about five more, and maybe I should have woken Keri to eat them, since they would spoil by morning. But I was enjoying this time to myself, so I let her sleep.

Next, I checked the pantry, where my searching hands discovered a half-eaten package of uncooked macaroni, some spaghetti, and a package of what felt like egg noodles. Everything else was spices and flour, except for a box near the back of the pantry that seemed to contain a dusting of graham cracker crumbs, the kind used for baking.

I decided to boil water and cook some of the egg noodles. But when I went to look for a pan, I pressed my hand on her stove for support, and felt electric burners instead of gas. Which meant I had no way to heat up the water.

This is when the new reality hit me so hard I nearly lost my balance. I sat down on the linoleum and put my head in my hands. My stomach was growling like a lion and I had nothing to put in it. I had no way to procure something to put in it. Sure, I could soak pasta in water and wait a couple of hours to choke that down. I could eat the ghastly chicken nuggets. But this food wouldn't last long.

Even if I wasn't afraid to die, starvation seemed like a pointless way to go about it.

I climbed to my feet and found my way upstairs, twice nearly tripping over junk on the floor. But eventually I located the bed, and the adjacent night stand, where the bottle of lemon vodka stood. I took a generous pull and sat down with my head in my hands.

When I finally looked up again, I noticed something strange—an orange glow that seemed to be hovering in front of my face. At first I thought it was a mirage, or maybe a dream, but when I turned around I could see the same orange through the window behind me. I'd been looking at a mirror.

From the vantage point of the second floor, it was clear the horizon was on fire. The idea that an American city in the 21st century might be devoured by an inferno opened a hole inside me that threated to swallow my physical hunger. The only way I could see to fill this emptiness was pour vodka into it, and with each swallow the world swam further away from me. It had been a mistake to visit the H-E-B. I should never have listened to that high school nerd explain why everything was broken, why the store shelves would never be restocked. What did he know? A country of 330 million people did not survive on a one-day food supply. There had to be more somewhere, if only—

And that's when it occurred to me: the idea that reshaped the trajectory of my life (and this story) forever.

The next morning, Keri and I went looking for Jimmy Jameson.

NINE

I awoke to the sounds of searching, a frantic rattling like someone shaking a bottle of pills. The room was bright and pink with color, the slopes of laundry piles thrown into relief by sunrise. Keri was in the bathroom, kneeling on the floor, her head pushed into the cabinets below the sink.

"What are you doing?"

She didn't respond or appear to hear me.

"Keri?"

"Fuck," she replied. "Fuck. Fuck. Fuck!"

She stood up, not bothering to close the cabinet, and marched in my direction. Grabbed her weed pipe from the nightstand and took a long, powerful hit. Her eyes closed and she held the smoke in for so long I thought she had swallowed it. Her hands were shaking noticeably.

"What's wrong?"

She looked at me with narrow eyes. This was not the same woman who yesterday morning had brought me a joint and a Bloody Mary.

"I'm hungry. I see you had dinner without me."

She glanced down at the vodka. It was a large bottle, but I had put a serious dent in it the night before.

"And you drank my booze."

"I ate one chicken nugget and a few pieces of edamame," I said, which wasn't exactly the truth but close enough for this conversation. "Then I felt so guilty I put them back in the freezer."

"You should have eaten them. They're totally gross now. And how did you like the habanero peppers?"

No wonder my mouth had gone into nuclear meltdown.

"You couldn't even get the lid back on the bottle. Did you eat them straight?"

When I chuckled at my ignorance, Keri cracked a tiny smile.

"So what are we going to do?" she asked. "My stomach feels like it's digesting itself."

"Do you not have family nearby? Someone who might have food?"

"My mom moved to Waco with some asshole. Which might as well be California since we have to walk."

"Well," I said. "Then we'll have to see what else we can find."

"Why would there be anything today if there wasn't yesterday?"

"Probably there won't. But I have a plan."

"And what is that?"

"Do you know how to get to Jimmy's place?"

She thought for a moment, her eyes looking out the window.

"I think so. I've been over there a few times to swim. But why would we walk so far?"

When I explained my idea, Keri's face brightened, as if it had been covered by rain clouds that were now melting away. Still, her hands shook so noticeably that she stuffed them into her pockets.

"You think he'll go along with it?" she asked me.

"I don't know why not. He's going to starve like the rest of us if he doesn't do something."

"Well, shit," she said. "Let's go!"

* * *

The streets were less crowded than the day before. We saw a woman walking a tiny dog, a bearded guy rollerblading, some dude in a blue jumpsuit looking through garbage cans. The sky was partly smoky and even at ground level there floated a fine haze that, if not for the acrid smell, could have been mistaken for fog. The roads looked like they had been staged for a science fiction film, cars frozen in place as if time had been intentionally stopped. Keri was a slow walker and puffed on a joint as we crept along. I took a couple of hits myself to dilute the passage of time.

We brought the dwindling bottle of vodka with us, loaded into a plastic Walmart bag along with the pasta and the graham cracker crumbs. My hunger was desperate, alive, a parasite eating me from the inside.

I'm young enough to have come of age when the Internet had already changed the world. I researched college projects on Yahoo! and followed current events at FoxNews.com. I've never subscribed to a newspaper. My first cell phone was a high school graduation gift, a handset in a black bag I carried with me everywhere and charged with the cigarette lighter of my car. Text messaging was an even bigger game-changer, because then I could connect with friends and family without the burden of speaking to them. By the time smartphones arrived I was sending and receiving thousands of these messages a month. I became a chronic email checker and Facebook poster and sometimes I wrote hateful comments on liberal Web sites to piss off those smug bastards. And it's not like my experience was unique. You were probably the same as me.

So the silence we endured that morning wasn't simply the absence of sound. It was a profound isolation, a sense of withdrawal not unlike being denied a drug your body had come to depend on. In the most basic sense we understood what had happened to the world, but all the complementary information was missing. How many people were dead? What was being done to restore power? Was anyone in charge?

After we walked a half hour or so, Keri wanted to alter our route.

"I think it's more that way," she said, pointing with a trembling hand. "'Cause when you leave the club you turn right. I think."

"How can you not know your way around better than this?"

"I feel like shit," she said. "I've only been to his place a couple of times and always at night."

A couple of times we heard a car engine or engines, the sound floating to us over the tops of houses, distant and surreal. I wanted to believe these engines belonged to military personnel that would eventually deliver news to us, but we never saw the vehicles, so I couldn't say for sure what they were.

For the first time since the power went out I wondered about my sister. Jessica lives in downtown Kansas City and we hadn't spoken since my mother passed away, which was a little more than three years ago.

Our falling out was a product of my not visiting Mom in the hospital before she died. I'd already stayed a week with her in the ICU, sleeping awkwardly in that little recliner every night, bloated on tepid hospital hamburgers. By the time she went in for a routine checkup three weeks later, I was already back in Houston. So when Jessica called to say Mom was back in the ICU, I complained I couldn't fly to Kansas City every time she went in for another test. The next day, I was stroking a six-foot putt for birdie when my phone buzzed in my back pocket. I missed the putt, grabbed angrily for the phone, and refused to answer when I saw it was my sister. She called two more times before finally sending a text message, two words only: MOM'S DEAD. At the funeral Jessica wouldn't look in my direction, despite my attempts at apology, and she communicated the disposition of our mother's affairs through an attorney.

Our father left when I was three and Mom was pregnant with my sister, so Jessica is the only family I have. But whatever. She abandoned me. She could go fuck herself.

When I glanced at Keri, she looked worse than ever. We had been walking for what felt like an hour.

"Are we getting close?"

"Maybe we're halfway. I don't know if I'm going to make it, Aiden."

"You'll make it."

"I feel like I need to sit down. Like right now."

"Let's sit down for a minute, then."

We were on the sidewalk of a major thoroughfare. There were more people out now, and most of them appeared to be going nowhere, or at least not in a hurry to get there.

"I need some water," she said. "Why didn't we bring any water?"

"I guess I thought we'd be there by now."

She wasn't looking at me. Her hands were trembling worse than ever.

"I have to tell you something."

"What is it?"

"I'm . . . I'm sort of addicted to Oxy. Like, painkillers in general, but mainly I use Oxy."

"And you're out."

"Yes. But I'm hoping Jimmy will have some. He always has something."

"Let's hurry up and get there, then, so he can fix you up."

"Okay," Keri said, "but then what? Even Jimmy won't have, like, an endless supply."

I wondered why she wouldn't look at the new world as the perfect excuse to stop using but didn't see the point in saying it. You can't tell anyone to get clean. They either figure it out or they don't.

"I'm really scared, Aiden. I haven't been this frightened in my whole life."

I could tell Keri wanted to be held, so I leaned forward and embraced her. Her stomach rumbled. Neither of us knew what else to say, so we just sat for a while.

I was starting to wish I could have made this trip myself.

* * *

Later, we saw a 7-11 that Keri believed was on the way to Jimmy's place. Suddenly she was confident we were headed in the right direction. Her mood improved and her hands shook a little less.

"So how'd you lose your job?" she asked.

"Economy went south and the company cut back on payroll."

"I don't understand why the economy goes up and down all the time. Why don't people just keep buying stuff the way they always do? It's not like I ever want to stop."

"It's more complicated than people buying stuff."

"What else is it?"

"Like maybe the housing market goes to shit because people borrow money to buy a house when they know they won't be able to pay it back."

"So? I never got a bad mortgage. Why do I have to pay for someone else's problem?"

"I don't really know. But when people can't pay what they owe, banks don't have enough cash to go around, and that locks up the system."

"Seems like a lot of made up shit to me," Keri said. "Like one person freaks out and that makes someone else freak out and suddenly everybody stops buying shit."

Keri's childish grasp of economic theory was beginning to grate on me, so I shut up and hoped she would take the hint.

At that moment we were walking past a shopping center that housed a couple of deserted chain restaurants and fast food outlets like Jimmy John's and Smashburger. The center was anchored by a Whole Foods Market, where someone had put up a handwritten banner that said CLOSED: Out of food!

Keri hadn't spoken in a while, probably because she had taken the hint, and I didn't care for the silence after all. Without the noise of her voice to cover it, I could hear the awful sound of my mind unraveling.

"So," I said. "Your mom moved away with some asshole?"

"Yeah. She finds a new jerk every couple of years who will put up with her shit. This is the first time she's left Dallas, though, so maybe he's the one."

"Did she not treat you right?"

"She's just selfish. She didn't mean to have me, but she also doesn't believe in abortion. So here I am."

"Does she know what you do? What your job is?"

"She knows I strip. She gives me shit for it, but I think that's because I can do it and she can't."

"How did you get into it?"

Keri laughed. "Guys always want to know that. It's no fucking surprise. I didn't try very hard in school, so I can't get an office job. For a while I was a waitress at a nice restaurant. Every so often some rich asshole would leave me a giant tip and write his phone number on the receipt. I mean, I have nice tits and I'm not fat, so."

"You're a lot more than that," I lied.

"Sure, I am. Except I met you at Cinnamon, and that's why you were there, right? For the tits?"

"I was there because of Jimmy."

"Well, anyway. I was making decent money as a waitress, but after a while I got to thinking I could make a lot more money at a club. I started out waiting tables, but the real money is in dancing, so here we are."

"Do you like it?"

"No, I don't fucking like it. Guys shell out good money for me to sit in their lap, and for what? Why don't they watch free porn at home? Why don't they find themselves a woman who will make them happy?"

"Not everyone can find a woman like you, Keri."

"Don't say shit like that. They don't know anything about me. I'm just an empty shell to them. A body they can ogle and squeeze in all the right places."

Ahead, on the sidewalk, a family approached: Dad in the front, followed by his wife and three kids. All five of them wore backpacks. The dad and both sons carried rifles slung over their shoulders.

"Shit," Keri said. "Let's cross the street."

"I don't think they're dangerous. The guns are for protection."

"Aiden—"

I took her hand and kept walking forward. The two boys were young teens, maybe fourteen and twelve years of age. The daughter was less than ten. When we had almost reached them, the dad said something to his wife and put up his hands.

"We're not looking for trouble," he said in a manner that sounded rehearsed. "Just let us be on our way."

"We aren't looking for trouble, either," I said.

Keri and I veered off the sidewalk and into the street. The dad glanced at her as he walked by, and Keri noticed.

"Hey," she said.

All five family members turned toward her, and the dad stopped walking.

"You have any water?" Keri asked. "We're pretty thirsty."

"We have limited supplies," said the dad in the rehearsed voice again. The sons must have been given instructions on how to behave, because they both stared at me as if I were a terrorist. The daughter looked like she had been crying and might start again at any time.

"Just a swallow," Keri said. "We're parched."

The dad hesitated, and his wife didn't like it. She leaned close and whispered harshly in his ear.

"I'm sorry," said the dad. "We have nothing to spare."

Now the daughter burst into tears. "Daddy—"

"Let's go!" growled the dad. "Move! Now!"

As Keri watched them go, her face hardened, and I couldn't tell if she was going to cry or scream.

"That guy has been in the club," she finally said. "Like in the past couple of weeks."

"You think he recognized you?"

"Of course he did. But he couldn't give us a single sip of water because he didn't want his wife asking questions. Asshole."

After that, Keri didn't want to talk. I hummed a few bars of "Enter Sandman" to block the screeching sound in my brain. Pretty soon we turned left, which as far as I could tell was north.

"Anyway," she finally said. "I think we're almost there."

* * *

A few minutes later, at an intersection of two major roads, we turned east. The houses on our left were larger than others we had seen and were guarded by a stone wall about seven feet high.

"This isn't Jimmy's neighborhood," Keri said, "but we have to walk through it to get there."

By then it must have been nine in the morning. On any other Saturday we would have seen kids on bicycles, dads mowing front yards, families in minivans headed to soccer games. Instead the streets were littered with stalled cars but few pedestrians. I wondered if people remained indoors because they were afraid or because there was nowhere to go.

Eventually we reached the entrance to another neighborhood, where a couple of gates stood open, and Keri smiled.

"This is it! I remember that tree!"

Between the entry and exit gates stood a mesquite tree with a shape that made it look vaguely like a hand reaching for the sky. Like someone pleading to God. Keri hugged me and kissed me directly on the lips.

"We found it! Holy shit, we found it!"

The houses in this neighborhood looked so much alike that when we arrived at Jimmy's, neither of us was completely sure it was his. The most convincing bit of evidence was the black BMW coupe parked in the open garage.

"Jimmy drives a car like that," I said. "Let's see if he's home."

We hurried to the front door and knocked. Then waited. There was no answer.

"He has to be here," Keri said. "Right?"

"We drove to Cinnamon in his BMW."

I knocked again, louder this time. When no one answered, I tried opening the door. To my great surprise it was unlocked.

"Hello?" I said. "Jimmy? You home?"

When there was no answer, I took Keri's hand and led her through the door. The entryway was two stories high, overseen by a gaudy, gold chandelier I recognized from before. All the shades and blinds had been drawn and it was very dark. We crept forward, in the direction of the living room. It sounded like someone was snoring. Then a man stepped in front of me, feet spread wide, and with both hands pointed a pistol at my nose.

"Stop right there, motherfucker!"

I put up my hands. The gunman was Bart, Jimmy's strongarm. His black hair was a mangled mess and I could smell BO even from this far away. It was the second time in two days someone had pointed a gun at me, and again I felt that strange and disconnected sense of superiority.

"Dude," I said. "It's me, Aiden. I was with you on Thursday night. I'm Jimmy's friend from Houston."

Even though the light was poor, I could see Bart's eyes were bloodshot. His stance was unsteady and his hands wobbled perceptibly.

"I don't know what you're talking about."

"You're Bart. You brought Jimmy ninety grand while I was sitting with him. Then we partied all night long. This is Keri. She was there, too."

Bart's resolve wavered and he peeked around me.

"All right. Fuck."

He lowered the weapon and Keri breathed a hurricane sigh of relief.

"It's been a strange fucking time since then," he said. "You're looking for Jimmy, I take it."

"Yes," I said. Keri stepped out from behind me. I put my arm around her waist to make sure Bart knew what was up. "Also, we're hungry. Y'all have any food?"

"There's cereal and chips and shit in the pantry. I don't know if any of the meat is still good. We cooked steaks on his grill yesterday afternoon."

"Where's Jimmy?"

"He should be upstairs in bed. We have some visitors from the club. Amy is with Jimmy, and Chelsea's still, um, asleep on the couch there."

"Y'all partied like rock stars?" asked Keri.

"You could say that. Anyway, help yourself to whatever you like. I'm gonna lie down for a bit. Jimmy will be up later."

"Thanks," I said.

"I remember now," said Bart. "Jimmy was wondering where you went. Pretty amazing you found your way here."

"Keri led the way."

"Yeah," she said. "And we've got an idea we want to run by Jimmy."

"What is it?"

"Oh," I said. "It's not that big a deal. We'll just get something to eat and wait on Jimmy."

Bart's eyes narrowed. He looked at Keri and back at me. He wasn't used to being on the outside of things that concerned his boss.

And if I'm honest, it gave me pleasure to wield this tiny bit of power over him. It was a feeling I wanted to build upon over the coming days.

* * *

After that, Keri and I marched straight to the kitchen. In the pantry I found a package of Crystal Light lemonade and mixed myself a tall, powerful glass. I love to make it strong, so bitter it puckers your lips.

Then we built ourselves a breakfast of Ritz crackers and peanut butter and potato chips. Even after I felt full, I knocked back six Oreos, probably the most I've eaten in one sitting. They were a little stale, though, and double-stuffed. Double-stuffed Oreos are stupid. Why mess with perfection?

After we ate, Keri and I wandered into the living room. Chelsea was still out cold.

"What's up with her?" Keri asked Bart, who was on the couch with arm over his head.

"Heroin."

"Is she okay?"

"She's fine. I checked her pulse three times already. She was pretty stressed last night and smoked more than the rest of us."

"Jesus Christ," said Keri. "Chelsea will take as much as you give her. You should have cut her off."

"I'm not her dad."

"Yeah, all you care about is her cunt."

Bart sat up then, and I was about to intervene when I heard something above us. I looked up and saw Jimmy at the top of the stairs. He smiled and grabbed a handful of his disheveled hair.

"Look what the cat dragged in!"

Jimmy's face was sallow and pouchy and his eyes were barely open. But as he descended the stairs, it was clear his enthusiasm was undiminished.

"I can't believe you guys made it. I mean, shit. Isn't this the fucking balls?"

He swept his arms upward in a grand gesture.

"What's it like out there?"

"We slept in yesterday," I said, "and by the time we went looking for food, the grocery stores and restaurants had been picked clean. Today it's a lot quieter. I think people are starting to realize help isn't coming."

"The fuck you say. This isn't Baghdad. We don't just leave the lights off around here."

When Keri and I looked at each other, it was the first time I had seen Jimmy's electric smile falter. Like ever.

"What? You don't seriously think they're going to leave it like this."

"Who is 'they?'" I asked him.

"The government. The police. Engineers, baby!"

By now, Bart was sitting up on the couch, watching us. He didn't look surprised. I suspected he had feared the worst but withheld his concerns.

"When we were at H.E.B.," I told Jimmy, "this nerdy kid explained to us what really happened. It's not some small thing, man. It has to do with that star in the sky."

"Well shit," said Jimmy. "We already knew *that*."

"Yeah, but it caused something called an electromagnetic pulse."

"Who cares?"

"Why don't we sit down?" I said. "And I'll explain why we care."

* * *

Jimmy is a smiler. He smiles when he sees you and he smiles when he's pissed off and he smiles when he wraps his brand new 56-degree wedge around a tree. Jimmy is also not much of a sitter. He's more of a pacer. After

I explained the details of what the EMP had done, and the effort to repair every chip and transistor and transformer in the world, he jumped to his feet and traveled around the room as if he'd snorted four lines of coke.

"So now what?" he asked. "If we do nothing, we'll starve to death, right?"

By now Amy had come downstairs and was sitting next to Chelsea, who was still sleeping so deeply she might have been comatose. Bart sat next to Keri and me.

"I have an idea," I said.

"What is it?"

"The company I used to work for shipped stuff all over the country. But fuel costs were so high, and the need for our products so time-sensitive, that we built distribution centers in strategic places to make shipping more efficient."

"So?"

"So, H.E.B. and Albertson's and Walmart surely do the same thing. A place like that would be a lot bigger than a grocery store and wouldn't sell to the public. So if there's one nearby, it's probably still stocked."

Jimmy's smile, having faltered, seemed poised to recover. But Bart was not as impressed.

"Don't you think someone else already thought of that? Like people who live near one of these warehouses? They were probably knocking on the door yesterday."

"I don't know. Everyone who could bought food yesterday. And this is still just Day Two. Most people probably don't know what's going on or realize how difficult a recovery would be. They're just waiting for someone to turn everything back on."

"So what's your plan?" asked Jimmy.

"I think we should put together a group—loyal friends, people who owe you money, whoever you can trust—and take the place with force."

Jimmy's smile returned to its normal wattage. He laughed.

"Storm a Walmart warehouse like a platoon of soldiers? This isn't Mad Max, you crazy cat."

Bart, though, wasn't as skeptical.

"Hold on, Jimmy. If that H-E-B kid was right, we either need to head for the sticks to hunt deer and rabbits, or we need to find food in the city. And according to Aiden, the grocery stores are already empty."

"All right," said Jimmy. "But if we're wrong, and the government fixes this, we'll go to jail. They'll lethal inject us for treason."

"It's a risk," I agreed. "But if we wait for the government to show up and they don't, someone else will hit the warehouse first. Then what do we do?"

"This isn't a bad plan," said Bart. "A warehouse full of food means we could survive a long time."

"But not forever," Jimmy said.

"No, but long enough for everyone else to starve. By then there would be enough food for whoever is left. Right, Aiden?"

"Exactly. And we could save other people if we wanted. Like, if we controlled the warehouse, we could let in the people we choose."

"You're crazy. Both of you. Even if we manage to get, I don't know, five guys—"

"I'd say ten," said Bart.

"Ten guys. We have to absolutely trust them. We have to feed them until we get in. And once we're inside, and everyone outside is starving, won't the hungry people attack? We're talking about serious organization. That's the only way this would work."

"So you think it could?" I asked, feeling hopeful.

"Maybe it could work. If we ran it right."

"What about friends?" Amy said. Until now, neither her nor Keri had said anything for a while. "What about my family?"

"Who said you're invited?" asked Jimmy sharply.

Amy's eyes widened and she looked down at her hands.

"I'm sorry," he said. "Of course you can come, baby. But there will be hard choices to make if we do this. I want you all to understand that."

Amy nodded without looking up at him.

"We have a lot of work ahead of us if we're going to do this," Jimmy said. "We've got to find our guys and outfit them. I've got some guns but we'll need more. And—"

The harsh look in his eyes made me wonder if he had suddenly changed his mind.

"What?" I asked.

"So, Mr. Smart Guy. Maybe there's a grocery warehouse somewhere in Dallas. How are we gonna find it? It's not like we can hop on the fucking Internet."

I'd been wondering this myself. I was hoping Jimmy or Bart knew.

"If you put together a team," I said, "one of them is bound to know, right?"

"And what if they don't?"

"I know where one is," said a broken voice. For a moment I thought someone else was in the house with us, but then I realized the voice had come from Chelsea, who still hadn't opened her eyes.

"Are you sure?" asked Jimmy.

"Yeah. My mom lives like a mile away from a Walmart one. I'll tell you where it is, but you have to promise to take my mom, too. And whoever Amy and Keri want to bring."

Jimmy looked back at me and smiled. His whole body seemed to glow with electricity.

"See there?" he said. "Already this thing is getting harder to manage."

* * *

Even though everyone agreed with my plan, and that time was something we could ill afford to waste, the next step had not been to gather weapons or sit down and map out a strategy. Jimmy thought a better idea was to relax and recover from the drug-induced stupor of the past two days.

I understood the desire to rest. In the months since I lost my job, I've wasted time alternating between nights at the bar and days recovering from those nights. It's a terrible, debilitating cycle that robs a man of productivity, of his will to succeed at anything other than remain in the cycle. But that morning, for the first time in nearly a year, a worthwhile goal stood before me. I could see a real reason to put aside the bottle and do something constructive. And no one else would get off the couch.

At the first opportunity, Keri pulled Jimmy aside and explained her situation with the painkillers. He took her into the kitchen, and a minute later she was back on the sofa with a calm look on her face. Then Jimmy went back upstairs with Amy.

The living room was outfitted with a sectional sofa, gas-log fireplace, and a giant television. On either side of the TV stood huge shelves of Blu-ray discs; beneath it sat a couple of stereo components and an

AppleTV console. It seemed so pointless, so hopeless, to wonder if the television would ever be watched again. The Blu-ray movies were movies no longer. They were flat, useless discs. An ottoman stood between the sectional sofas, and on it lay an iPad, also useless. I'm not much of a reader, but I might have picked up a book to pass the time had I seen one anywhere. Instead I just stared out of habit at the dark television set.

What point, I wondered, was God trying to make with all this? And what would come next? There was no reason to report to work. No television to watch. There was no way to get news and the only method of available travel was by pedal or foot.

Some people, like the family we saw earlier, were taking proactive steps to survive. Maybe they were marching to a safe place in the country. Maybe they owned a cabin on a private pond where they enjoyed lazy summer afternoons, fishing or swimming or watching NASCAR on satellite television. The dad might be one of those preppers who had seriously contemplated the fall of Western civilization. I knew guys like this, men who approached survival like a video game. They acquired assault rifles and purchased supplies and preached to whoever would listen how, when the Fall came, they would be ready. While the rest of us easygoing city slickers lived paycheck to paycheck, buying food daily, never planning for emergencies, they were doing the hard and thankless work of survival.

Except I never saw it as thankless. I saw it as entertainment, as pleasurable for them as playing golf was for me. Because what sane person would prefer this life to the one we had before? Even if that family somehow manages to reach their hypothetical cabin in the woods, even if their supplies last for weeks or months, do they really want to live like settlers on the frontier? And what will happen when hordes of starving people from Dallas and Ft. Worth pour into the countryside, parents desperate to save their children, to save themselves? The father no doubt imagines he will sit on the porch and pick off these desperate souls with his arsenal of deadly force, but will he really? Will he possess the will to kill as many of his fellow humans as it takes? And if he can summon the will, has he stockpiled enough rounds of ammunition? Will his wife and kids be ready to take up arms while he sleeps? And if by some miracle this family manages to protect itself from the swarm of humanity, will they possess the strength to bury all the bodies? Will the children address their dad as Pa and their mother as Ma? Will they grow beans and potatoes and trade with other settlers for tomatoes and cucumbers? Will they honestly enjoy this new way of life, which seemed romantic while they were dreaming it in front of their glowing computer screens and television sets, or will they long for their earlier, pampered existence, when their children didn't lose a leg from a rattlesnake bite or die from an infection that could have been easily cured with antibiotics?

Will the survivors join together? Will they find a way to combine resources and knowhow to push humanity forward again? Or will God simply hit the reset button?

I looked away from the television and saw Bart and Keri were both asleep. Chelsea might have been awake, or not, it was hard to know with her. In fact, the loudest sounds I could hear, other than the high whistle of my own brain, was the deep and measured breathing of the sleeping humans in this room.

I wasn't afraid to die, but the more I thought about it, the more I wondered if my new plan was such a hot idea after all. If God wanted us dead, why fight the inevitable?

I stood up and went into the kitchen. Found the bottle of Jimmy's painkillers and washed two of them down with another glass of lemonade.

Then I went back to the sofa, lay next to Keri, and dreamt beautiful dreams.

GATHERING STORM †

TEN

Ever since being interrupted by a phone call while trying to take his own life, since his discovery of the star in the sky, the brain cells in Seth's skull had seemed to be mechanically separated from one another, as if the space between them had somehow expanded. This effect induced a disassociation with the physical world that transformed, for instance, the short walk to the daycare into a journey of Tolkien proportions. At the daycare he worried the woman in charge would refuse to release his sons, that she would smell alcohol or car exhaust or nausea on him. Natalie's appearance in the golf cart was so unexpected that for a moment he feared he was hallucinating her.

Shopping for groceries in near darkness would have been surreal even with the clearest possible head, and the wait in the checkout line had been soul-crushing. None of it would have been possible if Natalie hadn't taken the drink cart, but it was foolish of her to promise the vehicle to Blake. Seth wanted to overrule her decision but Natalie's venomous response had been immediate.

"I made a promise," she hissed as they stood in half-light near the register. "Someone might have taken the goddamned thing from me if it weren't for him."

"Don't you think that's a bit dramatic?"

"Look around this store," she said, "and tell me I'm being dramatic."

All his life, the way Seth had held depression at bay was to indulge self-destructive behavior—cheating on tests and faking grades in high school, stealing sales and manipulating his way up the corporate food chain, and most recently gambling away his family's financial solvency.

Though he hadn't realized it before, he understood now these obsessive behaviors had insulated him from darkness by pushing it into the background. But today something miraculous had happened. Today he had been set free from his self-imposed restraints by an event that was maybe divine or maybe pure luck. Either way, Seth was fairly certain this unexpected second chance didn't involve taking orders from his snooping wife.

He kept thinking about the phone call, how Thomas had offered to pay his debts, how he had promised to take care of Natalie. What would possess a man you didn't know to be so generous? Was he in love with her? Had Thomas planned to swoop in and steal Seth's family? Honestly, he had no proof of their infidelity. He'd inferred as much after reading two messages in her Gmail account. On the other hand, Natalie definitely believed Seth had cheated on *her*, which possibly explained why her behavior this morning had vacillated between needy and surly.

"Whatcha thinking about?" Natalie asked, having materialized behind him.

Seth realized he was standing in front of the open pantry, staring at spices and flour and boxes of Lipton soup. He turned to face his wife, who was smiling like she didn't mean it.

"What we're going to eat when our food runs out."

"Maybe it won't come to that," Natalie said. She stepped forward and put her arms around him. "Maybe the government is already working on how to fix this."

"I don't know. All these things that aren't working, there's something internally wrong with them."

"Do you think this might be a pulse?" Natalie asked.

At the word *pulse*, Seth's head jerked involuntarily, as if he'd been struck, and waves of understanding rolled over him. The first thing he'd done after reading Natalie's emails was look up Thomas Phillips, which is how he had learned of the man's success in Hollywood. His second screenplay, Seth now remembered, had been called *The Pulse*, which was a story about the death of technology by way of solar flare. And if today's events were similar to what had happened in the screenplay, it meant microchips and transistors everywhere had been rendered inoperable. But what was Seth to make of this new information? Was Thomas some kind of demon?

"A pulse?" said Seth, as if he didn't know. "What's that?"

"It's like a burst of electricity or something that kills all the computer chips."

"How do you even know what that is?"

"I think I saw a story on FOX about it. I can't remember."

Because Seth knew his wife was lying, it lent him a kind of leverage over her.

"You know more than me," he said. "So what happens if you're right?"

"I think it means the whole world is fried. Nothing can be fixed anytime soon and meanwhile everyone in big cities will starve to death when the food runs out."

"What do you think we should do?"

Natalie looked at Seth as if she expected him to already know the answer.

"I would think," he said, "that if things don't go back to normal soon, we'll need to get out of the city."

"And how would we do that? With no car?"

"I suppose we'd have to walk."

"How do we walk that far with Ben and Brandon? And where would we go?"

"I don't know."

"I'm scared, Seth. If the government can't fix this, I'm afraid it's going to be pandemonium and we don't have a backup plan."

"Who would have a plan for something like this?"

"Maybe we should have bought dry goods over the years, or canned food, put them in the garage just in case."

By *we*, she really meant *him*, as in Seth should have planned for the pulse. Even though his snooping wife possessed the information they would have needed.

"But we didn't," he replied. "So now we'll have to figure out something else."

Natalie didn't care for this answer or the tone of his voice or both. She looked at him coldly and walked away.

It was true Seth was guilty of far worse crimes than his wife. Had Natalie gambled away their savings? Had she stolen an unconscionable amount of money from her own father to fund a descent into financial madness? No. But it was also true that Natalie was a woman with champagne tastes, who never expected to work for a living, and that Seth for much of their marriage had secretly felt like an inadequate husband.

Natalie had already married and divorced when Seth first met her. She'd still been working in the office then, and he often saw her in the break room, reading a magazine or sometimes a book. Men always stopped to talk to her, but he never saw anyone sit down, probably because they were too intimidated to try. Seth wouldn't have bothered, either, only one day Natalie looked up as he walked by, and something about her eyes compelled the word *Hello* to pop out of his mouth. Before he could stop himself, Seth asked if he could sit down, and in that little beat of time, before Natalie answered, Seth saw how their futures were balanced evenly between her acceptance or denial.

She hadn't made it easy on him, but eventually they turned that initial conversation into a relationship. Over a period of weeks and months he grew to know the real Natalie, the girl of childlike hopes and dreams and fears hidden behind a façade of blonde beauty. Her father, then three years dead, had taken to his grave the security she enjoyed since childhood, and naturally she assumed Dan, her first husband, would step into that gaping hole. Instead she found him in bed with a tattooed bartender six weeks after their wedding. Natalie had married Dan for his money first and his Christian Bale looks second and had given little thought to what kind of man would drive a BMW M5 and wear solid platinum Swiss watches and spend more monthly dollars at the salon than her. In Seth, Natalie clearly was looking for something different, but she'd never been subtle about her desire to live a financially comfortable life.

He'd spent many, many hours blaming Natalie for his gambling debts. It was easy to do, because when she became pregnant, Seth proudly announced his wife could quit her job and assume the role of full-time mother. A recent promotion made it feasible, just barely, for them to get by on one salary...at least until they learned Natalie was going to have twins. By then Seth couldn't bring himself to retract the offer, and the only way to remain financially solvent, he realized, was to earn more money. To be more like Dan and less like himself. But since he didn't possess the looks or experience or social connections to land a more lucrative job, he had no choice but to find a second one. So on a few evenings each week he delivered soft drinks for a local bottling company and told Natalie he was "working late." Seth lied to his wife because he couldn't bear to admit financial impotence. He lied to himself by ignoring the way this deception only deepened his self-loathing.

But when Ben and Brandon were born, the moment he held those vaguely purple children, the darkness receded into the distance, and for the first time in his life Seth felt like a man. As he held back tears and watched Natalie nurse the boys, he promised himself the mother of his children would never have to work away from home again. And for a while it seemed like his plan would work, especially when his boss lauded his efforts and promised a bigger promotion the following year. All Seth had to do, or so he thought then, was stick it out for a while, work the two jobs, and eventually everything would be okay.

Which might have proven true if Natalie hadn't complained about being left alone with the twins all the time. Even when Seth was present, she froze him out with cold stares and silence and paradoxically spending most of her time sequestered with their sons. If Seth tried to join them, Natalie would hand over the boys and go find something else to do. If all that weren't enough, she began to refuse sex, rudely, a habit that dragged on for months.

Because he was trying so hard to give Natalie the life she wanted, and because she seemed so ungrateful for his efforts, Seth began to resent his wife. Whether she knew or didn't know about his job hauling cases of soda was not the point. The point, as he saw it then, was Natalie desired a certain lifestyle, and Seth knew only one way to provide that lifestyle. He was out busting his ass to make extra money, and she resented him for not being home. Eventually the darkness returned and became more oppressive than ever. He feared, if something didn't change, he would fall into a black hole of dread from which there was no recovery. So one night, when he wasn't delivering soda, and before he was forced to head home and face his angry wife, Seth stopped by the Indian casino to play a few hands of blackjack.

* * *

The boys shared a bedroom and a bunk bed. They alternated weeks on who got to sleep on top. Seth found Natalie in the room with them, sitting on the floor, playing backgammon. He couldn't remember the last time he'd seen the boys play a board game.

"Dad," said Ben. "When's the power coming back on?"

"I don't know."

"Even our iPads don't work," said Brandon. "I charged mine all night. I want to play Minecraft."

Natalie was focused on the board and didn't look up at him. When she rolled the dice he nearly yelled *Hard eight!* Craps being his second-favorite game after Blackjack.

"You might not be playing Minecraft for a while, son. But your mom and I are going to take care of you. You'll always be safe with us."

"Why wouldn't we be safe?" asked Ben. "Is something bad going to happen?"

"No," said Natalie. "Your dad is being silly."

She stood up and finally looked at Seth.

"Honey, can I talk to you for a minute?"

He followed her into the living room, the farthest point in the house from where the boys were playing.

"Are you trying to scare them?" she asked.

"Of course not. But they must know something is going on. I wanted them to know they're safe with us."

"Instead you scared them."

"They didn't seem very scared."

"Well, you scared me."

He couldn't tell if Natalie wanted to slap him or be held by him.

"I don't know what you want me to do," he finally said.

"At the grocery store I thought you had changed, you seemed confident then, in charge. But now you're back to your wishy-washy self, not sure about anything."

"What is there to be sure about? We don't know what the hell is going to happen. No one does."

"Maybe you're worried about her," Natalie said. "Your girlfriend."

"My what?"

"You think you're so goddamned smart. You think I don't know all about her? Working late, my ass."

Before the first, life-changing trip to the casino, Seth had been an amateur gambler, mainly betting on football games and sometimes a March Madness bracket at work. What hooked him that first night was winning three hundred dollars almost by accident, betting conservatively and squirreling away his proceeds instead of subjecting them to possible losses. The next night he returned to the casino armed with that $300, and somehow, miraculously, won almost $11,000 during a four-hour run. This time he doubled down, split hands, and in almost every case saw the cards he wanted. On the way home he kept looking at the check, issued in his name, an amount greater than he could make delivering soda for an entire year.

This is where he should have stopped. Any sane person would have. He'd gone to the casino on a whim and in two nights walked away with enough money to eliminate the need for a second job. There was no reason to put any of that money at risk.

But the rush of throwing down chips and waiting for fate to render judgment could not easily be given up. Neither could the attention of spectators, those casino-dwellers who were too chicken (or well-reasoned) to risk their own money and instead lived vicariously through Seth's brazenness. They cheered his wins and groaned at his losses, and sometimes a sexy young woman would rest her hand on his shoulder and squeeze when the dealer busted. In these moments Seth felt as though the darkness was banished forever. Sometimes it seemed he'd never known darkness in the first place.

Despite all this, he missed his wife. And one night, riding high after another great run, he wondered if he might purchase Natalie's happiness with two infinity diamond bands to wear on either side of her wedding ring. He presented the gift to her over an expensive steak dinner. She could have swallowed the rings and he wouldn't have been surprised. Instead, she cried. She hugged him and played footsie under the table, and on the way home performed sexual acts on him while he drove.

A few days later, when Natalie asked how he had paid for the gift, Seth smoothly invented a surprise bonus for all the extra hours he'd put in at the office. This answer induced a new bout of tears, during which Natalie apologized for being unsupportive and admitted insecurities of her own: She no longer felt sexy since bearing children and refused to believe Seth could, either. It was only a matter of time, she feared, before he would leave her for someone else. The way Seth responded was to push Natalie to the bed and make love to her, to breathe sweet words into her ear until she fell asleep in his arms.

The next day, when he should have gone to work at the bottling company, Seth was inspired to visit the casino instead. He bet modestly and intelligently and managed to earn back a quarter of what he'd spent on the diamond bands. A few days later he quit the part-time job. What was the point of backbreaking labor when he could earn a lot more money and have a lot more fun at the casino? Sure, he would suffer losing streaks, every gambler did, but by then all Seth had to do was break even until the big promotion came through. Then he could stop forever.

But that wasn't what happened. Losing nights began to outnumber winners and so began the long descent. By the time he finally landed the promotion, this additional income was only a fraction of what he was betting weekly at various casinos. By then he was also making regular trips to New Orleans, where the bets grew bigger, and where the losses proved even more staggering.

"My girlfriend," he said to Natalie, the blood in his face rising. "You think I have a girlfriend."

"I know you have a girlfriend. And now you can't even call to ask how she's doing."

"How do you know this, Nat? Where did you come by your scandalous gossip?"

The moral certainty in her eyes, that dark light, seemed to dim a little. The magnitude of her wrongness calmed him.

"Yes, I looked through your phone!" she barked. "What did you expect after all your goddamned sneaking around? And I'm glad I did, because now at least I know the truth!"

"You don't know anything. You have no idea what I've done for this family."

"Don't try to weasel out of this. I saw all the calls she made to you. Did you break up with her? Are there two girls nagging you now instead of just one?"

"JJ isn't a woman, for God's sake."

"So you *do* know who I'm talking about!"

"Yes. And by the way, I also snooped. Thanks for sharing your feelings with a high school boyfriend instead of talking to me."

By now the certainty in her eyes was gone, but the anger was not. Natalie considered her answer a long time before she replied.

"Thomas is an old friend. At the reunion I was so distraught I finally broke down and told him everything. I had to talk to someone, Seth, since you weren't talking to me."

"But everything you told him is bullshit, Natalie. I've never cheated on you."

"How can you stand there and *lie* to me? We've been married for eleven years!"

"*I am not lying to you!*" he bellowed.

"All right, then. Where do you go? Because I know it's not just work."

His hands were squeezing themselves involuntarily and Seth forced himself to stop.

"Some of it was work. I took a part time job when we found out you were having twins."

"A second job? Doing what?"

"Delivering soft drinks."

"You expect me to believe that?"

"I have the pay stubs to prove it."

"But that was so long ago. Didn't you get a raise when the boys were born?"

"I did. But not in time."

"Why didn't you tell me?"

"I didn't want you to worry," he explained. "I wanted you to feel secure."

"So you thought it was better to lie to me?"

"I didn't want you to think I wasn't good enough for you."

"But you can't still be working the second job. Not when you travel all the time."

She paused here, and the look on her face softened as she waited for Seth to explain himself.

"Please talk to me," Natalie said. "Help me understand. Because living with you has been hell the past few years. It wasn't just the hours you were gone, Seth. Even at home you were a ghost of yourself, moping around with this empty look in your eyes, like you didn't want to be a part of the family anymore. If you were working two jobs for me—for us—I can only assume you resented me for it. We should have sent the boys to daycare. I should have gone back to work."

He couldn't know if Natalie was performing or if her description of his behavior was accurate. What he did know was he'd been living with the burden of his failures for so long that now, as he prepared to tell his story, Seth could already anticipate the freedom of no longer carrying the secret alone. Of no longer being stooped by the burden of his insurmountable debt. Of being granted the second chance at life he'd wished for so many times. His heart thundered in his chest. His fingers tingled. His mouth tasted like pennies.

"Let me tell you why I was really home from work this morning."

* * *

By the time Seth was done, the two of them were sitting next to each other on the sofa, staring at the dark television, drained by the exposure of so much heartache. Natalie grabbed a bottle of caramel vodka from the freezer, and when she returned with it, he was shaken by the hollow look in her eyes.

"Honey," she said after a swallow of vodka. "What is this darkness? Where does it come from?"

"It's been there since I was a kid. I'm always afraid the worst is going to happen, so why not just get on with it?"

"But you—"

She began to cry again. Seth tried to put his arm around her shoulder, but she shrank away from him.

"I can't get this image out of my head where you're sitting in the car, looking at pictures of us, waiting to die."

How good it felt to hear her say this! For someone to express empathy for his pain!

"How could you do that? Just skip out and leave us all alone?"

"Nat—"

"It's such a chickenshit thing to do!"

"I already told you there was no other way to pay the debt."

"That's bullshit. There's always another way. And what if it had worked? The boys and I would be facing this terrible world with no husband to help us."

"Obviously, I didn't know all this would happen," he said and took a swallow of the vodka.

It seemed Natalie would never understand the terror he had overcome to follow through with his plan. To her, his failures were nothing more than a story, a set of poor decisions she could unreservedly judge. For Seth, the gambling debt was like cancer he had tried to carve out with a knife.

"I wish you would have told me. I wish we could have gotten you some help."

Instead of answering, since there was nothing more to say, he took another pull of vodka.

"What about now?" she asked. "I know you're hoping all this means the debt is gone, but are you still . . .you know . . .do you still feel suicidal?"

"No. I'm here to take care of you guys no matter what happens."

Natalie grabbed the bottle and swallowed more vodka. A long moment passed, and finally she lay her head on his shoulder.

"And we're here to take care of you."

Eventually the boys, with nothing else to do, came looking for them.

"We want to go outside," whined Brandon. "Can we at least play in the back yard?"

"Not right now," Seth said. "Not until tomorrow. We aren't sure what's happening and we want you to be safe."

"But I am so *bored*. Ben, aren't you bored?"

"*So* bored."

"You're going to be bored and sore in the bottom if you don't go back to your room and give your mom and me more time to talk."

"Fine. Ignore us. We'll just be playing backgammon!"

When they were gone, Natalie said, "I keep thinking about you in the car. How frightened and alone you must have felt. I'm so sorry, Honey. For everything."

Seth wanted to believe Natalie had come to understand the sacrifices he'd made. But just because they had finally confronted each other didn't mean the pain was gone, nor did it change the external dangers they faced. If the power didn't come back and they couldn't find a sustainable source of food and water, his family's odds of survival weren't good.

Still, Seth couldn't imagine a universe cruel enough to offer a second chance at life only to steal it back with a death as pointless as starvation.

The two of them were still on the sofa, nestled in each other's arms, when the universe knocked on the front door and offered an answer.

ELEVEN

A few miles beyond Durant, Oklahoma, on a stretch of road empty of stalled cars and stranded drivers, Thomas stopped to study the road atlas.

"We have some options ahead," he explained. "To avoid towns I think we should use the turnpike, but let's make sure."

His original intention had been to follow a route to Tulsa with the fewest number of towns. Each community they drove through meant a potential encounter with rural Americans who during the past decade had been arming themselves against a Federal government they now hoped would save them. But his chosen route, Thomas could see, would take them past an Army ammunition depot. The last thing they could afford was seizure of his car, but if they made it past the depot, it looked to be a clear and relatively fast drive to Tulsa.

When they were moving again, Skylar finally ended her self-imposed silence.

"You know why I came to see you? Why I wanted to talk about Kimberly?"

Thomas shook his head. Kimberly was the character Skylar had been set to play in *The Pulse*.

"Because I didn't want her to be so fucking helpless, and that's how you wrote her."

"I'm not a misogynist. But in a world like this—"

"I understand why you wrote it that way. If there is no law and order, you think common decency will go out the window. A woman needs a man at her side because there's no way she's physically strong enough to fend off sexual predators."

"And you don't agree?"

"I do now!" Skylar said. "I'm scared to death and I feel exactly the way I didn't want her to feel."

Thomas didn't know what to say. If the power didn't come back on, modern life could be rolled back two centuries.

"Everyone believes the world changed with #MeToo and Times Up," Skylar said. "And I'm so glad some of these assholes have finally paid a price for their shit. But hashtags and headlines don't collapse a power structure that has been in place forever. Even if a man is afraid to sexually abuse you doesn't mean he won't fuck you over. Like if I just head-lined a film that grossed a billion dollars, and I get paired in *Darkest Energy* with a man in his first leading role, and that guy *still* gets offered more money than me, what do you call that other than spite? From some pencil-dick executive who wanted to punish me for being more successful than him?"

"You're right. He punished you with dollars. Don't you think that kind of man will take even more advantage now?"

"Look," said Skylar. "*The Pulse* was terrifying and compelling because of how plausible it was. I mean, we're living it right now, so I would say it was pretty fucking real. And I wanted to play a powerful, resilient character who was the most a woman could be. I wanted her to be strong even if I knew, in real life—like right now—she would be at a physical disadvantage. I didn't want to be the fantasy love interest for an insecure screenwriter who never got the girl. Because a girl is not a prize. Does that make sense?"

Thomas wondered if her questions about the reunion had been to confirm he was the insecure screenwriter she suspected. And it was true that for much of his life he *had* been that guy. But now?

"In an ideal world I want to play roles where women exist on their own terms, even if I acknowledge at this moment in time I'm pretty much dependent on you."

"I understand," Thomas said. "It just didn't seem realistic to expect the average woman to defend herself against alpha men who could behave without consequence."

"You're probably right. It's fucking depressing. But is your nonstop downward spiral really a film anyone wants to see?"

Thomas smiled gamely. This was precisely what he feared Skylar would say when she landed in Dallas—that neither she nor anyone else would be able to stomach the truth of a pulse-ravaged world. But stark reality was what he had intended to deliver. Pretending as if a technology apocalypse could be solved by a handpicked gaggle of airbrushed twentysomethings was not the story he was trying to tell.

"But I appreciate you letting me stay with you," Skylar said. "I'd be fucked otherwise."

They were approaching the turnpike entrance, which was adjacent to the ammunition plant. To his great relief Thomas did not see evidence of an Army presence, at least not until they had almost reached the interchange, where a lone soldier in fatigues observed the road with a pair of binoculars. As they reached the bridge, the soldier pulled one hand toward his face.

"Did you see that?" he said to Skylar. "That guy had a radio. Like a walkie-talkie."

"So?"

"So maybe the Army *does* have a plan. Maybe they have equipment that still works."

"Yay for them."

"I'm saying maybe there's a reason to hope after all."

"You think?" Skylar deadpanned. "Aren't the large transformers that run the electrical grid manufactured overseas? Doesn't it take like a year to get a new one?"

Thomas blinked.

"And that's if you wanted it yesterday. Now we need thousands of them. Have you forgotten your own screenplay?"

Honestly, he was surprised she had read the script closely enough to remember such detail.

"Whatever plan the Army has isn't enough. Nothing will ever be enough. We may as well be on our own."

* * *

The turnpike turned out to be so empty that for much of the stretch Thomas pushed the speedometer to near eighty. Even when the road ended at Henryetta, when they entered U.S. 75 again, stalled traffic remained sparse compared to the same highway in Texas. By this point nearly all drivers had abandoned their vehicles and were walking in the median or on the shoulder, some headed north, some south. Many of them gestured to Thomas to stop, but he avoided eye contact as much as possible.

When they eventually approached Tulsa, a diffuse cloud of black smoke rose from the horizon and widened as they grew closer. Once again the road became congested with stalled cars.

"So how are we going to find her place?" asked Skylar.

"I think I see a gas station up there," he answered, pointing. "I'll stop and see if they have a Tulsa city map."

"All right."

Eventually, on the east side of the road, a Conoco sign resolved itself. A small crowd of people loitered in the parking lot.

"I know it was my idea to come here," Skylar said. "I'm the one who said survival wasn't enough, and now I'm talking like there's no point to anything. I'm sure that's confusing."

Thomas nodded.

"But all I've been able to think about on this trip is your screenplay. You wrote this shit and then it happened, which is already weird and disturbing. Then it turns out you were right. Everything so far has happened like it did in the opening pages of your script. And if you keep being right, it means the ending will also be the same, which is Everyone Dies™, the end. So even though I think we should help Seth and Natalie, at the moment I feel torn between trying to survive and giving up. Does that make sense?"

"It makes perfect sense."

"So let's see if we can find that map."

In the Conoco parking lot, several overweight men wearing various patterns of plaid shirts and dirty jeans stood near a row of disabled pickup trucks. Another fellow was slightly less heavy, dressed in a black golf shirt and gray slacks. Above them, the sky was gray with smoke.

"So I'll stay in the car," Skylar said, "while you run in and get the map."

"I'm not leaving you alone with a bunch of men we don't know."

"Didn't we just talk about this? You think one of them is going to abduct me while you're inside?"

Thomas rolled his eyes. He reached under his seat for the gun and shoved it into his pants.

"That's a mighty fine vehicle you got there," said one of the men when Thomas shut off the ignition. "First runnin' car we seen since that red pickup went by."

"Texas plates, too," said another man. "You must be far away from home, boy."

Thomas opened his door and climbed out. He looked at the men and smiled.

"Here to help a friend. How are you guys?"

"Been better," said one. "I'm supposed to be on a rig down in Okmulgee this morning, but instead I'm stuck here. Want to give me a ride? Behind your pretty lady?"

"We just came through Okmulgee," Thomas said. "And now we're going the other direction, I'm sorry to say."

"You come all the way from Texas?" said another man. "Same thing going on down there as here?"

"Dallas is on fire. Planes down everywhere."

The man whistled ominously.

"If it's like this everywhere," he said, "we're in for some shit."

Thomas shot a look at Skylar, who smiled as if today was a day like any other. Against his better judgment, he turned away and went into the store, where he found a wary-looking man standing behind a counter that was cluttered with cigarette boxes and ads for Red Bull and a messy pile of spent lottery tickets among silver shavings.

"I got me four winners," said the man. "One of them is five grand. I'll sell it to you for a hundred bucks right here and now."

"No, thanks. But I'll take a Tulsa city map if you've got one."

The man pointed to a stand of maps behind a giant plastic tub of beef jerky.

"Sure do," said the man. "Hundred bucks cash."

"Excuse me?"

"Supply and demand, mister. I got the supply and you got the demand. You want the map or not?"

Thomas grunted. He'd put a small amount of cash in his pocket and kept the bulk of it in the car.

"Well shit," said the man as he watched Thomas flip through bills. "Any man who'll pay a hundred bucks for a map can probably afford two."

When Thomas went back outside, the men had moved closer to his car. The fellow in the golf shirt was leaning against the passenger door.

"Didn't know we were in the presence of the Hollywood elite," said the man. "I hear you're the guy who wrote that movie about himself and got rich off it."

"It was luck," Thomas said. "Now if you'll excuse us—"

"Miss Skylar and me was just getting acquainted. Really she was getting acquainted with all of us. Weren't you, sugar?"

But the alarm in Skylar's eyes was obvious.

"Sorry," he said. "We need to get going."

"I don't know," the man in the golf shirt replied. "I don't think we're ready to—"

Thomas reached into his pants and pulled the gun free. He didn't point it anywhere in particular, but the man in the golf shirt jumped as if he'd been bitten.

"Hey!" he said. "No call for a gun. It's not every day people like us get to meet a famous actress."

"I was polite before. Please back away so we can get going."

"You ain't the only one who's carrying," said one of the other men. "You best be careful if you come through here again, Tex."

"I have no quarrel with any of you," Thomas said. "But we're on our way to help someone."

"'Quarrel,'" said another of the men. "You sound just like one of them elitists."

But the men made no further move to harass them, and soon Thomas and Skylar were back on the highway.

"Jesus Christ," she said. "Is that what it's like to live here?"

"This is what it's like when they don't have to pretend anymore."

As Thomas drove closer to Tulsa, Skylar studied the map and eventually deciphered the nomenclature of city streets. The east-west streets were numbered. The north-south streets were given alphabetic names.

To his relief, one of these was named Braden. The intersection of 77th and Braden seemed to be where Natalie's house would be located.

And finally, nearly eight hours after the appearance of the new star, Thomas stopped the Mustang in front of an idyllic residence that did not betray the adversity that had corrupted its interior. The grass, freshly mowed, was a dark and dense green. Flowers bloomed in weedless beds near the front porch and spilled onto the lawn. The window shutters and front door had been given a fresh coat of paint. It was obvious someone cared about this house. Someone was proud of it.

"Thomas?" Skylar said.

He turned and looked at her.

"Shouldn't we hurry up? This is a hell of a lot of smoke."

She gestured upward, and Thomas was alarmed to find the sky almost completely overcast. The smoke was so thick, in fact, he could barely make out the new star, which by now was in the western sky and starting downward. The acrid odor tickled his nose.

"I'm wondering what's going on inside the house."

"You and me both," said Skylar. "But whatever happens, it needs to be soon."

Thomas nodded and stepped out of the car. His heart thundered in his chest.

TWELVE

There was a part of Skylar that knew how absurd it was to compare the awful reality she was currently living to a story Thomas had written. But how could she not? She'd come to Dallas to discuss *The Pulse* just in time for a real pulse to happen. And even if it was all coincidence, wondering about it at least distracted her from the horror that lay ahead.

Now she was standing in front of a house they believed to be Natalie's, which was a whole different kind of distraction, a scene that would be either awkward or terrible depending on what had happened to Seth after the old world ended.

Thomas knocked again, harder this time. Finally, there were sounds behind the door. The lock clicked audibly. The door swung open.

A man appeared. His face was pink and ruddy, his hair disheveled. He was medium height and build except for the pouch of his gut.

"Holy shit," said the man.

"Who is it, Seth?" asked a woman somewhere out of sight.

"How did you even?" said Seth before he turned away from the door and shouted inside. "He came all the way here."

"Who did?"

Now Seth faced them again and looked toward the street.

"So you have a car that runs. You drove all the way here. I can't believe it."

Up to this point the man had not acknowledged Skylar's presence, but when he finally looked more closely at her, his eyes widened in a surprise of recognition she had learned to expect from people who weren't in show business. In the typical fashion he blinked and opened his eyes even wider, as if to reconfirm the appearance of a familiar face in unfamiliar context. She returned his look with the bland, non-threatening smile that diffused tension in encounters like this.

"Seth, who is it?" the off-camera woman said.

"Your high school friend. Thomas."

"Thomas?" said the woman. "I don't understand what you're saying."

Seth looked back at them.

"I guess I should thank you for coming, especially after everything that's happened. Honestly, I can hardly believe you're standing here."

He was looking at Skylar as he said this.

"Seth, who is it really?"

Now the door opened wider, and Skylar saw Natalie for the first time. She was pretty in the way of large-featured Texan women—wide, sloping nose, big eyes, plenty of foundation. Brittle hair that had been bleached for decades.

"Seth, what is going on? How did—"

When Natalie looked at Thomas, her eyes narrowed visibly, as if she didn't trust them. But when she saw Skylar, all the muscles in her face appeared to lose tension and her mouth fell visibly open.

"Holy shit!" Natalie said. "What is wrong with my manners? Please come in, both of you."

She jerked the door open. Thomas motioned for Skylar to enter and he followed. Natalie led them to the living room, where she gestured at a sofa and two chairs, but no one sat. On the coffee table stood a bottle of liquor.

"You must be Seth," said Thomas, extending his hand to shake. "And yes, of course I came. I promised. I'm so relieved to see you're all right."

Skylar noted how Thomas was subtly taking credit for the decision she had forced him to make.

"Natalie," Seth finally said. "One thing I didn't tell you was my backup plan in case the insurance didn't come through: I asked Thomas to pay the bookie in Dallas if my claim was denied."

"Oh, Seth."

"I know it seems ridiculous, but the last thing I wanted was for Jimmy to come looking for you. And I couldn't ask my dad. You have to understand how desperate I was."

"But still," Natalie said. "Why did he—"

"Because he called me. He tried to talk me out of it and I wouldn't listen. But I did ask him to help you and the boys after I was gone. I never expected him to follow through after all this."

The four of them stood there while seconds of unbroken silence slid by. Finally, Natalie looked directly at Skylar again.

"And how did you end up here? This is like a dream."

"I was visiting Thomas in Dallas. In fact, we were just leaving the airport when, you know, when it happened."

Skylar reached out to shake Natalie's hand. Whenever she met someone this way she felt ridiculous.

"I'm Skylar," she said.

"Of course. I've seen you in lots of stuff. I'm Natalie."

They shook for what felt like an awkwardly long time, and then Natalie addressed Thomas again.

"It's so thoughtful of you to come. Wasn't it dangerous to drive this far? What did you plan to do when you made it?"

It was obvious that both Natalie and her husband had been drinking. And who could blame them, considering the circumstances? Still, alcohol was not going to simplify this conversation.

"Take you back with us," he said.

During the drive, after Thomas ignored the ailing man on the highway, Skylar had retreated inward. Those empty hours, she understood now, had given her a chance to face reality and muddle through stages of grief. It was nearly impossible to accept she would never see her family again, that she would never see Roark again. Everyone close to her was in L.A. or New York; her entire life, in fact, was split between the two coasts. Now, because of a decision that could be generously described as impulsive (reckless was more like it), she was stuck in the middle of nowhere with a man she barely knew.

The quiet nature of the disaster only made things more awful. In Dallas, the EMP had behaved as a proper apocalypse, where planes fell out of the sky and the horizon erupted into flames. But Skylar's emotions had bottomed out when they crossed into Oklahoma and the array of stalled cars mostly evaporated. It was so difficult to reconcile the untouched countryside with the awful reality of the EMP that she had nearly collapsed into tears. Only pride held her together. A refusal to reveal weakness to Thomas, to betray herself as the damsel in distress he expected.

She wanted to believe he was wrong about the reach of the pulse, that its effects were not as widespread as he feared. As they approached Tulsa, Skylar kept hoping they would discover cars driving and traffic lights blinking and planes streaking across the sky. But it hadn't happened. And if two cities so distant from each other were burning uncontrollably, that meant the same scene was being repeated across the country and maybe around the world. She couldn't wrap her mind around the horror of it.

"Thomas," Seth said. "I appreciate you coming here. Honestly. But as you can see, we are fine."

"Sure, but for how long?"

"We stocked up at the store this morning. We have food."

"For a week? Two? Then what?"

Skylar pictured the supplies Thomas had shown her. It was impossible to know how long this food would last with six people consuming it, but to her that didn't matter. The most important thing was to help others. Not sit on a mountain of calories while everyone around you starved.

"This is just like your screenplay," said Natalie. "Isn't it?"

Thomas looked embarrassed, as if the pulse had been his fault.

"So far it is. And after I wrote the script, I was so freaked out I gathered a bunch of supplies in case something like it ever happened."

"So did we," said Seth.

"I'm saying I have food and water and propane to last for weeks or months. We came here to help you survive."

"Thank you for that," said Seth. "But we can't just leave. We have family nearby. Everything we own is here."

Thomas didn't seem to comprehend this. Meanwhile, Natalie was staring at Skylar as if her presence was impossible.

"I know this is difficult to hear," Thomas said, "but the world out there is ending. There's a huge fire moving this way. The smoke is so thick you can't see the sky."

"You should see his safe room," Skylar said to Natalie. "It will take your breath away."

"Pretty soon there won't be any more groceries to buy," Thomas explained. "Running water will be gone in a day or two. What will you do then?"

It was impossible to read the emotions on Seth's face. He might have been defiant or distraught.

"Honey?" Natalie said.

"We'll go to my parents' house in Edmond. They live on the edge of town and my dad has plenty of guns. We can hunt for food if we have to."

"That's the next logical step," said Thomas. "But you have to know everyone with a gun will do the same thing. How long will small game last with thousands of people hunting?"

"We can plant a garden—"

"You'll starve to death before anything grows. And if you don't already have seeds, where will you get them?"

Seth's hands opened and closed. Skylar looked at the vodka bottle, which was standing uncapped, and wondered just how drunk the two of them were.

"Unless your safe room is the size of a Walmart," said Seth, "there's no way you can feed us indefinitely."

"No. Not indefinitely. But in three months there will be options for whoever is left."

The terrible reality of this statement halted the debate between Thomas and Seth.

"Dad?" said a voice from behind her. Skylar turned and saw two young boys standing at the front of the living room. They were seven or eight years old and sandy-haired.

"What's going on?" one of the boys said.

"Nothing," Seth answered. "Go back to your room and we'll come get you in a little while."

"We've been in the hallway listening. Why are we going to starve? Is it because the electric is out?"

"Brandon—"

"It's all dark outside. It smells smoky. Something really bad is happening, isn't it?"

"Brandon. Ben. Please go back to your room. Your mom and I will take care of you. You don't have to worry."

"We should go with them," said Brandon, who pointed in the direction of Thomas and Skylar. "They came here to help, right?"

"Brandon, I'm not going to tell you again."

"Fine! We'll just play board games and starve to death!"

When the boys were gone, Seth looked back at Thomas, and it was obvious his will to refuse had evaporated.

"Look," he said. "Even if we go with you, how are you going to fill up with gasoline to get back?"

"I have twenty gallons in the trunk. We'll refill the tank before we go."

"And you have enough room for all of us in your sports car?"

"It won't be comfortable. But if the boys sit in your laps, we'll all fit."

"What can we take with us?" asked Natalie.

"I'm afraid not much of anything," Thomas said. "It will be cramped as it is. We need to get on the road soon, anyway. There's still that fire to contend with, and it'll be dark in a few hours."

"But what about my grandmother's wedding dress? It's been in my family for seventy years. What about our pictures of the boys?"

"Most of our pictures are on the computer," Seth said. "They're lost anyway."

"We can't just leave *every*thing behind."

Seth turned to his wife and put his hands on her shoulders.

"Natalie. We have to make some tough choices here."

"I don't see why—"

"If we leave now, we may never see our families again, never see any of our friends. If we can do that, we can live without a few pictures."

Natalie stared at him a long moment before she answered. Then she looked over his shoulder and met Skylar's eyes.

"I guess you're right," she said. "I guess I need to remember what's really important here."

Skylar held Natalie's gaze for a long moment and then looked away. The reality of being in this unfamiliar place, under circumstances that were impossible to believe, returned to her with such force that she nearly lost her balance. This was really happening. Her old life was over and this was her new one, whether she wanted it or not.

She was not the kind of woman who took the world as it came to her. She had fought off the hormones of teenage guys, who first pretended she was a boy and later wanted her to be a slut. She battled her parents when they tried to separate. When her own agent called Skylar an "ungrateful feminist brat" during *Darkest Energy* contract talks, when he took the side of the studio executive (who turned out to be a fraternity brother), she had publicly fired him. A stunt like that could have killed her career, but she would rather have quit altogether than cash in her dignity.

Today she had convinced Thomas to get off his ass, to drive here and save this family. If everything went well, the six of them would roll into Dallas after dark, hungry and ready to eat. This felt good. It felt right.

But she wasn't so sure what came next. Would the six of them hunker down and wait for the world to end? What would happen when other people, thousands of people, ran out of things to eat? Would the world, as it had in the screenplay, break into desperate groups who fought over declining food stores and clean water and whatever gadgets survived the pulse?

Ever since she had been snatched from teenage obscurity, since her face had begun to appear on billboards and magazines and televisions across the world, Skylar had wrestled with the meaning of it all. The amount of money she earned was ludicrous, embarrassing, yet there were assholes with a hundred times more. A thousand times more. She refused to accept less than she was worth but could not reconcile these amounts with the abject poverty that millions or billions of people endured every single day. Didn't that qualify existence itself as absurd? As basically pointless?

But luxury wasn't just about things. It was also a freedom of mind, the time and comfort to explore deeper concerns like science and philosophy and love. She was a reader of Feynman and Hawking and Brian Greene. She was a student of the mind. She was fascinated with the hard problem of consciousness, of why a human could be sentient when a supercomputer was not. At least yesterday she had been fascinated with it.

Today she was simply trying to survive.

THIRTEEN

My Diary, by Natalie Black
May 16, 202-

It was nearly midnight by the time we reached Dallas, and I seriously have never seen darkness like that. Beyond the beams of our headlights, basically nothing was visible, except the sky, which was both black and bright with stars. So many stars.

The first thing Thomas did after he pulled into the garage was grab a bunch of candles from the safe room. Not long after, we sat down to a quick and gloomy dinner of hamburgers and tater tots that had been in the freezer but were nearly thawed. Thomas cooked everything on his propane grill, which he was afraid would be stolen while he was away. After we ate, he rolled it into the garage.

Later, while Seth kissed the boys goodnight, I asked Thomas for a pen and paper. It was late, but my mind was racing, and I wanted to write down everything that happened on the drive while it was still fresh. Maybe you know this by now, but candles aren't really that bright. I feel like I should be writing with one of those pens you dip in a jar of ink.

Anyway, before we left our house, I grabbed a couple of pictures of the boys, despite what Thomas had said. Then we went outside, where the smoke was so powerful and dense it looked like a tornado was about to touch down. I had a decent vodka buzz going, and everything had taken on this heightened sense of reality, like that photo app on my phone when I switch the filter to Vibrant.

Then, before we could even climb into the car, the shit hit the fan.

The shit in this case being Frank, the jerk who lives across the street. Frank smiled when he saw us, that mean way he smiles when he's making fun of someone's shoddy lawn care or talking shit about the single guy who lives next door. Frank thinks everyone but him is bringing down the neighborhood, even though he mows his lawn at 6:30 in the morning and idles his Harley in the driveway when he's not planning to ride it anywhere.

First, he asked where we were going, and when no one answered, he asked if he could "borrow" a jug of gasoline for his motorcycle. Then he recognized Skylar. You could almost see a switch flip in his mind, like he just hit all grapes on the slot machine. She smiled back in this empty way, like she's so jaded about being the most beautiful woman in the world (I mean she is pretty hot). You could tell Frank felt dismissed, because next he asked what she was doing in Podunk, Oklahoma and even offered his "services" to her . . .as if there were anything a famous actress could possibly need from him.

I could see Thomas was about to intervene, which meant he would have to stop fueling the car, and that's when Seth politely suggested Frank go find something else to do. Frank's response was to pull a gun out of his pants and point it at my husband.

Not ashamed to admit it: I shrieked like a little girl. Brandon yelled and Ben started crying and my heart raced until I thought it would burst. Frank wanted the car so he could take his family to some cabin in the woods. That's where they planned, as he called it, "to ride out the storm." They needed a car to get there and couldn't believe when the Mustang appeared in front of their house like a gift from God.

All this happened fast, because the next thing I knew, Thomas was standing behind Frank, pointing a gun at the back of his head. Frank never even saw him coming. It was like a movie.

Then Thomas made Frank lie down on the ground while Seth poured in the rest of the gasoline. Even after we got in the car, Thomas wouldn't let him up. He wouldn't give Frank his gun back, either. And Frank begged. Just take out the bullets, he said, but leave me the gun. It's the only one I have, he said. But Thomas refused, which was pretty cold if you ask me, because how will Frank defend his family or hunt for

* * *

May 16, 202- (later)

Sorry, I heard Seth coming earlier. For now, I want to keep this private so I can work through my feelings. In a way, I think this journal could be a record of what happened, like for posterity, for my family and maybe even the world at large. But if I thought someone would look at it now, I doubt I would be very honest.

So, let me finish the story of the trip. As we drove out of the neighborhood, the sky was so dark it looked like the sun had gone down. There wasn't enough room to put up the convertible top, so we made the boys put their heads down and breathe through their shirts. I felt terrible for them. It's hard to get through your head that a city is on fire, instead of just a building, and that nothing can be done about it. No sirens, no fire trucks, no Army help, no nothing. And I kept thinking, if we ever came through here again, our house and all its memories would probably be gone. ☹

(I guess emojis are over, too. Handwritten ones are just not the same.)

Thomas was worried about some folks who saw him earlier, so instead of the typical route to Dallas, we stayed on the turnpike all the way to Hugo. The stalled cars became less numerous, and Thomas drove faster, and eventually everyone relaxed. I played I-Spy with the boys, and Skylar told them about her show on Nickelodeon. I didn't even realize she was on that, but the boys did. They perked up and asked her all sorts of questions about Jeffrey, who I always found effeminate and way too friendly to children. That's something I won't miss: creepy children's TV shows.

By then, it could almost have been any old road trip (albeit in a crowded car), when I heard this strange whistle right behind me. Then a chunk of road flew up, and I heard the crack of what we realized was a gunshot. Seth pushed the kids into the floorboard and threw his body on top of mine while Thomas sped up and weaved the car back and forth. I honestly thought we were going to die. Or lose the car and maybe be raped. Seth said the gunshot came from very far away, and that the people shooting were cowards or kids or both. We never saw them, and no one else fired at us. But I didn't let down my guard again until we got here.

Thomas drove even faster after that. We kept the boys down as much as we could, but they complained a lot, and by the time we reached Texas it was dark, anyway. We began to see more stalled cars, and every five minutes some family appeared in the headlights, waving like crazy, as if we could do anything for them. There was no more room for anyone. That didn't stop people from approaching us, though, and a couple of times Thomas was ready to pull his gun again. But he didn't.

I should also mention that Seth brought his own gun, and a pocketful of bullets, which he kept hidden. He said our family could use insurance of its own, like if Thomas didn't follow through on his promise to help us. It seems like all Seth thinks about anymore is insurance.

Eventually, we left the highway and crossed a bridge, and not long after we turned into a neighborhood dense with trees. Again I felt like we were living in a movie, that scene where the audience cringes while a naive family drives into a nightmare. But instead of monsters, Thomas was worried one of his neighbors would see us or hear us. He was especially concerned about Larry, this scientist guy who worked at the particle accelerator near Wichita Falls before it was destroyed.

Speaking of my hometown, I should explain about Thomas and the high school reunion. I know it sounds awful, but by that point I was so upset about Seth's infidelity (or what I thought was infidelity) that I hoped someone would flirt with me. The mixer was held in the back room of an Applebee's, and there were maybe forty or fifty of us total. I couldn't believe how hot Michele Cobb looked. Like way better than high school. She must have had Botox and maybe a boob job, I don't know. The only reason I noticed Thomas was because she was talking to him, if that tells you anything. But then he glanced over Michele's head and looked straight at me, like we'd known each other for years, and nodded in the direction of the bar. I was a bit tipsy and overwhelmed that a man I didn't recognize would be so forward. But then Thomas joined me at the bar, where he said:

So, Nat, did you ever figure out how to spell dependant?

(I still don't know if I have it right or not.)

It seemed impossible to believe this classy, handsome man had gone to our school, but anyone who knew I couldn't spell dependant (dependent??) had obviously been a friend. And I couldn't remember him!

Anyway, I giggled, and said I still wasn't sure how to spell it.

You were such a good English student, he told me. Your papers were so well-written. And then it would appear, like a pimple in the middle of the page. Dependent with an A!

Ah, shit. Now I remember. I'll go back and fix it later.

You know, he said. I was hoping you would come. And here we are, having a drink together.

So where do you live now? I asked. California? Because you seem like you're far from home.

I live in Dallas, he said, but I was in L.A. a few weeks ago.

Oh yeah? Doing what?

Having lunch with Ryan Gosling. He may be the lead in my new film.

I'm sure it sounds like he was trying to impress me, and I soaked it up like he knew I would. I might have slept with Thomas had he made any sort of move. Eventually, Michele Cobb got curious (or jealous) and walked over. She threw her arms around both of us, drunkenly, and I guess my hormones must have been on high alert, because I nearly jumped out of my skin when her hand brushed my boob. Thomas laughed, and I laughed, and Michele didn't seem to care for that. She pranced away in a huff and left the two of us together.

As I stood there, looking at Thomas, I wondered if I really would be willing to cheat. Until the past couple of years, Seth has been an amazing husband and father. It was me who caused the problems, who couldn't get her mind right after the boys were born. Maybe it was post-partum depression. Maybe I still missed my father. But I couldn't stop thinking how something was very wrong with my life, that I had inadvertently picked the wrong path and was doomed to be unhappy forever. It never occurred to me that

FOURTEEN

"**W**hat are you writing?" Seth asked Natalie.

He had awoken just minutes before in a state of disorientation so profound that he wondered if he had died after all, if the day's bizarre events had been a last-gasp death dream. But eventually his mind cleared and he discovered, by flickering candlelight, his two sons sleeping in the bed beside him. They were facing away from each other, probably because Brandon was a snorer and Ben hated it.

Once he felt stable enough to stand, Seth wandered back to the room he'd be sharing with Natalie. Only instead of sleeping, she was bent over a stack of paper, writing something. Naturally he was curious what had captured her attention, but when his wife looked up, she immediately turned the paper over.

"Nothing. Just some notes about . . ."

Seth watched, amused, as she struggled to invent a lie.

"All this is so huge, Seth. Life-changing. World-changing. Someone needs to write down what's happening."

"But I can't read it?"

"Maybe later. This is also how I feel inside, about us and what you did. I don't know if I'll ever feel comfortable sharing it. The whole point of keeping a journal is to work through your feelings."

"That's all behind us now, Nat. I'm sorry for what I did, but we have a chance for a fresh start because of all this."

A little while later they crawled into bed, and when Seth put his arm around Natalie, he tried not to notice her body stiffening beneath him.

"Do you hear that?" she asked.

"Hear what?"

"The static. Or maybe it's like a ringing. Or both."

"I don't hear anything."

"I heard something like it this morning when I was in the golf cart," Natalie said. "I thought maybe it was stress."

"You're hearing it again?"

"I'm not sure it ever stopped. Maybe it got quieter or I didn't notice it for a while."

"Probably it's stress," he said. "What could be more traumatic than this?"

"I'm scared, Seth. I know we made it here, and I know Thomas has lots of food and supplies. But if this is how it is now, like if the power doesn't come back on, what are we going to do?"

"We'll survive. We'll do the best we can for our boys and ourselves."

"But I want to go shopping. I want to travel to Europe. I want the boys to go to college and become doctors or engineers."

Seth understood what she meant. The idea of never being able to set foot inside a working casino again was horrifying.

"Maybe it won't be like this forever," he said.

But honestly, Seth hoped he was wrong. He hoped things never went back to the way they were.

After all, he wasn't cut out for the real world.

FIFTEEN

Thomas was standing in front of the safe room, having just closed its door, when Skylar approached.

"Still hungry?" she asked.

"No. I wasn't sure if . . ."

He trailed off. Skylar Stover, the actress, was looking at him plaintively, and for a moment he thought he could see through her, as if she weren't standing there at all. As if he were imagining her.

"I wasn't sure if I should lock this door," he finished.

"Who are you trying to keep out of there? Us?"

"Not you. Anyone desperate enough to break in and steal."

"And you think that might happen tonight."

"Probably not, but at some point the threat will be real. Starvation will change people. It will turn them into monsters."

"Then don't let them starve. When your neighbors run out of food, help them."

"We can't help them all."

"You keep saying that. Like you don't care who dies."

Driving all day had left him shattered, and he was worried sick over whatever Hell loomed ahead. But somehow Thomas still noticed Skylar's profile in the flickering candlelight, like the jutting curve of her chin that was somehow both strong and feminine, or the faint presence of her upper lip, a feature that strengthened the character of her mouth in the opposite way of collagen injections and plastic surgery. Skylar was surely exhausted and emotionally spent, but when she smiled, he could see she was a person who smiled easily, and when she spoke, her words always carried meaning. After dinner, when she volunteered to clean the dishes, the candle beside the sink threw her into such flattering light that she finally caught him staring.

"If we try to save everyone," he explained, "we'll all die. There's no way to sustain the current population without technology."

"You sound like a documentary."

"I'm being realistic."

"What are you hoping for?" she asked. "What if the six of us outlast everyone else? What then?"

"I don't know."

"In your film, the whole country is gone except angry little towns that guard their farms with machine guns."

"Maybe it won't be like that," he said. "Maybe the damage isn't as widespread as it seems. Or there's an easier way to fix the broken things."

"I thought you were being realistic."

"I don't have answers, Skylar. But I don't want to die, either. I don't want you to die or Natalie and her family to die. Isn't that enough? Why not focus on us instead of whatever is going on out there?"

"Because selfishness is why this even happened. Enough people knew the risk. We could have prepared. Instead we fought with each other over stupid things and now everything we ever cared about is gone."

Skylar's bottom lip quivered. Her eyes glistened through tears.

"I did it, too. I made more money than I could ever spend, and what did I do with it? Invested it. Put it in the bank. Gave some to charity but compared to how much I made? I could have done more. You could have done more. The fucking capital class could have done more. And you know why we didn't?"

Thomas didn't think he wanted her to answer.

"Because we are selfish. Greedy little animals."

She stepped forward and pressed her index finger into his chest.

"But I won't be an animal anymore."

STATIC (IN AIDEN'S MIND) ├

SIXTEEN

I stood there staring at the dark form of a man, my lips puckered from the bitter taste of lemonade. My chest felt tight, like I couldn't breathe. Static roared in my ears.

"Is this death?" I croaked.

"You wish, loser. It's time to go."

But when I tried to move, my arms and legs wouldn't respond. They felt locked in place, paralyzed, the way they do in nightmares.

"Aiden, man. Get up."

The figure in front of me wasn't there. My eyes weren't even open. I woke to find myself on the couch, Jimmy pressing on me, shaking me.

"Dude, you were out cold," he said. "You wouldn't wake up."

"What time is it?"

"Shit, man. I don't know what time it is. Afternoon. We're gonna put your plan into motion."

My head felt bulky, like it had increased in size. My ears screeched. I was starting to worry that sound would never go away.

"How long have I been asleep? What have you guys been doing?"

Jimmy moved to the ottoman and smiled.

"Glad you asked. I made a list of dudes, just like you said. These guys either work for me or owe me money or both. I picked them based on where they live and the chance we can find them. It's not like I could get them out of my phone, so Bart and I went through old mail and did our best."

"That's great," I said, not feeling great about Jimmy's list or anything. My brain was like a lead weight sinking to the bottom of the ocean. The plan to siege a grocery warehouse seemed, after my nap, like a hopeless waste of time and resources. The EMP hadn't happened by accident: God clearly wanted the world to end. Who were we to fight against His wishes?

"So this is your list," said Jimmy.

He handed me a sheet of paper, which contained several names, addresses, and a crudely-drawn map.

"Bart and I each have five guys to find. You have four. I assume we won't get them all, but hopefully we'll end up with something close to ten."

"This is going to take a while."

"A day or two at least," Jimmy said. "But it's not like we've got much else to do."

"You mean besides get high?"

"Yeah, well. That's only fun for so long. Eventually we have to figure out how to move on from all this."

I could have asked him why anyone would want to move on, but Jimmy's not that kind of guy. He sees the world in simple terms and debating the relative merits of survival wouldn't compute. The EMP presented a challenge to be solved. Until then, little else would matter.

"Anyway," he said. "I'm also giving you this."

Jimmy handed me a pistol. It was a SIG Sauer, similar to my own.

"I figure each of us should try to find one guy this evening. We already heard some gunshots like an hour ago, and I bet it'll get worse after dark."

"Gunshots?"

"And there's another fire going on a little west of here. Couple of miles away. I think people are looting."

"If that's the case," I said, "maybe we're too late."

"No way to know. But the longer we wait, the less chance we have. I also heard a few running cars. I don't know if they're police or military or what. Bart tells me older cars may still work if they have a mechanical ignition."

"I hadn't thought of that."

"Me neither. But if he's right, and we see someone with a car, we could motivate them to donate it to our cause."

"If we had a car," I said, "we could round these guys up in a few hours instead of a few days."

"Exactly," Jimmy said, smiling.

"So are we going now?"

"Yep. Just get yourself something to eat, drink, whatever. I see you already found the lemonade."

He pointed at my glass on the coffee table. It was half empty.

"Chelsea whipped up some mashed potatoes if you want a home-made dish. Speaking of, the girls are going to stay behind. Too risky for them to be out."

"Where's Keri?"

"In the kitchen. Bart is taking a shower. The water is still hot, but we're losing pressure. You might want to rinse off before you leave. Then the girls will fill the tubs and all my bowls and buckets so we don't run out of water."

A lot had happened while I was asleep. I didn't see how anyone had the energy for it. But unless I wanted to take the SIG and shoot myself in the head (an idea more alluring than you might think) there was little choice but follow the plan.

"Okay. I'll wash up first."

"You can use the shower in the west bedroom. Back that way."

Jimmy was right. The pressure was so low I could barely rinse shampoo out of my hair. But the water was hot, and I stood beneath it for what seemed like forever, wondering if it would be the last hot shower I would ever enjoy. To this day I haven't had another one.

* * *

For my trip to Dallas I brought three T-shirts, two pairs of jeans, five golf shirts, and five pairs of golf shorts. Unfortunately, I'd already worn all these clothes at least once, so I grabbed a T-shirt that smelled the least offensive and my other pair of jeans. I hadn't noticed till after the shower, but the clothes I'd been wearing since Thursday evening reeked of cigarettes and booze and B.O.

After I brushed my teeth and applied deodorant, I felt almost normal . . . except for the low-but-constant screeching sound that seemed to originate deep in the bowels of my brain.

"Well, hello, handsome," Keri said when I walked into the kitchen. "You clean up good."

Judging by the light, it was maybe five o'clock in the afternoon. Bart and Chelsea were at the kitchen table. Jimmy stood in front of the stove, drinking what appeared to be a cocktail.

I found a paper plate and carved myself a heavy spoonful of mashed potatoes. There was also a box of crackers and a plastic jug of beef jerky. I helped myself to a few pieces and sat down to eat. I was ravenous.

"Any questions about your assignment?" asked Bart.

"What should I know beyond the names and addresses?"

"The first guy on your list is less than three miles away. Mitch Brown. If he decides to come there's one other guy you might try. He's two more miles to the south. That'll leave you a longish walk back here."

Keri sat down beside me.

"I still don't know if this is a good idea," she said, and leaned into me. "But I don't see what the alternative is."

"The alternative is we eat all of Jimmy's food and then starve to death."

"Geez," said Chelsea. "Downer alert."

I wasn't surprised by the untroubled mood in the kitchen. No one here was accustomed to the routine of an 8 – 5 work day, the rhythm of family life, or even obeying the law. Bart and Jimmy understood the gravity of the crisis, but they also believed our plan was achievable, and didn't appear worried. Chelsea and Keri seemed oblivious to the risks we faced, or the consequences for failing to succeed. Probably they were both high on opiates.

When I finished eating, I folded the list and dropped it into my pocket. I shoved the gun into the back of my jeans and smiled like all this was perfectly normal. I didn't imagine my mind as a spool of fishing line that was slowly being unraveled and pulled into the dark ocean.

"Ready to head out?" I said.

"I'm going to check on Amy before I leave," Jimmy answered.

"Gonna finish this dinner," said Bart.

Several bottles of Smart Water stood on the kitchen island. As I grabbed one, Keri walked over and hugged me.

"Please be careful. I'll miss you while you're gone."

I looked down at her blonde hair and perfect cleavage and felt split nearly in half by competing emotions. One part of me could imagine playing this silly game, returning to Jimmy's house with both my charges in tow, celebrating with scotch and sex.

The other half of me was sickened by all this nonsense, especially how Keri had contorted our two days of drug-induced debauchery into a faux relationship. Her behavior reminded me of the time I watched, in a single weekend, an entire season of *The Bachelor*. I could never understand why twenty-five women would refer to the preselected guy as "their boyfriend" and "the man I'm going to marry" when they had spent a grand total of six hours with him. The desire to formalize such a fleeting connection seemed absurd and desperate and I was thrilled to be getting away from Keri and everyone in the house for a while.

You could definitely say I was there for the wrong reasons.

* * *

I found my way out of the neighborhood by reversing our original route. The wind, which had been almost calm during our journey to Jimmy's, was blowing steadily from the south. Also, the haze was thicker than before and carried a harsh, chemical odor that made me wish I was breathing through a surgical mask. On my right I saw a black tower of smoke rising into the sky, and I wondered for the first time if the whole city might burn to the ground.

As I neared the gated exit of Jimmy's neighborhood, I heard gunshots. A quick and distant pop-pop-pop. My hands reached behind my back and felt the reassuring weight of my weapon. I stopped for a moment and looked at the map, memorized the next two navigation points, and put the paper back in my pocket.

On the main road I felt vulnerable the way a child might. It seemed like I was in another country. Another world. The stalled cars on the road might have been Hollywood set pieces, the haze generated by digital effects. The ambient silence was so profound, so unusual, that the whole city felt like it had been trapped under a giant dome. After a while I noticed the distant sounds of people talking, someone shouting, dogs barking. It made me think the city wasn't so much silent as forsaken, as if it had been abandoned and left for dead.

For years I'd been convinced climate change was a hoax, that China and the liberal media had purposely stoked the fears of uninformed citizens to undermine American economic dominance. I came to be this way because, like my friends and family, I believed most of the news on TV was fake. No matter what the "scientists" said, there was simply no way humans could measurably affect Earth's enormous atmosphere. But then thousands of commercial airliners had come down at once, and smoke from fiery impact sites had grown thick enough to make breathing uncomfortable, and I wondered if all this time I'd been wrong about the human impact on our planet.

The real problem, which I came to understand as I walked ghostly streets north of Dallas, was all the people. There were too many cars to drive us and too many planes to fly us and too many farting cows to feed our desperate little mouths. The only way to fix the problem was to cull the herd, and that's exactly what the EMP was meant to do. It was like a modern version of the Great Flood, only this time God also wanted to get rid of nonstop news coverage and social media and working shit jobs for corporate overlords. Only the chosen few would survive.

If you're wondering what makes me special, you should know I'm His perfect candidate. I'm happy to assist. I'm ready to kill.

See, I've been angry for longer than I can remember. Angry that a company would fire me instead of more deserving losers. Angry that my sister had exiled me over a stupid mistake. Angry that the promise of America turned out to be a lie. Every generation in my family was more affluent than the one before, at least until I came along, even though I'm the smartest person my family has ever produced. It's almost as if the entire enterprise was a big joke. As if, on television, the Hollywood elite made America look shiny and full of promise, but down here in the trenches, where real folks lived, the place smelled like shit.

But finally there were no elites to steal my dignity and no government to fuck me over and no police presence I could detect. God had put power back where it belonged: into the hands of the people. Into the hands of His chosen.

My brain whistled and screeched and I smiled a pleasant smile.

At the first major intersection, on the other side of the road, five or six men were clustered in front of a nursery. One of the men was talking to the others, gesturing wildly. I turned south and kept walking. The animated man banged loudly on the nursery door. He yelled at someone to let him in. Eventually there was a gunshot, and the men broke open the door. One after the other they disappeared inside.

I began to see more people, almost all of them men. Some were in pairs, some on their own. I came upon a shopping center, a folksy collection of shops and restaurants built to look like log cabins, all of which appeared deserted. At the south end of the center stood a Subway restaurant, where a woman emerged from the doorway looking panic-stricken. She was maybe thirty, dressed in a stretchy T-shirt and high-waisted jeans. She looked like the kind of woman who was always trying to lose ten pounds.

"Sir!" she yelled. "I need your help!"

Her brown hair was long and had been thrown together in an unruly formation on top of her head.

"I don't have anything to eat."

"I'm not looking for food," she said, as if she hadn't just stepped out of a Subway. "I need insulin. My daughter is sick and I'm completely out."

"She's diabetic?"

"Of course she's diabetic! She seemed fine yesterday, but today she didn't wake up from her nap!"

"You don't keep extra insulin for emergencies?"

Her eyes seemed to bulge out of their sockets. I thought she was going to rear back and hit me.

"I could always drive a block to Walgreen's and get it. But I walked down there today and it's like a bomb went off."

I hadn't thought of this before, but it made sense. If Jimmy hadn't been around to fix her up, Keri would have tried to steal pills. That's how desperate she was.

"Please!" the woman said and put her hand on my arm. "I need help!"

"Let go of me."

"Please, sir. My Hailey is going to die if I don't get insulin."

"What do you expect me to do? I don't know where to find any."

In the distance I heard that terrible high whistle again, the sound of anger and insanity, the voice of God. I reached behind my back and felt the reassuring steel of my gun. The pistol was hard and smooth and carefully designed, whereas this woman was a mess.

"Please!" she cried.

"Get out of my sight," I said, and pushed past her.

"You bastard! Fuck you!"

The gun was hidden under my shirt. Blood pounded between my temples as I turned toward the woman again. The whistle screamed in my ears. Was this my first test?

I gripped the weapon and pulled it free of my pants. Slowly, deliberately, I pointed it at her head.

"Oh my God!" she screamed and threw her hands in the air. "Please don't shoot me!"

My finger slithered over the trigger. There was no one to stop me. America was a big, fat blob of ignorance and debt, and the bill had finally come due.

"Please," said the woman. "My poor baby. She's got no one but me."

"That's too bad, because you are a shitty parent."

Rivers of mascara-stained tears poured out of her eyes. Her sobs were choked by congestion.

I closed one eye and mimed a gunshot. All at once the screeching in my head disappeared.

"Bang."

While the woman screamed, I placed the gun, safety still on, back in my pants.

Then I turned south again and smiled a Jimmy Jameson smile. For years, liberal snowflakes and social justice warriors had thwarted the American merit system. Their socialist agenda had weakened the country, exposed a soft underbelly, and it was time to make things right again.

I wouldn't be so merciful next time.

* * *

Eventually I reached a bridge that crossed the George Bush Turnpike. Beneath me, people walked along the access road or sat against a concrete retaining wall. I might have jumped to my death if not for a chain-link fence adjacent to the sidewalk.

Instead, I sat down to rest and considered the woman with the diabetic child. Even if she was a moron for letting the insulin run out, the problem was larger than one worthless woman. There were a million other idiots who every day made terrible choices that incurred no consequences. Liberal college professors who taught students to hate America. Simpleminded voters who elected presidential candidates based on nothing more than hope and change. Postmodern scientists who pretended as if theirs were the only facts that mattered. I had been raised to believe in a merit system, a country where the best would thrive, but the only happy people I knew were those who contributed nothing.

Now there was no room for emotion. No quarter for political correctness. You either survived or you didn't. You either won or you lost. No more trophies just for showing up.

By the time I reached the first name on my list, dusk had nearly fallen. The sky was striated into layers of orange and pink and gray that made me think of the Grand Canyon. Mitch Brown's neighborhood had been new in the 1980s, rows of single-story ranch houses that no one here could afford to maintain. A white pickup stood in the driveway, and when I finally knocked on his front door, Mitch didn't answer. Eventually I wandered into the back yard, in case he was grilling dinner. He wasn't.

This beautiful new dusk, filtered through the haze, made the world look dreamlike. Unreal. It was absurd to believe we could find ten men this way, walking the streets of a city made enormous by single-passenger commutes. I looked straight up, as if answers might be found in the sky, and saw stars twinkling through the haze. I considered how many suns must be out there, and how any of them could blow up with no warning. The more I thought about it, the more I could appreciate how something that appeared stable on the outside could be volatile on the inside . . .that a star, or anyone, could blow in an instant, killing everything around it. Everyone around him.

I walked out of the back yard and found myself on Mitch's driveway. The light was so low I could barely read the map. If I went looking for the next guy, Paul Wilkins, I'd be out well after dark. That didn't seem like a good choice, so I decided to head back.

I was stuffing the map into my pocket when I noticed a man approaching from the house next door. He was broad-shouldered and muscled, dressed in a red polo and jeans. It was dark enough that I couldn't see his features clearly. Other than his size there was nothing special about him, nothing noteworthy to describe.

"Hey, there," said the man. "You know Mitch?"

"I came here looking for him. You know where he is?"

"Not sure. He works in McKinney. Maybe he never made it back."

I had no idea where McKinney was, nor did I care. The whistle in my brain rose again, screeching, shrieking.

"You need him for something? You come here on foot, you must really have wanted to talk to him."

This man meant nothing to me. His presence here was pointless. He was fat waiting to be trimmed.

"It doesn't matter now."

"What doesn't matter? Mitch got something you need?"

When I reached for my gun, the world turned black and I nearly lost my balance. For a moment I thought someone had hit me. But I quickly recovered and pointed my weapon at the man's head.

"Hey," he said in a terrible voice. "Hey, buddy. I didn't mean nothing. I was just looking out for Mitch."

Like I said, it was dark and difficult to see features on the man's face. Without a face he hardly registered as a man at all. My gun was pointed at the shape of a head and I wondered if I would feel remorse. If I would feel anything at all.

But I had been chosen for this and there was no turning back.

I flipped off the safety. The man's knees buckled.

"Please, buddy. Please. I don't want to die. Please don't shoot me."

I stared at this crouching figure, this miserable beggar. For such a big man he was awfully chicken-hearted. I stepped closer, pointing downward at his head. My finger wrapped around the trigger. The whistling in my ears faded until I could barely hear it at all.

"Please, man. Please don't kill me."

The sound of the gunshot was enormous. Unreal. It seemed to echo around me in a spreading wave. Blood and bone and brain matter splashed into the grass. The body buckled and reached as if trying to find its missing head. I watched, transfixed, as these animal arms and legs began to comprehend a new reality and slowly lost their will. What did it feel like when consciousness was replaced by nothing? Did it feel like a warmth or glow, a kind of full-body euphoria? Did the terrible sound finally end?

I was still standing there, considering the body, when a screen door opened. A figure staggered out of the same house, what appeared to be another man. This fellow was shorter and slimmer than the meathead I had executed. Instinctively I backed away from the body, and when this new man saw why, he fell to the ground and began to make an awful sound. It was something between a wail and a scream and I couldn't bear to hear it.

"Why did you do that?" said the fellow, his dark face looking up at me. "Why did you kill my Tanner?"

Then the man rose to his feet.

"I loved him! He was only trying to protect me! Why did you hurt him?"

My head felt expansive again, like when I ate mushrooms with Keri. My mind whistled and shrieked. The gun felt heavy, like gravity was trying to take it from me.

"Why?" the man cried again and took a step forward.

With great effort of will I raised the gun and pointed it at the approaching figure. It stopped walking and put up its hands in a protective stance.

"Don't do it! Please! He was only trying to protect me."

I couldn't stand there forever. Eventually someone would come looking to see what had happened.

"What's your name?" I asked, but somehow I already knew.

"Mitch!" it cried. "Of course my name is Mitch! What do you want from us?"

"Mitch Brown?"

"Yes! How do you know me?"

You might think, after the day's events, that I'm a bad guy. But I don't believe in bad guys. Instead, I think good guys are sometimes forced into tough choices.

What would you have done, right then, if you were me? Maybe it wasn't Mitch's fault that I killed his friend, but how could I take him to see Jimmy after what I'd done? What I'm asking you is, if you were in the same situation, would you have let Mitch live? Or would you have corrected the problem so it couldn't come back later and ruin your life?

The guy would have starved to death in a few weeks anyway. That was the entire point of the EMP. So what I really did was save him a lot of unnecessary suffering.

Honestly, I think I did Mitch a favor.

SEVENTEEN

By the time I headed north again, the new star had fallen below the horizon, but still the sky glowed faintly orange. I took this to mean the fires were closer, no doubt propelled by the strong south wind.

Over the tops of houses and trees I heard a rising swell of sound that had to be people. A mob of them marching somewhere. Maybe looting. The mob was too far away to resolve individual voices, but I didn't need to hear words to sense the collective anger and fear. It was the second evening since the EMP, after all, and still there was no sign of the government. No news at all. Nothing.

Gunshots erupted, a few quick pops at first. Then an enormous staccato roar that sounded like automatic weapons fire, followed by a crash of metal and glass. I reached for the reassuring shape of my own weapon, caressing it with my fingertips the same delicate way I like to touch myself.

It was difficult to believe I was walking the affluent streets of a major American city. I could have been an unwitting actor in the most realistic post-apocalyptic film ever made, and in a leading role, no less. Except this movie was real life and the director was the Almighty Himself.

When I finally made it back, Jimmy opened the door with a drink in hand and smiled ferociously.

"Dude!" he said. "I have good news!"

Beyond Jimmy, candlelight flickered in the living room, and from that direction I could make out a number of enthusiastic voices. I stepped inside and locked the door behind me.

"So what's the news?"

In the living room I counted three new faces, all male. One of them, a slick cat in a vintage *Star Wars* tee, was holding court with Keri. In the moment before she saw me, I could tell she was riding an opiate wave and basking in the fresh attention of this new slick fellow. She was admiring him the way she had admired me during our first night together, drunk on vodka and high on X, and I decided Keri wasn't attracted to a person so much as an experience. Even when she finally looked up and saw me, when she smiled an oversized smile, the light in her eyes dimmed a little. Probably because she was eager to move on to the next experience.

Then she was in my arms, hugging me, kissing my neck.

"Aiden! You were gone so long! I'm so happy you're home."

I didn't know how to take this public demonstration, especially since everyone knew Keri and I had only just met. I also wondered if I looked different to her, to any of them, now that I was a killer.

"Thanks for missing me."

"I totally missed you!" she squealed.

"So what's the news?" I said again to Jimmy.

"We have a truck. A '76 Ford pickup."

"A working vehicle? Are you serious?"

"She needs a new fuel filter," said another of the new faces. This guy was older and very thin, except for a tight and hard-looking beer gut. I later learned his name was Nick. "So she runs a little rough."

"But that bad girl runs!" exclaimed Jimmy. "We can find a fuel filter soon enough, but the point is we have bona fide transportation!"

"Where's the truck now?" I asked.

"We left it at Ed's place," said Jimmy. "Didn't want to put it at risk until we're ready to go. So tomorrow morning we'll head out on foot, grab the pickup, and find the rest of the cavalry. And then food warehouse here we come!"

* * *

The three new guys were Aaron, Ed (Keri's friend), and Nick. Ed was an acquaintance of Aaron's, and hadn't been named on the original list, but he did happen to own the pickup and was invited to come along.

It made sense that Keri had gravitated in his direction, since among the new recruits Ed's ownership of the pickup elevated him to savior status. Nick was a weapons enthusiast whose buddy owned a gun store. The buddy, Nick claimed, could outfit us with military-grade gear, which everyone believed was necessary to take the warehouse.

"You could see what it was like out there," Jimmy said. "We're thinking we should make our move tomorrow."

"I heard gunfire," I said. "A lot of it."

"We heard that, too," said Bart. "Might be Army troops. I'm wondering if buildings like this grocery warehouse will be guarded."

"No way to know," I said. "All we can hope is, if there are military or police somewhere, they're too busy with looters to mess with us."

"I'm more concerned about the guys who work there," said Ed. His T-shirt clung to his muscular, wiry frame like cellophane, bending Vader's red light saber across chiseled pectorals. "Big dudes who pick and load merchandise and know where every entrance is, every window. You think they didn't get the idea, after the power went out, to grab their families and hole up in that building until help came? Or didn't come? They see that food every day. They know what it means."

Jimmy looked at Chelsea, who was drinking what appeared to be a margarita.

"You've driven past this place before, I take it?"

"Sure," she said. "All the time."

"How many people work in a place like that?"

"Fuck if I know. Hundreds, maybe? The building is huge. And lots of trucks."

Looking back, it's funny to remember how naïve we were, a group of poorly informed idiots with no military training planning an assault on a building we'd never seen before, not knowing what weapons we'd be carrying or how many men would be in our group.

Eventually I wandered into the kitchen, where a citronella candle was burning. Someone had made a new batch of mashed potatoes and a pot of black-eyed peas. Scattered on the island were packages of chips and crackers and cookies that had been severely picked over. I made myself a bowl of potatoes and peas and grabbed a bottle of water. There were only three of these left.

While I spooned carbs into my mouth, I opened the pantry and discovered it was nearly barren. All I found were spices, more lemonade mix, and bottles of vinegar and olive oil. Also, on a lower, darker shelf, I discovered a wet mess of what looked like Mitch's brains. I would have inspected more closely if Keri hadn't walked up right then, looking at me with wild eyes. I shut the pantry door and stood in front of it.

"There you are!" she squealed. "I leave for a minute to use the bathroom and you just disappear!"

"Where's all the food?"

"We've been eating it," she said and leaned into me, like we'd known each other for years. "Isn't that what it's for?"

"Has anyone here thought about what we're going to eat tomorrow, though?"

"Aren't we going to the Walmart place tomorrow?"

"That's the hope," I said. "But what if something goes wrong? What if we have to wait another day?"

She pushed away from me, her face wounded, as if I were scolding her personally.

"Jimmy told us to eat," she said. "And you wouldn't even be here if it weren't for me."

"I know that. I'm just saying we'll run out of food soon and everyone will be hungry."

"And I'm telling you Jimmy said eat."

"All right. Sorry I said anything."

"No worries. So how do you like those black-eyed peas? I made them!"

Everyone else was still in the living room and eventually we rejoined them. Amy and Chelsea were sequestered at one end of the sectional sofa, while Bart and Aaron were deep in conversation at the other. Jimmy, Ed, and Nick stood at the fireplace, drinks in hand.

"Yo, Aiden," said Jimmy amiably. "You should hear about the weapons Nick's friend has."

"A bunch of old school automatic rifles," said Nick. "And maybe an RPG."

At that point, Bart and Aaron joined us. Bart was still haggard, his cheeks bloated and heavy-looking, as if he were on a bender.

"So Mitch wasn't home?" he said. "That's weird because he hardly ever goes anywhere."

"Maybe he got hungry and went looking for food."

"He probably wouldn't go anywhere without Tanner. That's his, um, boyfriend. Lives next door."

I didn't like the way Bart was looking at me.

"Mitch is a smart guy," said Bart. "He went to like engineer school or something. We should swing by tomorrow and see if he's back. We could use a guy like that."

"That means bringing his boyfriend," I said. "You really want to add two more?"

"We agreed on ten," Bart said. "You got something against Mitch?"

There was no way any of them could have known what happened to Mitch. But I got the feeling Bart wanted to turn the group against me.

"Jimmy's kitchen is nearly empty," I said. "We're basically out of food, and we have to fit everyone plus weapons into a single pickup. We still have others on the list. Why go back for someone we already checked on?"

Luckily for me, Jimmy agreed with my logic.

"If we have enough time," he said, "we can think about Mitch. But we've got to be quick about this. If we're not in that Walmart place by tomorrow night, all of us are going to be hungry. So let's get some rest and be ready for tomorrow. Gonna be a big day."

* * *

The "couples" were given bedrooms, while our three new recruits crowded on the sectional sofa. Keri wandered into our room and collapsed on the bed. I went into the kitchen for a bottle of water, but by now they were all gone. When I tried filling a cup from the faucet, there was almost no pressure.

I expected Keri to be out cold when I returned, but as soon as I climbed into bed, her arm slithered over me and her hand went straight between my legs. Unlike our previous hazy encounters, I was fully sober for this one and instantly, violently turned on. Keri loved my newfound intensity and matched it with her own. I knew everyone in the house could hear us and didn't care. Something inside me had hardened, had evolved, and I used it to tear into Keri while slick Ed was forced to listen from the living room. Tomorrow I would use the same hardness to move against the Walmart warehouse, and if Bart was still giving me shit by then, maybe he would inadvertently take a round to the face. The way Mitch had taken one to the face. As Keri clutched my shoulders and cried my name loud enough for everyone to hear, I remembered the stricken faces of my victims, the fear in their eyes, their terrible pleas for mercy, and when I pulled myself from Keri, I aimed it at her face. The gun kicked in my hand, and suddenly blood was everywhere, in the grass and in the sheets and splashed across her lips while I towered above her, a commanding figure, freshly emergent in my wet new skin.

EIGHTEEN

When I opened my eyes it was already light outside. Keri's head was still buried under a pillow, so I climbed out of bed and put on a shirt and shorts. I was already hungry and hoped to find something to eat before the others were up.

But when I reached the kitchen, I could see it was too late. Everyone but Keri and Chelsea was already there.

"There's the big man," said Jimmy. "You put on quite a show last night."

Bart and Aaron laughed.

"She still alive?" asked Ed.

"She's fine."

I glanced around the room, indifferently, hoping to spot a snack that had been overlooked.

"Food's gone," said Bart. "Early bird gets the stale Cheetos."

"So what's our plan?" I asked Jimmy.

"Leave in an hour or so. Take only what we can easily carry: our guns, bottles of water, lighters, a few candles. It's about three miles to Ed's place. The more I think about it, the more I think we don't need more guys. We have six now, not counting the women, and Nick's buddy makes seven. If he really can supply heavy weapons, I don't think we need more personnel. And like you said, how do we fit them all in the truck?"

"A smaller force means our eventual defense will be limited," said Bart.

"Look," Jimmy said. "This whole thing may be a long shot, but it's also the best idea out there. Play it right and it might work. Except it's time to stop talking and start doing."

It was easy to see why Jimmy was successful. When you looked around the room, you could see belief in every pair of eyes. We were a gang of nobodies, with no special skills, but somehow we would make this work.

And I planned to play a vital role.

* * *

When we walked out the front door, Jimmy didn't even bother to lock it. Judging by the wistful smile on his face and the way he kept looking over his shoulder, I think he was afraid he might never be back.

We were nine, six men and three women, walking in a crooked line through an upscale suburban neighborhood. The wind, if anything, was stronger than the day before, and above the horizon of rooftops, leaning plumes of smoke were visible in nearly every direction.

On the main road, foot traffic was heavier than the day before. We saw people in pairs and in large groups and everything in between. Some were carrying weapons openly and others were not. Several people on bicycles went by, heads down, pedaling furiously. Only twice did I see a woman walking by herself, each of them overweight.

The sound was a constant hubbub, like what you might hear at the county fair . . .minus the music and periodic rush of roller coasters. Communication between the various groups was sporadic, but within them it was constant. Emotions ranged from fear to freedom. I wondered how many people saw this event as a break from the monotony, as escape from their dead-end jobs. I wondered how many realized the world was over.

Keri took my hand as we grew closer to one of the looming plumes of smoke. The windows of a Shell station had been broken and were exhaling smoke in an anemic way that made me think the fire had been worse earlier.

"Look at that," Jimmy said, pointing. "Someone tried to steal gasoline."

Because of the smoke I hadn't noticed, but when I looked more closely I could see three steel discs—covers for the underground fuel tanks—had been removed and cast aside.

Beyond the immediate intersection stood a small shopping center anchored by an urgent care clinic. As you would expect, the doors of the clinic were hanging by their hinges and several windows had been broken—obviously because of whatever pharmaceuticals and supplies had been present there.

You have to remember it was Sunday, only forty-eight hours since the EMP. It remained difficult to believe people had already been looting. But unlike a blizzard or the aftermath of a tornado, when you could already see a recovery coming, in this case there was no information at all. And fear had rushed to fill that vacuum.

We walked another mile, through the next major intersection, and then turned south into Ed's neighborhood. By that point an hour had passed, I would guess, and a little while later we stood in his garage, marveling at the pickup.

It wasn't much to look at, this old Ford, its black paint peeling in armies of paper-thin curls. There was a dent in the rear fender and the tailgate was warped. Three of us could fit in the cab and the rest would ride in the bed. All the weapons and ammunition were meant to fit back there as well, which meant it would be a tight fit to say the least.

"Your buddy lives south of Denton," said Jimmy to Nick. "Which means we've got an hour drive to his place and then another hour to his gun shop?"

"At least," said Nick.

"So let's stop wasting time and get on it."

We were all hungry and thirsty, you remember, so Ed grabbed anything we might eat or drink. The nine of us shared three bottles of red Gatorade, a box of Triscuits, five stale chocolate chip cookies, and the debris at the bottom of a box of Corn Flakes. Dessert was a quarter bag of white powdered doughnuts.

After that we climbed into the truck: Ed in the driver's seat, Jimmy shotgun, and Amy squeezed between them. I wasn't thrilled to be stuck in the back with the other common yahoos. I was a winner, a leader, and they were all low-energy losers.

Finally, Ed turned the key, and the revving, mechanical sound was nothing short of surreal. It felt like months since I'd been in a running car. When the engine caught and roared to life, I was overcome with optimism so profound I nearly cried out. Keri threw her arms into the air and let out a pleased screech.

As soon as Ed pulled out of the garage, though, the engine hic-cupped and almost quit. At the same time I noticed a man walking toward us. He was a few houses away, his hand raised into the sky. I saw Jimmy confer with Ed and then turn back toward the man.

"We're in a hurry, guy," he yelled out the open passenger window. "Sorry."

"Hold on!" the man yelled back. "My daughter is—"

Ed gave the engine more gas and we shot down the driveway, into the street. The pickup lurched forward as the man ran toward us, yelling. The engine nearly died and then snarled to life again. The angry man got within twenty yards of us before Ed finally pulled away.

Soon we emerged from the neighborhood and turned west onto the main road. Heads turned, people pointed, and a group of three men began walking toward us. With six of us in the truck bed, and three up front, it was obvious we didn't have room for anyone else, but that didn't stop the men from approaching. Ed accelerated away from them, but it wasn't like he could fly down the road, not with all the stalled cars in the way.

"Hey," said Bart, sitting across from me. "Maybe we should make our weapons visible to discourage idiots from approaching us."

I nodded and pulled the Sig from the waistband of my jeans. Nick and Aaron saw the point and followed suit.

Sure enough, when Ed slowed to negotiate a glut of stalled traffic, another group of men approached us. Each one was dressed in camou-flage and carried a rifle.

"Where y'all headed?" asked the shortest guy, who was walking ahead of the rest and the apparent leader.

"Nowhere," shouted Bart.

"Maybe you could take us along," yelled another of the men, this one much taller and broader across the shoulders. "We're looking for someone to tell us what the hell is going on. Like the police or the Army."

Ed couldn't get through the intersection without driving onto the sidewalk. But the curb was tall, and as he eased over it, the group of men gained on us. The engine idled and choked so roughly I nearly fell over.

"We haven't seen any cops or military," barked Nick. "I bet they mobilized south of here, where the city is burning."

"Then take us there," said the short guy. "We want answers. Otherwise shit is about to get real."

"Shit already is real," said Bart. "Now just go on with your business."

"Our business is to make sure this is still the United States of America. Be a patriot, mister."

Ed was over the sidewalk now. The men began to fall behind us as the pickup accelerated through the intersection.

"It's in your best interest to help us, jackwagon," said the short guy.

Bart's response was to raise his weapon higher, a clear message to back off. When he did, the short guy shouldered his rifle but didn't quite point it at us.

"*You want to see who's a better shot, asshole?*" he screamed.

"Move this fucking truck!" yelled Bart.

The pickup lurched forward. The short guy in camouflage raised his weapon higher, as if he might fire, but one of his buddies reached over and pushed the barrel downward. After an exchange of words, the two of them turned away and went back to patrolling their claimed corner.

Ed learned from that experience to approach intersections with more speed. It was a hell of a ride with nothing to hold onto but the side of the truck and each other. We agreed to be vigilant about watching for interested parties and made it to the Dallas North Tollway with no more trouble.

The tollway is a major arterial that connects Dallas with its northern suburbs, and by then it was conveying a massive number of refugees from points south of us. Many of them walked in the median, but plenty were on the road surface as well, threaded between stalled cars, looting them for food and valuables. We kept our weapons visible to discourage anyone from approaching the truck. In the direction of the airport, smoke in varying shades of white and gray and black boiled into the sky, where it was eventually absorbed by a dark cloud deck that seemed to promise rain.

None of us had anticipated quite so many pedestrians on the highway, so we decided to exit at Eldorado Parkway. Here we found more strip malls, grocery stores, and gas stations on corners.

When we crossed a short bridge, Bart thumbed southward and said, "That's Lakewood Village. Big houses on the shoreline of Lewisville

Lake. Would be a good place to ride this out, I think. It's isolated and protected by water on three sides."

"A Walmart warehouse would also be a good place to ride this out," I suggested.

Soon we reached a second bridge, a long stretch of road over gray, choppy water. I realized Bart had a point: If you posted sentries at both bridges, you might protect the area from refugees and looters. How strange it was to think of the world in wartime terms when only days before I had been playing golf and making out with strippers. It had never occurred to me how fragile our society was, how civility and order barely covered our animal instincts. God had forced us to look at ourselves, and the reaction had been desperate and feral. We would either starve to death or kill each other and then starve to death. Except for the chosen few. Except for me.

Eventually we turned onto a ribbon of blacktop so narrow that trees stretched over us like a canopy. As we sped down the road, I imagined it was 1944 and we were in a Jeep, sneaking behind enemy lines. The sky was dark and seemed close enough to touch. The trees were so dense I expected, at any moment, a squad of Nazi soldiers to burst onto the road. Each one of us gripped his weapon a little tighter and opened his eyes a little wider, as if it were obvious something terrible was about to happen.

Finally, we reached the end of the pavement. Ahead stood a metal gate, beyond which the road became dirt. Off to the right stretched a long gravel driveway where a two-story house loomed, bluish gray, surrounded by trees. The garage was open and a red pickup was parked inside.

"Stop!" a voice yelled. "This is private property! Identify yourselves or I will take you down."

"Mack," said Nick loudly. "It's me. I brought some friends. We need your help."

"Nick," Mack said, as if in confirmation. "I can't believe you came all the way out here. What's your business?"

"We know where there's a lot of food and we need your help to get it. We're going to put together an assault and we want you to come along."

Finally, a figure emerged from the trees, a short, heavily-bearded man dressed in a flannel shirt and ratty jeans and a camouflage trucker hat. His rifle was shouldered but he didn't point it at us.

"Let me guess," he said. "You're talking about the Walmart DC."

NINETEEN

When Mack invited us into his house, my first notion was to walk straight for the kitchen and find something to eat. I wasn't exactly starving, but my hunger was magnified by the knowledge that I was unable to satisfy it.

Mack didn't seem to care, though. We gathered in his living room, where he revealed how he'd known our plan before we explained it.

"The idea of taking refuge in a Walmart distribution center sometimes comes up in the prepper forums. Most of the sheeple don't even know it's there. And it's stocked with enough food to feed a lot of people for a long time."

"That's our thought as well," said Jimmy. "We're hoping we can enlist your help."

"So tell me your plan."

"If we approached with enough firepower," I said, "we should be able to overcome whoever might be there already."

"Maybe so," said Mack. "You should assume Walmart built contingency plans for an event like this. They would expect to be a target. There could be men with rifles. There might be families. You'll need to develop strategy and a tactical plan and treat this like the hostile invasion it is."

Right about then the house began to creak under sudden, gale-force winds. Through the windows I could see trees thrashing and leaves swirling in light so low it might have been dusk. A moment later, that all disappeared behind a gray veil of pounding rain. The sound of it was something like a roar. In the old world, this is the time I would have pulled out my smartphone to check the radar or a local news live stream.

"Shit," someone said.

"Exactly," said Mack. "You need contingencies for the weather. You need to understand what the building looks like and how to approach it. You need to decide exactly when to mount your assault."

"When?" said Aaron. "We're hungry as hell. Every minute that goes by, someone else might get there instead of us."

"I know it seems like a long time to wait," said Mack. "But I would recommend a nighttime assault. This building will sit on a large asphalt lot, and there may be little cover."

I hated the way everyone was looking at Mack. As if by offering a couple of suggestions, he had become our leader.

"You go there now, even in the rain, and it may turn out to be a suicide mission. So let's sit down and sketch what the building might look like, where the entrances might be, and then develop a tactical assault plan."

"Sounds great," Jimmy said. "Don't you think so, Aiden?"

"Sure. Of course."

"We don't want to shoot anyone if we don't have to," Jimmy added.

"Speak for yourself," I said.

"That's admirable," Mack replied. "But the folks already in the DC will understand what's at stake. It's a giant building full of food."

I looked around, waiting for someone to react to what I had said, but no one was even looking in my direction.

"Assuming we have superior weapons," I said, louder this time, "we should be able to fight our way inside. After that, if someone tries to approach, we obliterate them with machine gun fire."

"You mean you plan to stay there? Long term?"

"It's where the food is. And once we get in, surely with the right weapons we can defend our position."

"That's where you're wrong," Mack said. "I don't care how much firepower you have: When you are ten and they are ten thousand, you will lose. Especially when you are well fed, and they are starving to death. And we're not talking about a bunch of pansies from California, neither.

We're talking about Texans who have been arming themselves to the teeth ever since BHO's stint in office."

"I thought you said this was a popular idea," said Jimmy.

"Depends. Some Walmart DCs are more remote, but this one is on the northern edge of a metropolitan area about to eject seven million hungry people. If you somehow manage to get inside, the next thing you should do is grab as much food as you can and find somewhere else to wait it out. Ideally, it would be off the beaten path, because in a week the city will be a shit show. The problem is how to move supplies without being discovered."

"How long do you think it will take?" Jimmy asked. "You know, for everyone to—"

"Starve to death? No one keeps much in the pantry anymore. I'd say in a city this size you're looking at a fifty percent mortality rate within three months. Seventy-five in six months. By a year out, I'd say you're north of ninety percent dead. In the meantime it'll be like *The Walking Dead* around here. So what we should do is grab enough food to feed the folks in this room for ten to twelve weeks."

"Don't forget about my mother," Chelsea said.

"You understand," said Mack, "the more people we bring, the more food we have to haul away. There's just no chance for a small group to survive inside the DC. Staying there would be a death sentence."

"That's pretty much what we already have," said Ed.

Mack nodded.

"This tough old world just got a lot tougher."

* * *

A bit later, Mack led us to his garage, where he pointed to a steel door mounted to the concrete floor. It looked like the entrance to an underground storm shelter.

"The weapons I sell in the store, the legal ones, aren't military grade. They're look-a-likes that became popular when the Kenyan was elected. For any reasonable advantage, we'll want fully automatic weapons and high capacity magazines."

Mack had brought a large, white candle with him, and a book of matches, both of which he handed to Nick.

"Light this while I open the door here."

Mack retrieved a key from his pocket, unlocked the door, and descended into darkness with the candle. When he reappeared, he handed Nick a heavy-looking military rifle. The butt and handle of this gun were made of a polished, amber-colored wood. It turned out to be a Norinco 56 S.

Mack retrieved other weapons: A Norinco 56 S-1, an HK-91, two AK 47s, and a Norinco RPG. In case you're wondering, RPG is short for Rocket Propelled Grenade.

Outside, the wind shrieked through the trees, and rain pounded the roof so hard it sounded like gunfire. The layering of this noise over the continuous whistle in my ears made me feel chaotic. I wanted something to eat. I wanted to be an agent of a change in this strange new world. I wanted a reason to kill again.

Later we took our weapons into the house, where Mack demonstrated their proper use and handling. The rifles, he explained, had been sourced overseas, built for wars that were ancient history to me. I was impressed by the lot of it and eager to get going. Jimmy, by contrast, seemed amused.

"Where did you get all this?" he asked Mack.

"That's my business. But there is an active market for weapons like these."

"Unless you're planning to break into Fort Knox, why own actual military rifles?"

"Aside from using them to wage war on Walmart?"

Jimmy smiled.

"Look," Mack said. "This event may be a surprise to you folks, but some of us have been prepping for years. If that star hadn't gotten us, it woulda been a solar flare. Or a nuke detonated over Kansas. Ever since America turned weak, ever since city folk got used to electricity and iPhones and groceries on demand, it was bound to happen."

Mack looked around at all of us, clearly pleased with his speech.

"And now here we are," he added.

But I wondered why, if he was so prepared, Mack was even bothering to help us. Unless it turned out he was low on food himself.

* * *

Eventually, the weather cleared and the sun came back out. Mack grabbed some paper and a pencil and sketched a rectangular shape.

"A building like this probably doesn't have many windows," he said, pointing. "There may be an office up front, and if so it will be the facility's weakest point. But the rest of the place will be a huge concrete shell. The loading docks will be garage-style doors. If I were defending the building, I would post men near these docks.

"Chelsea, it looks like your mom's house will need to be our staging area. You women will stay behind. We'll post men at the DC and make as many trips as we can back to the house. If we fill a whole room full of high-calorie, protein-rich food, it should be enough for the ten people in this room—plus your mother—to get through the worst of the shortage. Each trip will be dangerous, though, especially if other folks discover what we're up to. They will beg and eventually they will try to steal.

"Honestly, it's a huge risk to stay anywhere near the city, but I don't see another option, not with one pickup and the roads as crowded as you claim. We'll need to stay out of sight and be ready to fight when the shit gets real. Hopefully it will be enough.

"Now," Mack continued, "let me explain how I think we should approach the DC."

* * *

As the day wore on, I wondered if my stomach would digest itself. The hunger pangs were like earthquakes flattening whole city blocks of internal machinery. And I wasn't alone.

"I am fucking starving," Keri finally said. "Don't you have any food around here, man?"

"I hadn't been to the store in more than a week," Mack said. "And I've eaten all the junk in my pantry over the past couple of days."

"So your speech about being prepared, that was all bullshit?"

"I've got weapons. I've got a shitload of ammunition. But I've been out of a job for five months, and when I got low on funds I ate my supplies."

Keri looked at me and smiled ghoulishly.

"A survivalist who can't afford the apocalypse," she whispered. "Now there's the economy sticking it in your eye."

Since evening was still hours away, there was a lot of time to kill. Mack taught us offensive maneuvers and how to split our attack into separate formations, which would force anyone in the DC to divide their defense. When he was done, Keri and I walked outside, where we sat in a bench swing on the front porch.

"I don't know about you," she said, "but I'm glad this got pushed back until later."

"I thought you were starving."

"I am, but I'm also scared. Aren't you?"

I could have told her about God's plan to end the world, about my special role in the new order, but I don't think she would have understood.

"Of course I'm scared," I said. "But if you think you're hungry now, wait until tomorrow or the day after that."

"Why don't we climb into the truck and drive somewhere else? Where there's less people and more food. Like a farm or something."

"You think a farmer will be thrilled with ten people who want to squat on his land and eat whatever he's growing?"

"I don't know. But two days ago there was enough food to feed everyone. It can't all be gone already."

"It's not gone. It's just far away. We already talked about this."

Keri abruptly stood up and marched off the porch. The loss of balance pushed the bench's gentle pendulum motion into disarray.

"I know we already talked about it!" she cried. "I was hoping you could make me feel better and not rattle off more depressing facts. I'm scared, Aiden! I'm scared this isn't going to work and maybe some of you will get hurt or killed."

The frustrating thing was Keri understood what we were up against. That she wanted me to supply her with bogus platitudes made her seem like a child.

"I don't like this any more than you," I lied. "But we have to take risks if we want to live. And it's not like you'll be on the front lines. You don't have to worry about anything."

"I'm worried about losing you, Aiden. Can't you see that?"

"I thought you were more concerned about running out of painkillers."

At this Keri smiled a bitter smile.

"I have problems same as you," she said and stepped onto the porch again. As she stood over me, I was sorry for what I had said, only because she might never wrap those killer legs around me again.

"But at least I'm willing to talk about them. If you keep your problems bottled up long enough, eventually you'll explode."

She marched away, into the house, and for a while all I did was contemplate the loneliness of a nearly-empty world. The way Mack talked, it was like he had *wanted* something like this to happen. Why? Because the old world made him feel ostracized? Or because, in this new one, he had been promoted to the top of the food chain?

I closed my eyes and imagined empty cities overgrown with trees and vines, freeways crumbling, bridges collapsing, the disappearance of all Man had wrought. My mind shrieked like a tea kettle. I wondered how much longer I could go on like this.

When I finally went back inside, the rest of the men were standing in the living room, guns in hand.

"Aiden," Jimmy said. "Nice of you to join us. It's time to go."

"I thought we were going after dark."

"While you were outside swinging," Mack said, "we decided to gather recon while it's still light out. We'll drive past the DC on the way to Chelsea's mother's and see how closely the building matches our expectations. Then we'll go back there after dark to execute the plan. Sound good to you, Colonel?"

"Sounds great," I said, wondering how it would feel to shoot Mack in the face. "Let's go kick some Walmart ass."

CABIN FEVER ┼

TWENTY

Before the pulse, Skylar had endured her fair share of personal disaster, and the way she preferred to suffer was in the familiar topography of her own mind. When Roark moved out, she inverted her days, popping Ambien to sleep the light away and sitting all night in front of the TV watching childhood favorites like *Pretty Woman* and *Big*. Not to cheer herself up, but to remember that life was not art, that life was wonderful and messy and, most of all, unpredictable.

But now she wished the opposite. She wished yesterday had comprised the first two acts of a film. She hoped today was a newly-written third act, that a studio executive had ordered Thomas to replace his original dark ending with a sappy one where the effects of the pulse were erased.

She couldn't stop thinking about her parents and specifically her father. Over the past several years his health had deteriorated, starting with the quadruple bypass that robbed him of vitality that never fully returned. A year later his right knee was replaced, then a hip, and now he made jokes about Terminators and Bionic Men. But Skylar wasn't amused. Every time she drove past a cemetery, every time she saw a funeral procession, she found herself fighting back tears. Because one of these days it would be her turn to sit in a dark limousine, staring down the barrel of a life in which her warm-hearted father was no longer a part.

Now, for all she knew, her parents were already dead. A plane could have gone down in Manhattan or her father could have collapsed trying to make it home or anything. Anything could have happened and there was nothing she could do about it. Nothing but sit here at the kitchen table and watch Thomas and Seth argue about the boys playing outside. It was Saturday afternoon, the day after the pulse.

"I already explained why we shouldn't go out there yet," Thomas said, closing the back door. This confrontation was taking place not ten feet from where Skylar was flipping through a recent issue of *Entertainment Weekly*, which so far had contained four mentions of her.

"I'm sorry I don't share your anxiety," Seth said. "We didn't see any neighbors."

"But I told you Larry is nosy. I hardly ever see him without those stupid binoculars around his neck."

"And I'm telling you we didn't see any Larry. We didn't see anyone."

"But what if *he* saw *you*? Maybe he comes over here with a gun, or maybe he tells someone else and we end up with twenty people outside."

"If that happens," Seth said, "we deal with it. We have weapons, too."

Natalie was in the adjacent living room, holding a book in her lap Skylar had never seen her open. She was staring out the window and didn't seem to care that guns and potential violence were being discussed in front of her young sons.

"Look," Thomas said. "I don't enjoy telling anyone what to do—"

"Then please don't. When you asked us to come here, you didn't say we'd be on lockdown."

"I don't mean for it to seem that way. But our choices over the coming days and weeks will mean the difference between life and death."

"It's not like my boys can sit inside and play Xbox all day. They need something to do."

"I have a pool table upstairs," said Thomas. "And board games."

"I hate board games," said Brandon. "Especially backgammon."

"Me too," said Ben. "If we can't play Xbox do you at least have Nintendo Switch? That runs on batteries."

Seth laughed. "Let's go upstairs, boys. We can play Monopoly."

"What's Monopoly?" asked Ben.

"It's a game where you buy streets and houses and charge people money when they stay there."

"What kind of game is that?"

"The way to win is to own all the property so you can drive up the cost of living and tell everyone what to do."

Skylar caught Seth's eyes and smiled at him. She liked that analogy, comparing their absurd living conditions to a board game. Maybe Seth wasn't as provincial as he seemed. Maybe he would prove to be an ally here.

After Seth and the boys disappeared up the stairs, Thomas collapsed into a chair across the table from her.

"I'm not an asshole," he said in a low voice. "I'm just trying to keep everyone safe."

"You're living in fantasy world," Skylar said. "You can't lock a bunch of strangers in your house and expect everyone outside to fend for themselves. Let's go talk to your neighbors. Get everyone together and come up with a plan to get through this. Like long term."

"I don't know my neighbors. There isn't enough food. We already talked about this."

In the living room, Natalie stood and looked briefly in their direction. Skylar wondered if she was upset with someone here or missing family she had left behind or in shock. Natalie walked toward the kitchen but then veered into the hall and out of sight.

"I thought you were a nicer person," Skylar said. "I thought you were more empathetic."

"No matter what I do it will be the wrong thing."

"As if it's up to you who lives and dies. As if you're God."

"I'm not the only person who prepared. There's a whole culture of people who expected something like this to happen, and the prevailing opinion has always been to get the hell away from everyone else so they don't take you down with them."

"But even wild animals cooperate, and we humans are self-aware, for heaven's sake. We can make complex decisions. And all you care about is your own stomach."

"You can't focus on the philosophical if you don't satisfy the biological."

"Maybe so," Skylar said. "But would you really let the light go out forever because you're too selfish to share?"

"The lights are already out."

"That's not the kind of light I mean," Skylar said, and got up to leave.

TWENTY-ONE

Natalie's silence was nothing she consciously decided, but when every moment in this house was worse than the one before, what was there to say? The more she withdrew, the less necessary it felt to interact with the exterior world, and by now she felt almost no desire to speak at all.

The first problem was her husband's obsession with Skylar. There was a reason *Life . . . Unexpected* never disappeared from Seth's Continue Watching list on Netflix, and it wasn't his affinity for low-budget movies. The idea of Skylar Stover being here in person seemed to have blown his mind. He couldn't stop looking at her.

Maybe he was noticing Skylar's breasts, barely contained by the stretchy fabric of her tank top. Maybe it was the waterfall of her hair, which somehow looked theatrical and glamorous no matter how she chose to wear it. It might have been her perfect thighs or sculpted calves or the generous-but-tiny curve of her butt. All she knew was Seth couldn't stop staring at her and it was driving Natalie mad.

By now it was Sunday morning, somewhere in the dead zone between breakfast and lunch. Natalie was at the kitchen table, buzzing a little from a fresh taste of the limoncello Thomas had served after dinner last night. Ben and Brandon were playing The Game of Life with Skylar in the living room while Thomas read a paperback on the sofa. Seth was upstairs at the pool table. Natalie didn't see anything wrong with a little day drinking, especially since it seemed to dampen the ringing in her ears, and anyway what else was there to do?

"I don't understand this game," said Ben. "The job I get and the amount of money I make is based on luck."

"Real life is sometimes like that, too," Skylar explained.

"But my dad says you have to work hard if you want a good life. That we have to get good grades in school if we want to make lots of money."

"Your dad is right about that."

"But if I work hard, it's not luck."

"And she has a better job than Dad," Brandon said, pointing at Skylar. "You make like a million dollars, right?"

Natalie looked up and watched Skylar fumble for an answer.

"She's a beautiful actress," Ben pointed out.

"Exactly," said Brandon, brow furrowing with the gravity of philosophical insight. "And that's not hard work. She was born beautiful."

"Even in acting you have to work hard," Skylar finally said.

"Really?" said Brandon. "I was in a school play last year, and that didn't feel like work to me."

"Imagine being in a play for fifteen hours a day. And having to tread water in a swimming pool for six hours while the director tries to film three lines of dialogue your costar can't seem to get right."

"That still doesn't seem like work," said Brandon. "That seems like fun. How do I get a job like that when I grow up?"

Skylar glanced up then and caught her staring. Natalie looked away, at the wall, at Thomas, who was also looking at her. Then she realized: They expected her to say something. Ben and Brandon were talking about school and careers as if the power would eventually come back on, as if the old way of life had simply been put on hold. But how could Natalie explain reality to the twins when she wasn't ready to face it herself?

She went into the kitchen, where the bottle of limoncello stood, and quietly poured herself another small glass. Judging by its flavor, so light and sweet, the liqueur couldn't be very strong. She poured one more little swallow and went back to her seat.

Until now she had ignored the magazines fanned across one end of the kitchen table, but as she tried to enjoy this fresh and heady rush of limoncello, Natalie began to suspect everyone knew she was drunk. And the sound in her ears had returned, louder than ever, clamoring like a school bell as she reached for the nearest magazine. Here was a smiling Tom Hanks. A feature on someone named Darren Aronofsky. A picture of Skylar Stover in a tight-fitting red dress, her hourglass figure nearly a cartoon. What did it feel like to live every day in a body like that? How wonderful must it be to reach for Skylar's voluptuous figure among tangled bedsheets, to discover swells and curves of radiant skin, breath hot and humid, the soft touch of warm fingers—

"It's so cool you're a famous actress," Brandon said. "I used to watch Jeffrey every night before bed."

"Me, too," said Ben. "You were our favorite."

"You mean Electric Eric was your favorite. Music Madison was *my* favorite. Because, you know, she was so pretty."

Brandon looked up at Skylar, blushing furiously. She smiled gleaming megawattage back at him.

"Thank you, Brandon."

A sharp sound startled Natalie, then. Startled all of them.

Someone had knocked on the front door.

"Everyone please be very quiet," Thomas said. "This is exactly what I've been worried about."

And then to Natalie specifically, he said: "Maybe you could take the boys into your bedroom? Just in case?"

"I'll do that," said Seth, who came padding down the stairs.

When the boys were gone, Thomas approached the door. The entryway was around a corner from the kitchen and Natalie couldn't see it.

"Hey there," Thomas said. "How's it going?"

"Been better," said a man's voice. "I'm going around the neighborhood to see how everyone is getting along. You remember me? I'm Matt."

"Sure," said Thomas like he didn't know the guy at all. "I'm doing all right so far."

"Have plenty of food?" asked Matt.

"I wouldn't say plenty. If all this doesn't get fixed soon, I'll need to work on my fishing skills."

"Are you kidding?"

"Well, no, I mean—"

"I got some kids who are pretty hungry," said Matt, "so none of this seems very funny to me."

Natalie heard a rumble of thunder. She looked out the window and wondered if it might rain.

"Sorry," Thomas said. "It's a tough situation."

"I've been thinking, if everyone in Lakewood Village combines our food supplies, maybe all of us will have a better chance to survive."

"I don't have a lot of supplies," Thomas lied. "I just hope the power comes back on soon."

"I figured you'd be like that," Matt said. "You don't come to the HOA meetings. You don't come to the monthly barbecue. I guess you like your privacy."

"I pay my yearly dues," Thomas said. "And I travel a lot, so."

"A real jet-setter you are."

Thomas stood there with the door open, saying nothing. Natalie wondered what was happening, why the two men were staring at each other for so long.

"Well," Matt finally said. "I better run before I get rained on. Guess I'll see you around."

"Sure thing," said Thomas.

As he closed the door, Natalie tossed her magazine across the table and reached for another one. A moment later, white light flashed through the windows, followed by a house-shaking clap of thunder.

"Holy moly!" yelled Ben, who was already approaching from the hallway. "That was loud!"

"Boys!" whispered Seth. "Keep quiet!"

But the twins had reached the window, fascinated by a curtain of rain crossing the lake.

"Look at that!" said Brandon. "Here it comes!"

A moment later rain was upon them, falling so heavily the nearby lake receded from view. The roar of the storm made Natalie think of her honeymoon in Niagara, where she and Seth had taken a boat tour to the falls. As they kissed theatrically under the spray, Natalie felt like a movie star, almost lovely, the way she felt before fat and gravity conspired to make her look like a middle-aged woman.

In the early part of their marriage, Seth had somehow been able to look past her declining beauty, and she basked in the glow of his attention. But as years went by, and especially after she gave birth to the twins, Natalie could no longer ignore what she saw in the mirror. The less attractive she felt, the more difficult it was to believe Seth could desire her. Or that she could desire him. Instead of waiting every night for the boys to go to bed, instead of anticipating a kiss or the delicate touch of his hand on her thigh, Natalie nodded off in front of the television earlier and earlier, as if someone had drugged her. It was obvious now she had slept through much of Seth's descent into gambling addiction. That her waning sexual desire had inadvertently enabled him.

"Mom," said Brandon. "Can you believe this storm?"

Natalie didn't trust herself not to slur, so instead of answering she simply nodded.

"Mom, are you okay?"

All at once the world was spinning around her. The roar of the storm distorted the sound in her ears until it was a high-pitched whistle. She wasn't in love with Seth. She had drifted away from him long before the gambling addiction took hold. Even while he apologized for his actions, while he came clean to her, Natalie had hidden her own failures.

"I'm fine, honey. Just tired."

A figure approached from the hallway and she saw it was Seth.

"Look at that rain," he said from the living room. "Can you imagine if there was a tornado? With no radar, we'd never see it coming."

Thomas and Skylar joined her boys at the windows. Natalie's heart beat in her brain. She had never felt so left out, so alone. She stood up suddenly and her chair screeched across the floor.

"Nat, are you okay?"

Seth looked at her carefully, waiting for an answer, but if she opened her mouth nonsense would tumble out. And what was there to say? She didn't belong here. The whole scene was too much to bear.

She staggered out of the kitchen. Grazed the wall on her way to the bathroom and a picture frame exploded on the floor. Voices called after her. Footsteps followed her. She locked the bathroom door and vomited into the toilet.

As Seth pounded on the door, asking what was wrong, Natalie hated herself. How pathetic was it that the end of the world wasn't the worst part of her life?

Then she heard someone else talking. Someone who turned out to be Skylar.

"Seth," she said in the tender and husky voice that was her trademark. "Why don't you give her a little space? She could probably use it."

"She could probably use my *help*."

"Honey," Skylar said, "you should let Natalie process this in her own way. Believe me, I know how she feels."

Natalie wanted to open the door and scream *How could you possibly know how I feel? Look at your life and look at mine! You have no idea how I feel!*

Instead, she kneeled forward and vomited into the toilet again, her ears whistling like a kettle. Something was wrong with her. Like really wrong.

Like she was losing her mind.

TWENTY-TWO

It was three days now since they'd come here, or the third day . . . Seth had never understood the proper way to increment time like this. Since they arrived early Saturday, and now it was Monday morning, did that mean it had been two days? One? Three?

The heat was unbearable and Seth was losing his patience. He had finally convinced Thomas to open the windows, and at first enjoyed the feeble breeze that followed. But now the house was flooded with humidity so dense and oppressive that Seth imagined he could see it gathering in corners and pooling against the ceiling.

If the heat wasn't bad enough, Natalie's silence was driving him nuts. After her meltdown yesterday morning, after sleeping away most of the afternoon, Seth was sure she would have come to him with an apology. But no. She wouldn't leave the bedroom and wouldn't speak when he stopped by to see her. She acted as if the pulse was his fault, something Seth had inflicted upon her personally. Worst of all, she wouldn't even interact with the boys.

After dinner last night, after he downed two glasses of bourbon, Seth found Skylar standing at the back windows and summoned the nerve to approach her. By then the boys were in bed and Thomas was upstairs. Moonlight gleamed on the rippled surface of the lake and she didn't seem to notice him.

"I'm sorry about Natalie," he finally said. "Thanks for helping with the boys."

"I can't imagine how hard this must be on them," Skylar answered. "When the world is turned upside down and even adults don't know what to do, where does that leave a child?"

"I know what you mean. I feel so bad for them."

Skylar stood there saying nothing. For a while all Seth could hear was wind whistling past the window.

"When I was a little girl," she eventually whispered, "I thought grownups knew what they were doing. Not all of them, but I was sure a select group of smart people knew how things worked. It didn't seem possible to live in a world with cars and planes and bridges and the Internet if there weren't people, you know, in control of it all."

Seth couldn't think of anything clever to say, so he waited for Skylar to continue.

"I got into acting when I was young and did my first big picture when I was only fifteen. It was a rude awakening. The director was a big deal and I went into the shoot thinking he was one of those 'in control' guys. But he was a basket case. The whole project was an unorganized disaster, and I kept thinking there was no way all this megaphone yelling and standing around in the freezing cold could turn out to be a real picture. But then the movie won two Oscars, including Best Director. And that's when I knew."

"Knew what?"

"That grownups weren't so different from children. That everyone was as lost as I felt. Until that point I had been a good little girl, totally not rebellious because I was afraid to disappoint my father. But the idea that the best and smartest people in the world were as flawed as I was made me wonder why I was bothering to be proper. Why not snort coke and fuck men twice my age and spend two drunk weeks in Copenhagen with a dude who could barely speak English and liked me to shove steel balls up his butt?"

Seth nearly laughed, but when Skylar looked at him there were tears in her eyes.

"I understand how Natalie feels," she said. "The world is falling apart and no one is coming to fix it. No one is in charge. If the government was, you know, a bunch of thoughtful people with the country's best interests in mind, this wouldn't have happened. Someone would have made smart choices to keep us safe. But instead the government is burdened by small men with small minds whose only thoughts are for corporate donors."

"Personally," he said, "I've never trusted the government. It's too bloated and wasteful with my tax dollars."

"Come on, Seth. That's just a talking point you've been trained to repeat. Do you honestly think anything happens in government without the consent of private money?"

To Seth, this was a typical argument made by the liberal elite, which was to blame the problems of society on someone else, either Republican congressmen or large corporations that did what they were designed to do—make a profit for stakeholders. Liberals never wanted to assign blame where it belonged, which was on people who wouldn't lift a finger to help themselves, who lived on welfare and food stamps at the expense of taxpayers like him. Or they wanted to blame natural events on humanity's failures. Whether the pulse had been divine intervention or a celestial accident, it definitely hadn't been caused by humans.

He would have liked to explain all this to Skylar, to talk sense into her pretty liberal head, but he worried that arguments coming from him would sound poorly reasoned and unintelligent compared to her own. She was a beautiful and articulate actress and he was an average man who barely graduated from a mediocre college. Also, he was enamored with her.

Before he could decide what to say, Seth realized they weren't alone. He turned around and saw Thomas looking at them from across the kitchen.

"I'm going to bed," Skylar said, and walked away.

Now it was the middle of Monday morning, what normally would have been the beginning of a new work week, and Seth was on the living room floor with the boys playing Monopoly again. Natalie was still in bed, Skylar was at the kitchen table, and Thomas had disappeared into the garage.

Seth was struggling to focus on the game because he couldn't stop sneaking glances into the kitchen.

"I don't understand why we can't go outside," said Brandon.

"We just can't."

"Why?"

"Brandon, I already—"

"But Dad," whined Ben. "It's so hot in here."

"I don't care how hot it is. You are not going outside. We don't know what's going on out there, and I'm not sure it's safe."

"Yes, we do!" said Brandon. "I can see out the window. Let's go swimming in the lake! That would feel so good."

Seth looked into the kitchen again and found Skylar smiling back at him. A book was open in front of her and he wondered what she must think of him, playing board games and denying pleasures to the twins.

"No."

"Are we going to sit here and play Monopoly for the rest of our lives? I don't even like this game, Dad."

"Me, neither," said Ben.

The problem for Seth was he agreed with his sons. It was miserable indoors and looked comfortable outdoors. They could be fishing off the dock or swimming near the shore or just sitting in the grass, enjoying the breeze. Who was to say this Larry guy would see them, and why would it matter if he did? If he came by later, starving and armed, he would be outnumbered and easily overpowered.

"Dad, pleeeaaaase," said Ben.

Seth heard a sound and looked up to find Skylar standing above him. She was wearing a pink tank top and cutoff shorts, and seeing her smooth, delicate thighs at eye level made the boys and their pleas seem distant, unconnected to this moment. What he wouldn't give to reach for those thighs, to feel their silky texture against his fingertips. Natalie's own legs had given up their slim sensuality in favor of a robust, industrial girth more suited to domestic labors than wrapping themselves around Seth's midsection.

"Let's take them outside," said Skylar, who seemed oblivious to his longing.

"Are you serious?"

"But be quiet about it," she said to the boys. "Can you do that?"

Ben and Brandon nodded ferociously. Seth tried not to notice how, from this angle, he could see two inches of leg above the ragged hem of Skylar's shorts. Her underwear, if she was wearing any, could be only millimeters out of view.

"Then let's go," Skylar said.

When they reached the back door, the dead bolt was locked, but Seth knew Thomas kept a key on the molding above. He watched over his shoulder for someone to discover what they were doing, but no one else was around.

"All right," he told the boys. "Let's go. Quietly. I mean tiptoes."

The difference between indoors and out was a revelation. On the porch it felt at least ten degrees cooler than the kitchen. Seth hadn't realized how much he was sweating until wind pressed his shirt against his skin, which felt cool as ice.

"Dad," said Brandon. "This is amazing!"

"Can we walk down to the water?" asked Ben. "Please?"

"Sure."

When the boys were out of earshot, Skylar said, "Ever wonder how it would feel to be a fictional character?"

Seth desperately wanted her to think he was intelligent and was careful with his reply.

"Isn't that sort of your job?"

"I mean what if none of this is real? Thomas already wrote one film that basically came true. Maybe this is another."

"How could something like that even happen?" asked Seth. "Isn't a screenplay just words on a page?"

"Movies are just pixels on a screen, and they look real, don't they?"

Seth smiled and stared into Skylar's sea-green eyes. He couldn't imagine how a man might approach her. Or attempt to kiss her. What sort of armor did a woman wear when she was desired by every man she met?

"I think maybe this is all bullshit," she said. "That's why I want to meet this Larry character. It's time for the villain to make his first appearance."

"That's his house," Seth said, happy to possess knowledge Skylar wanted. He pointed past a huddle of mesquite trees and a ridge of honeysuckle. As they walked toward the lake, Larry's back yard became more visible. It was heavily wooded near the water but opened to an expanse of grass that approached his enormous brick home. There was an outdoor kitchen that appeared to border a swimming pool.

"I think he might be cooking something on the grill," Skylar said. "See that smoke?"

Even though he wanted nothing more than to impress the young starlet, Seth wondered about the wisdom of Skylar revealing her presence to Larry or anyone else nearby. Even if Thomas was being dramatic about his food supplies, the presence of the world's most famous actress would surely attract visitors the way bugs were drawn to light.

The boys reached the shoreline and raked their fingers through the shallow water.

"Dad!" cried Ben. "There's something gross floating on the lake."

"Shhhh!" Seth whispered hoarsely. "I told you to be quiet!"

"But Dad!"

"I'm going to walk over there," said Skylar, pointing toward Larry's house.

"Are you sure that's a good idea?"

"What's the big deal. I'm sure he—"

"Hi, there," said a voice.

Seth had been so busy shushing the boys and negotiating with Skylar that he hadn't noticed a figure approaching along the mesquite tree line. It was a man with wiry arms and a paunch of a gut, dressed in a blue Polo knit shirt and khaki cargo shorts. His hairline was receding from two directions, as if the forehead and crown were in a contest to reach the middle of his scalp. A pair of binoculars hung from a strap around his neck.

"I'm Larry. I live next door."

Larry reached forward as if to shake their hands, and that's when he finally recognized Skylar. His face crumpled in a way that might have been reverence or disgust or both.

"Oh, my God," he stammered. "I'm . . .I'm so pleased to meet you."

"Nice to meet you," said Skylar in a cheerful voice that was nothing like her normal speaking tone.

"I don't underst—oh, wait! You signed on for that film Thomas wrote. Are you guys, like, dating now?"

Skylar stepped backward and crossed her arms over her chest.

"Um, no. I wouldn't say we're dating."

Larry smiled. Seconds elapsed while they stood there looking at each other. Seth hoped *he* didn't come across to Skylar this way, so creepy and silent and staring.

"I can't believe you're here," said Larry ponderously. "I love your work."

"Thanks."

Beyond Skylar the boys approached, and everyone turned to watch them.

"Dad," called Brandon. "The water has something floating on it. Like dirt."

"Yes," said Larry. "The wind is carrying a fine grain ash. If it contaminates the water and kills the fish, that will pretty much seal our fate."

When they were near enough, Seth grabbed his sons and pulled them close, his arms slung over their shoulders.

"I'm Seth, by the way. These are my two boys."

"I was wondering why I hadn't seen Thomas since all this happened," Larry said. "I didn't realize he was hosting guests."

Larry leered at Skylar again, who, judging by the look on her face, had concluded this journey outside was a mistake.

"Thomas doesn't talk to me often," he said. "But he did tell me about *The Pulse*. It's a lot like this, isn't it?"

Larry gestured in a general way, over his head and toward the lake behind him. In the distance, clouds of smoke climbed into the air.

"I thought the rain might have put out the fires," he continued, "but it didn't."

"Well," Seth finally said. "We just came outside to get some air. Probably should head back inside. Right, Skylar?"

"For sure."

"Why would you go indoors?" asked Larry. "My house is like an oven."

"I don't want my boys to breathe all this smoke."

"From here, though, it looks like your windows are open."

"I'm going to take them inside. Just to be safe. It was nice to meet you."

"You, too."

Larry turned to Skylar and reached again for her hand, which he clasped between both of his own.

"I'm so glad to finally meet you," he said. "I was a science consultant on several films and met several actors. I even met Roark once."

Skylar didn't answer, but the horrified look on her face left no doubt about how she felt.

"Let's go," Seth said. He let Skylar walk ahead of him and pushed Ben and Brandon behind her.

"Come by if you need anything," Larry said as they shuffled away. "Like if you need to borrow a cup of sugar."

Seth raised his hand but didn't turn around. He knew they'd made a very bad mistake and wasn't sure what to do about it. Larry was even stranger than Thomas had made him seem, and eventually there would be a price to pay for having put themselves on his radar.

But what? Would he come for Thomas' food? Convince others to come?

"And I'll do the same," Larry added.

TWENTY-THREE

It seemed all his life, Thomas had been failing to please women.

One day when he was twelve years old, his mom picked up the phone and found herself talking to her husband's mistress. The girl, barely out of college, explained how his father had been fucking her every morning while pretending to be at the gym. The way his mother handled this unexpected news was to get drunk and wait for her husband to come home so she could stab him with a broken beer bottle. And though she hadn't gone through with her plan, she did kick his dad out of the house for a while, and Thomas had spent those terrible weeks doting on his mother even as she verbally abused him for it. She growled and yelled and broke down in angry tears, and all the while he convinced himself she didn't mean to say those things, she didn't mean it when she slapped him across the face, she didn't mean it that one awful morning while she sat in front of her vanity yanking at her tangled hair and hoarsely whispered words he could still hear today: *I hate you, Thomas.*

With time he came to understand why he fell so hard for women like Natalie and Sophia: It wasn't true love unless you were forced to work for the tiniest bit of affection. And when he finally met someone devoted to him, Thomas was put off by it. As early as their second date he knew he would never love Gloria the way he should love a wife, but she was beautiful and driven and wanted desperately to be married. They suffered five years avoiding conflict (and eventually each other) before Gloria summoned the nerve to leave him. Because for Thomas to leave her would have meant another failure.

Today smoke loomed on the horizon, and soon flames would reach the shore of the lake, and then what? Would they be forced to leave? Would the water protect them? Would they be overrun by hordes of starving people? There was no way to know. To spend even a single moment thinking of anything else seemed frivolous.

But Thomas couldn't help himself. He wished he knew how to comfort Natalie. He resented having to order Seth and his boys to remain indoors. And his relationship with Skylar was a disaster. She had flown here, ostensibly, to discuss his screenplay, but her obvious flirting at the airport hinted at a possible romantic interest he never would have imagined. And there was no use pretending he wasn't flattered by her attention. This was a woman who was every man's fantasy, who had flown halfway across the country to have an in-person conversation that could easily have happened over the phone. Who now loathed him for refusing to share his food.

She thought he was being selfish. Inhuman. And she was right about him, that was the hell of it. There was an animal side of Thomas willing to share food with everyone in the neighborhood if it meant Skylar would sleep with him. That he would consider sacrificing the life of everyone in this house for a half-hour sexual fantasy made Thomas feel exactly like the monster she believed he was.

On top of all that, he enjoyed being around her! What he wouldn't give to relive the airport scene, when their easy camaraderie had melted the tension of an anxious first meeting. If not for the end of the world, everything might have been different.

Now, it was Monday evening, and the mood in the house was dark. Skylar was upstairs with a book. Natalie remained in the bedroom, mysteriously mute. Thomas himself had passed much of the day building an inventory of the safe room and preparing estimates on how long their group of six could expect to survive on the current food stores.

Ironically, out of everyone in the house, Seth and the twins seemed most at ease. It was two days now since Thomas had admonished them for going outside, and he assumed Seth would be tempted by the bright sunshine to give it another go. But somehow this had never happened, which was the lone bright spot in an otherwise awful afternoon.

Yesterday Skylar had mentioned a love of Asian food, so Thomas was boiling water and chopping onions for tonight's dinner of curry and rice. Yes, it was a cheap ploy to earn her approval, but what did he have to lose? And so far it appeared to be working, because a few minutes ago Skylar had finally come downstairs. She was sitting on the sofa, reading, of all things, *Alas, Babylon*.

When he was done with the onions, Thomas walked past the kitchen table, where Seth and the boys were playing Sorry!. Through the back windows he could see clouds of smoke against the setting sun.

Thomas heard a knock then, quick three raps, that he recognized immediately but refused to acknowledge.

"Someone's at the door," Skylar said from the living room. "Maybe you ought to answer it."

"I'll get it," said Seth.

"Seriously?" Thomas replied. "*I* will answer it. And please be quiet. Just like when Matt was here before."

He knew who was at the door. Even when the electricity was on, Larry preferred to knock. He was the kind of man who considered himself more cultured than most, when really his personality was adolescent and celebrity-obsessed.

"Hi, Larry," Thomas said as the door swung open. "This is some crazy shit, isn't it?"

Larry smiled his typical creepy smile. He was a physicist and had been one of the leaders at the particle accelerator in Olney before it was destroyed. Today, he worked for an overseas corporation with a German name Thomas couldn't remember.

"Crazy?" Larry said. "Do you say that because of the improbable supernova? Or because this reality is so similar to your new screenplay?"

Thomas didn't understand how a person could effect a manner both erudite and slimy.

"I don't know how the government plans to respond, but if they don't come soon I'm afraid—"

"You know there won't be a response," Larry said. "It hasn't been that long since we talked about this. Don't you remember?"

One night several months ago Larry had lured him onto his patio, which was how Thomas had come to know the man's role at the particle accelerator. Larry had also told stories about his years in Los Angeles and all the celebrities he met while working as a science consultant. But Thomas didn't remember talking much about his work.

"Maybe," he said. "I had just finished another draft of *The Pulse*, so it's possible I—"

"I'm not surprised you prepared for an event like this," said Larry. "You were pretty spooked by the idea."

Thomas remembered drinking a lot of scotch. Possibly more than he intended.

"Anyway," Larry whined, "if you've invited a family to stay in your house, you must have put away more food than I thought."

"A family?"

"They seemed like nice people. Seth and his two young sons. I'd love to say hello."

Larry grinned.

Now here was Seth, yanking the door farther open before Thomas could react.

"Hey, Larry."

"Hello, Seth! Oh, it smells good in there. What are you guys cooking?"

Thomas was so furious with Seth he could barely think straight, but it was the wrong time to let emotion get the better of him.

"We do have a little food," he said to Larry. "But we are being frugal with it, because who knows how long this will last?"

Larry's creepy smile widened, stretching from ear to ear, as if it was in danger of splitting his face in two.

"Maybe we should invite him for dinner," said Seth inconceivably. "I bet he'd enjoy some curry."

"Yes, I *would*," replied Larry. "And it would be lovely to speak with Skylar again."

The words *Skylar who?* arrived at his lips, and it was all Thomas could do to contain them.

"Let him inside!" trumpeted Seth, who grabbed at the door, who exhaled a sour cloud of whiskey breath.

Thomas jerked the door away.

"So now you know," he said to Larry. "There are six people here, including two children. Six people I have to figure out how to feed."

"So you have enough for six but not seven?"

"What I mean is we're on our own. Everyone is."

"But everyone didn't prepare for the apocalypse the way you did. I can't believe you would decline to help a hungry neighbor."

"It's only been three days. Surely you're not out of food yet."

Larry stepped forward. The smile on his face faltered into a grimace. It was horrifying.

"Even if I can survive on Bisquick for another day or two, I'm still going to run out. I walked to H.E.B. after the rain yesterday and the place looked like a bomb went off. What do you expect me to do?"

"I don't know, Larry."

"You expect me to stay home and starve while you get drunk and make curry for your celebrity girlfriend?"

"I expect you to take care of yourself. The way I'm taking care of my guests and myself."

"I'm not the only one around here who's running low," Larry countered. "Maybe I should tell everyone in Lakewood Village about your little party."

"Get out of here," Thomas said. "And don't come back."

Larry leaned to one side and pretended to look beyond him.

"Give Skylar my regards."

"Get out," Thomas said and shut the door.

When he turned around, Seth and the boys had disappeared. Thomas marched into the living room, where Skylar sat alone.

"So you went outside?"

"Yes, I did. What are you going to do about it?"

"That's a mature response. You realize your pointless act of rebellion will probably get us killed."

"What's so pointless about talking to a neighbor?"

"I told you what he was like! What would you have done if he attacked you? What if he tells someone else and a bunch of skeezy men show up here?"

"You mean you wouldn't protect me?" Skylar said, and pretended to theatrically fan herself. "What will I ever do without a man?"

"Not this shit again. That isn't what I meant."

"You act like you want the best for us, but you don't include us in a single decision."

Thomas balled his fists and walked in the direction of the kitchen, where he was greeted by the sour smell of onions and a pot of water rapidly boiling itself away. He switched off the gas and stomped into the hallway. When he barged into the bedroom, looking for Seth, he discovered Natalie on the bed, writing something.

"Sorry," Thomas said. He wondered what she could be writing or why she had chosen now of all times to do it. "I'm looking for Seth."

Her response was to level her eyes at him, eyes so sad and empty that he should have stopped and talked to her. But he couldn't do that for a number of reasons, the primary one being the behavior of her stubborn and defiant husband, who along with Skylar seemed determined to sabotage the environment that was keeping them alive.

The other downstairs bedrooms were dark, so the only place left to look was the game room. When Thomas reached the top of the stairs, he heard fierce whispers and found the twins huddled under the pool table.

Seth himself stood between the table and the bar, brandishing a handgun. Flickering candlelight lit the scene like a nightmare. When Thomas raised his hands and took a step backward, the two boys screeched.

"Daddy, no!"

"Seth," Thomas said. "Put down the gun."

"We're tired of listening to you, Thomas. You're not being reasonable and we're all suffering."

"You're scaring the boys."

"They don't understand what's going on. Natalie is so upset she won't speak to anyone. You shouldn't treat us this way."

"Seth."

"You caused all this to happen."

Beyond the raised surface of the bar, Thomas noticed the top of what appeared to be an open liquor bottle.

"What do you mean I caused it to happen?"

"Your screenplay. You wrote this. It's your fault."

Thomas noticed Seth wasn't pointing the gun at him anymore. His hands had fallen to his sides, and his weapon was aimed generally at the floor.

"Did Skylar tell you that?"

"Don't patronize me. Just because I'm not some hotshot Hollywood writer doesn't mean I'm stupid. Your whole shtick is to write shit that comes true."

"That's ridiculous."

"Is it any more ridiculous than all this happening in the first place? A new star shows up and that's it? The end of the world?"

Thomas blinked, and for a moment reality seemed to disappear. He lost his position in space and wobbled on his feet. He realized, as if for the first time, how alluring it would be if Seth and Skylar were right. If he had caused this, if Thomas had thrust them into some kind of alternate fictional reality, maybe all he had to do was wait for the inevitable happy ending. Because American studios didn't fork over millions of dollars to make the feel-bad thriller of the year. In a movie everything would work out well in the end.

"Maybe you're right," he said to Seth. "Maybe all this is my fault. But we still have to live it. And there's no reason to scare them."

He pointed under the table.

"You don't tell me what to do with my sons," Seth blurted.

Thomas stepped forward. He looked down at the gun again but was convinced Seth was bluffing. His eyes were dull and uncertain and Thomas wondered how much he would remember tomorrow.

"Maybe it was a mistake to bring you here," he said. "I was only trying to help. You're welcome to leave if that's what you want."

"We can't," said Seth, breathing through his teeth. "That's the whole problem. We're trapped here now. In this stupid movie of yours."

Where had he gone so wrong, Thomas wondered, that the people he was trying to help felt like prisoners?

Eventually he went downstairs and found Skylar still in the living room, devouring *Alas, Babylon* as if it were the most riveting novel ever written in English. She didn't look up as he walked past.

Even if Natalie had killed most of the limoncello, several ounces remained, and Thomas dumped all of it into a tumbler. All he was trying to do was make the best of a bad situation, and somehow everything kept getting worse. He poured a bit of olive oil into the skillet and dumped in the chopped onions. Miraculously, in the pantry, he discovered a single can of coconut milk. Which meant this was the last batch of curry he would ever make.

While the onions sautéed, Thomas brought the water to boil again for the rice. He heard something behind him and found Skylar standing there, *Alas, Babylon* hooked under her arm.

"What are you cooking?"

"Curry. Doesn't it smell good?"

He tossed in sliced carrots and red peppers and stirred them with the onions.

"Are you making that because I said I liked Asian food?"

No woman could respect an earnest man. The better approach was to impress without seeming to try.

"Will you stop?" she said.

"Stop cooking?"

"Stop trying to be so fucking perfect!"

"I'm sorry. Would you be happier if I treated you like shit? If I was more of a bad boy?"

"Stop trying to bend the world into the shape you want!"

The curry paste would burn if he didn't add the coconut milk. He used an opener to puncture the can and poured milk into the skillet, where it erupted into a cloud of steam. Surely Skylar would see reason when she sat down to eat a hot meal.

"Don't you get it?" she said. "It doesn't matter if you wrote this world or if it's just a coincidence. The outcome for us is the same. You behave as if you're in control of everything that happens. You treat everyone as if they're characters in your story. Why don't you try being real for a change? Or at least vulnerable? I think everyone in the house would appreciate it."

This was finally enough. He threw the empty can into the sink and pointed his spoon at her.

"Give the sanctimony a rest. You pretend the only reason you came here was to tell me how wrong I was about the script, as if your work is somehow more authentic than mine. But then you accept twenty million dollars to dance like a puppet in front of a green wall. You have all the money a person could ever need. You could make art films for the rest of your life. But you don't. Because you're as shallow as anyone else."

Skylar stared at him. The curry simmered.

"So yeah," Thomas said. "Maybe I could use a reality check. But so could you."

"I think I'll go to bed."

"You haven't eaten anything in hours. Why not sit down and have some dinner?"

"Sorry, but I'm too tired to be hungry."

Skylar walked out of the kitchen while Thomas methodically stirred. A little while later the rice was ready, and he scooped some onto a plate. He added curry and took his dinner to the table along with a glass of whiskey.

Thomas didn't waste any time with the drink. He knocked it back in a couple of swallows and toyed with onions and carrots and peppers. When he first conceived this meal, he had imagined how Skylar might smile at the chopsticks, an unexpected taste of refinement injected into the anxious boredom of their days. Now, sitting here alone, the chopsticks felt ridiculous. He pushed vegetables around his cooling plate and thought about what Skylar had said.

How on earth could she accuse him of being a control freak? All his life Thomas had tried to be a kind and honest and empathetic man. He wanted people to be happy, not miserable. Was the problem Skylar's? Was she so upset that she couldn't see reason?

Or was there something off-putting about Thomas that he was too blind to see?

TWENTY-FOUR

Ever since her career had begun to take off, Skylar had imagined her life as a flight of stairs. The steps themselves represented great events and milestones, while the space between steps was like the excitement of defining a new challenge and the anticipation of achieving it. Believing she would always reach the next step meant a life never wanting for hope.

But had she been fooling herself? Was her staircase really just a net worth calculator? And what did it matter now? Because the pulse had halted forward movement, had ensured all remaining steps would be back down the stairs. The smallest slip meant a tumble toward some destination too far away and terrible to see.

Until now, the worst hardship she'd ever endured was the summer when her father, after an awful fight with her mother, fled to their lake house. She was fourteen then, prone to emotional turmoil, and the idea that her parents might divorce sent her spiraling toward full meltdown.

While her father was away, she lost her virginity to a baseball player who had followed her around school ever since spring break and who, when she finally kissed him, squeezed her boobs like he was trying to drain juice from them. One afternoon, during the third week of her father's absence, Skylar walked over to the baseball player's house and watched a movie about an asteroid crashing into Earth. This time, when his squeezing hands reached between her legs, she hadn't pushed them away. She still remembered his arms on either side of her, smooth and hard and shimmering, his face gone red with concentration. His piston thrusting ended as a woman and her father in the film cowered before an enormous tidal wave, and Skylar wondered what her own father would think if he knew, at that very moment, a thick-headed baseball player was squirting his own wave inside her.

"How's the book?" a voice asked. "I see you've almost finished."

She looked up. Thomas was carrying a plate of breakfast, about to sit across from her.

"It's fine."

Today was Tuesday, four days since the pulse, though to Skylar it felt more like forty days. The sun was out and the sky was a smoky shade of blue. Natalie and Seth and their two boys were nowhere to be found.

"You know," Thomas finally said. "You don't have to read that."

"No? Should I read your screenplay again instead? So I'll know what happens next?"

"I'm saying you don't have to read anything like that at all. It obviously upsets you."

Skylar could feel her coherence dissolving into something like haze. Her head seemed to inflate with the pressure of it.

"You come across like this sweet guy, but I'm not sure you feel human emotions at all."

"That's where you're wrong," said Thomas. "Because I'm pretty fucking pissed at you and Seth right now. Inviting that nutcase for dinner just to prove a point."

"We didn't *invite* him."

"By revealing your presence, that's exactly what you did. And probably half the neighborhood before it's all over."

"Let me say this one more time," Skylar said, "since you don't seem to get it: There's no reason to survive this if it can't be on our own terms."

She spent most of the day in her room, sprawled across the bed, reading the rest of *Alas, Babylon* and then staring at the ceiling. In the book, months after a nuclear war had obliterated most of humanity, the protagonist's girlfriend longed to be married. In a study of contrast, following their wedding on Easter Sunday, the protagonist had hunted down and killed a group of havoc-wreaking men in the manner of frontier justice. The obvious point being that the new order of things was the old order of things. The invisible armature of civility had been blown apart by nuclear warheads, leaving behind a daily struggle for survival that left little time to dwell on philosophical concerns.

But *Alas, Babylon* had been written in the 1950s, and the world had come a long way since then. Women had come a long way. Skylar was going to survive or she wasn't, but she definitely wouldn't place her destiny in someone else's hands.

For dinner Thomas made sandwiches and a side salad of black beans, corn, and diced tomatoes. By then no one was spending much time in the common areas of the house, choosing instead to sequester themselves in bedrooms or the game room upstairs.

Skylar didn't make a decision to leave. Instead, she inched toward her departure one move at a time. When no one was in the kitchen, she found a plastic container and shoveled some of the bean and corn salad into it. She grabbed several bottles of water. After dark, when the candles and lanterns had been extinguished, she stuffed her dirty clothes into the Hello Kitty bag, along with the water and corn salad and a box of Raisin Bran she found in the pantry. Then she lay on the bed and stewed in the hypocrisy of stealing supplies to support her fight for independence. She thought about her parents. She wanted to believe Manhattan had been evacuated, that right now her mother and father were headed somewhere safe. But even if the Army had arrived, there was no way to transport two million people off the island. Her parents were left to their own devices, which meant their fate was sealed.

It was something like midnight or maybe 2 a.m. when Skylar finally climbed out of bed. As quietly as she could manage, she carried her bag out of the bedroom and down the hallway. The kitchen and den were lit by silvery moonlight, which produced shadows that were both dramatic and confusing, because one of those shadows made it seem as if a person was sitting at the kitchen table. But why would someone sit there in the dark? She walked past the kitchen and approached the front door. Turned the deadbolt until it slipped free, and now all she had to do was open the door and walk through it. All she had to do was reach for the knob and turn.

But was someone really in the kitchen?

If someone was, they'd probably come over to look when she opened the door. She decided to check, just to be sure.

"Was that a suitcase?" said a woman's voice.

Skylar's heart nearly thumped out of her chest.

"Natalie!" she hissed. "Why are you sitting in the dark?"

"I'm here to watch a crazy woman give up food and water and shelter for the chance to be raped or killed."

Skylar had never imagined she would see anyone before she left and had constructed no story to explain what she was doing or why she was doing it.

"Is it really that tough being stuck here with us?" asked Natalie. "Are we such poor company that you'd rather wander around Dallas until you're taken hostage?"

"It's nothing to do with you. And I don't plan on being taken hostage. I can fend for myself."

As Skylar stood there, staring at the dark form of a woman, Natalie's face began to resolve itself in the moonlight. She might have been smiling.

"You want to sit down and tell me how you plan to do that?"

"Sit down?"

"If you need to go," Natalie said, "I won't tell anyone I saw you."

This couldn't be a sign, could it? Natalie's presence here this late at night?

"Maybe I'll sit down for just a minute," Skylar finally said, and lowered herself into a chair. "But you have to tell me why you're sitting alone in the dark."

Now Skylar remembered she hadn't heard Natalie speak aloud in something like two days.

"I've been feeling very strange. My ears have been ringing a lot, and I thought I was going crazy, but maybe it's stress. I'm so overwhelmed I can hardly get out of bed."

"I know what you mean. This is the worst—"

"It's not that," Natalie said in a shaky voice. "I don't love my husband."

"Hey," Skylar said, and reached across the table for Natalie's hand. "He's struggling like all of us are. Maybe you should cut him a little slack."

"Before all this, when Seth was gambling away our life savings, I thought he was cheating on me. And part of me wanted it to be true, because then I would have a legitimate reason to leave. Instead, he felt so guilty he tried to kill himself to get the money back. How could I not love him for that?"

Skylar squeezed Natalie's hand and waited for her to continue.

"He wants the best for us," she finally said. "But I don't want him. Honestly, I'm not sure I ever loved him the way you're supposed to love a husband, and for that matter I didn't love Dan, either. I married him before Seth, basically because my dad died."

Skylar noticed Natalie's own hand was squeezing a little tighter.

"That's why I sit out here in the middle of the night. Because I need Seth now more than I ever did, and I've never wanted him less."

"Natalie," Skylar said. "I am so sorry. But why do you think you need him so much? Because of all this?"

"Yes, because of all this! If we split up, what would we do with the boys? Split them, too?"

"Well, no, but—"

"Even if we didn't have the twins, I don't think I could make it through this on my own. But I take it you do."

"I think I could," Skylar said. "At the very least I want to try."

Natalie made a blustery and frustrated sound.

"You know what I think? I think you're so used to living like a princess that the idea of having to struggle is too much for you. Like this is your way out, walking into Hell in the middle of the night."

"Natalie!" Skylar whispered fiercely and jerked her hand away. "How can you say something like that? You don't know anything about me."

"I've seen pictures of you in those stupid magazines. Like at the Oscars when your boobs spilled out of your red dress. How much did that diamond necklace cost? Or was it on loan from Fred's?"

"So you've seen a couple of pictures of me in a magazine and think you know who I am? Weren't you the high school beauty? It's been twenty years and Thomas still remembers drooling over you in English class."

Natalie's eyes narrowed but she didn't say anything.

"You know who I was in high school?" Skylar said. "A nerd in Drama no one wanted to kiss. One asshole said my lips were so thin it looked like I had them surgically removed. The only way I made it into pictures at all was because a film director bumped into me on the street. And I was cast as a ten-year-old kid even though I was fifteen."

"I guess you hadn't blossomed into your body yet."

"I'm pretty sure you know I have implants."

Natalie appeared to nod assent.

"And they're silicone, which don't last forever. What happens when they leak? Do I call the warranty hotline?"

"It still makes no sense to go out there and be hungry and maybe get raped," Natalie said. "You're one of the most famous women on earth and you must know you'll attract unwanted attention."

"I guess that's part of the point. My life has been so privileged the past few years. It's made me soft and spoiled and I'm tired of it."

"Why be a movie star if you don't want a privileged life?"

"Because I love it," Skylar said. "Not saying I don't. But another part of me can't get past the unfairness of it all. Do you know how hard I fought to be paid as much as men less talented than me? And even then I felt like shit because of all the actors who struggle to get noticed, who get paid almost nothing. Meanwhile I make more money for a single film than most will earn in a lifetime. And do you know why that is?"

"Because you're talented and gorgeous?"

Natalie said this with emphasis and Skylar couldn't tell if she was being genuine or sarcastic.

"That's nice of you to say, but no actor is a million times better than another. I get paid so much because a couple of films turned my brand into something studios could count on. Show business used to be like a family, and a lot of people could make a good living at it. Now it's a fucking machine like everything else. A few of us get lucky and live like royalty while everyone else earns peanuts."

"So that's what this is about?" Natalie said. "You feel so terrible about being rich and famous that you might as well walk into post-apocalyptic hell as a way of forfeiting your good fortune?"

Skylar looked out the window, at the lake where moonlight glinted off the rippled surface like a sprinkling of snow. She wasn't sure why she wanted to leave.

"In high school I had a group of Drama friends. Beth and Deidre and Molly were the big three, each one more popular than me. Now all of them are mothers, Beth is divorced, and they have jobs and drive minivans. We met for drinks a few months ago and they were so excited to have time to themselves that all three of them got falling down drunk. They smoked cigarettes and wanted to buy pot and you could feel the desperation coming off them in waves. And I thought, well this is a Thursday. I felt so privileged and mean and all I wanted was to go home so I could be around people more like me. Now my high school friends are going to die and here I am, privileged again, and Thomas is making curry, and I just want it to stop. That's all. I just want it to stop."

She was still staring out the window.

"Skylar," Natalie said. "Look at me."

She reluctantly turned away from the window.

"I can understand feeling guilty about your success compared to your friends. But if they really wanted to act for a living, who better to know than you, right?"

"Deidre was going to move to Hollywood before she got pregnant, but—"

"It doesn't matter. If any of those women wanted to be in a movie bad enough, you could have made it happen. At least once. Which means something is different about you than them. You gravitated toward making movies and they were more interested in starting families. Unless they asked for help and you refused, this guilt of yours is bullshit. It's just another way for you to be aloof, to feel sorry for people who aren't you."

Skylar's reflexive urge was to lash out at Natalie, who until then she had dismissed as naïve and unsophisticated. Here was a woman whose husband donated the family's savings to a casino right under her nose and she only suspected him, predictably, of cheating on her. As if adultery was the worst thing that could happen. What the fuck could she possibly know about Skylar's life and how she felt?

Still, she held her tongue and eventually conceded there might be some truth in Natalie's words. Because Deidre and Molly and even Beth could have joined her in Hollywood. She could have helped them. But in the end her friends had been more interested in traditional lives than being in films. They'd wanted stable relationships and families and to watch their kids grow up.

"I resented my friends for being so conventional," Skylar said. "And all they ever did was complain about how difficult their lives were. But today they would kill to have those miserable lives back. It makes me wonder if people are ever really satisfied."

"Did you want to switch places with them?"

"No. And now I feel so alone. Other than my parents, my brother, I don't have anything to care about or anyone to care for."

Skylar had never spoken these feelings aloud to anyone, not even Roark, whose desire to be a father, she had believed until it was too late, hovered near zero.

"You could change the things you care about," Natalie finally said. "I mean why did you come here to see Thomas? And don't say it was to talk about his screenplay."

"That was part of the reason. In his first project, the women were strong and intelligent. They were integral to the story. But *The Pulse* wasn't like that at all. He made it seem as if a woman couldn't do anything on her own."

"I understand your point," Natalie said. "Women haven't spent generations fighting for equality to watch it all wink out of existence along with electricity.

"But you've got to face the truth here, Skylar. The very qualities that made you so successful in the old life will make you vulnerable in this one. My husband can't take his eyes off you, and he's one of the nice guys. For that matter I can't take my eyes off you, either. Your face, your brand, whatever, will make you a target. You walk out of this house without some real way to protect yourself, and you're asking for trouble."

Natalie's arm slid across the table surface. She took Skylar's hand into her own.

"And I get why you're frustrated with Thomas. He's a little too proud of himself for being prepared, especially because it only happened by sheer luck. He seems to think he needs to do something or be in charge somehow. But there isn't anything to do. We're either going to stay here with his supplies, or someone is going to take them from us."

"But I don't want to sit here. I want to do something."

"If we survive this, there will be plenty to do."

"And Thomas is being selfish. He won't share with anyone."

"He's sharing with us," Natalie said. "I'm sure his original plan was to keep the food for himself. How many people does he need to feed before you're satisfied?"

As much as she didn't want to, Skylar saw her point.

"He's been pretty damned generous if you ask me," Natalie added.

"Maybe you're right."

"And in the meantime, while we wait this out, is it really so wrong to be close to someone? Wouldn't it be nice to let down your guard? To feel the touch of someone else?"

Skylar studied Natalie's eyes, the shadowy contours of her face. Was she talking about Thomas? Or herself?

"You must really have wanted to meet the guy to fly here instead of just calling him."

"I did want to meet Thomas. And I think I would probably like him if not for all this."

"To me, it's hard to blame someone whose heart is in the right place. He wants to shield you from disaster. He wants that for all of us. Is it so wrong to give him a chance?"

TWENTY-FIVE

My Diary: Natalie Black
May 19? 202-

S o I just sent Skylar to Thomas.

All this time, I thought I was intimidated by her, by how beautiful and intelligent and put together she seemed. But when she tried to explain how hard it is to be a famous actress, I realized she's just as lost as everyone else. Eventually we got to the heart of her pain, which is her guilt about not having children, and how that ship has probably sailed. Maybe it has. It's hard to imagine why anyone would bring another child into a world like this, at least on purpose. But there's no way to know what the future will bring, and in the meantime, we ought to look for hope where we can.

The problem with sending her to Thomas is, when she held my hand at the table, I realized why I'd felt so unsettled around her. I don't know how to say this exactly, but I think I'm attracted to her. Like sexually.

If that sounds impossible to you, imagine how surprised I am! Although when I finally acknowledged my desire, I realized how deeply I had buried the truth. All my life, I've been trying to create an ideal suburban life because it's all I knew, and because I wanted to be the daughter my dad imagined I was. But that hasn't exactly worked out, has it? And if you think I'm blinded by Skylar's physical beauty, or drawn to her celebrity, that's because you didn't feel the electricity that jumped between us when she touched me. I could barely see her in the dark, but the texture of her hand, so soft and smooth and delicate, was nothing like the touch of a man. And once I started thinking about her hands, I couldn't help but imagine how soft she must be everywhere, how her skin and her curves and her everything would feel beneath my fingertips, how it would taste against my tongue.

But when you've just realized something unexpected about yourself, like life-altering, the last thing you want to do is immediately tell someone else. Especially someone who's given no indication she feels the same way. Someone who is only here because of her attraction to Thomas.

After she went to his room, I tiptoed over and listened while she woke him up. Thomas didn't seem upset. Then again, would any person on earth be unhappy to wake up and see Skylar Stover standing there?

Seth hasn't slept with me the past two nights because I've been so quiet. After I made that mistake with the lemoncello (that doesn't look right but how else would you spell it?), I've had to do a lot of soul searching. But now that I finally understand what's been wrong all this time, I feel free in a way I can scarcely remember. Like ever. Even that horrible ringing sound has mostly gone away. And if you want to know the truth, I'm so turned on by the memory of Skylar's hand that I need someone to touch me. So, I'm going to find Seth. I know that seems crazy, but I don't know what else to do. I'll let you know.

May 20, 202- (later)

I wish I knew what time it was. Without clocks, it's impossible to know if it's midnight or four in the morning. Anyway, Seth was sleeping on the floor in the boys' room, because the bed wasn't wide enough for all three of them. I knew he wouldn't be able to see me in the dark, so instead I curled up and wrapped my arm around him and pretended not to feel whiskers when I nuzzled into his neck. Eventually, when he was fully awake, I asked him to take me into our room and make love to me.

Seth is attentive in bed, and he always visits "downstairs" before climbing on top of me, but tonight that experience was brand new. When I ran my fingers through his hair, I pretended it was Skylar's hair, and when his tongue roamed against me, I imagined it was hers. It was easily the most intense orgasm of my life. I know Seth was pleased with himself afterwards, and I tried to seem as if I loved him inside me. But after Skylar's delicate touch, it was impossible not to notice his rough skin and the sharp angles of his arms and legs and the stiffness of his, well, you know.

When the light comes up, I'll head to the kitchen and see what I can scare up for breakfast. Poor Thomas has been handling all the food himself, and no one has been eating with him or helping him. Probably today will be different, since he and Skylar will be on good terms, but what am I supposed to do? How am I supposed to feel? If this were the normal world, I would eventually talk to Seth, and probably we would get divorced. But this is a completely new reality, and for the moment I see no option but stay the course.

Don't feel sorry for me, though. I may be in a tough place, but I'm not upset.

Because for the first time in my entire life, no matter how ironic it may sound to say this, I feel like everything is right with the world.

TWENTY-SIX

When Thomas woke to find Skylar standing over his bed, carrying a flickering candle, his first thought was something terrible had happened. Larry had broken into the house or Seth had gone outside again or maybe someone was sick. He panicked and sat up in bed and rubbed sleep out of his eyes. But when he opened them again, he could see Skylar was smiling.

Something about her had changed. Her face looked relaxed and free of tension that had been present since the pulse. But before he could ask what had happened, Skylar glanced at the open expanse of bed beside him.

"Do you have room in there for company?"

He blinked.

"Yes, of course."

Skylar stood the candle on his nightstand. She vaulted over him in one leaping step and soft-landed in the jumble of comforter and sheets. It was too hot to sleep under the covers, but he couldn't part with them, either. Most nights he slept in boxers and clutched the comforter like a lover.

Now Skylar was on her side, mere inches away, and Thomas was conflicted like a man who had won the grand prize without knowing how or why. Locks of blonde hair dangled in front of her eyes. Her gauzy pink tank top stretched across feminine curves he was helpless not to notice.

"I'm sorry about before," she said.

"Sorry about what?"

"For accusing you of trying to be perfect."

"I'm not perfect, Skylar. Not by a long shot."

She scooted closer. Brushed her foot against his. Her cleavage was a fault line that stretched into infinity. For the first time since he could remember, the dampness of sheets, the constant sheen of sweat on his skin, ceased to be unpleasant. Instead, the humidity that hovered between them seemed charged with electricity. And still he wondered what had brought her here, why she seemed to have forgotten about the desperate state of the world.

"I don't know what's going to happen," she said. "But in the meantime I guess we don't have to be miserable every second."

And when her hands reached for him, as she pulled him on top of her, a voice in his head announced in something like all capital letters, HOLY SHIT I'M GOING TO HAVE SEX WITH SKYLAR STOVER. But once this salacious bit of gossip had been acknowledged, his hands and mouth found their usual rhythms and wandered into the usual places. And if there was a subtle-but-unmistakable human odor associated with sweat and the absence of proper hygiene, if her tank top was damp as he tossed it to the floor, these organic sensations only heightened the immediacy of his arousal. For the first time since the supernova had appeared, Thomas could imagine a future in which he was not constantly miserable.

On the other hand, he might have been misled by the primal relief of entering Skylar, or by watching her eyes roll back while she thrust against his body with the brute force of a woman determined to enjoy the entire length of him.

It was easy to be happy during a moment of sexual bliss.

He would lean heavily on this memory during the difficult days that followed.

DC ASSAULT ┼
(AS REPORTED BY AIDEN)

TWENTY-SEVEN

According to Chelsea, the Walmart distribution center was on the other side of Melissa, an exurb northeast of McKinney. She couldn't tell us which street the building was on, but she did know you had to drive past a landfill to get there. With that information Ed deduced the approximate location.

We left Mack's place around 4PM so we could scout the DC in daylight. Ed, Mack, and Jimmy rode in the pickup's cab and the rest of us climbed into the bed. My mind whistled like a kettle. The hard shell of my skull shrieked. A dull knife of pain poked into the space behind my eyes, and I wondered for the first time if something was physically wrong with me.

By now weapons had been assigned, and the semi-automatic rifle I'd been given was clearly meant as an insult, since most everyone else was carrying a full auto. The pistol was shoved into the back of my jeans.

From Mack's place we drove east through a rural region where stalled cars were less numerous than other areas we'd been. At one point we passed a pickup traveling in the opposite direction, an old brown Chevy with four men piled in the back. The men carried handguns and one of them offered a knowing nod. Only two days had elapsed since the EMP, and already a new order was understood. One class of citizens was armed with guns and transportation that gave them a fighting chance to survive. The other would probably starve to death before summer was over.

At the Highway 75 intersection we headed north, and the road was a disaster. Ed honked his horn repeatedly to move people out of the way. They were single walkers, married couples, families, the elderly. At one point a small BMX-style motorcycle passed us, steered by a girl who could have been twelve or twenty. People carried backpacks and duffel bags and rolled suitcases behind them. Some carried nothing at all. Fear rose from this mob like waves of heat. People yelled at us for help. They threatened us. One guy claimed Army tanks were approaching from the south.

Fortunately the drive to Melissa was only five or six miles, and by the time we exited 75 at TX-121, we were making good time again.

When Chelsea figured out where we were, she began to babble directions. Eventually the truck slowed down, and Mack motioned us to lower our weapons. Then, at long last, I spotted it: A driveway labeled with a blue-and-white sign that looked like this:

WAL★MART
Distribution Center
*OUR PEOPLE MAKE THE DIFFERENCE

Because of the tree line, and because the DC was set well back from the road, I caught only a short glimpse before it vanished from view. The building was uniformly white and enormous. When we reached another break in the trees, I could see the facility was divided into two separate buildings, one of which was taller than the other, like maybe three stories high. A large propane tank stood on the front lawn, along with taller, cylindrical tanks that probably held fuel.

Standing atop of one of these taller tanks was a man wearing a brown shirt and jeans and holding a rifle. Beneath him a crowd of people had gathered on the other side of a chain-link fence. The entire scene was visible to us only a few seconds and then was hidden by trees again.

"Did you see that?" said Bart. "They got guards just like we thought."

A couple of minutes later we turned into a neighborhood of condos and duplexes. One more turn brought us to the home of Chelsea's mother, where we climbed out of the truck to stretch our legs. Though nightfall was still a couple of hours away, the overcast sky made it seem as though the sun was already going down.

Chelsea took us inside, where she found her mother napping on the couch. Here was a wispy, graying woman who clearly had not been expecting company.

"Oh, Chelsea!" she shrieked. "Oh, my God! I didn't know if I would ever see you again!"

"Everyone," Chelsea said, "this is my mom, Marie."

The mother cast a wary eye upon our motley crew and especially the rifles.

"Mom," Chelsea said, "these friends of mine are going to visit the Walmart warehouse tonight. We think there will be a lot of food."

"I wondered about that," said Marie. "Danny Armstrong walked over there this afternoon, but I don't know what came of it. He lives next door."

"I'm sorry for bringing weapons into your home," said Jimmy. "But we think the Walmart building might be well-guarded. In a situation like this they ought to share their supplies."

"I agree," said Marie. "But won't it be dangerous to force your way in?"

"It will, but we won't take the girls with us."

"And if they're able to bring back food," Chelsea said, "I was hoping you'd let us crash here for a while."

Marie didn't love the idea of taking in so many guests, but after Jimmy gently reminded her of the desperate reality she faced, that everyone faced, she relented.

Soon, the men were outside again, standing next to the pickup, while Mack explained our next steps.

"As you could see, people already want inside the DC. That means our assault will come from the rear of the property. I'm willing to bet there's nothing but pasture back there, but we won't know until we arrive.

"And we can't just drive all the way to the property, because they'll hear us coming. So we'll need to leave the pickup far enough away to maintain stealth, but close enough that we can retrieve it in a timely manner. This interval will be important, because the civilians outside may approach the building when they realize something has changed inside.

"The next problem is exactly where to approach. Those guards are probably employees familiar with the campus. Our advantage will be surprise and hopefully superior weapons, but we won't know the exact nature of our assault until we're familiar with the layout.

"We'll split into two teams and coordinate a staggered approach from different angles. When the guards realize an attack is in progress, their attention will be drawn to Team One. This could make it easier for Team Two to approach the building and breach the security perimeter.

"Men, our biggest ally, the darkness, will also prove to be a major obstacle. That's why it's important to locate all guard positions while it's still daylight and hope they maintain those at night.

"Visibility could be even worse inside the building. Any lanterns or fires may be extinguished as a last-ditch defense. And if we get inside and can't see, all hell could break loose. These people will know their way around their building. We will not.

"As far as teams go, let's put Ed, Bart, and Aiden on Team One. Nick, Aaron, Jimmy, and me will be Team Two. We'll see how these teams work during our scouting run and make any changes before tonight. Questions?"

* * *

On the drive over, the difficulty of what we were trying to do finally became tangible enough to scare the shit out of everyone. We were traveling west and hadn't gone far when we found an unpaved road that ran north and south. From there we were close enough to catch glimpses of the DC, its rectangular bulk reflecting orange hues from the sky. We were maybe a half-mile away, but I wondered if the guards could hear our engine running and our tires crunching over gravel. Or for that matter if they could hear the ever-present screeching of the world, if that awful sound had wormed its way into their heads the way it had lay waste to mine.

On our left stood unimproved pasture, brown grassland dotted here and there with mesquite trees and the occasional oak. When we discovered an unlocked gate guarding the entrance to a forgotten-looking dirt road, we turned and found a place among some trees to hide the pickup.

From there we approached the DC on foot: Mack and Nick; Jimmy and Aaron; Bart by himself; Ed and me at the rear. What a smug bastard the slick cat was in his hip jeans and his lean frame squeezed into a shirt too small for him. He probably thought he was better than me.

He was probably a godless, libtard Democrat who voted for Killary and Obummer and took money from George Soros. He was everything wrong with America. He deserved to be shot.

The trees grew denser the farther we walked and my mind began to wander. What would it be like inside the warehouse? Would there be lemonade? What sort of food would I eat first? Something canned? From a bag? A box? I wondered if I would ever eat another pizza. I tried to understand the appeal of pizza. Nothing more than bread and sauce and cheese but put one in front of me and I would eat the entire thing. I pictured the whole world as a pizza, where you could take a bite of anything, anywhere, and it would taste like your favorite slice. In fact, when I looked down, the texture of the ground had changed. It was softer, springier, and coming up on my right was a large, brown boulder that might have been made of pork sausage. But it couldn't have been. Right? Except beyond the boulder lay a series of red, oily discs, flat on the ground, that anyone could have mistaken for slices of pepperoni. And large cacti shaped like chopped bell peppers, and concrete slabs that looked like onion slices. Brown, crusty cliffs loomed in the distance, as if we had stumbled without knowing into a large, structural basin. Eventually the ground began to change again, the cheese giving way to a red, gooey swamp, and I realized the entire surface of our planet floated on a great lake of blood, which in a perfect world would have contained the blood of every person who had ever wronged me, like for instance my absent parents and my disloyal sister and every slutbag who never returned my calls. And all the liberal elites who made me feel stupid and provincial. I was so hungry I could imagine falling to my knees and slurping this blood right off the ground, laughing the way a hyena laughs while he devours his prey alive.

Eventually our progress slowed and then stopped altogether. Mack turned around and raised a finger to his lips. I thought he might invite us to fill our bellies with pizza before the attack, but when I looked around, the food had disappeared. All I saw were the other men standing in a narrow grove of trees. Through branches and leaves, the rectangular bulk of the DC loomed enormously. We were closest, at that point, to its northeastern corner. Mack and Nick and Aaron crept closer to the edge of the trees, using binoculars to look for any posted sentries. They observed for a few moments and then returned, encouraging us to gather into a rough circle, like the shape of a pizza. Where the hell was the pizza?

"So the problem we have," said Mack, "is a buncha semi-trailers parked at the docks. These will provide cover for the guards, while our approach will be made across a wide-open lawn and parking lot. The only cover we'll enjoy is darkness, but as I said before, that will make it more difficult to identify our enemy targets."

"If they're well-armed," said Ed, "this attack sounds like suicide."

Mack nodded. "I know it seems like every weekend warrior nowadays owns a military rifle, but most of these weapons are toys compared to what we're carrying. Even so, we don't have a lot of ammo. This means we must shoot efficiently."

Speaking of ammunition, each of our weapons was loaded with a 30-round magazine. Because I was carrying a semi-automatic rifle, and couldn't fire as rapidly, I hadn't been given a spare. Mack was carrying the RPG, while Bart wore a backpack that held three grenades.

"I'll tell you one thing," Mack added. "I underestimated the size of that building, even after seeing it from the road."

We retreated into the trees a bit and moved westward until we were more centrally positioned. There were two main buildings, remember, this flatter-looking one and the taller one at the southwest corner of the campus. Eventually, Mack stopped again. It was a good thing, too, because I was ready to point my rifle at Slick Ed and fire away. If I cooked his arms and legs, they might taste pretty good.

"All right," Mack said. "Let's spread out and put fifteen yards between each of us. Then we'll approach the tree line. I want every one of you to scan the perimeter of the building and look for movement. Watch for legs moving below those trailers, for movement on the roof. Look for any surface feature up there that doesn't belong. We'll do this for a minute or so and then regroup."

From what I remember, our movements weren't that loud, and we were at least three hundred yards from the building. In fact, as we spread into the new formation, I was fed up with all the careful preparation. I didn't understand why we wouldn't storm the building then, in the daylight, and force the guards to show themselves. I wondered why we even called them "guards." We were talking about a handful of forklift drivers probably armed with hunting rifles and pistols and maybe a consumer-grade AR.

"All right," Mack said. "I see a—"

You never imagine the sound of a bullet from the terminus of its journey, not unless you're a soldier, which I certainly am not. So the brief and powerful whistle that coincided with the crack of a gunshot did not register at first as a recognizable event. Only when I heard fierce and frightened curses, only when I turned and saw a body convulsing on the ground, did I realize what had happened. That's when I heard a second bullet and saw, not thirty feet from me, a spray of blood as Aaron's head jerked sideways with the force of deadly impact. For a moment he just teetered there, a sickening grin on his face, while blood poured out of his nose and a chunk of cranial bone fell away from his ear. Something about that bone fragment finally registered as DANGER in my brain. I dropped to the ground and made myself flat.

"Fall back!" I heard a voice yell, which I now know belonged to Bart. "Fall back now!"

But I couldn't bring myself to move. The only course of action that made any sense was to stay low, out of sight, to not make myself a target. But then I heard a third gunshot, and someone screamed "Nick!" and finally I got the message. We were being picked off like Coke cans in target practice. The shots were being fired from a considerable distance. Just because we couldn't see the guy didn't mean my magnified head wasn't the next target.

I rolled sideways and onto my feet, where I scrambled deeper into the trees and caught up to Ed. The two of us ran blindly back the way we had come, at least until we spotted Bart and Jimmy huddled near the ground. Somehow Bart had grabbed a pair of orphaned binoculars.

"Stop and sit down," he hissed. "Listen for any sound. We need to know if they're following us or not."

"Holy fucking shit," said Ed. "They shot Aaron. Holy fucking—"

"I said *shut the fuck up!*"

Even when Ed stopped talking, our gusting breaths made it difficult to hear anything.

"We have no chance against that sniper," I finally said. "He's standing on the roof of that warehouse playing a goddamned video game."

"Maybe so," said Bart. "But I'm starving and thirsty and we don't have shit for supplies."

"We're low on energy and not thinking straight," Jimmy said. "Whereas those guards are well fed and enjoy better visibility. But they are missing one ingredient the rest of us will bring when we make our move."

"And what's that?" asked Ed.

"Desperation," Jimmy said. "Because if we don't get inside that building, the rest of us will die like our boys just did."

* * *

Seeing the spilled blood of fellow soldiers brought focus to my desires. Where minutes before I had been ready to shoot one of my own men, a real opportunity had finally arisen to fire at someone else. Also, I was pissed off. Why would God choose me to facilitate His plan and then intentionally cut our team in half? It made no sense. I began to wonder, for the first time, if God really played an active role in my life. Had my journey from unemployed graphic designer to member of this assault team been *my* doing? Was I the one in charge?

It was time to find out. Time to assume command.

"Why don't I take your binoculars," I said to Bart, "and sneak back to the tree line in a different spot? The sniper probably found us so easily because of the way we spread out. Maybe I can locate him this time before he finds me."

"You're willing to do that?"

"Sure. I'd rather go out guns blazing than starve to death."

"It better be soon," Jimmy said. "You're losing your light."

Until then I hadn't noticed the rapidly approaching darkness. There was also a towering cloud structure behind the DC, dark and flat at the bottom, brilliantly pink in its upper reaches.

"Bart," I said. "Hand me those binoculars."

While I looked for a new spot to survey the roof, the screeching in my head began to sound more like a ringing, or a high-pitched tone you might hear during a weather alert. A sense of destiny wrapped me like a warm blanket, as if this assault had somehow been arranged for my benefit. As if I were the hero of this subplot.

Eventually I found a suitable position and crouched near the ground. I pushed the binoculars into an open space and hoped the rest of me was hidden by branches and leaves. I found the northeastern corner of the building and panned westward. The light was so low it was difficult to tell where the roof ended and the sky began, especially because, through the lenses, the approaching storm seemed close enough to touch. Its popcorn cloud formations had become a pinkish, dusky gray and the smell of rain floated on the wind.

I couldn't see how anyone could hide on the roof, as featureless as it was, at least not until I reached the middle portion of it. That's where I discovered a single row of what appeared to be exhaust ducts.

Adjacent to the closest one, if my eyes were not deceiving me, stood a rifle mounted on a tripod. As far as I could tell the gun was pointed right at me.

I blinked.

Rolled violently away.

The crack in the air might have been thunder, so close was the storm, but the explosion of nearby dirt verified the arrival of a bullet. Had I moved a second later, I would have been dead. Instead, I saved myself.

Which made the truth so obvious. *I* could be my *own* God!

"He's at the middle of the roof!" I hissed. "By the exhaust duct. Cover me. I'm going in!"

The deliverance I felt in the next moment electrified me so thoroughly that as I sprinted out of the trees, down the slope of grass, it felt like my conscious mind had spread beyond the boundaries of my body. As gunshots rang out the world seemed to slow down and become drained of color. My footsteps on the ground were thunderous, the air in my ears a gale-force wind. Only when I reached the parking lot, when I saw a row of handholds mounted near a corner of the building, did I realize rain was pouring out of the sky. By this point, because of his angle, the sniper could no longer shoot at me from his original position. I kept waiting for other guards to appear, to be riddled with bullets, but these ground-based sentries were nowhere to be found. I darted between a semi-trailer and the exterior wall of the DC and found the handholds again. They turned out to be rungs of a ladder that stretched all the way to the roof. Without bothering to stop and rest, I slung the rifle over my shoulder and began my ascent. Through the torrential rain I saw

Bart and Jimmy and Ed approaching, firing in bursts toward the roof. Hopefully their assault would occupy the sniper while I climbed.

On the way up my arms and legs seemed to take on weight, and my energy ran out just as I reached the last rung. Rain roared on the steel roof. Below me I heard loud voices and someone pounding on a door. What I didn't detect was a response, like other voices or return fire or any sort of resistance.

Finally, when my muscles had recovered, I summoned the energy to push my right hand upward, where it slapped against the wet steel surface of the roof. Rivers of rain poured out of my hair and into my eyes.

Amid all this chaos, a voice emerged. At first the identity of the voice didn't register because I was concerned only with the message itself.

"Come any closer," said the sniper, "and I'll blow your fucking brains out."

Then reality poked through my confusion, and I marveled at this unexpected twist.

The sniper was a woman.

TWENTY-EIGHT

"**I**f you wanted to kill me," I shouted back at her. "You could have done it while I was out in the open."

"I tried. Conditions were poor."

"Still, you murdered three of our group without so much as a warning shot. I can't leave you up here to keep firing at us."

"Warning shot? Your friend was carrying a grenade launcher!"

I saw her point, but nonetheless we remained at stalemate.

After seeing that first armed guard, the one who stood on the fuel tank, we had assumed the DC would be well-defended. But a lack of commotion on the ground suggested a much smaller force. If Jimmy and Bart and Ed were already inside the DC, that left the sniper up here alone.

It's difficult to overstate the surreal nature of the scene at that point: rain pouring down in buckets; me clinging to ladder rungs, the weight of my wet clothes threatening to peel me away; a chick sniper who had fired with impunity upon fellow American citizens. And possibly strangest of all: I was intrigued by this woman.

"It's true we came here expecting a fight," I said, "and maybe you had every right to shoot at us. But it sounds like the rest of my group is inside the building now. You can't stay up there forever."

"I can wait as long as it takes."

"Maybe so. But I haven't eaten an actual meal in two days and I'm out of energy. Why don't you follow me down so we can talk?"

"If I come down, and your people are in charge, I could be executed. In that case I'd rather do it myself."

"So do it, then," I said.

She didn't answer. The roar of rain remained deafening and unbroken by a gunshot.

"What's your name?" I asked.

"I'm not telling you my name!"

"If I guarantee you won't be killed, will you come down with me? I'll explain what you did and why."

"Like that's going to work."

"Fine. Stay up there forever."

By that point the rain was beginning to relent, and I heard something that might have been a laugh. But my hands were at the limit of their stamina, and I couldn't wait there any longer. I was about to start back down when I looked up and saw a face peering at me.

And whatever you call the unspoken communication that sometimes passes between strangers, where connection is achieved by nothing more than a glance, it happened to me then.

"If you want to be the hero," she said, "now's your chance."

"Just be careful. These rungs are slippery."

* * *

When we were both on the ground, I got my first full look at the woman who had tried to kill me. Her face was pale and plain-looking, her red hair tied in a knot behind her head. Her eyes were a dusty shade of blue, like they had been colored with chalk.

"What's your name, soldier?"

"Paige."

I noticed she hadn't brought the rifle down with her, but that didn't mean she wasn't armed.

"All right, Paige. Hand over your weapons. I can't bargain for you otherwise."

She was wearing a camouflage rain suit and black boots. From the right boot she removed a handgun, what looked like a Beretta, and from the left she retrieved a green-handled combat knife.

"Thank you," I said. "There must be a door somewhere nearby?"

"That way," said Paige, pointing to her left.

I motioned for her to walk in that direction, and we trudged along the edge of the building, feet splashing in puddles on the concrete sidewalk. By then it was nearly dark, and I didn't see the entrance until we'd almost reached it. The door stood open and beyond it lay even more darkness, tinted I thought by a faint green glow.

"Jimmy!" I yelled. "Are you inside?"

An echoing rustle of feet followed, and then someone answered.

"Aiden?" growled Bart.

"It's me," I said. "And the sniper."

"Good work. Bring Paige in here. We need to have words with her."

* * *

Entering the DC was like stepping into an underground cavern so enormous its true dimensions could only be guessed. Light was supplied, as Mack had suggested, by what appeared to be a collection of propane lanterns and candles. On our left, the grid-like skeleton of a vast shelving unit seemed to flicker into and out of existence. Ahead, in the lit area, a sizable crowd had gathered. Today I know there were eleven members of three families, all of whom were connected to the DC by someone who worked there. Paige was number twelve and the guards assigned to the front of the building brought the total to fifteen.

I expected Jimmy and the others to approach Paige with suspicion or anger, but the three of them had already discussed her fate with the DC's occupying group. Jimmy stood beside an officious-looking black man who wore spectacles, slacks, and a short-sleeve white button down.

"Aiden," said Jimmy. "This is Anthony. He and Paige are in charge of the families staying here. We've just negotiated a deal with them. They'll supply us with food and bottled water in exchange for gunning down our men."

"What did you expect her to do?" shouted one of the warehouse employees.

"Fair enough," growled Jimmy. "Just don't forget we have three dead men out there."

I had the feeling Jimmy was bluffing about our downed soldiers. It didn't seem like he cared much for Mack and Nick, and the only reason

Aaron had come along was because he owed Jimmy money. We were lucky to be inside the DC and I'm sure Jimmy knew that.

"It's time to gather supplies these men will carry back to their truck," Anthony explained to his people. "Deion and Mike, please bring me two cases of canned chicken, a box of tuna in pouches, and a case of Vienna Sausages. Also grab a case of Chunky Soup, something with vegetables. Fred, bring me three boxes of bottled water. Michela, please grab a box of potato chips."

The light sources, which seemed bright when you looked at them directly, pushed back the darkness in a rough sphere of maybe eighty yards in diameter. This was a blip when compared to the DC's interior space. Luckily, the occupying families had already worked out a method where Tiki torches, the kind favored by white supremacists, were lit and used as makeshift flashlights. Soon the runners were off to find their assigned supplies while the rest of us stared at each other. The idea of food awakened a raging appetite that recalled the blasted pizza landscape. My stomach made sounds loud enough for everyone to hear, but the shrieking of my brain was nearly silent, at least for the moment.

"We've been here since Friday night," Anthony finally said. "We knew to come because of Mr. Miller. Her dad."

Paige nodded. "He'd been worried about a possible EMP for a long time. He taught me and everyone who worked here what to do if one ever happened. I thought there would have been more of us, honestly."

"Where's your dad?" I asked her.

"I think maybe his pacemaker didn't hold up. Found him in the shower."

"I'm sorry."

"Thank you," she said. "But this is what he prepared me for."

"Where did you come from, exactly?" Anthony asked Jimmy. "What's it like out there today?"

"Getting worse. Dallas is burning and the fire line is moving this way. The roads are packed with refugees."

"I wish you would reconsider your strategy," said Anthony. "Every trip you make into or out of the building will jeopardize security for all of us. Can't you bring the rest of your group here?"

"In a week," Jimmy said, "you could have a thousand people on your front lawn. We don't have enough personnel or ammunition to repel a crowd of that size."

"We should get as far away from the city as possible," Ed added. "I don't think any of us can imagine what it will be like if a million hungry people come through here."

"But carrying food makes one a target," Anthony said. "And water is heavy."

"There are plenty of small lakes nearby," Ed replied. "And stock tanks to water cattle."

"Water like that would need to be purified," said Paige.

There was a presence about this woman that made me want to be near her. I wished everyone else would leave so we could become better acquainted.

When Anthony's people returned with food and water, it was time to carry these supplies to the pickup and back to Marie's. We decided two of us should go and the other two would remain behind to help with security. I volunteered to stay, and unfortunately so did Ed.

At that point, the plan was for Bart and Jimmy to return the following day, park the truck closer, and this time pack it full of supplies. On his way out the door, Jimmy stopped and shook my hand.

"Aiden, what you did today was incredible. You're either one tough son-of-a-bitch or batshit crazy."

"Maybe both," I said.

Then Jimmy and Bart took their boxes and disappeared into the darkness, promising to return the following afternoon.

But I didn't see Jimmy again for four days, and by then Bart and Marie were both dead.

TWENTY-NINE

As Ed and I sat on the floor and shoveled canned chicken into our mouths (oh how heavenly it tasted), Anthony explained the layout of the DC.

The entire campus, he said, totaled a million square feet, though three hundred thousand of that had been sealed off by the time we arrived. The restricted area was the Perishables building, which stood three stories high and was the first building we'd seen from the road. On Friday, when the first families arrived, they harvested as much fresh fruit and vegetables as they could and then locked the doors. No one had been over there since. Anthony spoke of the place in hushed tones, as if the building were haunted, but his fear was well-founded. Before the power went out, the Perishables building had functioned as a giant refrigerator, its interior held at a constant 37 degrees Fahrenheit. A hundred thousand pounds of rotting meat, ill-contained, was an ecological disaster waiting to happen. No one was allowed near the doors.

Paige's shift on the roof ended when it was too dark to see, and in her place a couple of men were assigned to ground-level positions. When Anthony asked one of us to volunteer, Ed and I glared at each other until he finally relented. A little while later, Paige offered to give me a tour of the dry goods warehouse, which was my new home.

She led us by Tiki torch into the darkness, turning first right and then left. She was wearing a purple TCU T-shirt and a snug pair of jeans. In the flickering light I could see she was very fit but curvy at the hips, which is the most important place to be curvy.

Paige explained the DC's design, how much of the building ran on automation, but that wasn't why I had asked for the tour.

"Is there somewhere we could sit down? I could use time to digest all that chicken."

We were walking between two rows of giant shelving units whose grid-like skeletons disappeared into the darkness above us. When we reached the end of one, Paige balanced the torch inside a corner support column. Then we sat down on the concrete floor, our knees mere inches apart.

"So your name is Aiden?"

"Yes," I said and extended my hand to her.

"I should thank you for before," she said as we shook. "For being friendly after what I did."

"They were pals of Jimmy's. I didn't really know them."

"Still," she said. "I killed three men and I feel awful. It's hard to believe this is the world now."

I liked the intense way she looked at me.

"Do you regret shooting them?"

"What kind of question is that? Of course I regret it."

She stared at me and I stared back at her.

"Because I wouldn't."

She looked away from me, at something in the darkness, and the flickering torch lit her face in amber hues.

"It's true I had no choice. Our defense couldn't match those weapons."

"That's not what I mean."

"Then what do you mean?"

"I'm talking about how it felt."

"It felt like my life was in danger," she barked. "That's how it felt. I couldn't let your guy set up the grenade launcher and take shots at us."

The conversation did not proceed the way I expected. Others had probably heard us.

But I was convinced Paige was hiding her real feelings about the matter from me.

And maybe from herself.

* * *

That first night I slept on a couple of cheap, fuzzy blankets that barely cushioned me from the concrete floor. At some unknown hour I woke with an emergency need to have a bowel movement and was directed to an employee bathroom so far away from our campsite that I nearly didn't make it. Imagine sitting on a cheap commercial toilet in a tiny stall while holding a bug torch to keep the darkness at bay. Certainly the experience was a far cry from what I was accustomed to in my own home, where I had installed a heated toilet seat and could use my phone to browse Tinder profiles to my heart's content. At least someone had thought to grab a case of wet wipes from the warehouse floor. The wipes were individually wrapped, and printed on the label of each were these instructions: TEAR, UNFOLD AND WIPE, DUDE. ALSO SWEET FOR FACE, HANDS, PITS & DUDE REGIONS. Leaving aside the missing Oxford commas, which already was a crime against humanity, I wondered how the losers behind Dude Wipes felt about their super hip labeling now that flushing the toilet meant pouring a gallon of water into the tank. Because the world would no longer tolerate bad taste and frivolous marketing. It was a serious, deadly place where only the strongest were meant to survive.

In the morning, Ed and the others returned from overnight guard duty and found themselves a place to sleep. I spoke to Anthony about how much fresh water was being wasted in the toilets, so he asked Deion and Mike to dig a latrine on the back lawn. Then he took me outside, where we walked in the direction of Perishables. Layers of sunrise smoke hovered near the ground like fog. The murmuring of the crowd floated above us, disembodied and restless, mixing with the screech in my ears to produce a vivid sense of being observed. As if I had stepped onto the stage in front of a studio audience.

Even though the Perishables building was locked, there was an entrance road nearby that had drawn a crowd on the other side of the chain link fence. The lookout point, instead of a fuel tank, was the check-in station for arriving tractor-trailers. People in the crowd began to shout as we approached.

"Come on, now. Some of us have been waiting here for two days. Have some mercy, man!"

"My baby hasn't eaten since Friday and we have nowhere else to go!"

"This is America. We don't turn our backs on the needy!"

Anthony looked at the ground and spoke to me in a low voice.

"Don't acknowledge them. We engaged a few yesterday and it went poorly."

"What did you say?"

"That our duty was to Walmart. That we can't hand out inventory without a directive from Bentonville."

"Bet that went over like a load of bricks."

When we reached the check-in station, a tired-looking man met us at the bottom of the steps. He eyed my gun and extended his hand to shake.

"I'm Emmitt," he said. "Pleased to meet you."

"Aiden. So what's it like out here at night? Do the people go home?"

"Some do, some don't. But there's more coming all the time. Yesterday they was all down at the east end, but now we got people over here, too. I keep telling them Perishables is locked down, but it's like they don't believe me. Like we got magic cooling units that run on fairy dust."

"That building wasn't refrigerated!" someone at the fence line yelled.

I looked over and spotted the man, who was wearing jean shorts, penny loafers, and a button-down shirt meant to look like the U.S. flag. Perched upon his head was a red cap with the words MAKE AMERICA GREAT AGAIN embroidered in white. His fingers were hooked through the fence and his face hovered between his hands.

"You don't refrigerate a warehouse three stories tall!" he crowed. "Think about the power bill. It don't make no sense!"

"Say," Emmitt said to me. "That's a nice weapon you have. Think I could use it at night? Beats the hell out of this hunting rifle."

I'd resented my semi-automatic weapon since it had been assigned to me, but suddenly I was possessive of it. Still, being able to loan the rifle to someone else made me feel important.

"Sure," I said. "No problem."

After Emmitt left, Anthony and I climbed into the check-in station. It was about the size of a kid's tree house and windowed on three sides. Since we could talk without being heard, I asked Anthony how he planned to control the crowd as it grew larger.

"Would you ever hand out food, at least to the especially needy?"

"Aren't all of them especially needy?"

Maybe they were. I couldn't have cared less. The only reason to give them anything was as a defense strategy.

"What about children only? Or some kind of lottery?"

"All that would do," Anthony said, "is create a situation of Haves and Have Nots. Where that discrepancy lives, violence follows."

"But this whole scenario is one giant Have versus a thousand Have Nots."

"Sure, but the DC represents order. The old way of things. They won't attack until they've lost hope the world will go back to the way it was."

Anthony was an intelligent man. You could see it in his fastidious manner and the careful way he considered his words. But he was also a hopeful man. A dreamer. Despite reality staring him in the face, he wanted to believe order would return.

"Yesterday," he said, "I heard a helicopter in the distance. I believe it may have been a Black Hawk, the type of chopper used by the U.S. Army. Hearing this machine gave me hope the government has a plan to restore order. That they will come here to gather supplies and distribute them in a fair manner."

"But what if that doesn't happen?"

"Did you know Walmart owns over twenty-five percent of the entire U.S. grocery market? We run nearly 5,000 retail locations serviced by 44 grocery distribution centers. If you want to feed hungry people right away, wouldn't this be a great place to start?"

"Or maybe if Walmart and factory farms hadn't devoured local grocers and growers, the food supply would live closer to the people who consume it."

"Anyway," Anthony finally said, "Good luck. Someone will relieve you at lunchtime."

Do you ever get the feeling you don't exist? That the words you speak aren't heard by others?

Eventually, I turned toward the crowd. The new star had just emerged from the horizon of trees in the east. It was no longer a discrete point of light but smeared by striated layers of smoke. Also, I noticed a light dusting of ash on the ground, as if snow had fallen the night before.

I opened the front window of my perch to let in air, and so I could point my rifle through it if needed. It wasn't long before people began to approach the fence and lob questions in my direction.

"Sir," a woman said. She was young and thin and disordered. Her two weepy children were under the age of five. "It's my fault I let the grocery shopping slide. My husband and I had been fighting for three days, and after he left for Phoenix I fed my kids out of the freezer. Now I've got nothing, and the stores are empty, and we walked three miles to get here. My two-year-old daughter just walked *three miles,* and this is not even her fault. It's *my* fault! Won't you please help us?"

And it wasn't just these two kids who were upset. Sporadic crying and yelling were common across the crowd. A few groups had put down blankets on the grass, as if digging in for the long haul. Someone opened a case I hadn't noticed before and began to strum a guitar. All this noise was awful. My mind reeled with the chaos of it.

To focus myself, I picked out obese humans in the crowd and imagined how it would feel to point my rifle at their fat bellies.

For once in your life you deserve to be hungry! I might yell at the enormous middle-aged woman wearing a bright red T-shirt that read I'M A LUCKY DEVIL! How wonderful it would feel to shoulder my rifle and fire rounds into her sickening, bloated carcass of a body. The mewling sound of her pleas would be like musical harmonies I could punctuate with the thundering drum of my weapons fire. I imagined pumping breakbeats into her shapeless figure until she was nothing but a cooling blob of fat and meat.

Eventually, Deion came along to replace me while I went inside to get a snack. Eating in front of the crowd, as you might imagine, was strictly prohibited.

By then two of the dock doors were partially open, and visibility inside the DC was much better. I could see, in addition to the shelving units, a network of miniature elevated highways, which someone explained were conveyors that had been used to move merchandise across the warehouse. When I asked about the open dock door, and the risk of attack from someone in the trees, Mike said this:

"When Paige is on the roof, no one is worried."

That made me think of Aaron's stricken face, how she had killed him with a single shot from three hundred yards. With trees in the way.

"Why don't you take her some lunch?" Mike said.

In the common area I found a jar of crunchy peanut butter and a loaf of wheat bread. I prepared sandwiches, grabbed two cans of soda, and found my way to the ladder again. It was no easy feat to climb while carrying the box of food.

"Coming up," I yelled. "Don't shoot."

"I listened to you struggle the whole way," said Paige. "You must be part turtle."

"Good thing I brought two sandwiches because this turtle is hungry."

Paige smirked and grabbed at her food.

"I hope this isn't crunchy," she said, taking a huge bite. "I hate all that gravel in my peanut butter."

"You know that's what it's made from, right? Peanuts?"

"So? Coffee is made of beans, but I don't want them rattling around my cup."

The flirty banter was a good start, but I wanted more from her.

"Sorry about yesterday," I said. "I was just curious—"

"Don't worry about it."

"Okay. But I want you to know that I would never tell anyone if—"

"You should probably head back down," she said. "Mike could use help with that latrine."

Paige finished the sandwich and resumed her position behind the rifle. In the distance we heard a couple of gunshots, followed by a few more.

"Imagine having to hunt for food," she said, "after being able to buy it under cellophane your entire life. Most people have no chance. They can't shoot well enough."

"How did you become such a good shot?"

Paige sipped on her soda and didn't look at me. Her father would be at the center of any answer, I guessed, and his death was still a fresh wound. But I hoped it was a wound she wished to dress.

"I was an only child," she finally said. "And my dad obviously wanted a son. He taught me to play golf and throw a football and how to shoot. For some reason I happened to be good with a gun. In competition, I beat the shit out of dudes all over the country, so at eighteen I decided to join the Army. Being a paper puncher gets old because the targets don't shoot back."

Paige looked at me as if she expected judgment, but this is exactly what I wanted to hear.

"Then my dad wouldn't let me enlist. He was an officer during the Iraq war, and what he saw over there soured him on government. We're talking about the most conservative, grounded man I've ever met who came home calling George Bush a puppet and Dick Cheney a traitor. He said going to war was like pouring gasoline on a fire America was pretending to put out. That it was never about liberation or fighting terror. It was a money grab. It was a video game the Pentagon had been waiting years to play."

"What did you think?"

"I thought he was nuts. Why did I train ten years if not to help us win a war?"

"So what happened?"

"He cried and told me about the families we wrecked, about the innocent children we murdered. He made me watch Dwight Eisenhower's speech on the military-industrial complex. He was convinced the biggest threats to America weren't external, that rich special interests were devouring our Republic from the inside. And all this was before Trump. When Trump was elected, he got drunk and said 'They finally did it! The serfs picked their new king.'"

"Sounds like he watched a lot of fake news."

"Maybe so. But I loved him and agreed not to join the Army."

"What did you do instead?"

"Became a teacher. I picked first grade so I could reach students while they were still young enough to believe what I said."

"But you kept shooting?"

Paige's eyes narrowed and she didn't answer right away.

"Obviously, I kept shooting. You train to do something your whole life, you can't just quit."

"You said you were bored with paper targets, so I just wondered what you shot at instead."

It took me a moment to realize I'd gone too far, but before I could retract the question, her eyes went blank and she looked away.

"I'm starting to think we shouldn't bother trying to hold the DC," Paige eventually said. "The south wind is getting stronger and pretty soon either fire or smoke will drive us away. Maybe it's better if we leave the place on our terms."

The image of wandering from town to town, the two of us against the world, imbued me with such confidence that I ignored good sense and leaped.

"I don't care where I end up," I said. "As long as it's with you."

She looked at me like a bug, like a pest that needed swatting. Her lips arranged themselves into a pitiful smile.

"You've lost your mind."

"Maybe I have."

* * *

It was no surprise when Jimmy didn't come back on Monday. As tired as we all were, the motivation to return for longer-term supplies had surely diminished. But by Tuesday, Ed and I were convinced something had gone wrong at Marie's house.

"Maybe I should walk back there," said Ed in the evening after Paige had come down from the roof.

"That would be brave," she said, "but also pointless."

"Because they aren't worth saving?" I asked.

"Because Jimmy and Bart were well-armed. If they ran into trouble, it didn't end well."

"If we stay here much longer," said Ed, "it's not going to end well for us, either."

Anthony had been standing at the open dock door and walked over when he heard us talking.

"We may face another battle soon," he said. "I have seen some heavily-armed civilians in the crowd. They seem to be scouting our defense."

"I haven't seen anyone out back," said Paige.

"Still, we should be careful. I don't think anyone should leave the campus until we're all prepared to go."

"Just so we're clear," I said, "our weapons are part of the reason you're able to adequately defend this place. If me and Ed decide to leave, that's our business."

Anthony's eyes narrowed and he stared at me while silent seconds elapsed. This was the moment of truth: Either I had earned enough respect for him to take my challenge seriously, or I hadn't.

"Very well," Anthony said. "You should be in control of your fate. But if you choose to leave, I don't think you should approach the DC again. The situation outside is too volatile."

"Fair enough."

When I looked at Paige, she rolled her eyes. She underestimated me. Just like they always do.

Just like you always do.

* * *

For days, the weight upon my mind had been building, the noise in my mind swelling, and after the failure with Paige I knew my time at the DC was coming to an end. There was nothing left for me there except food and water, which would have been good reasons to stay if not for the constant chatter of the crowd, which had begun to sound almost like a ticking clock. Like a bomb waiting to explode.

So I developed a plan. A big, beautiful plan. A plan that began with Ed, whose effortless, casual charm made me feel stupid and unaware. He was a grifter. A liar.

But he did happen to carry an automatic weapon, along with two 30-round clips. Combined with my own clip, that meant 90 total shots, minus the one I planned to use on Ed.

With an automatic weapon and 89 rounds, I could put on a show. Not total carnage but entertaining nonetheless.

If you're wondering how I lured Ed away from the building, that's the most brilliant part of the entire story. He did it to himself! On Wednesday night, I agreed to guard the rear perimeter with him, and after a couple of hours of mindless pacing, Ed remembered something I'd totally forgotten.

"You know what?" he said, gesturing toward the looming shadow of the forest. "The rifles Mack and Nick and Aaron dropped are probably still out there. We could use more good weapons if an attack comes."

"I'm sure Jimmy and Bart grabbed the guns."

"Maybe. But they were carrying a lot of food. And it was almost dark. I think we should walk over there and check."

So we did, each of us armed with a rifle and a canvas bag to carry back any guns and ammo we found. The wind blew steadily. An odor of smoke swirled around us. Ed crept across the parking lot and into the grass beyond it, carefully ascending a knoll beyond the pavement. I followed. The silhouette of the tree line loomed like a many-limbed organism ready to absorb any creature that grew too close.

When we reached the trees, Ed slung his rifle over his shoulder and pulled the flashlight from his pants. A moving circle of dirt and fallen leaves and root systems appeared. I watched, transfixed, as Ed voluntarily offered his life. Why wasn't he more cautious? Why would he trust me?

I could barely hear Ed when he finally spoke, so loud was the shrieking of my skull.

"Let's see," he said, pointing. "I think we were more that way. Don't you? Aiden?"

When he turned around, Ed discovered the barrel of a rifle pointed at his nose from a distance of two yards. The night was so dark he was nothing more than a silhouette.

"Hey, man. What are you doing?"

"I'm killing you."

"Hey, man. Don't do that. Not after all this. Please?"

Ever notice how even the biggest jerk turns friendly when bargaining for his life?

"You think you're so fucking slick. First you tried to move in on Keri, and now you're doing it again with Paige. Is that your thing? Steal a guy's girl to make yourself feel like a big shot?"

"What do you mean? Keri adores you, man."

"The hell she does."

"And Paige, I mean, she's not—"

"She's not what? Good enough for me?"

"She's not into dudes, man. She likes girls."

"Bullshit. How would you know that?"

"She told me. We were talking the other night, and I don't know, it just came out."

I'm no dummy. I know some women really are gay. But the ones like Paige, they're too lovely to be that way. It's like they do it on purpose to deprive men of the chance to be intimate with them.

"Have you been asleep the past few years? We don't think about women that way anymore."

I jerked my rifle forward until it was mere inches from Ed's nose.

"You talk an awfully big game for someone with a gun pointed at him."

"Aiden," he answered. "I didn't say anything. I'm at your mercy. Please don't kill me."

I couldn't tell if he was serious or trying to make me feel unstable. When someone replies to your interior thoughts, it's hard to know what to believe.

But by then it didn't matter anymore.

I fired. A single shot. Ed's silhouette toppled over and his flashlight fell in an arc toward the ground, where it came to rest pointed straight at its owner. The body made awful, screechy, liquid sounds, and I would have abandoned the flashlight if not for the weapons and ammunition that theoretically were nearby.

After a few minutes of searching, I discovered the swollen bodies of Mack and Nick and Aaron. Mack's rifle was threaded between thick fingers, and when I tried to wrench it free, the wooden sounds of skin tearing and bones splintering dropped me to my knees. From here I could see pink foam leaking from his nose and I wondered if I was dreaming. Because in a way none of it seemed real. Would anyone believe I had murdered three people since the EMP? What if it had all been some kind of grand hallucination? Why did I need Mack's gun when there were two other rifles nearby that had been thrown free of their owners?

A little while later I trudged out of the trees and eased down the slope with an automatic rifle slung over each shoulder and the canvas bag in my hands, into which I had stowed all the new ammunition. The RPG would have been killer (haha), but it was awkward and I didn't know how to fire it. Still, two rifles and 269 total rounds could inflict plenty of damage.

I approached the DC with care, in case any of the other guards had come around back, but none had. I stowed my newfound cache in an out-of-the-way spot near the door and resumed my position along the rear wall.

For hours I stood there, staring into darkness but not really seeing. Instead I pictured a beautiful sunrise marred by the chaos of a thousand displaced humans who might be sleeping or crying or praying. I realized how pointless that was, praying, asking for help from an imaginary guy in the sky. Why had I wasted so many years believing He cared about me? Where was the evidence? A loving God would not have allowed my old life to deteriorate into chaos. He wouldn't have permitted His followers to suffer at the hands of the powerful, to fall prey to the lies of the rich, who pretended to care about our interests in order to get our votes. There was no God. There was only filthy, stinking humanity that had frittered away its chance at greatness. Who chose short term gains over long term prosperity. I was as guilty as the rest, of course I was, but in the morning I would use my new weapons to acknowledge the truth no one else was honest enough to admit.

The world was over. There was nothing left to live for. No more reason to struggle.

I was ready to go, and on my way out I would take a few with me.

Start the dominoes falling.

Hasten the departure.

* * *

Sometime before dawn, as patches of indigo appeared in the eastern sky, I became aware of a strange, new chemical odor. A little while later, ash began falling in clumps, like dirty snow, collecting on my head and in the fine hair of my arms. The sound of the crowd rose from a murmur to a low roar.

Eventually Paige walked out of the DC and ascended the ladder. She didn't even bother to say hi or relieve me from duty. But I didn't care anymore. All I wanted from Paige at that point was her position on the roof, because being up there was integral to my plan.

When I walked inside, Anthony was pacing near the open dock door. He could tell something was different. I wondered if he would ask where Ed was, if he would discover the truth in my reaction.

Instead he said, "Aiden, follow me."

We marched out the dock door, toward the edge of the building. The air was so smoky I could taste it, and our footsteps stirred ash into a cloud that hovered near the ground. I wondered if I was being marched to a punishment of some kind, if I was being banished to the crowd. Imagine the irony of feeding me to the humans I had targeted for mass murder!

When we finally reached the corner, I could see the mob had swollen enormously, its restless energy barely contained by the illusion of our control.

"You gotta let us in, man!" someone yelled. "The fires have reached McKinney!"

"That smell is the tire plant! The smoke is toxic!"

Anthony pointed toward a tall, broad-shouldered man lumbering toward us. The weapon in his arms looked like mine. The bulk of his chest suggested body armor. I had no idea what was happening.

"We can't breathe this air for long," the fellow growled when he reached the fence. "Let us have some food or there will be hell to pay."

Anthony was clearly concerned about this man and his intentions, rather than me. He approached the fence and spoke in a voice so low I could barely hear what he said.

"If we open our gates, the supplies inside will be wasted. Chaos will reign. People will get hurt."

"What do you think is happening out here?" said the angry man.

"I understand people are desperate," Anthony said. "But help is coming."

"Help? From where?"

"From the U.S. Army. The other day I heard a helicopter, what I believe to be a Black Hawk—"

"Listen here, Professor Plum. I've seen two of those choppers myself. They aren't landing. They aren't helping anyone. They're surveying the carnage so they can report back to whoever is in charge. We put binoculars on the closest one and saw a guy taking *pictures*. With a *Polaroid*. Help is not coming. You're sitting on a mountain of food and you are going to let us in."

Anthony was facing away from me and I couldn't read his expression, but the disbelief in his answer was obvious.

"I—" he said. "I cannot—"

"You *will* or there will be hell to pay."

The notion that the government, or some version of it, was unable or unwilling to help us seemed like the most obvious thing in the world. But Anthony was clearly shaken by the news. He walked backward a few feet and surveyed the crowd. He raised his hands into the air, and like magic, the roar of conversation grew quiet.

"Listen," he said in a loud, deep voice. "I can bring food to you."

The cheering that followed made it impossible for Anthony to go on. While he waited, I reviewed the details of my plan. The first and most important step was to get on the roof as soon as possible.

"My men can bring the supplies with carts and dollies," Anthony eventually said.

"Just let us in, fella!" yelled someone. "We'll come to you."

"Please understand: The food inside will become useless if order breaks down. Anarchy will put your safety at risk. Think of the children."

I assumed the man who threatened us would have been pleased by this announcement. Instead, he turned around and disappeared into the crowd, which to me seemed ominous.

Deion and Emmitt were ordered to remain at the west entrance, while Mike manned the east side with an older guy whose name I had forgotten. Anthony asked me to follow him back into the DC. His face was solemn, his eyes uncertain.

"You're really going to bring them food?"

"I don't know," he said. "My speech bought us time, but minutes only."

"That guy could be bluffing about the helicopters."

"He did not seem to be bluffing. And if no one is coming, my strategy no longer makes sense. Maybe we should grab supplies and evacuate before the decision is no longer ours."

The last thing I wanted was for Anthony to give up so easily. I needed more time. When we reached the building, I appealed to his sense of order.

"If we're going to evacuate, let's do it on our terms. I'll go to the roof and help Paige watch the crowd while you and the others round up supplies."

Anthony looked at me for a long time before he answered. Could he see through me? Could everyone?

Was this even happening?

"Yes, Aiden. Go join her. When I decide how to move forward, I may need your help again."

As I climbed the ladder, the rifle slung over my back, I looked up at the sky and marveled at the amount of smoke and ash in the air. Its presence had been increasing gradually for days, but this was like someone had closed the flue of the world. As if the smoke, having nowhere to go, was rolling backward with an odor so sharp it burned my nose.

Eventually I reached the roof and saw Paige lying behind her rifle, eye pressed against the scope. I quietly shouldered my own weapon. The sound in my mind compressed itself to a lone, high whistle. A gunshot fired this close might ignite the crowd, but how else was I meant to get Paige off the roof?

There was a way to solve this riddle if only I had more time.

But time was suddenly more precious than I knew.

"We've got a problem," she said, and coughed into her fist.

* * *

Like the rest of us, Paige had realized something was different that morning, and she'd been carefully scanning the northern and eastern trees for movement.

"Someone's in there," she said. "At least two groups."

"Can't you shoot at them the way you shot at us?"

"Maybe. But what if Jimmy and Bart decided to come back?"

This seemed unlikely, but what if she was right? What if the women had come, too? Was Keri out there, waiting for her chance to see Dead Ed again?

"So what do we do?"

"All we can do is wait," she said and coughed again. "Even if I knew none of them were friendly, they're too deep in the trees to get a clear shot."

I looked where her scope was pointed but couldn't make out a thing. Also, my throat was feeling ticklish, and I coughed a few times to clear it. The noise in my head became heavy and dense: a ragged membrane of dissonant wails. The window for maximum destruction was rapidly closing. If something didn't happen soon, it never would.

"Anthony wants to cut and run," I eventually said. "Maybe you should go down there and talk sense into him."

"He's right. We can't stay here any longer. But I don't want our escape cut short by whoever is in the trees. Shit, I've lost them."

"Both groups?"

I shouldered my rifle and watched the tree line. I swept right and pointed my rifle at Paige. My finger slithered onto the trigger. Her skull would be beautiful in pieces.

"Oh, shit," she said, her eye still pressed against the scope. "It *is* Jimmy."

I swept back left again. Toward the trees. Violins between my ears, strings shrieking.

"They're about to walk clear of the tree line," said Paige. "They've got Jimmy out front. And a woman. Two women. Using them like shields, those fuckers. Like the women aren't even human."

"You mean you can't take a shot?"

"Not yet," she said. "Not unless I can make a clear kill. The sound of gunfire could start a riot out front."

I finally saw movement at the tree line, and then Jimmy emerged, followed by two women. From this distance they were little more than shapes, but their shuffling gait suggested all three were either exhausted or in bad physical condition.

And behind each one of them was a man carrying a rifle. As the six of them grew closer, I realized one of the men was the fellow who confronted us at the fence. I didn't recognize the other two.

"Watch the entire tree line," Paige said. "They could be trying to distract us from an assault. Who the hell are those women?"

As the group continued its approach, I heard someone shouting.

" . . . deserve a right to eat the same as you! We are not here to fight, but we must protect our families! I repeat: We are not here to fight!"

"I could hit at least one of them," said Paige. "Maybe two. But I can't get all three before the other one starts shooting. They might kill Jimmy and those two women."

Was she asking if I would let Jimmy and the unknown women die in exchange for killing the intruders? If so, my answer was a resounding yes! Only what then? There was still the matter of the 269 rounds. A herd of people I was meant to cull.

"Let's go down and meet them," said Paige. "You first and I'll cover. We should be able to reach the ground before they make it around the corner."

Did she know I had pointed my gun at her? Would she fire while my back was turned?

I walked toward the stairs and closed my eyes and waited for the blast. But none came.

The ladder didn't face the tree line, which meant we could descend without fear of being shot. On the ground we hid behind a semi-trailer. Eventually the approaching group stopped at the corner of the building.

"We are not here to fight!" one of the men yelled. "We were in the woods behind the warehouse and discovered this man approaching from the east. He says he's been here before. He says you supplied him with food and water. Why shouldn't we be treated the same?"

"Where are your other men?" I yelled back.

"Watching from the trees. They have orders to attack if this doesn't go well. We are well-armed. I advise you to help us."

I looked at Paige. Her face was unreadable. With this automatic rifle I might overwhelm the group with a barrage of fire, but that meant killing Jimmy myself. And possibly inviting an attack from their other men.

"Approach slowly," I said instead. "Make any sudden moves and my sharpshooter will be forced to take you down."

"We are aware of your sniper. We are not here to fight."

The first movement I saw was Jimmy rounding the corner. His face was bruised, and blood was crusted beneath his nose and one of his eyes. Then two women followed, and one of them, I noticed, looked familiar, even if I couldn't place her.

Soon the six of them were standing before us. Anthony had apparently heard and emerged slowly from the open employee door. He stood beside Paige and faced the men.

None of this was turning out the way I had hoped. I was thwarted. Disillusioned. My mind was a universe of chaotic, screaming nonsense, and I swore I could taste, of all things, lemonade.

From this awful disorder Anthony's composure emerged.

"I am Anthony Williams, manager of this facility. Paige and Aiden have been helping protect our interests."

"Billy Pate," said one of the men. He was the angry guy from before, the one at the fence. "This here is Thomas Phillips and Seth Black."

Upon hearing this exchange, Jimmy appeared to come to life. He craned his neck to look backward.

"So your name is Seth Black?"

Seth was shorter and softer-looking than the two other men. He would have been more at home in a cubicle, I thought, than a battlefield.

"So what if it is?" Seth said.

"You here from Tulsa? Have a wife named Natalie?"

"I'm Natalie," said the other woman, the one I didn't recognize.

The defiant look on Seth's face changed to one of confusion.

"How do you know us?"

Jimmy turned directly toward Seth and smiled. I could see blood in his teeth.

"I'm Jimmy Jameson. You owe me $213,000."

The look on Seth's face, upon hearing this news, was something close to horror. I couldn't know the incredible circumstances that had directed the paths of these two men to cross, or that Seth had come all the way from Tulsa the previous Friday, *after* the EMP.

And I surely didn't understand what role Thomas had played in our lives thus far, or in events that were still to come.

But I do now.

JOURNEY ⊢

THIRTY

Larry Adams had always known he was special. When he was eight years old, during one of his father's nightly visits, he asked:

"Daddy, what is dark?"

His father, distracted, hadn't answered. But when Larry asked again later, he was given this uninspired observation:

"Dark is the absence of light."

And that was true, anyone could say so, but it wasn't really an answer. You could see dark in outer space, too. Was the dark between planets and stars the same as the dark in his bedroom, late at night, when his father turned off the night light and shut the drapes? Was dark the absence of anything? That couldn't be right, because even when his room was completely dark, the dresser was still there, the bed was still there, his father was still there. His hands could feel in the dark. His ears could hear. What if dark to your eyes was the same as silence to your ears?

In high school physics he finally learned the answer, or the beginning of the answer. Light and dark weren't just about seeing or not seeing. Light itself was *made of stuff*, of particles called photons, and the way you saw an object was to bounce photons off it in order to ricochet some of them into your eyes. And the crazy thing was, all the photons that didn't travel directly into your eyes were invisible. Invisible! They flew right past your nose at the speed of, you know, light, but unless they struck your retina they might as well be dark.

That was it. Larry was hooked. And though math had never been his favorite subject, he immersed himself in standard calculus and tensor calculus and differential equations and differential geometry. In vector spaces and function spaces and Fourier analysis. Partly because he couldn't get answers to big questions without mastering the proper tool set, and partly because losing himself in the labyrinth of mathematics helped him forget the social failures of high school. Helped him forget Jillian's cruelty, forget how the other high school starlets ignored him, how they looked upon him the way Larry might look upon an ant. Eventually he moved on to higher education, to important work at Fermilab and the NTSSC, and he almost never thought about Jillian's 10th grade note, which Larry had opened with such hope but instead left him shattered. *Stop staring at me all the time. My boyfriend says you are a FUCKFACE. P.S. Don't W/B!*

But during his last weeks in Olney, when stress and alcohol had gotten the better of him, Jillian's note was all Larry could think about. He lost his grip on reality and sent those terrible messages to the news anchor. He resented celebrity, the idea that certain, lucky people were elevated to royalty for nothing more than an accident of genetics. None of them seemed to understand that *he* was special, that if anyone should be considered royalty, it was him.

After the supercollider was destroyed he fled to California, specifically Barstow, where he installed himself in a cheap hotel room and waited for law enforcement to come calling. But law enforcement never arrived. Eventually Larry found his way to L.A., where he frequented hotel bars like the Andaz and the Marquis and Chateau Marmont, hoping to meet a beautiful actress, a real-world starlet. That never happened, but one fateful afternoon he found himself in a conversation with Lynda Obst, a powerful producer who hired him not once but three times to offer advice on high-budget science thrillers. On the sets of these films he was sometimes within shouting distance of female leads like Natalie Portman and Emma Stone and Jennifer Lawrence, which on its face was a dream come true, but in practice was profoundly disappointing. Because the actors never spoke to him and the directors never listened to him. *No one* listened to him. Even Ms. Obst, who respected his technical expertise, picked dramatic license over scientific accuracy every time. Larry couldn't understand what was so boring about reality. Reality was spectacular and mesmerizing and, he believed, a story worth telling. The double-helix structure of DNA, the core code of life on earth, was by itself more fascinating than anything Hollywood could produce. But no one seemed to care.

He would have quit after the Obst films if the money wasn't so good. Instead, he began "advising" for other producers, and when he wasn't working he drove up and down Sunset in his convertible Bimmer, until one day the last fleck of glitter fell away and suddenly he was sick of L.A. Sick of everyone preening, of looking for just the right angle, sick of ground-floor celebrities soaking up Instagram likes and retweets of their clever turns of phrase while cobwebs gathered on Larry's own Twitter feed. He returned to Texas, built himself a large house on a lake, and pretended to consult for a fictional German manufacturer. But there was no work. Just the slow, measured descent of a man who discovered that his wildest dreams were less rewarding than whatever darkness lived at the bottom of a bottle of scotch.

But the supernova had made things interesting again. Now, all the shallow people who over the years had wronged him were going to die. For that matter, Larry himself would probably die, which would have been fine if not for the miraculous appearance of Skylar Stover in the house next door. The idea that Thomas Phillips, of all people, was holding court with such a lovely woman was enough to drive Larry bonkers. Even worse, when he dropped by to say hello, Thomas wouldn't let him through the door.

Larry was not a superstitious man, but he didn't see how Skylar's appearance could be a coincidence. It had to have been arranged. Sometimes he imagined a great wheel in the sky, as if the universe was a game of roulette that turned and turned until one day the ball landed on you. Larry had been waiting all his life for a chance to win. He wondered if today was finally that day.

On Monday night, after Thomas refused to let him in, Larry had walked home and poured himself a stiff scotch. He simmered in failure and looked for Skylar in old celebrity magazines and masturbated furiously. The next morning he was awakened by a headache so powerful it rang like a bell between his ears. He made more instant pancakes and saturated them with real maple syrup and downed a breakfast shot of Bailey's. He sat on his back porch and stared at the green water of his swimming pool. He wondered about the plan Blaise had proposed. It was a long walk, fraught with danger, but what other choice did he have?

Larry imagined himself on the road, strolling beside Skylar. Their arms, beaded with sweat, sometimes brushed against each other, electrifying him, electrifying her. He realized he was getting hard again and went inside to relieve the pressure. Afterward he inspected the empty shelves of his pantry and finally his mind was made up.

Even so, it took several more hours and fingers of scotch before he summoned the nerve to walk down the street and talk to Matt Bernhardt. Matt was a thick-headed redneck who already had canvassed the neighborhood looking for food, and who resented the success of others. He had been sitting in his back yard, tending to a bed of coals, cooking something that looked like a dog (but couldn't possibly be a dog). When he heard about Skylar and the family Thomas was hosting, Matt replied by clapping Larry on the shoulder and smiling a ghoulish smile.

"You done good, Professor. Want to come along when we liquidate his stock?"

Larry had shaken his head violently. Just because he despised Thomas didn't mean he wanted to physically steal from him.

"No problem at all," said Matt amiably. "Me and my men will go in after midnight. Feel free to stop here in the morning for breakfast, assuming there's as much food as you say."

Matt noticed Larry looking at the fire.

"You hungry now?"

In fact he was starving, but the skinned animal smoking on glowing coals was definitely a dog. Or a coyote. Or something else he refused to eat.

After he left Matt's yard, Larry walked back up the street and into a dark grove of trees. It was nearly pitch black beneath the canopy of branches, and progress was slow. Eventually, he stumbled into the white fence that bordered Blaise's heavily-forested property. Blaise himself was sitting on his back deck beside the green glow of a propane lantern.

"If that's a man," Blaise said, "identify yourself. Otherwise I'm gonna use you for target practice, don't you know."

"It's me," Larry said. He emerged from the trees into a small clearing. "I'm the only person who ever comes by."

"Can't be too careful. Any luck with the screenwriter?"

"Nope. You were right. He won't share anything."

"That's a smart man who wants to survive."

Only one chair stood on the back deck, and Blaise was sitting in it. Larry, hungry and exhausted, took a seat on the rough wooden slats.

"I guess there's just one option left."

"And you still want to go through with it," said Blaise in his abrasive, East-coast way that could have been a statement or a question.

"I already spoke to Matt. He's going over there tonight."

"How much food you think there is?"

"I don't know," Larry said. "But he's got five people staying there and no one seems very worried."

"Not even the two young boys?"

"Sure. Whatever."

"You must really be in love with this actress," said Blaise.

"What's that supposed to mean?"

"You're willing to starve a family of four just to get close to her."

"They're not going to starve. We're taking them to an even larger supply of food."

"How many times I gotta tell ya? This here plan is no slam dunk."

Larry stood up and loomed over Blaise. The gnawing sensation in his gut made it hard to think clearly.

"You asked me to recruit someone," he said. "To help carry the weapons and ammo. When I mentioned Thomas, you said fine."

"I never said steal food from babies."

"They're like eight years old."

"So you got no problem marching a couple of eight-year-old kids through thirty miles of blazing heat."

"How else was I supposed to get them out of the house except remove their supplies?"

"You coulda asked that Matt fella to go with us. He's been keen for a fight ever since the lights went out."

"Matt is volatile."

"Plus, he's not a fancypants actress."

"Fuck you," said Larry.

But Blaise needed food like anyone and eventually shut his mouth about the kids.

"So I should expect you to bring them by in the morning?"

"That's the hope," Larry said. "Thomas doesn't have the guts or weapons to fight Matt. He won't have any choice."

After he was home, Larry, by candlelight, poured another healthy scotch. He imagined their arrival at the warehouse, the great rows of groceries, Skylar's immense gratitude, her open arms.

Larry, she whispers. *How can I ever repay you?*

I just wanted you to be safe. I want you to be happy.

Oh, I am. *I* am *happy. And now I want you to feel as good as I do.*

He poured himself even more scotch and climbed into bed and let the darkness wash over him.

Dark is the absence of light, said Skylar when she came up for air. *But* you *are the light, Larry. We need you. So be good to yourself. Be good to yourself. Be good . . .*

THIRTY-ONE

Thomas awoke violently, slick with sweat, confident he was being watched. An inexplicable interval passed where the alternate reality of his dream flickered in the shadows of the candlelit real world. Based on the dark windows, on the silence of the house, it was still sometime in the middle of the night.

In the dream he'd been in his office, bathed in the pale glow of his Mac display, trying to imagine the next scene in an epic screenplay that was nearing completion. But he sensed a stranger in the corners of his peripheral vision, waiting for Thomas to type so he could rush forward and inflict unspeakable agony upon him.

Even as the dream receded, his emotions remained. Thomas lay there feeling for all the world like he was the target of a malevolent plot.

On his left, at the distant edge of the king bed, candlelight flickered over Skylar's sleeping form. She lay on her back, and her limbs were spread away from her torso as if she were falling from a great height. He remembered the way she had clutched his shoulder, her hot breath in his ear. It was a strange thing, this life. Sometimes it really *did* feel scripted, like someone behind the curtain was pulling the levers of the world to extract the maximum human drama from every scene.

He heard a sound, a rustling that might have been Skylar, except he hadn't felt her move. Maybe Natalie or one of the boys was awake. Maybe one of them had wandered into the kitchen to get a drink of water or something to eat. Probably he should get up and investigate, but already the sound was fading from his memory and Thomas was drifting away, sitting in front of his computer again, only this time it was no computer . . .it was an old Underwood typewriter. The power was out and this was his only chance to save the world. He was banging away, one letter at a time, when he heard another rustling sound, this one much louder than the first and definitely not anything that had come from Skylar.

Then a hoarse, whispering curse: "*Fuck!*"

Thomas sat upright. He was dressed in a pair of boxers and nothing else. Maybe it was Seth. Maybe he was up looking for food. Or booze.

Thomas reached on the floor for his T-shirt.

"*Will you shut the fuck up?*" someone whispered.

Now, his shaking hands could barely fit the shirt over his head. Ripples of fear crawled like insects up his spine. Someone was in his house. Someone who wasn't supposed to be here. He reached under the bed for his gun.

Thomas owned the weapon for exactly this purpose, but now that he was called to use it, his limbs felt heavy. What if the intruders carried their own guns? How many were there? What were they doing?

They were here to steal food. Or water. Or whatever.

He rolled out of bed. Crept toward the door. Listened for more whispering, for any sounds at all. Were they in the kitchen? The safe room? Locking up was part of his evening routine, but had he forgotten last night?

Thomas reached the door, which was closed, and wondered what to do. Explode into the hallway and order the intruders out of his house? He didn't want to shoot indiscriminately when he had no idea who was there. Maybe it was teenagers. A husband and wife. He turned the knob and pulled open the door, barely, just enough to peer into the hallway. It was too dark to see anything, but he could smell them, whoever they were, strangers in his house, thieves trying to take his food, trying to steal the security he had so carefully prepared.

He thought he heard them in the kitchen. That's the first place anyone would go. No one would even know to look for the safe room. He stepped into the hallway and turned to the right. He'd taken maybe three quiet steps when he heard a voice directly behind him.

"That's far enough," said a man. Thomas felt the barrel of a gun press into the back of his neck. It was cold and hard and he thought he might faint. "Hand over your piece."

"Who the hell are you?" Thomas said in the steadiest voice he could muster.

"I said hand over your piece, asshole."

Thomas held out the gun. The man took it from him and then pressed forward with his own.

"Move," he said. "Into the kitchen."

In a film, the hero would execute a sudden, brutal move that would disable the intruder and use him as a human shield against whoever was in the kitchen. But Thomas was so paralyzed by the presence of deadly force against his neck that he could barely put one foot in front of the other.

The kitchen was pale with moonlight, and when he turned the corner, Thomas saw the silhouettes of two other men standing near the table.

"Honestly, I'm glad you woke up," said the guy behind him. "We can do this a lot faster now that we don't have to sneak around."

The other men chuckled and one of them switched on a flashlight that blinded Thomas. His arms jerked up involuntarily. He thought they were going to shoot him.

"You got flashlights," the guy said. "You got spare batteries and candles and lanterns and more food than an army could eat. You know somethin' about this whole thing ahead of time? You some kinda spy?"

"I prepared," Thomas said through clenched teeth.

"Funny how you didn't say nothing about being prepared when I came by a few days ago," said the man behind him.

As he turned around, Thomas finally realized the armed man was Matt, the same Matt who on Sunday afternoon broached the idea of a neighborhood food collective.

The flashlight painted Matt's shape in grayscale hues. He was a little taller than Thomas, and his beard had grown in rough patches. He was dressed in a flannel shirt and jeans.

"I've got a family here," said Thomas. "These are my supplies. I was only trying to protect them."

"If you were more of a neighbor," said Matt, "you mighta told people this could happen. Maybe we could have prepared, too. Maybe it could have been, you know, a *community effort.*"

"I didn't know this would happen. I prepared in case it did."

"Sounds like some fake news to me," said one of the other men. "I been waiting for you elitists to take it on the chin. It's high time the common man got his."

"By stealing?"

"Your kind has been stealing from us for years," said Matt. "Lookin' down on real Americans like we ain't as good as you. But the world ain't slanted in favor of the educated liberals no more. Now we're back to God's original design: Survival of the fittest."

"The world is what you make it," Thomas said.

"You got that right," said Matt. "It's a world where our families get to live a lot longer now that we have all this food."

Matt nodded at the two other men.

"Go on and carry that outside. When you come back, bring them other boys and let's speed this up."

The two of them carried their loads away, and without the flashlight the kitchen was returned to moonlit shadows. In the distance, Thomas could hear the men talking to someone outside. He remembered all the trips he'd made to Sam's wholesale club, to Home Depot, all the shipments from Amazon. The guys at the liquor store assumed he was throwing a party, at least at first. Later one of them asked if he was trying to kill himself, which was said in the manner of a joke but didn't seem like a joke. In the end, it had taken weeks to stock the safe room, and Thomas had been so proud of his preparation that he'd driven 250 miles to "save" a family he could no longer feed.

"Will you please leave something for us?" Thomas asked Matt. "There are children here."

"'Fraid not. You knew this would happen and didn't tell anyone."

Right about then, a couple more men ambled into the house, and Matt directed them toward the safe room. As they walked away, down the hall, Thomas saw movement on his right and realized one of the twins was walking toward the kitchen. He could barely tell them apart during the day and in this light it was impossible.

"Brandon? Go back to bed, son."

"I'm Ben," said the boy. "I thought I heard my daddy. Is he awake?"

"No, he's not up. Go back to bed."

But Ben kept walking and eventually rounded the corner, where he saw Matt. Thomas instinctively put out his arm and stepped in front of the boy to block him from the gun.

"Hi," said Ben. "Who is that?"

"I'm a neighbor. Me and Thomas are friends."

Thomas looked back at Matt and saw with some relief that he'd hidden the gun behind his back.

"His name is Matt. He came over to borrow some food."

"But I thought we weren't sharing the food," said Ben. "Since there's no more to get."

"Thomas changed his mind. He's a real nice guy. Ain't you Thomas?"

"You could say that. Anyway, Ben, why don't you run back to bed? Your dad isn't up and you don't want to be tired in the morning."

Behind Matt, more men walked by, stooped by the weight of supplies.

"Okay," Ben said, watching the men. "But is that guy really your friend?"

The enormity of what was happening was still taking shape in Thomas' mind. He hesitated just long enough for the truth to be evident, even as he countermanded it with his words.

"Of course he's a friend. Now, get back in bed, all right?"

When Ben was gone, Matt brought the gun out where Thomas could see it. His smile twinkled in the moonlight.

"Wish I could be around when that kid hears the truth," Matt said. "I bet you made yourself out to be a real hero, didn't you? Except you ain't no hero. You're just an elitist who thought it was fine to live high on the hog while the rest of us starved to death."

By now Thomas was no longer afraid for his life, not in the short term, anyway. Matt was clearly enchanted with the idea of him going hungry.

"Rich people fuckin' over the common man," Matt added. "I'd say that's as American as apple pie."

* * *

By the time Matt and his men had left, Thomas could see the first colors of dawn peeking over the horizon. He found a broken window in his study, which was how they had gotten into the house.

He shuffled to the safe room to see what was left, but of course the men had taken everything. There was no water, no food, no alcohol. His supply of candles and flashlights and batteries was gone. Everything was gone, save a few empty boxes and bags left on the floor like fallen soldiers. The stark emptiness of the safe room frightened him in a primal way that made him want to strike out at something, anything. Matt had even taken his handgun, though there was another under the front seat of his car.

He kept thinking about the car.

On its face, a working vehicle seemed like a valuable commodity, but the problem with driving it was the attention it would attract. By now it was Wednesday morning, five days since the pulse, and people were beginning to run out of food. They would take to the streets and eventually flee the city. They would be armed and desperate. An innocent-looking family in a convertible would be an obvious target.

And by the way, he'd spent nearly his entire gasoline supply on the trip to Tulsa. Even if the roads were clear they wouldn't get very far.

There was no way to recover from the loss of his supplies. He could try to catch fish from the lake, or hunt for food in the trees, but these gestures would do nothing more than pass time and preserve false hope. No matter what he did from this point forward, Thomas and every one of his guests would surely starve to death. And it was all his fault.

Eventually he found his way back to the bedroom. In the early morning light Skylar's curves were thrown into dramatic relief, and her skin shimmered, slick with sweat. Thomas climbed into bed and stared at the ceiling. He could smell smoke. He thought about what Matt said before he finally left.

"I know you're mad about this, and maybe you got more guns stashed somewhere. But this is your one warning: Don't come looking for your food. If we see you coming, any of you, we'll shoot. This is a matter of life and death, and I'll do whatever I need to protect my family."

Thomas had said nothing.

"You don't even know where I live, do you?"

Thomas hadn't answered, but Matt had correctly interpreted his silence.

"Just take your people and leave," he said. "Get on the road and out of the city like everyone else. Don't come looking for me."

What kind of a man stood idly by while thieves walked away with his very existence? Why the hell had he brought Natalie and her family here? He'd doomed them. He'd doomed himself. The only way to survive something like this was to stay away from everyone, to be lethally selfish. But Skylar was right: Who wanted to live in a world full of selfish survivors?

He didn't know what to do. He felt like a helpless child. He couldn't bear to lie there suffering alone.

"Skylar."

She twitched at the sound of his voice, but only a little.

"Skylar!"

Now she shook awake and sat quickly upright, as if he'd given her a bump with imaginary shock paddles.

"Oh my God, Daddy!"

Thomas reached for her hand. It was soft and warm. He didn't deserve to touch her.

"I was dreaming about my parents. Their building was on fire. The whole city was."

Thomas felt like he would burst if he didn't spill the truth.

"I wish I could bring them here. I wish they were safe."

"Skylar, I have something to tell you."

"What is it? Did help come?"

"Someone stole our supplies last night."

"They what?"

Thomas opened his mouth to answer, but Skylar pressed on.

"Is this a joke? Are you making fun because I want you to share your food?"

"It's not a joke."

"But how?" She sat up in bed and looked at him carefully, searching his face for the truth. "How could that happen? How do you know this?"

"I woke up while they were here."

"Someone seriously broke into your house? How did they—"

"A window in the study. And I didn't lock the safe room last night."

"But you woke up and still—"

He briefly explained his encounter with Matt and the other men.

"Oh my God."

"We don't have anything left. It's gone. All of it."

She climbed out of bed, completely naked and unconcerned.

"How could you have let this happen? What the hell are we going to do?"

He wanted to hold her. He wanted her to understand that no matter what happened, everything would be okay.

But he couldn't. No matter how hard he tried, Thomas would never be able to make everything okay. He had failed again. The way he would always fail.

"I can't believe this. What are we going to do?"

"I still have the water well," he muttered. "And maybe we can catch enough fish to feed ourselves."

"Catch fish. You think we can catch fish."

"If that doesn't work, we'll have to leave. We'll have to get out of the city and look for food."

"Where, Thomas? Where will we go?"

"I don't know. Maybe—"

"Maybe? You know there's nowhere to go. Too many people, remember? Not enough game. We're fucked. All of us. Fucked."

This exchange made Thomas think of his mother, the hate in her eyes, the sarcasm that dripped from her voice like candlewax that burned the sensitive skin of his ego and left scars.

"I should have left when I had the chance," Skylar said cryptically. "This is what I get for expecting a man to take care of me."

It was only hours since Thomas had made love to her and already Skylar loathed him.

"This whole time you pretended to be in charge, like you were the only one who could save us. But you can't even take care of yourself."

THIRTY-TWO

N ow Skylar was sitting on the back porch, watching the sun gradually illuminate smoke clouds above the lake. She didn't want to be in the house. She couldn't risk the chance of Thomas walking by wearing that miserable expression, the hapless look of guilty resignation.

It was a strange thing to suspect death was coming but not be able to see it or feel it. In the present moment Skylar wasn't even hungry. She felt a little grimy, and could have used a shower, but she wasn't overly concerned about it. Which was a far cry from her old routine. On days when she was expected to make a public appearance, preparing hair and skin and nails could consume most of a morning.

As frustrated as she was with Thomas, as hopeless as she felt about the general state of the world, one (slim) prospect for liberation remained: that all this was a dream . . . or perhaps a fictional scenario that could be ended or changed.

Before *Thomas World*, which she had seen mere days after Roark's phone call from Iceland, Skylar had never questioned the reality of the world. The idea seemed so implausible, especially because in pictures like *The Matrix* or *Inception*, farfetched and complicated reasons were given to explain their artificial worlds. But the protagonist in Thomas' film had built a simulation to satisfy unrequited love. Which was, if you were going to ordain your own reality, the only good reason to do it.

Afterward, when Skylar read the story behind *Thomas World* and how it mirrored the author's real life, she also learned he'd written a new screenplay. And once she became attached to the project, Skylar amused herself by wondering if her involvement in the film had somehow been preordained.

She'd been in New York at the time, leaning on her parents for support. And when she was ready to fly to Los Angeles, Skylar decided to assert her free will by engineering outcomes that defied reason. Instead of going straight home, she requested the meeting with Thomas. Instead of a perfunctory and professional lunch with him, she suggested a weekend of conversation and brainstorming. And she wouldn't play coy. She would flirt unreservedly. She would flaunt her free will to whoever might be watching and in the process unburden herself from the shameful farce of her marriage.

Then she landed in Dallas, and planes began to fall out of the sky, and Skylar wondered if the universe had called her bluff. Because her "spontaneous" decision to discuss a post-apocalyptic screenplay turned out to be the very thing that saved her from a real-life apocalypse.

In a film, when you pushed a protagonist's life out of balance, her task was to make things right again. But every time she took a step to find peace, her actions generated a new complication. Could Skylar identify a similar pattern in the events since the pulse? Did the appearance of the supernova signal the beginning of her story? Had the various incidents since then moved from positive to negative to positive again, like a swinging pendulum that powered the narrative engine of any film?

Last night she had given herself to Thomas, had finally lowered her guard and forgotten her fears, and the world had responded by stealing their food supply. What Hollywood cliché was more celebrated than a young woman in a horror film being killed as soon as she dared indulge her sexual self? If there was a better metaphor for the essence of the patriarchy, Skylar didn't know what it was.

Probably none of it was true. But how else was she meant to pass the time except hope it was all a big joke? Yesterday she had been ready to pack her bags and leave, but now, as the rising sun cast clouds of smoke in violent colors, Skylar understood that idea was suicide. And suicide would be an awful, pointless end to her story.

While she sat there, waiting for a reversal, Skylar's mind floated away, across the country, across the ocean. How different the old world had been! How luxurious. Like her extremely modern marriage to Roark. They would never have bothered with a legal union if not for a shared commitment to avoid the typical Hollywood relationship mistakes.

Instead of expecting pure fidelity, Skylar suggested an open sexual relationship with one restriction: No affairs with costars, and nightly phone calls when shooting at a distant and exotic location. Like for instance Reykjavik, Iceland. Because the most dangerous threat she could imagine was not some random sexual encounter but rather Roark in close quarters with another actress for fifteen hours a day, and then being sequestered in the same hotel every night. So it wasn't a shock when a friend emailed Skylar blurry pictures of Anne Roberts and her husband kissing on the rugged coast of the fjord Hvalfjörður, not when he had failed to call her the three previous nights.

It hurt to know Roark had violated their agreement, but what she could not accept, what angered her still, was how predictably their breakup had unfolded. She guessed the tabloid headlines before they were written, because she'd read them so many times before. And when she finally asked why he slept with Anne (as if it mattered) Roark's lame answers only angered her more.

It's time to go our separate ways, he'd said. *We're never in the same place. We're never together. We're still so young.*

So young? It's not like you're under lock and key. You can fuck almost anyone you want.

Maybe that's not what I want. Maybe I want to be faithful. Maybe I want to give myself to someone.

Just not to me.

I guess not, Roark said.

Send her my love, then. I hope you two become soulmates on the set of Iceman 2.

Whatever, Skylar. You may have the world fooled with this snobby attitude, but I know better. I know why you refuse to love someone.

Refuse to love? I loved you!

You loved the idea of us. You wanted the world to love the idea of us. You wore me like an expensive dress.

Roark—

I can't be married to someone who doesn't want to have a child.

Then he had hung up. Or she had hung up. It was hard to remember. She'd knocked back two Lortabs with a glass of wine and had gone to sleep for what seemed like days. Later she flew to New York in a prescription fog and camped in her old room like a teenaged girl. Her mom brought her soup. Her dad sat on the edge of the bed and squeezed her ankles. And by the way her parents were dying. Her lovely parents were dying and now Skylar was in the process of dying and she was never, ever going to hold a baby in her arms. She was never going to inhale her baby's smell or feel the grasp of her baby's fingers or feel the bite of her baby's gums on her breast or—

"Hello," said a voice.

Skylar looked up and saw a man standing over her, smiling a creepy smile.

"Oh," she said. "Larry."

"You must have been deep in thought. I called to you before I walked over here."

"I was thinking about my parents."

"I'm sorry," he said. "As bad as it is here, I can't imagine what Manhattan must be like."

Skylar didn't bother to ask how he knew where her parents lived. She could tell from his unpleasant manner that Larry was the kind of guy who enjoyed a running fantasy behind his creepy black eyes, even while he was looking you in the face and carrying on a conversation. At public events these men were always present, a row or two behind the screaming teenaged girls, observing Skylar with a certain pompous removal, as if they were above the adoration that had brought them to see her in the first place. She imagined Larry had saved every copy of *Us Weekly* he'd ever received in the mail, indexed by date, that he paid for premium digital subscriptions to People.com and TMZ and the Daily Mail, that he towered over Reddit as an expert on all things Skylar Stover or Scarlett Johannsson or whatever famous actress was the object of his current fantasies. His obsession was smeared all over his oily face.

"The whole world is shit," she said. "Doesn't matter where you are."

"What do you mean? Did you guys run out of curry?"

Skylar smiled. Larry's genuine personality, the jealous and hateful side of him, lay so close to the surface he could hardly contain it.

"We've run out of everything," she said. "We're going to starve just like you."

Larry appeared to think about this, as if the obvious outcome might not be so obvious.

"Maybe not."

"Really? Did the power come back on while I was daydreaming?"

"No," said Larry. "But I have a friend who knows where all the food is."

"I don't know what you're talking about."

"His name is Blaise. If we help him carry weapons, he'll take us to the warehouse."

"What warehouse?"

And when he explained the plan to her, Skylar smiled again. Smiled widely.

"So it finally came," she said.

"What finally came?"

"The next scene in the film. The reversal."

Larry stared at her for a minute, curiously, and when she imagined how a celebrity-obsessed creep like him would behave when he realized he was trapped inside a genuine Hollywood production, Skylar laughed out loud.

"What are you talking about?" Larry finally asked.

"Does any of this strike you as authentic? Mass extinction by way of supernova? Sounds more like something Thomas might write, don't you think?"

Larry's brow furrowed, either in concentration or anger.

"You're making fun of me, aren't you?"

"Don't be so arrogant," Skylar answered. "Why would everyone in the world be out to get *you*?"

THIRTY-THREE

When Seth opened his eyes to the slope of Natalie's naked shoulder, his first thought should have been pleasant. Should have been relief. His wife hadn't uttered a word in something like two (or three?) days, and then last night, unexpectedly, she had come to him. She asked Seth to make love to her and seemed to enjoy him in a way he hadn't known in years.

But instead of relief he felt dread. His body resonated with guilt, as if he'd done something terrible. His left side hurt, his tongue was glued to the roof of his mouth, and every cell in his body seemed to have been drained of water.

Gradually, memories began to surface. Like Natalie sitting against the headboard, writing something in the journal she refused to share with him. Seth had wondered what was going through her mind but didn't want to jeopardize their newfound harmony, so he stared at the flickering candle and didn't feel harmonious at all. Really, he had wanted to rip the pages from her hands and read them aloud, or maybe dip them into the candle flame and watch them burn.

Seth didn't believe he would do either of those things, but his memory of the evening was broken, and pieces were missing.

Carefully, so he didn't wake Natalie, Seth turned over. Looming before him in the morning light was a bottle of whiskey. An open bottle that was at least half gone. Next to the bottle sat a key.

The key.

Seth couldn't remember where the key had come from, but he knew for sure what door it opened. Had he snuck into Thomas' room? After Natalie had fallen asleep, had he—?

Skylar had been there. She'd been lying on her side, one leg draped over Thomas, and in the flickering candlelight Seth could see her naked ass and possibly more in the shadow between her legs. It wasn't fair. It wasn't fair that Thomas, for nothing more than a quirk of fate, was allowed to sleep with Skylar while Seth himself was not. He wished he could run his fingers along the jutting ridge of her hip. He wished he could know what it felt like to be with a woman so sexy and lovely and admired. But he couldn't stand there holding a candle forever. Instead he inspected the top of a dresser and a chest of drawers and the countertop in the master bath, looking for the key, but where he finally found it was in the pocket of Thomas' shorts.

Seth vaguely remembered unlocking the door to the safe room, standing among shelves of food and water and paper plates and candles. And booze. He grabbed a bottle of Jack Daniel's by its neck and went back to the bedroom where Natalie lay sleeping. He climbed into bed and swallowed occasional pulls of whiskey and wondered why the world always worked against him. Like for instance the pulse. The new star had not only saved him from a suicide attempt but also, miraculously, forgave every cent of his gambling debts. But instead of becoming a hero to his wife and children, instead of protecting them from the perils of this new world, Seth was mooching off Thomas. He was not the architect of their safety but a passive observer. What seemed like a miracle had really been a curse, a component of the plot to deny his every desire and turn him into the butt of every joke.

"Why is there a bottle of whiskey on the nightstand?"

Seth opened his eyes and saw Natalie facing him, propped on one elbow. He must have fallen asleep again.

"I—"

"What key is that?"

While he grasped for an answer, Seth realized he could hear voices elsewhere in the house. Animated voices. Loud voices.

"I drank some whiskey to help me sleep," he finally said.

"Because sex wasn't enough?"

"Why won't you let me read your journal?"

"Because it's private. Everything in this world isn't about you."

Anger rose in him like a tide. He'd been so full of hope when Natalie came to him last night, and just look at what happened. Nothing ever turned out the way he wanted. Nothing.

"You're right," he said. "It's all about *you*, Nat."

"So when you gambled away our fortune, when you stole from the boys' college fund, that was for me?"

"I fucked up, Nat. People do that. They fuck up. But at least I tried to fix the problem. I was willing to give my life to make sure you would be taken care of."

"Oh, for the love of God. You're asking me to thank you for attempting suicide?"

Why couldn't Natalie ever acknowledge all the good things he did? Why did she only harp on the bad? His stupid parents had been the same way, always punishing him for innocent crimes like inadvertently breaking his sister's arm or shooting through their car windows with his BB gun, without ever recognizing his positive contributions—things which had surely been numerous even if he couldn't at the moment recall any specific examples.

"Why did you marry me?" he asked her.

"Because I loved you."

"I think you wanted security. You married me for what I could provide instead of for who I was. Maybe you loved me but you didn't really *like* me."

"Look, Seth. I don't know how to tell you this. I mean, I only just realized it myself, but—"

"You don't love me anymore?"

Natalie's eyes blurred behind tears.

"That's not . . .I mean . . .it's more complicated than—"

"It's actually not, Natalie. It's not complicated at all. Either you love me or you don't."

She didn't answer. She just stared at him. And in her eyes Seth saw, for the very first time, indifference. Pity.

"Just answer the question, Natalie."

"You're right, Seth. I don't love you anymore."

The sensation generated by this declaration was full-body numbness, as if she had submerged him in a dark pool of frigid ocean water.

There was nothing in the world without Natalie and the boys. There was no other reason to exist. What did she want if not to survive this apocalypse with him?

He rolled out of bed and grabbed the bottle of whiskey.

"Seth," Natalie said. The pity in her voice threatened to shatter him. "Don't walk away from me. It's not what you think."

But he did walk away. He marched out of the room and into the hall and into an empty bathroom.

"Seth, please!"

The world turned glassy as his eyes filled with tears. How would they go forward from here? What about the boys? How was he meant to be their father in this dead world next to a wife who didn't love him?

Seth took a pull of whiskey and then another. The soreness in his left side flared immediately into something like fire. The conundrum he couldn't resolve was he felt like a powerless victim, yet cognitively he knew many poor outcomes had been produced by his own dumb choices. Fortunately, he was in possession of the whiskey, and after a few more pulls, a radical new idea took shape: All Seth's problems had been inflicted upon him, while all his good fortune was a product of his own design. It was absurd to think anyone would ever choose to impose bad circumstances upon themselves. A person would only ever try to make his situation better, never worse.

Seth remembered how his father had overlooked him in favor of his brother, how his mother had overlooked him in favor of his sister. And the only reason he'd managed to win the heart of a woman like Natalie was because she'd been hurt by someone better than him. Her perfect match was a wealthy man, a confident man, a man who got noticed on the street. Seth carried too much subcutaneous fat and insecurity to be noticed on the street. He wore clothes for utility instead of appearance. The only time he ever truly felt like a man of means was when he was gambling his family's money away. When he was playing blackjack or poker or craps, *he* was the man who was noticed. He was unpredictable and dangerous; he was a mistake women loved to make. Gambling had seemed like an escape from the darkness, but in the end this deception had been unsustainable. The darkness was always going to win.

Voices again. Voices outside the bathroom door.

"Seth!" someone yelled. It was maybe Thomas.

He didn't answer. He never wanted to leave this room again.

"Open the door!"

He reached forward and turned the knob. The door opened. Thomas and Skylar and Natalie stood in the hallway.

"So it was you," Thomas said.

"It was me what?"

"You left the door unlocked. To the safe room."

"No, I didn't."

"Honey," Natalie said. "The key was next to the bottle of whiskey you took."

"This key," said Thomas, holding it up for everyone to see.

"I'm pretty sure I locked the door."

"I'm pretty sure you didn't," said Thomas. "And you know how I know? Because men broke into the house last night and found my supplies. The safe room was unlocked and they took everything. Which means we have nothing. We don't have a single thing to eat."

Even though this didn't seem like a thing that could have happened, Seth wasn't surprised it had. Because everything he ever touched turned to shit. That's how the world worked and the way it always would.

"Do you understand the gravity of what you've done? We could starve to death. Your *children* could starve. Do you realize that?"

"But surely—"

"The only choice we have now is to set off on foot."

"On foot?" asked Seth. His mind was chaotic, swarming with confusion. He didn't understand what was happening.

"Larry seems to believe there's a Walmart grocery warehouse about a day's walk from here. It looks like we don't have any choice but follow him there."

"A warehouse?"

"Yes, and it's being guarded by someone. We may have to fight our way in."

"Fight our way in?"

"Maybe you should give the whiskey a rest," said Natalie. "It's a long way to go in the blistering heat. It's going to be hard on the boys, and I'll need your help."

"All right," Seth finally said. "I'm sorry about the lock. I thought I—"

But Natalie had already turned away from him. She disappeared into the hall, and soon Thomas and Skylar followed.

Seth stood there alone with the bottle of whiskey. Humiliated. Shamed.

Somehow, he had to make up for what he'd done. No matter what it was, no matter the sacrifice, he had to fix what he'd broken.

Because the end was coming. It was closer than ever now.

The only question was what form it would take.

THIRTY-FOUR

Watching Seth walk out of the bedroom, carrying the bottle of whiskey, had been like watching a metaphor for her marriage playing out in real time. It seemed impossible Natalie had ever given her heart to this man, and maybe that was part of the problem. Maybe she never really had. Maybe Seth, subconsciously, had always known the truth it had taken her a lifetime to discover.

Maybe you loved me, he'd said, *but you didn't really like me.*

It was true Natalie longed for security, that since her father's death she'd been trying to reestablish equilibrium in her story. But she was no gold digger. She had loved Seth for his humility and his devotion toward her. In a way she was like a prize to him, a victory he finally secured over lifelong self-doubt. She had loved being his prize.

Hadn't she?

Or had Natalie convinced herself she loved it in order to restore balance? Balance that was impossible to achieve because of her denial about who she really was and who she could really love. She wondered, for the first time, how many lives and relationships had been strained or destroyed because a person was either in denial or purposefully hiding who she was.

While Natalie had sat in bed, listening to the ringing in her ears, she heard voices again. Loud voices. Someone else was in the house.

She found her clothes near the bed. When she pulled a shirt over her head, the smell of smoke and body odor struck her in the face. Why hadn't she noticed the rank stench of her clothes before then?

Eventually Natalie had walked out of the room and toward the voices, toward the kitchen. There she found Skylar and Thomas and a man she'd never seen before.

"Think about it," said the man. "A million square feet of food just sitting there. Imagine how many people it could feed."

"So what's the catch?" Thomas had asked.

"The building is guarded by employees with guns, which is why Blaise needs our help. His friends have already scoped the warehouse, but they need better weapons and ammo to make an approach. If we help carry it all, Blaise will make sure we're well rewarded."

"This sounds like a way to get ourselves killed," said Thomas. "It sounds like suicide."

"As if we have a choice," Skylar said angrily.

"Blaise says there's a thousand people already waiting outside. He thinks whoever is guarding the place will back down if presented with a real threat."

Natalie had trouble following the conversation. She didn't see why any of them would go anywhere with a stranger and his friend when there was already plenty of food here to eat.

"Excuse me," she'd said. "But what are y'all talking about?"

"We're talking about our only chance to survive," said Skylar. The way she had looked at Thomas made it clear something had gone wrong between them again. "Now that all our food is gone."

"What do you mean our food is gone? There's a whole room of—"

Thomas looked at her gravely.

"Someone broke in last night," he said. "They took everything."

"He left the safe room unlocked," Skylar offered, pointing at Thomas.

And that's when Natalie understood what had happened. In another time she might have covered for Seth, might have lied for him. But he had betrayed her too many times. Guilt washed over her, threatened to push her to the floor. The key. The *key*.

"No, he didn't," she said.

"The door was unlocked," Thomas replied. "When I woke up they were already in the process of carrying it all—"

"It was Seth."

"What do you mean? How did he—"

"Seth has your key. He went into the safe room for whiskey last night. Seth left the door unlocked."

* * *

After Thomas confronted Seth in the bathroom, the only thing left to do was decide whether or not to go with Larry and Blaise. But there was little room for debate. Thomas offered to turn on his generator, which meant a working pump and a steady supply of fresh water. He could even run the air conditioner. But the idea of dying a slow, comfortable death enchanted no one. Eventually, Thomas agreed going with Blaise was their only realistic chance to survive. He found two backpacks and two large green grocery sacks that had come, ironically, from Walmart. All these bags were stuffed with empty water bottles Thomas had recovered from the trash. Larry claimed Blaise had means to fill them.

Natalie feared for her children. She feared for herself. Every day in Dallas had been hotter than the last, and she didn't see how they could walk so far under the blistering sun.

"Why don't we take the car?" she asked Thomas.

"It would draw too much attention from desperate people on the roads. And we can't all fit. And the gas tank is nearly empty."

After this Natalie went to the boys' room and told them what had happened.

"I knew that man wasn't his friend," Ben said.

"Which man?" asked Natalie. "You saw a man?"

"I woke up when he was in the house. Thomas told me he was a friend."

"You're a smart kid, Ben. Both of you are. And now I need you to be the biggest boys you've ever been. We have a long way to walk today. It's going to be very hot. Can you be big boys for Momma?"

She could see the two of them imagining the walk as a great adventure, but their enthusiastic nodding threatened to break her heart into little pieces.

When Natalie returned to the kitchen, Seth was there. He seemed to have composed himself, but he was clearly still drunk.

"I'm here to help this family however I can," he said. "Even if we aren't exactly a family anymore."

There were many things to say, but now was not the time.

* * *

"Daddy, I'm hot," said Ben, who had been glued to his father ever since they left the house. The boys were always drawn to Seth in times of stress and it drove Natalie mad with envy. Only the young could love so blindly. What if they knew their father was to blame for this sudden, desperate turn of events? Would they still believe he walked on water?

"How much farther is it?" said Brandon.

Seth looked at Larry, who was on his left, walking next to Skylar.

"Just a few minutes to Blaise's house," said Larry. "But after that we have another, much longer walk.

"Does Mr. Blaise have anything to eat?" asked Ben. "I'm hungry."

"He might have some bacon left," said Larry. "We'll ask before we leave."

"I still don't know how the boys are going to walk thirty miles," Natalie said to Seth in a voice that was meant to be a whisper, but which everyone heard anyway.

"Thirty miles!" Brandon squealed. "How far is that?"

"It will take all day," said Seth. "But we'll stop and drink water and rest so you don't get tired."

"I probably haven't walked thirty miles in my whole life," mused Ben.

Natalie noticed how Larry kept looking at Skylar, as if he wanted to say something to her. Natalie wondered if it ever got old, always being seen, always being noticed; she wondered what it felt like to be so universally desired.

But if the world stayed this way, if no one came along to fix the broken things, being famous would become a relic of the past, just like the Internet and electricity and air travel.

Her stomach growled and her ears rang. Her feet already hurt. But Seth's failure had opened a vacuum of security left for Natalie to fill, and she hoped like hell she was up to the task.

"I think I know who this guy is," Thomas said when they veered away from the road and into the woods. "I saw him at a town hall meeting a few months ago. Were you there, Larry?"

"No."

"Apparently he owns quite a bit of land, and a real estate developer offered to buy it for a couple million dollars. But this guy thought he was being chased off the peninsula by the wealthy elite."

"Blaise does own a lot of land," Larry conceded.

"Is he from the northeast? Like Rhode Island, I think?"

"That's him."

In places the trees were so dense and choked with vines that they were forced to travel in a single-file line. But eventually the seven of them approached a white fence, which Larry explained was the border of Blaise's property. A few minutes later the shape of a roof emerged among the canopy of trees, and finally they stepped out of the forest and onto a wispy Bermuda lawn.

"Nice of you folks to come by," said a voice that Natalie located to a back porch and more specifically a chair. The man's accent was a harsh Northeastern drawl.

"These people have agreed to accompany us to the warehouse," said Larry.

"That's good news. Are we ready to go, then?"

"My boys are hungry," Natalie said. "Do you have anything they could eat before we go?"

She was close enough to the porch now that Natalie could see Blaise roll his eyes at this request.

"Sure," he said. "Let's throw a party all day and leave tomorrow. Or maybe Friday."

"Please," Natalie said. "If the boys don't eat, they won't have the energy to walk so far."

"Oh, all right. I'll cook a batch of bacon. But wait much longer and we'll be walkin' after dark."

A few minutes later Natalie found herself in a tiny kitchen, where Blaise stood over an old white stove, peering through a cloud of steam at an enormous cast iron skillet. She guessed Blaise was thirty-five, his head and face covered in stubble that might have been a week old. The boys and Seth were sitting on an ancient sofa in the living room while everyone else stood in a wide arc around Blaise and watched him cook. The smell of frying meat made Natalie's mouth water.

"Where did you get the bacon?" asked Thomas.

"Cured it myself. Beverly was her name. I got bread, too, as long as you take it dry."

"I think I saw you at a town hall meeting once. Your name is—"

"Blaise Bailey Finnegan III. My friends call me BBF. Where your visitors from?"

"Tulsa," Natalie said. "Thomas brought us here."

"So I'm curious," said Skylar to Blaise. "How do you know what's going on at a warehouse thirty miles away? Did you just come from there?"

"Nah. Spoke to my friend, Tim, on the radio."

"The radio?"

"It runs on tubes and batteries. I seen this comin' for a while, don't you know. Lots of us did."

"Have you talked to anyone else?" asked Skylar. "About what's going on in other places?"

"Couple of hams on the East Coast and one guy in Washington State. It's the same everywhere. The fellow in Boston said half the city was on fire. The guy in Washington saw a mushroom cloud in the direction of Seattle."

Natalie took in a hitch of breath.

"Like an atomic bomb?"

"Maybe. An even worse problem is nuclear reactors. If you don't have water to keep the rods cool, they melt down. And if you don't have working pumps, you don't have water. Since the pumps are run by electronic controls . . .well, you can see where this is going."

"Like Chernobyl," said Larry.

"Probably worse, because at least the Ruskies sealed their place with concrete. Down the road from here, about a hundred miles, sits Commanche Peak. If no one stops it from melting down, it'll probably explode and send fallout all over the place."

No one said anything for a moment. They all stared at the floor.

"If that's true," said Skylar. "Why bother with the warehouse?"

"Maybe the wind will blow the fallout away from us. Or maybe they got some failsafe I'm not aware of. Either way, we can't just sit around and wait. We gotta act as if we're going to live. Which is why we need to get the heck on the road."

Blaise transferred bacon from the skillet onto a heavy yellow plate. The bacon had been cooked so thoroughly it looked more like strips of wood than food. While Natalie made a plate for each of the boys, Blaise pressed more bacon into the skillet.

"Do you have anything to drink?" asked Brandon. "With this bread it's hard to swallow."

"All's I got is water," Blaise said. "In this here jug. It may taste funny but it's clean. Came out of my pond."

Natalie found cups in a cabinet above the jug. She half-expected the water to be tinted brown, or contain solid pollutants, but it was as clean as Blaise had promised.

"Just so all of you knows," he said as the second batch of bacon began to fry, "this whole thing is one systematic conspiracy."

"What whole thing?" asked Skylar.

"That light in the sky isn't no star. It's some kind of weapon built by the government. They did this to us because they didn't like the way things was going."

"Blaise," Larry said. "We talked about this. The supernova is not a local event. It's—"

"They've been working toward this for years," said Blaise. "We're supposed to be the richest country in the world and the roads are like the Middle East. When I moved here from Providence I busted two tires on the way. The government is sneaky and liars and they rip the people off. Where the heck you think our taxes go? To the military and fat cats who run the companies. They got some fancy city in the tropics and right now rich people from all over the world are going there while the rest of us starve to death. From all over the world. It's always been rich against poor. Then came the Internet and us poor saps could talk to each other like no other time. They knew a revolution was brewing, so the fat cats had to kill social media and all that. They had to make it so we was in the dark again."

Natalie got the feeling Blaise had been rehearsing this speech for a while, and as crazy as it sounded, there was a certain paranoid logic to his theory.

"You're talking about neoliberalism," said Skylar, who always behaved as if she knew something about *every*thing.

"Am I?"

"The counterculture in the 60s rocked the foundation of power. Everyone knows the wealthy elite don't care for democracy. Their solution was to destabilize education, because poorly-informed citizens can be tricked into voting away their livelihood. Even social media was a tool to separate us. They mined our data and turned our posts into battlegrounds."

Blaise turned to face Skylar directly. Bacon grease dripped from his spatula to the floor.

"So the actress is a thinker," he said. Natalie bristled and tried not to be jealous.

"What I'm saying is the wealthiest families already had complete control. Why destroy technology that took thousands of years to produce?"

"Okay, but look here: With a thing like this they got rid of pollution and overpopulation in one bold stroke. The planet couldn't take two billion Chinese and Indians driving cars and running factories. So the fat cats built themselves cars and planes and boats that wouldn't be fried by this pulse deal. All of us coulda had shielding built into our shit, but we didn't. You think that's an accident?"

It was all a little much for Natalie to consider, especially when they were about to walk thirty miles toward a warehouse she knew nothing about, carrying weapons she hoped would never be fired.

"But like I said," Blaise explained, "some of us prepared. Some of us are ready to fight back."

"How would you, though?" asked Thomas. "If they've already set sail for paradise and we're on foot?"

"Because they gotta come back for the food. All over the world are these giant warehouses where they keep the supplies. They store it under our noses, in broad daylight, and when they come for it we're gonna be ready. I own a high-powered assault rifle, I own a 12-gauge double barrel shotgun, I own a regular shotgun, I own a regular hunting rifle, I own a 9mm, a .357, a .45 handgun, a .38 Special, and I own an M-16 fully automatic ground assault rifle."

Blaise smiled proudly, but for Natalie it was too much. The ringing sound rushed into her ears again. The force of it snapped her neck.

"We can't do this," she said to Seth, to all of them. "We can't. Our boys will be in danger. All of us will. We can't do this."

"Nat," said Seth.

"Don't you 'Nat' me, Seth! You left the door unlocked! You doomed us!"

"Nat—"

But she couldn't stand there any longer. She marched out of the kitchen and into the living room. Natalie was suddenly sure all this was a joke, that it couldn't be real. She felt certain, if she ventured away from this movie set, she would find a hidden crew that had been filming them all along.

Across the living room stood a dark doorway. Beyond it loomed a long hall that stretched away on her right. From there she walked until she reached another doorway, this one on her left. It opened to a bedroom that was more shadows than light, drapes covering the only window. In front of that window stood a desk. A large rectangular box sat on the desk, a piece of equipment with knobs and dials that made Natalie think of the ancient stereo in her parents' living room. The cylinder of a microphone stood before it.

So this was the radio. It looked real enough, but it couldn't be. It was a set piece. A prop.

Natalie had never accepted the reality of this awful new world. Not really. The journey from Tulsa to Dallas had been a rush of blind fear and adrenaline; afterward, during the quiet days in Thomas' house, she'd been so consumed with personal drama that she barely considered what would happen if and when his supplies ran out.

She heard a footstep behind her. If Seth tried to placate her with more bullshit, Natalie thought she might—

"Mommy?"

Standing in the doorway was her baby boy, little Ben, a quiet child who opened his mouth only when there was something important to say.

"What is it, honey?"

"I'm scared."

"I know. I'm scared, too."

"Are you going to leave us alone?"

Natalie leaned down and looked her son in the eye. She was so consumed by her inability to face reality that she was failing this child and his twin brother.

"Ben," she said. "There's not a chance in the world I would leave you alone."

"But you don't want to go with us to Walmart. Where will you go instead?"

"I'm coming with you. Of course I am."

"Will it be dangerous?"

Natalie stared into Ben's blue eyes. The idea of lying to protect his feelings seemed hopelessly obsolete.

"Yes," she said. "It will probably be dangerous. But your dad and I will make sure you are far away from any of that danger. Okay?"

"Okay."

"I need you to be as brave and as strong as you can. We have a long walk ahead of us today."

"I will," said Ben. "You will be so proud of me. I will be so brave and strong."

Natalie took his small hand in hers and hoped she could be the same.

THIRTY-FIVE

Thirty miles didn't seem that far, really. In an earlier, better time, Larry had occasionally visited a gym where he walked uphill on a treadmill at four miles an hour, a pace that if matched today would put them at the Walmart warehouse well before sunset. But they probably wouldn't walk that quickly, not while shouldering bags full of weapons and enough water to keep them alive. Not while dragging along a couple of kids and their drunk dad. A more reasonable pace seemed like three miles an hour, and any slower meant they wouldn't make it before dark. Stretched before him lay a full day under the brutal sun, an obstacle that might have proved insurmountable if not for the luxury of making the trip alongside the lovely Skylar Stover.

Larry, Thomas, and Blaise each carried a handgun. Blaise had also produced a military-style rucksack and another canvas bag, into which he placed the extra weapons and ammo. Annoyingly, Thomas had come prepared with additional bags and nearly two dozen empty plastic water bottles. Into these Blaise poured purified water from his pond, along with three large jugs of his own. Was it enough to keep them alive for an entire day in the humid Texas heat? There was no way to know and no way to look it up.

If there was any part of this disaster Larry mourned the most, it was the potential knowledge lost in the ruins of the pulse. All the work over the past century to develop and refine the Standard Model, for instance, would be lost to the fight for survival. Hardly anyone cared about quantum physics before the pulse, and half the country didn't understand the most basic outcomes of science, like Darwin or climate change. How did these uninformed rubes expect to survive? How many knew how to grow crops or cure meat?

A half-hour or so later, the eight of them were full of bacon and water and taking their first steps toward the warehouse. Blaise wore the rucksack and carried a Walmart bag. Seth had unexpectedly volunteered to carry the other heavy bag, which was slung over his shoulder. He looked like he might collapse under the weight of it. Larry and Natalie and Skylar all wore backpacks, and Thomas carried the other Walmart bag.

As Larry waited for the physical placement of the group to shake out, Thomas pulled a map from his pocket and studied it.

"So where is this warehouse again?" he asked Blaise.

"Off 75 near Melissa."

Thomas peered at his map as if to verify the accuracy of Blaise's claim. Skylar walked beside him, or sometimes slightly behind, and seemed to have forgiven Thomas for the loss of his supplies. Larry seethed. Why didn't the deserving man ever get the girl? Why did posers and fakers always get the girl? Was Skylar attracted to Thomas because he'd written it that way? Did she really believe all this was a story?

Eventually, the eight of them reached the end of Blaise's long, gravel driveway and turned east on Eldorado. The road was mainly empty, though Larry could see a couple of abandoned cars shimmering in the distance. Already the heat was dense, oppressive, and it couldn't have been much later than 10:30. Hazed hovered around them in barely-moving layers. The air was still. Their footfalls on the asphalt were swallowed by the ringing in Larry's ears.

"It's crazy how quiet it is out here," said Blaise. "I thought there would be more people on the road."

No one said anything. Larry was ready for water and their journey had only just begun.

"I guess none of you people ever imagined how something like this could happen?" said Blaise.

When no one answered, he plowed on. Larry had heard it all before.

"A lot of us knew it was coming," crowed Blaise. "All the economic upheaval, all the racial problems and terrorism, we knew the center wouldn't hold. Those fat cats have been planning this for a long time."

"There's no way to plan something of this magnitude," said Skylar. "Too much could go wrong."

Larry wondered why Skylar didn't volunteer her own hypothesis, why she didn't turn around and blame Thomas for everything. Probably because she didn't really believe it.

Soon Larry saw movement on the horizon, what appeared to be three or four people walking toward them. But something wasn't right, because the individuals in the group looked enormously tall, like giants.

"It sure seemed like everything was on a downward spiral," said Natalie. "Every day there was a mass shooting, or an immigrant invasion, or a virus, voter fraud—"

"Spreading misinformation to own the libs," said Skylar.

"Sure," said Natalie. "Socialist nonsense from an actress worth fifty million dollars."

"This is what I'm talking about," said Blaise. "You're doing their work for them."

"Look," Skylar said. "I don't need—"

"They manipulate you with the media!" cried Blaise. "For a while it was terror. Blow up an airplane or a strip mall and you get three hundred million people frightened for their way of life. The sheep in the suburbs are so put off by the randomness of it that they'll gladly give away their right to privacy and due process."

"Sheep?" said Natalie. "What are you talking about?"

"I'm talking about the fat cats who pit you against each other so they can steal your money in broad daylight. The only time the middle class ever got a fair shake was after the Second World War. But They just couldn't stand it, all these happy people enjoying their lives. Take Walmart as an example. They put all these small shops out of business, all these nice places where you could buy interesting things from interesting people, and now everyone is making peanuts so some fat cat family in Arkansas can hoard a hundred billion dollars. They put up these big boring stores and sell us cheap crap that we have to buy because no one has money anymore. The fat cats are so smart they got us thinking it's a *privilege* to shop at Walmart, like it's as American as apple pie, and meanwhile all the flags and patriotic crap they sell comes from China. People don't recognize that all those low prices are going one place and that's to fat cats who laugh all the way to the bank. And yes, I can see someone is coming."

Larry had been pointedly looking at the approaching group, hoping to distract Blaise from his rant. By now he could see the four of them were on horses: three men and one woman. The men were carrying rifles across their laps and the woman held a handgun at her side. When they were maybe fifty yards away, the man in front raised a hand.

"It looks like they want to talk," Thomas said.

"I don't care," said Blaise. "Let's keep going."

"If we ignore everyone," Thomas said, "we'll look suspicious. And we're carrying weapons. What are they going to do?"

"I don't trust other people," said Blaise.

"If that's the case, what are you doing with us?"

"Good point," Blaise said, and raised his hand to the group.

The man in front, stocky and heavily bearded, nodded in recognition. The group eased their horses across the road until they were only a few yards away. In order from left to right stood the three others: a leaner and younger fellow, a bearded man who was maybe ninety pounds overweight, and a petite woman whose blonde hair was tied into a ball behind her head.

"I'm Kirk," said the lead man. "Where are you people from?"

"Are we required to identify ourselves?" asked Blaise. "Are you operating in an official capacity?"

"Brother," said Kirk. "There ain't no *official capacity* anymore. We are protecting the peninsula from refugees. And two of our men, back at Little Elm bridge, are Frisco PD if that makes any difference."

Despite his aversion to government, Blaise seemed impressed by this announcement.

"I'm glad to know the peninsula is being looked after," he said. "I live just west of the entrance to Lakewood Village on the south side of Eldorado. I own several acres of land there."

"Thank you for that," said Kirk. "And the rest of you?"

"I'm Thomas Phillips. I live on Stowe Lane. The others are my guests, except for—"

"Larry Adams," Larry blurted. "Live next door to Thomas."

"May I ask where you folks are headed?" asked Kirk.

"Off the peninsula," said Blaise. "Is that a problem?"

"I reckon that depends on where you're going. Refugees have set up along the east side of the lake. The park over at Hidden Cove is swarming with them. With this heat I think things are about to get bad real quick."

"What about the smoke?" Seth asked, sounding delirious. "It seems thicker this morning."

"It is," said the second man, a lean, muscled fellow wearing a tight T-shirt and expensive-looking jeans. He looked completely out of place on a horse, like he would rather be on a patio bar wearing shorts and flip flops and leering at every woman who walked by. In fact, he appeared to be leering at Skylar now.

"The fire line stalled out for a few days," the man continued, "but now it's moving again and has reached The Colony. When it starts creeping up the lakeshore we'll be facing a big problem."

As if we aren't already facing a big problem, Larry imagined himself saying.

"We have men stationed at both bridges," Kirk said, "but if the refugees come hard enough we won't be able to hold them off."

"There's not enough food here for the existing people," Skylar said, "let alone thousands more."

"No one's gonna care when their babies are burning," said Kirk. "They'll run to safety, wherever that takes them."

This was a perfect example of how Thomas had let ego get the better of him. What if Lakewood Village had been overrun by thousands of starving people? How would he have protected Skylar? He couldn't have. He was in over his head. All of them were.

"Speaking of food," Kirk said, "we've been asking people to donate their remaining supplies so we can create a ration plan. Several groups are fishing around the clock to provide a supply of new food. You're welcome to join if you have anything to contribute."

"All our supplies were stolen last night," Thomas said. "Several men broke into my house and carried everything away."

Kirk flashed a knowing look at the second man.

"That was probably Matt Bernhardt," he said. "He's set up in the Clark place at the southeast corner of the peninsula. His men are well-armed and patrol the property around the clock, but they'll run out of food just like everyone else. That's when they'll come after us, I reckon."

"We have weapons same as them," said the heavyset man. His smile was broad and littered with flecks of chewing tobacco.

"If we turn on each other," replied Kirk, "everyone's gonna lose."

"Which is why we're leaving," said Blaise. "The situation here is unsustainable."

"Maybe so," said Kirk. "But I can't say I like your chances. We send out men every morning, but all the stores and restaurants have been stripped bare for days. The roads coming up from Dallas are packed with refugees. My men said the tollway was like a war zone."

"We still want to see what's out there," said Blaise. "Even if it's a risk."

"That's your prerogative. Check in with our men at the bridge and they'll note you as residents. The main fellow up there is Billie Joe."

"Thank you," said Blaise.

"Excuse me," said the young guy in the tight T-shirt. "Are you Skylar Stover?"

Larry, standing just behind Skylar, stepped forward. His need to protect her from overconfident creeps felt biological.

"Yes," she said. "Thomas is a friend of mine."

"Holy shit!" said the third man. "I didn't even recognize you. You're a lot smaller in real life than in the movies. How'd you end up in Lakewood Village?"

Larry glared at him. At all of them. As if Skylar could ever care about these plebeians! Why did she waste time answering their questions?

Finally, they continued east, past a few large homes and vacant fields. It would have been a clear day if not for the smoke, yet nowhere Larry looked could he find sky that could believably be called blue. And for the first time during this entire ordeal, he felt a tickle in his lungs from breathing smoke.

No one spoke for a while, and beyond the sound of their footfalls, the silence was overpowering. Larry had never considered until the pulse how much he'd come to depend on the constant hum of the world. Refrigerators clicking on, cars going by the window, mobile phones buzzing, hard drives whirring, the quiet roar of a distant highway, a plane flying by, the shriek of air brakes, the screech of tires against concrete, the lovely whisper of a beautiful woman's voice, a man yelling *Get out of the left lane, fuckface!*

The makeshift security gate was a row of six hay bales arranged to create an entrance and exit. Once they were through it, the bridge stretched before them, six lanes of bright concrete marked here and there with vandalized cars. By now the smoke was so thick the eastern shore of the lake was shrouded in a dreamlike haze.

"Well," said Blaise. "This is it. If any of you have second thoughts, you'll want to turn back now."

"It's too late for that," answered Larry. "Let's go."

As they left the peninsula behind, as land disappeared beneath the bridge, Blaise began to tell a long, improbable story about his confrontation with a Rhode Island judge over a speeding ticket. Larry didn't even pretend to pay attention. His consciousness reached past Blaise's northeastern drawl to listen for the gentle lapping of waves beneath them. Haze hovered over the water like fog. In the distance he saw, or thought he saw, a group of boats on the water. As Blaise lied about his verbal attack on the judge, Larry, grimy now with sweat, imagined diving straight over the low wall of the bridge. He would take Skylar's hand in his, they would slice into the water, and together the two of them would find a new life in the murky depths of the lake. He imagined how they might adapt. Evolve. In such low light their eyes would grow large and sensitive. Their ears would discover new sounds, like the ringing chimes of freshwater fish. The two of them would grow gills and webbing between their hands and toes. Eventually their legs would fuse into great, green tails, and Skylar would shed her clothes, her beautiful round breasts swollen with milk that he would drink and drink and drink....

Larry looked over at Skylar and saw her staring straight at him. He smiled seductively before he realized he was erect.

Bits of conversation floated by as they approached the eastern end of the bridge. A mass of humans had gathered along the shore on both sides of the road. When Larry looked closer, he noticed several men and a few women standing in waist-deep water with fishing poles in their hands.

A young, frightened-looking couple broke away and approached them. The two might have been newlyweds.

"Sir," said the groom. He was tall and lanky, dressed in a T-shirt and shorts and flip flops. "You just came from the other side of the lake? Is it safe over there?"

"People are starving over there the way they're starving here," said Blaise, continuing to walk.

"I mean from the fires. We keep having to move north, and I don't know what's going to happen if we can't stay on the lake anymore."

"First of all," Blaise explained, "that's not the other side of the lake. That's Lakewood Village, and they aren't letting anyone on the peninsula who isn't a resident. You should carry as much water as you can and go find somewhere else to set up camp."

"But it's so hot," the bride said. "We need the lake to stay cool."

"I'm sorry for you," said Blaise. "We have to keep moving."

For a while they walked without speaking, and though Larry tried to keep his eyes on the road, he was helpless not to examine this new world that was both familiar and bizarre. Here was a Sonic and a Subway and a Starbucks. A bank and a church. And in every green space, like baseball diamonds and soccer fields and vacant lots, families were camped under the brutal and still rising sun. Mothers clutching babies and a man yelling at another man and a skinny, bearded fellow playing an acoustic guitar. Larry noticed there was order to the way people had settled themselves, clusters of white families and Hispanic families and black families, an arrangement that seemed perfectly natural when there wasn't a cultural pundit nearby to render judgment.

A little while later they passed a long, open field that was bordered near the road by power lines. A couple of the poles stood near each other, connected by a horizontal third, which made them look like uprights on a football field. Suspended between these poles were three cylindrical power transformers, painted gray and charred near their tops. One of them had been split down an apparent seam.

The damage from the pulse was almost inconceivable. He wondered which nearby star had gone supernova. He wondered exactly how far away it had been. Anything inside twenty-five light years would eventually kill them all, because an onslaught of gamma rays would erase the ozone layer. Even one hundred light years might not be far enough to save humanity in the long term. Irradiation by cosmic particles could cause widespread cancer and genetic mutation that would lead to a mass extinction event or change the course of evolution. None of this could be known, or even measured, which in a way rendered their struggle meaningless. If Larry could get sick and die in weeks or months, what was the point of anything? Why fight to survive? Why not renounce social norms and become a merman and marry a beautiful mermaid actress?

He wondered if these strange thoughts were his own, or if someone had written him to look like a creep. He considered that his sense of time passing had become untethered from measured time. Without clocks or the rhythms of life, if Larry wasn't watching television or counting the minutes until his first whiskey of the day, these discrete points and units became meaningless. Time's passage lost focus until it became the ringing of a giant bell that threatened to shatter his brittle reality into a billion tiny pieces. Timey pieces. If he didn't keep track, he would quickly forget which day it was. Which month it was. Did measuring time really matter when a civilization lapsed into chaos? Clocks and calendars, after all, weren't tangible objects. They were mental constructs meant to organize and approximate reality. And when the math didn't add up, you added leap years to make it right.

They began to see more people, all of them headed west. Larry guessed these were thirsty refugees looking for the lake.

"Look up there," said Blaise a bit later. "See those two men? They seem to be carrying real weapons. Take your guns off safety and keep them ready. Got it?"

"Sure," said Seth. "But won't they leave us alone if we leave them alone?"

"You think this is some kind of friendly morning stroll?"

Seth looked wounded. And green with nausea. Maybe Larry could put him out of his misery. His hand drifted to the butt of his gun. He stroked himself.

"No," Seth said. "But—"

"But nothing. This is a mission through hostile territory to procure supplies. I've been watching every group and individual since we crossed the bridge. Have you?"

"Daddy," Brandon said. "I'm scared."

Seth grabbed his son by the shoulder and pulled him close. Larry realized his hand was in the wrong place and gave it a rest.

The two armed men were dressed in head-to-toe camouflage, as if splotchy green shirts might help them blend into the dense underbrush of brick houses and asphalt streets. One was portly and the other was nearly obese. Where, Larry wondered, had these men purchased their clothes? Did it make logical or economic sense to produce military activewear in sedentary sizes?

"Can we help you, gentlemen?" said the man on the left.

"Just passing through here," answered Blaise in his northeastern drawl. *Here* sounded like *Heah*. "We don't want no trouble."

"Just passing through, huh?" said the other man. "What's an armed Yankee doing in Little Elm, Texas?"

"I live here," growled Blaise. "Why is that your business?"

Your sounded like *Yaw*. The heavyset mercenaries didn't like it.

"Where exactly do you live?"

"I own a few acres on the peninsula, but I consider myself a citizen of Little Elm. This man behind me, Thomas, lives in Lakewood Village. So does that one. His name is Larry."

"All right," said the first guy. "What's your business this far east?"

"We're scouting for food," said Blaise.

The two men looked at each other and burst out laughing.

"Scouting for food," said the second guy. "That's hilarious. You and three million refugees coming up out of Dallas."

"If you don't mind," Seth said unexpectedly, "we'll be on our way."

The second man stopped smiling and approached Seth.

"Who the hell are you, asshole?"

"Seth Black. Do you swear like this around your own children?"

Larry waited for one of the fat soldiers to shoulder his weapon. Silence rang in his ears.

"Why don't you folks move along," the guy finally said, nodding toward the east. "Can't wait to see all this food you're gonna find."

Blaise looked at Seth with admiration before the group resumed their march. Larry wished Skylar would look at him like that. After they stopped for a water break, hoping to impress his mermaid princess, he offered to relieve Seth of the canvas bag. But Seth refused.

Eventually Larry noticed another glut of people moving toward them in the westbound lanes, threading their way through the graveyard of abandoned cars. Some of them were stopping to inspect the various vehicles, which had surely been plundered days ago.

"We're coming up on 423," said Blaise. "It's the first north-south road that would be carrying a lot of refugees. Stay focused and don't get caught off guard."

On their left, a Lowe's Home Improvement stood well back from the road, and Larry marveled at all the people streaming toward the building. As if today was the day to finally fix those leaky gutters. Ahead he saw FM 423, and sure enough a dense mass of humanity streamed northward, more people moving together in one direction than he'd ever seen.

"Based on what Kirk said about the tollway," Blaise said, "I think we should head north here."

They reached the intersection and merged into the river of humans. On Larry's right, a woman carried a baby girl in one arm and held hands with another daughter who was maybe six. A rope of brown hair was tied behind the woman's head. She was wearing a tank top and yoga pants, as if the advancing fires had interrupted her pounding miles on the treadmill. She met his eyes with a look that was both pleading and hopeful.

"Hey there, honey," said a grimy-looking man to the young mother. "You need a rest with that little girl? I could carry her for you."

"That's very kind, but I'm doing all right."

"Why don't you let me help? A woman got no need to be alone in a world like this."

"I'm fine," the woman said in a bright voice. "Really."

"Things ain't the same as they was before. You women are gonna need to learn your place again."

In front of Larry, in an abrupt motion, Seth yanked his handgun free. He pointed it at the man, who was soft around the middle and dressed in a ratty-looking plaid shirt and jeans. The man's eyes grew wide at the sight of the gun.

"Shit, fella. I'm just trying to help the woman. Put away your piece."

Around them, the gun seemed to have a ripple effect, as if it were a stone Seth had thrown into the water. People began to spread away from them in all directions. Blaise made grunting sounds of disapproval. The baby girl whimpered and began to cry.

"She said she didn't need help," said Seth.

"Well, she does. Even if she don't know it yet."

The grimy fellow melted into the crowd and disappeared.

"Thank you," said the woman. She switched the baby from one arm to the other and kissed her on the cheek. "I'm Melanie."

"I'm Seth. And I hate to say this, but that guy is right. Things aren't the same as they were before."

"I know that," said Melanie, looking both flustered and frustrated. "Believe me."

"Where's your . . .I mean their . . .?"

Forgotten in all this, at least for Larry, was the older daughter, who continued to walk straight ahead in robotic fashion. Her face was empty, her features slack, as if she had checked out of reality. Or maybe she was entranced by the ringing in her ears.

"His office is in Arlington," said the woman. "He is . . .he *was* an attorney. We live in The Colony and waited as long as we could, but he never came home."

"I'm sorry. It's an impossible situation."

Larry seethed. Seth had left the safe room unlocked. Seth was a zero. Larry was the hero. Larry was the reason these poor saps knew about the Walmart warehouse in the first place. Why didn't Skylar realize this? Or anybody? Not one person had thanked him for his generosity.

"Do y'all have any idea what you're going to do?" asked the woman. "Where you're going to go?"

"Not really," said Seth, the lie pouring out of him like cold, fresh water. "You?"

"No. Autumn woke me up. That's my baby. She was coughing in her crib and I realized we had to get out. Houses at the end of my block were burning. The smoke was like a wall. I didn't even think to grab my wedding rings. We saw other people headed for 423, so we followed them, and here we are."

A disturbance of some kind rippled through the crowd. Fifty or sixty yards ahead, people were beginning to shift left, toward the west side of the road. After a moment Larry realized a narrow band of water, nothing more than a creek, passed under the road where a bridge was. From here Larry could see the creek was lined on both sides by refugees, who eagerly slurped water with their hands or directly into their mouths.

"Oh, gosh," said Melanie. "My girls haven't had anything to drink since we left. I think we better stop. I don't know when we'll see more water."

"Good luck," said Seth as they drifted away.

"We can't afford to pick up stragglers," Blaise growled. "I didn't think I needed to explain that."

"You don't," said Seth. "Just keep walking."

They continued northward for a while, picking their way through individual stalled cars and the occasional traffic pileup. Larry wondered how long it would be before someone moved the cars out of the way. He wondered if anyone ever would.

By now the sun was directly overhead, and the bald patch on his head felt ready to ignite. Each time they walked past a water hole or creek, more of the crowd peeled away to hydrate. Twice Larry saw women, both elderly, collapse to the ground. He didn't feel sorry for them. Frail old people had nothing to offer this new world.

423 ended at the intersection of another road, U.S. Highway 380, and walkers were scattering both east and west. Others were sitting or standing or lying on their backs in the fields of tall grass beyond the road surface.

Larry heard snatches of conversation like:

" . . . never going to find enough game with this many people. Every family has a gun."

"I wish the Army was here to get things under control. This shouldn't happen in America."

"Don't wait for the government to save you. Save yourself."

Most of the walkers ended up going west. Some of those resting in the field looked like they might not get up. Larry wondered why more of them didn't notice Skylar. How could anyone miss her? Even beaten by the heat, she shined brighter than the midday sun. He wanted to run into the field with her while daylight glinted off grass as high as their hips, butterflies floating on thermals, Larry's convective love for Skylar ascending to the upper reaches of her heart. If he could somehow prove what a perfect match they were, Skylar would have no choice but love him.

"We're headed that way," Blaise finally said, pointing east.

Someone ahead of them mentioned the Dallas North Tollway. As if road names mattered anymore.

"Blaise?" said Seth. "Are you okay?"

Until then Larry hadn't noticed, but when he looked more closely he realized Blaise was walking slower than before and touching the side of his rib cage.

"Yeah," growled Blaise. "I'm fine. You focus on you and I'll focus on me."

"Sure, man. I just wanted to check."

Blaise grunted and trudged on. But the farther they walked, the worse he looked, and Larry began to wonder if he was going to make it. Thirty miles was a long way. And if Blaise gave up, perhaps Larry could assume a leadership role. Maybe that's what it would take to earn the reward of Skylar's favor. Maybe his role in this production would finally be given the screen time it deserved.

He grinned like a madman. He put his hands on his ears. He thought he might scream.

* * *

Based on the sun looming almost directly overhead, Seth guessed they had been walking only a couple of hours. But the way he was wilting under the sun made it seem like days. Ever since they left Blaise's house, he had leveraged all his energy to project confidence and courage, and this expenditure had nearly broken him. His left side hurt as if someone had punched him there, and the sweat on his skin smelled like pure whiskey. His was the worst kind of sickness: the self-inflicted variety. He deserved every minute of this misery. He had earned it.

By now Seth realized his marriage was truly over. That much had been obvious when he helped the woman in the crowd and Natalie rubbed her head as if embarrassed for him. The only thing that stopped him from following Melanie off the road was his fierce love for Ben and Brandon. The more his boys suffered, the worse his own pain became.

He would see them safely to the warehouse, even if it meant his own life. After they were safe Seth would move on. Release them from his failure.

They were headed east now on U.S. 380, where wider pavement and fewer walkers made private conversations possible. To relieve his despair, Seth asked Blaise about the warehouse and his friends staged there.

"The guy with the radio is Tim. He's from Michigan and knew the Fall was coming same as I did . . .that's why he moved to Melissa in the first place. He's joined forces with these two other men who live down the street, typical Texas cowboys who hunt and fish and dream of whichever pickup they want to buy next. Couple of days ago the three of them scouted the warehouse and found a crowd of people camped in front of it, as well as the guards, who they suspect are former employees. A couple of the guards are carrying military rifles. They won't let anyone past the fence."

"If we have to fight our way in," Natalie said, "how is that better than going hungry?"

"It probably won't come to that," said Blaise. "If they was hungry enough, a crowd that size could easily take the building. Which I'm sure the guards understand. The idea for us is to show up with heavy weapons and negotiate a truce."

"What if they refuse?" asked Thomas.

"Then you have to ask yourself how bad you want to survive."

Seth looked down at Ben and Brandon. Their features were slack, their eyes vacant. His heart felt like it might break in two. The heat was like a giant hand that threatened to squash them into the road like bugs.

"Anyway," said Blaise. "Let's sit down for a minute if you guys don't mind. I'm getting pretty hot."

After all the tough talk, it seemed impossible Blaise would be the one who faltered first. But something was clearly wrong with the guy. His gait had slowed and he was listing to one side. He held his rib cage as if someone had punched him.

"Blaise," Seth said. "What's wrong?"

"Nothing's wrong. Just need a little break. Let's have some of that water, why don't we?"

They all sat down for a moment, slurping hot water from a gallon jug, while refugees walked by looking at them. Seth wondered why Larry, who seemed to be friends with Blaise, wasn't more concerned.

"You sure you're okay?" asked Seth.

"Maybe I had too much bacon. I wasn't ready for this heat."

Seth didn't see how this could be the explanation. He looked at the others, hoping someone else would speak up, but it was clear the heat had compromised them all. What would they do if Blaise couldn't go on? Leave him behind? Would Tim and the other men help them if their partner didn't show up?

A little while later they were headed east again, but progress was a lot slower than before. Crops grew on both sides of the road, but Seth, not being agricultural, had no idea what they were. In any case they didn't look ready to harvest, but refugees were inspecting them for edible food, anyway.

Eventually they walked past a sign that announced the tollway intersection. Ahead, Seth could see a mass of humanity, thousands of people, shuffling northward. Some of them turned to walk this way but most didn't.

"As we approach the tollway," Blaise grunted, "keep your weapons handy. Like visible. Best way to ward off unwanted attention."

The number of people streaming toward them continued to increase. Men carried hunting rifles or sidearms or long, sheathed knives. Frightened fathers shepherded wives and children, who sometimes carried babies wrapped in blankets or pushed strollers inside which pallid, frightened faces shrunk from the sounds of footfalls and conversation. Fierce young couples, hollow-eyed older couples. A single heavyset woman who took slow, struggling steps.

At the tollway intersection, the mass of humanity became overwhelmingly dense. Seth didn't see how they were going to cross through it. But soon they found a gap big enough to squeeze into, and he directed the boys to fall in line behind him. Natalie followed. Eventually Seth could see the tollway was divided by a wide grass median. The northbound walkers were split into two streams, and between them, groups of people had set up camp in the grass. A few of these groups were huddled around narrow columns of white smoke. Some people looked up as they walked by. Most didn't.

The smell of these desperate and displaced humans was overpowering, the ripe body odor and simmering pools of unseen piss and clouds of flies swarming around little brown mounds of shit. Near the center of the median, a grim family sat near a bed of coals, two boys and a girl with their parents, nibbling on bones that may have belonged to the family dog.

No amount of theoretical discussion could have prepared Seth for the reality of this many refugees. Cognitively, you could know how many people lived in a city, but a number like seven million was abstract until you were immersed in the reality of it. What had been so difficult to believe over the past several days, while Seth feasted on snacks and played games with the boys, was abundantly clear now: Most of these people were going to die, and sooner rather than later. There was no easy way to feed them. The only sources of water were streams and small ponds, but with so many people clustered around these, the water would be drained or contaminated quickly.

Still, these problems might conceivably have been solved except for one missing ingredient: organization.

Seth imagined all the minutes he'd lost sitting at traffic lights that were poorly timed or couldn't measure the flow of cars. He remembered the frustration of standing in long lines on election day or being bumped from an overbooked flight to New Orleans or being denied access to his bank account when the Web site was down for maintenance. At least three times a month he stood over the meat counter at The Fresh Market and examined cut after cut of perfect ribeye steaks, hoping to discern a difference between them. As if any cut would taste better than another after he had cooked it to an exact internal temperature on his three-thousand-dollar infrared grill. Seth could see now, when it was too late, that what appeared to be an inelegant and disordered culture had actually been a kind of genius, thousands of years of accumulated knowledge that allowed millions of humans to live nearly on top of each other. His daily frustrations and disappointments with life had been misguided. He'd been spoiled by living in the most advanced civilization in human history.

Enduring a hangover in the midday heat was bad enough without his misery being aggravated by fear, but it couldn't be helped. Seeing thousands of homeless citizens terrified Seth. Until Friday these people had been quietly living their lives, raising families and working jobs they hated or maybe loved, eating hamburgers and French fries and barbecue and tacos. Until Friday they had been safe. Now they were eating nothing or possibly their own pets and they were anything but safe. All because of a cosmic event that most had never considered.

Eventually the eight of them emerged from the eastern river of walkers. Natalie rubbed her head and stared at the sky like someone hoping for salvation.

"We should probably rest again," Blaise said.

"I don't think we should rest," said Seth. "We don't have anything to eat and have a long way to go still."

"I need to sit down."

"You said we shouldn't be on the road after dark," Skylar reminded Blaise.

"I'm going to sit down. I suggest you folks do the same."

Blaise angled toward the road shoulder and wandered into the grass. His arm was wrapped around his midsection. His face was pale and tinted green. He lowered himself to the ground and bowed his head.

"I don't know if I'm going to make it."

Finally, Larry walked over to where Blaise was sitting.

"What's going on, man? You thought the children would slow us down and now you want to pull up lame?"

"Watch that mouth," said Blaise.

"We're not even halfway there. What happens if we show up without you? Will your friends even help us?"

"Bring those guns and they will. That's what they need."

"They're expecting you," said Larry.

"Look," Blaise said. "I got cancer in the pancreas. Doctor told me I didn't have but a couple a months. I've been on pain meds but those ran out, don't you know."

"Shit," said Larry. "I had no idea. Maybe you should drink more water."

"We barely got enough to go around. If anyone gets more it should be the kids."

"But we need you."

"And I'm telling you it's not worth it."

Seth glanced at Natalie. She looked lost. Horrified. Ben saw her face and opened his mouth as if to speak, but he didn't speak. Thomas and Skylar exchanged glances. No one seemed to know what to do.

"Listen to me," Blaise said to them, and to Thomas specifically. "I'll show you on the map where the warehouse is, where Tim lives."

"Come on," said Larry. "Get up."

"Explain to him what happened. He'll understand."

"Blaise, seriously."

"And one more thing," said Blaise. Now he motioned for Seth to come closer, as if he wanted to share a secret.

But Seth was afraid to approach, as if cancer might be catching.

"Please."

Reluctantly, Seth stepped off the road and into the grass. He knelt near Blaise. Larry had moved out of the way but was trying to hear whatever was said.

"If I can't make it," Blaise whispered, "I want you to take me out."

Seth stood up. He looked at Blaise and then Natalie and then all of them. Why wouldn't he ask Larry to do this?

"You can't be serious," he finally said.

"I'm dead serious."

Blaise rocked forward and gingerly pushed himself to his feet. Even standing he wasn't fully upright.

"When people are hungry enough, they'll do what they have to do. And I like how you've handled yourself so far. You turned out to have balls. You got to promise me."

Everyone was looking at Seth as if they expected him to explain what Blaise was asking for.

"That's not going to happen," was all he would say.

"I'll do it myself if I can. But I'm afraid I won't have the energy. Or the nerve."

Seth was horrified to see Blaise on the verge of tears.

"Let's just go," he finally said. "You're gonna be fine."

But Blaise wasn't going to be fine. It was possible he wouldn't make it another twenty steps, let alone twenty miles. And the idea that someone in this group might die today, involuntarily, made Seth realize just how foolish he was. His pathetic attempts at self-destruction seemed absurd next to the authentic pain of a man suffering from a life-threatening disease. Why would any healthy human being take his own life? What the fuck had he been thinking?

"Can I at least carry your bag? Maybe you'll have a better chance of making it?"

"Any way you want it," said Blaise.

* * *

Thomas didn't need to hear Blaise's voice to know what he had asked Seth. The clue was in his follow-up: *When people are hungry enough, they'll do what they have to do.*

During his research for *The Pulse*, as he browsed subreddits like /Preppers and /Survival, Thomas had run across several threads about cannibalism. *That's going too far*, most seemed to believe. *I don't want to think about eating Grandma.* This was one of the many reasons why Thomas had considered their movement more like entertainment than preparation and why his own safe room had been little more than hubris. If he'd really believed the shit could hit the fan, he would have developed an actual strategy to deal with it. And once the shit did, in fact, hit the fan, he could have treated that shit with the proper respect and deference. He could have kept the shades drawn and the candles out of sight and he should never have let Skylar talk him into driving to Tulsa. If a single action had sealed their fate, it was bringing six more people into their lives. Even if his neighborhood had been overrun by refugees, two people could have lived in the safe room for days or even weeks if it meant the difference between life or death. But he had wanted to impress her. He wanted her to like him.

He always wanted women to like him.

Skylar, walking slightly ahead, now drifted backward until they were side by side. Her swaying hand brushed his.

"You think he's going to make it?" she whispered.

"I don't know. He seems to feel pretty awful."

"Why don't you help him?"

Skylar smiled like a woman with a secret. It wasn't a friendly smile.

"Like how?"

"You know how."

"I'm not a doctor."

"No," she said, "but you play one on TV."

"Skylar."

"What?"

"That's not funny anymore."

"You're right," she said. "It was never funny. But it's the only thing that makes any sense to me. It's our only way out of this."

"What is our only way out?"

"You have to fix it. Put things back the way they were."

Thomas looked down at his feet. He looked at the road ahead. He imagined humankind as an egg protected by a shell that was hard but easily broken. Maybe cracks had been visible for years, but the pulse had finally shattered the shell, and now the animal nature of their species was pouring out. The mess was spilling everywhere, coating everything, and it was only a matter of time before hungry neighbors began to turn on themselves, before they were forced to consume each other. Probably it had already happened. Blaise knew that as well as anyone.

Skylar, on the other hand, seemed happy to ignore reality, even as they walked deeper into the sticky, yellow slop of it. She appeared to believe the egg could be unbroken, that the arrow of time could be reversed. She expected Thomas himself to do this. He wished he could. He wanted to make her happy. But he didn't believe there was any chance that a fairy-tale reversal was possible, either for his relationship with Skylar or the world at large.

A half hour or so later, they saw another large group of northbound walkers. But as they grew closer, Thomas noticed something strange: Nearly everyone was black. The group appeared to be moving in an organized way, as if being guided by an unseen hand. And when Thomas was close enough, he saw why: Armed men were posted along the sides of the road.

When two of these guards spotted Thomas and his group, they appeared to exchange words. Then one of them raised his hand.

"YOU MEN WANT TO PASS?" yelled the guard.

"YES," answered Seth, apparently because Blaise was too weak to project his voice. "HEADED EAST."

The guards raised their rifles into shooting position and addressed the throng of walkers.

"STOP!" one of them yelled. "All of you niggers behind this line, STOP NOW and let these white folks pass."

Dread bloomed inside Thomas, settling into his fingers and toes. Now he could see the crowd wasn't just black. There were Asians and Hispanics and Indians and a few Caucasians.

Somewhere to the south, he guessed, a terrible battle had been waged to arrive at this orderly procession of hatred. Was perhaps still being waged. Thomas looked up and down the road and wondered if he might spot possible cues, like duplication in the crowd, like artifacts where the scene had been stitched together by a digital effects team. Not because he was surprised something so backward could happen, but because there was a similar scene in *The Pulse* that had been faithfully recreated here.

Both guards were dressed in army fatigues and wore hats embla-zoned with the Lone Star flag of Texas. One guard continued to face the crowd with his weapon in firing position while the other spoke.

"Welcome to the Republic of Texas. We have always been a sover-eign nation illegally annexed by a tyrannical Federal government. While you are permitted to pass, we invite you, as white citizens, to join our great Republic."

Thomas was so taken aback by this announcement, by this bizarre mix of reality and fantasy, that he didn't know what to say. Even Seth seemed lost for words. It was Blaise who finally answered.

"Thank you for the kind invitation," he croaked. "We respect your sovereignty and also reject the oppression of the United States. But we are on a long journey and request passage at this time."

Thomas had written this scene one night after watching a shouting match on FOX News, after the passage of a law in North Carolina meant to disenfranchise black voters. He couldn't remember the details of the law or the argument on television, but what he did recall, with vivid clarity, was the smug look on the face of the FOX host as he defended a concept that any human with a pulse knew was meant to be oppressive. Here was a self-righteous jackass born into wealth, a genetic lottery winner, whose job it was to convince millions of loyal viewers to hand their money to advertisers of aspirin and herbicide and high-interest credit cards, and the most effective way to keep those viewers tuned in day after day was to sell the idea that brown people made the country poorer and dirtier. And Thomas wasn't stupid. He understood racism was alive and well all over the country. He could see it in the angry faces of rednecks who drove pickups jacked six feet above the road, as if to declare superiority by way of physical elevation. He could read it in the bitter expressions of the upper-middle-class elderly, who could remember brighter, cleaner days when those damned niggers had known their place. He could watch it on election day, when hordes of suburban parents piloted minivans to the local church and cast solid-red ballots to counteract the galling reality of a black man being elected (twice!) to the most powerful and important office in the world. Thomas could still remember the joy he'd felt the night of President Obama's victory, the rush of optimism that the United States (and humankind itself) had taken an evolutionary leap forward. He remembered the dignity with which that President had served his country, in spite of bitter opposition and resentment championed by Republican legislators. And of course he could recall the awful night, eight years later, when angry voters responded to Obama's Presidency by installing a hateful and disgusting man to replace him, as if to dishonor the office and, by association, the black man who served before. Still, he had never imagined, in modern times, that a well-known host could go on national television and defend state-sanctioned racism with little fear of retribution.

So it didn't seem like a stretch, during civilizational collapse and with no force to oppose them, that certain armed racists would attempt to reverse America's progress toward true equality. Thomas had written the idea into his script and now it had happened in real life. *If* this was real life. For the first time since the pulse, he was overcome by a genuine sense of déjà vu, as if reality had been overlaid by his fictional version of it. He wondered if Skylar was right. He wondered if this moment was really happening. But the problem with accepting such an idea was it left you with no course of action. What was there to do when you believed the world wasn't real? Sit down and wait for it to end? Behave in spontaneous and absurd ways? Live life as if it were fantasy? And what if you were wrong?

Unless a director appeared from nowhere and ended the scene, what could Thomas or anyone do? If they didn't pretend to be on the side of these racist "Texans," they would never make it across the road. They could be stripped of their weapons and supplies and made to join the group of walkers. Or engage in a very short and bloody gun battle.

"Very well," the guard finally said to Blaise. "You folks are free to pass."

When they were out of earshot of the road, Thomas waited for someone to comment on what had happened. But no one said anything. Even when he looked at Skylar, she would barely make eye contact with him. None of them seemed to know what to say or do.

For hours the landscape had remained unchanged, mile after mile of the same flat, dead pasture broken here and there by stands of trees. But now the road divided itself into multiple east and westbound lanes separated by a grass median. The surface changed to newly-poured black asphalt bordered by bright white concrete curbs. Soon they saw a 7-Eleven on the north side of the road, where a large group of people was gathered in the shade of the covered fueling area. Across the road, on the south side, Thomas saw a sizeable pond that until then had been hidden by trees. Several hundred people were gathered around it, all of them white or Hispanic.

As they walked past this gathering place, Thomas heard snatches of conversation.

" . . .entire area north of the George Bush turnpike between the tollway and 75 . . ."

" . . .Brett told me there may be a thousand bodies at Preston and Frankford . . ."

" . . .I don't understand where the army is . . ."

Indeed, Thomas had been wondering the same thing. The military had surely been hit hard, but some of their equipment was built to withstand a pulse. He knew from research that the Army had even developed plans to deploy small-scale EMPs for warfare use. So where was the military now? Called into action elsewhere? Waiting on orders? Or was the lack of presence its own kind of strategy?

By now the heat and smoke felt like a solid physical presence. At Colt Road they encountered another large group of northbound walkers, and Thomas was dismayed to see every single one of them was either white or Hispanics that were nearly white. What was the point of reaching the warehouse, of surviving the apocalypse, if the leftover world was a blasted landscape where armed idiots divided themselves by color like a box of crayons?

"We're not that far from 75," said Blaise a little while later. "Maybe two or three miles. Maybe I can make it after all. I feel a bit better."

"How much farther to the warehouse after we reach the highway?" Seth asked.

"Maybe ten more miles."

Considering their modest progress, this distance seemed to Thomas like an insurmountable obstacle. They stopped occasionally to drink water, but even so all of them were suffering in the heat. Brandon had cried off and on for the duration of the trip, while Ben walked stoically, as if the experience had matured him. Natalie spoke to the boys occasionally but was otherwise quiet. Larry was also quiet and lurked behind Skylar, presumably waiting for Thomas to disappear so he could finally make his move. Skylar herself seemed bemused by everything around her, as if she had experienced a psychotic break.

Eventually Blaise began to slow his pace again, and Thomas could see him wincing with every other step.

"How are you doing?" Larry asked.

"Been better."

"Are you going to make it?"

"Fuck if I know!"

Natalie took in a hitch of breath, as if offended by Blaise's language. But it was the first time he'd cursed in front of the children, and Thomas assumed he was in serious pain.

At Lake Forest Drive they encountered yet another group of northbound walkers, where a short man wearing a camouflage golf shirt thought Blaise had pushed him.

"Fuck you, Yankee!" yelled the man.

"Watch your mouth around these children," growled Blaise.

"This is the Republic of Texas," said the man. "Who's crying now, bitch?"

"You're gonna be the one crying if you don't step off!"

Thomas could see Blaise paid a high physical cost for raising his voice, and so, it seemed, could the angry man.

"Is the bitch Yankee not feeling well? Why don't you go back home where the bland food suits you better!"

Now, Seth raised his gun a little higher and leveled his eyes at the man.

"Why don't you move on, sir?"

The man looked at Seth's gun and walked away.

"That asshole punched me," Blaise said a few minutes later. "When we were in close. Right where it hurts."

"Are you feeling worse?" Larry asked.

Before he could answer, Blaise turned away from them and vomited into the grass. Brandon began to cry again, and Natalie picked him up to console him. Blaise's vomit was mainly bile, yellow and stringy, and there wasn't much of it. But that didn't stop him from dry heaving another four or five times.

"A lot worse," he finally croaked. "Don't think I'm going to make it."

"Yeah, you will," said Larry. "75 is just ahead, and after that we're in the home stretch."

"It's ten more miles after that. I don't know if I can walk ten more feet."

"We didn't come all this way to lose you, Blaise. These are your weapons. This was your idea. Don't stop believing now."

"Belief doesn't mean anything. Thomas, come over here with your map."

Blaise seemed to be sweating heavier than ever. His hands shook as he took the map from Thomas.

"The warehouse is on the other side of Melissa," Blaise said, pointing. "When you get here, you're gonna take 121 up this way. Tim's house is over here. You'll want to turn off the road here, on a street called Milrany, and just head straight north."

"As bad as the tollway was," Thomas said, "I'm not sure about taking 75. Might be a bad scene."

"Good point. If you don't like 75, just cross and take this road here. Looks like a state road."

Thomas nodded.

"Now, listen here. When you show up without me, Tim won't like it. He's not as reasonable as I am."

Blaise cracked a smile in spite of himself.

"So when you see him, say 'Ask the lonely.' It's a private joke and he'll know I trusted you."

"Okay," said Thomas.

"Okay. Let's get moving again. I feel a little better."

Twenty or so minutes later, as they approached Highway 75, Thomas could see a large crowd of people gathered near the intersection. He heard loud voices and the sound of an automobile engine. The crowd appeared to be yelling at walkers who were going by on the overpass. Eventually he could hear what was being said.

"No more tyranny!"

"This is a constitutional Republic, not a democracy!"

"Keep walking, niggers! Keep walking, gooks!"

Thomas had no clue how long they'd been walking. Eight or nine hours at least. They had trudged across the outer reaches of a city that looked like America but had devolved into a warped facsimile of her. Had the concept of a cultural melting pot always been fallacy? An uncomfortable arrangement forced on hostile tribes by naïve intellectuals who never understood the fear that lived in the hearts of their human brethren?

When they finally reached the intersection, Thomas could see the noise and movement of the crowd was primarily theater. The walkers themselves, as they traversed the overpass, were little more than disembodied heads and shoulders floating behind a vertical concrete barrier. Thomas saw no evidence of the automobile engine.

"I thought the refugees on 75 would be the problem," said Blaise in a voice that was somewhere between a rasp and a whisper. "But really it's these turkeys and their showboating."

"They're frightened," Thomas said. "They're grasping at whatever seems like order and strength. But it won't last."

A row of mercenaries stood facing the overpass. Once again Seth was forced to explain themselves and negotiate passage, this time out of the Republic instead of in. He invented a story about Blaise going to see his mother.

"Do you understand the risks you take by leaving?" asked the leader. "Repeated gun battles have broken out among the refugees coming up 75, and your safety beyond this border cannot be guaranteed."

"We understand, but my friend needs to see his mother before it's too late."

"Very well," said the leader. "You folks are welcome to go. But watch out for those boys with the truck. They're up to no good."

It was depressing, Thomas thought, that no matter how awful a man's own behavior was, he always assumed the other guy was in the wrong.

* * *

Skylar had never been a religious person, but for the first time in her life she could understand the allure of spiritual faith, how intoxicating it was to believe in something larger than yourself. The only way she had managed to walk so far in this heat was to consider their journey part of a larger plan (a story) that would eventually come to a satisfying close. But after so many hours without a change of scenery, without a reversal, Skylar's faith in reality as fiction had begun to falter. In a well-told story, something should have happened by now. Good or bad, something dramatic should have altered their trajectory. Instead, it was minute after minute and hour after hour of the same, flat, suburban desert.

She kept thinking about the disgusting scene with the racists, the river of minorities being forced out of the city. When they were finally allowed to pass, Skylar couldn't bring herself to make eye contact with anyone in the crowd, even though she wanted to. She wanted to explain how Thomas had written an almost identical scene in *The Pulse*.

Don't worry, she might have said, *this is just a scene in a film.* But Skylar had been afraid to do anything that might upset the course of events. If she broke the fourth wall, maybe the illusion would collapse and she would find herself back in the real world. Maybe she would cease to exist at all. How could she know?

The problem was she couldn't. She wasn't sure anymore (if she had ever been sure) that all this was a story. What if she had walked through that crowd of human beings, prisoners in their own country, having said nothing and done nothing? How could she live with herself?

In a typical tragedy it was easy to know who or what was to blame, and the obvious antagonist in this case was the pulse. But there were more factors to consider, because a similar electromagnetic event had happened in 1859 with minimal effect. In the years since, mankind had made itself uniquely vulnerable to these invisible attacks from space, and who was to blame for that? The primacy of the marketplace?

Capitalism, after all, was a reflection of life itself, of the will to survive. Even an educated woman like Skylar could not deny the primal desire to acquire resources, to maximize her chance for survival. Still, she was not an animal. She was a human being with advanced cognitive functions who knew constant growth and endless profit were unsustainable. And once enough people understood the limits of the marketplace, they should have been able to make corrections. Should have realized that a culture always striving for more would create an overstimulated population with little interest in deeper thought or meaning. By reducing success to sheer numbers, humanity had traded short-term achievements for long-term failure.

Had essentially committed suicide.

Skylar was losing focus. She was losing faith. She was losing herself.

When they reached the east side of Highway 75, a group of armed men stood waiting, loosely gathered around a white 70s-era pickup that had been ravaged by rust. One of the men, clean-shaven, grinning wide, approached Seth and Blaise as if he'd been expecting them.

"Hello, boys!" he said. "I'm Floyd White. Welcome back to the United States of America."

Skylar immediately understood what the Texas unit leader had meant about *the men with the truck*. Floyd was off-putting in a way that made her sweaty skin crawl. Natalie and the boys moved closer to Seth. Larry stood directly behind Skylar, as if using her like a shield.

"Hi," said Seth. "Got a sick friend here. On our way to Melissa."

"Oh, yeah?" said Floyd. "Where at, exactly?"

"Near Milrony."

"Mil*rony*?"

"Yes. Off 121."

"You mean Mil*rany*?"

"Right. That's it. I've never been there but I'm helping my friend."

"Can we give you a ride?"

Skylar heard Blaise grunt. She looked over to see him shake his head decisively.

"No ride," he croaked. "Make me sick."

"I get that, I get that," said Floyd agreeably. "But you could be there in minutes instead of hours."

As leery as she was of these men, Skylar wondered if this scene was the reversal she'd been waiting for. She cleared her throat. She wanted the ride.

"Thanks," said Blaise. "But we're just going to walk."

"Suit yourself," said Floyd. "But I'd take McDonald if I were you. Lots of shots fired on the highway this afternoon. People are desperate. They're hungry."

"Great," Seth said. He reached protectively for his boys.

"You people don't look too hungry," said Floyd. "You got any food in those bags?"

"No food," Seth said. "I can't even feed my kids at this point."

"We know you got rations over there," said another fellow, this one also tall but thicker around the middle. He wore a NASCAR-branded trucker hat. "And if no one is going to share, we're gonna go get 'em."

"We didn't come from McKinney," said Thomas unexpectedly. He'd been mostly quiet during the journey, probably because the safe room had been the sole source of his confidence. Skylar wished he would figure out a way to end this whole charade. She wished he would stand closer to her. "We started farther west but had to walk through that shitty Republic to get here."

"All right," said Floyd. "Just head that way to McDonald and then go north. Road turns into Highway 5 and will take you straight to Melissa. 'Bout nine or ten miles."

Skylar watched Seth nod and push his family in the direction Floyd had pointed. Blaise walked alongside them. Thomas and Skylar followed. Larry drifted behind her, his head cocked at a weird angle, as if listening to a song only he could hear. Their progress was painfully slow, and every time Skylar looked over her shoulder, Floyd was watching them like he might watch a ribeye cooking over an open flame.

"How are you feeling?" Seth asked Blaise.

"Like someone stabbed me with a knife. And I'm shivering, even though it's like a hundred degrees out here. I think this may be the end."

"It's not the end," said Seth.

For a while their walk was uneventful, and Skylar imagined an orchestral score playing in the background: dark strings floating above a heavy layer of bass. Before Roark betrayed her, Skylar had planned to visit him on location to hear the Iceland Symphony Orchestra perform Jóhan Jóhannsson's iconic score for *Arrival* live at the Harpa. But she hadn't gone and now she never would. Instead, she faced the bleak reality of never hearing Jóhannsson's work again, and possibly never hearing another piece of recorded music for the rest of her days.

Her faith waxed and waned, like the wind, like the signal of a distant radio station.

Natalie had been quiet for much of their journey, often staring into the distance like someone who'd lost her bearings. But now she drifted closer to Seth and spoke to him in a low voice. Eventually Blaise joined her and the three of them seemed to argue.

Finally, Seth stepped back and said, "I'm not doing it."

"See that golf course?" asked Blaise, pointing. "I'll stand in a bunker and you do what needs to be done. Then just cover me with plenty of sand. All right?"

The twins watched this confrontation with looks of quiet devastation. Thomas was also watching, at least until he glanced at Skylar to share a look of disapproval. She wondered if this was the reversal. It was obvious what Blaise wanted Seth to do. It had been obvious ever since he said, *When people are hungry enough, they'll do what they have to do.*

She wondered if Seth could. She wondered if *she* could kill someone begging to die.

They walked past an electrical substation that had been blackened by fire, past industrial businesses, past apartment buildings. A couple of times Skylar swore she heard an automobile engine, but the vehicle never appeared.

"I would say just leave me behind," Blaise said, and now he was crying. "But I can't bear the idea of someone desecrating my remains."

"Seth," Natalie scolded. "Please do something. The twins shouldn't have to hear this."

Skylar wanted to laugh. She wanted to cry. Natalie longed for independence from Seth but also expected him to take care of her.

"Nat, come on. This—"

But then they reached a place in the road empty of human interference, an opening of grass and trees and stillness. Blaise looked at it with eyes that were barely open.

"This is it, man. Just walk with me out there. Right in that little stand of trees. Everyone else can keep going. It won't take long."

Skylar watched as Seth considered a response. The look on his face could have been confusion or fear, at least at first. Then a transformation occurred, or so it seemed to Skylar, as Seth's eyes narrowed to slits.

"Fine," he said. "Start walking."

The silence, always oppressive, seemed to swell around them as Blaise raised his hand.

"Don't worry about me," he said. "I'll be all right without you."

"Dad," said Ben. "What's happening?"

"Just go on with your mom."

"But *Dad*—"

"I said go *on*, Ben."

Natalie ushered her sons forward. She rubbed her head as if suffering from a migraine. Thomas seemed to linger as if he were required to say something profound, but finally he turned and followed Natalie. Larry approached Skylar and whispered in her ear.

"Intense, isn't it? This scene?"

She recoiled. She could have spit on him.

"What?" he said. "I realized you were right about all this. I'm on your side."

"I don't have a side," she hissed. "Get away from me."

He looked at the ground, wounded, and then slithered toward Blaise.

"Is there anything I can do?" Larry asked.

"Nah. You done enough already. Just make sure you tell Tim what I told you. So he trusts you. Got it?"

"Sure. But Blaise, I mean, do you want *me* to—"

"Nah. Seth needs this more than you. He's been searchin' for redemption."

Larry gestured to Skylar, beckoning her to follow him. She replied with a look so threatening that he gave up and started toward the others.

Now she was left alone to watch the two men wander away from the road.

"I'll catch up with you in a bit," Seth said to her in a determined voice. "It'll be all right."

But if Seth expected her to walk away while he disappeared into the trees to shoot a man, he was fooling himself. Because this was it. This was the end of a very long scene, and Skylar was going to witness it. She wanted to be propelled into a grand, final act where the horror of this world would be resolved. Where all would be revealed. When Seth and Blaise were almost out of sight, Skylar stepped off the road surface and moved toward the edge of the forest.

The ground under her feet was uneven. The weeds were wispy and grew to hip level. A fine haze hovered in the air, as if immune to gravity. Skylar imagined what the ending might look like, how the final reversal would take shape. She lost her focus and could no longer see the two men. She couldn't hear them, either. She stopped and listened. Nothing. Seth and Blaise might have disappeared.

Eventually she leaned against a tree, and that's when she saw the two of them barely twenty feet away. Blaise stood a few yards ahead of Seth, facing away from him. Birds chirped and sang in the trees around her. A string section of cicadas rose like a wall.

"*Will you just do it already?*" cried Blaise.

"You don't want to say anything?" answered Seth. "You want me to just shoot?"

"Please just get it over with. I'm about to lose my nerve. You don't even have to dig a hole. Just cover me well enough that—"

"You boys aren't a couple of queers, are ya?" yelled a voice.

Skylar whirled around. She couldn't see anyone, but whoever had yelled sounded like Floyd . . .which was both unexpected and the perfect complication for this awful scene.

"Oh, God," said Blaise. "This is no good. No good."

"Just leave us alone!" yelled Seth in a general direction that made it clear he couldn't place Floyd's location, either.

"Can't do that," said the voice. "You're getting ready to shoot your man, are you not?"

"That's not your business!" yelled Seth.

"It's my business when my boys are starving. There ain't no reason why you can't turn your man over when he's passed."

Blaise moaned. He dropped to his knees and then sat down.

"What difference does it make to you?" yelled Floyd, who sounded as if he were closer now, though Skylar hadn't heard any movement. "Once he's dead, what does it matter?"

"It matters to him. Can't you find anything else to eat? It's too soon for this kind of thing."

"The stores are empty, and all the ranchers have pulled their livestock indoors. Or they've hired armed guards. And there ain't enough wild game to go around. You need to make a good decision here, or I won't be asking anymore. Understand?"

Blaise tugged on Seth's shoelaces.

"Come on, man. Don't let them do it."

"I won't. I won't."

"This is the way it's going to go," said Floyd. "You take care of your man like you already planned, and then you turn him over to us. In return, we'll drive your group to Melissa."

Skylar could see it now. They were rescued. Daylight was already beginning to fade and there was no other way to reach their destination before dark.

"Please," said Blaise. "Please don't let them have me."

Skylar watched as Seth turned back around. He raised the gun from his side and pointed it at Blaise. Pointed it at his face. Skylar took in a hitch of breath, and though she wanted to look away, she didn't. Because the entire point of coming out here was to witness the reversal, was it not? To solidify her faith? To know for sure this was a film? A fever dream?

"I've changed my mind," said Blaise. "I think I can make it. Let's keep walking and maybe . . ."

Seth's hand shook but he did not lower his weapon. A cold look came over his face, as if he could no longer hear what Blaise was saying. For that matter, neither could Skylar. She watched the weapon shimmy and shiver and she wondered if Seth would—

The sound of the gun was like the slam of a door, sudden and irrevocable. Blaise's body jerked as if he'd been hit by a baseball bat. Blood and bone burst out of the back of his skull in a fine red spray that made Skylar go weak in the knees. The body toppled over. Its arms jerked and its hands grasped as if reaching for someone. Skylar knelt and threw up. She moaned and wailed and wished she were dead.

Which was a terrible problem because she had never been more afraid to die.

The world couldn't be a film. Or a dream. It didn't seem possible that Blaise's death had been artificial. It had to be real. Which meant she was going to die. Death was the only true reality.

"Is it done?" said Floyd.

"It's done," answered Seth.

"Good. I'll send men over to get the body."

Skylar heard crunching grass and then Seth was standing over her.

"I told you to follow the others," he said coldly. "I'm not sure why you wanted to see something like this."

A little while later, after harsh, whispering negotiation between Natalie and Seth, the seven of them and Floyd climbed into the bed of the pickup. The other men rode up front with Blaise, whose body had been cruelly folded into the passenger seat. A shirt had been wrapped around his head and was dark with blood.

"We ain't bad men," said Floyd, casting an eye at the twins. "It's not like we go after innocent people. But if someone is going to check out anyway, I don't see the harm."

"You're right," said Seth. He sounded to Skylar like he was reciting someone else's dialogue. "If they're checked out already, what's the harm?"

Skylar stared at the smoky sunset and swallowed her nausea. To distract herself from reality she conjured the echoing choir of *Fordlandia*, another Jóhannsson orchestral masterpiece, meant to evoke Henry Ford's failed experiment to create a modern, capitalistic Utopia in the Amazonian jungle of Brazil. Jóhannsson's intent (she'd read on his Web site) had been to juxtapose the human hunger for technological progress with the magnificence of nature reclaiming itself. It seemed to Skylar that the rise and fall of Fordlândia was analogous to what was happening now, as modern society was quietly but violently shut down by the pulse. She wondered why humans continued to believe they could bend the world to their will when the opposite had always proven true. She wondered how she could have ever deluded herself into believing life was a film.

Floyd went on to explain, in coded language, how he and his men had acquired their other victims. He tried to elaborate about the cooking and cleaning process, but his limited vocabulary fell short of the poetry required to conceal the truth from two young boys. Eventually Floyd gave up and allowed them to suffer the remainder of the ride in peace.

When they reached Milrany, Floyd asked Seth where to turn next.

"We'll just get out here," Seth said. "I need to figure out how to explain this to Blaise's mom."

"Sure," said Floyd. "But can I ask you one question?"

"Of course."

"Where you going with all them guns? Because I know you wasn't bringing them to anyone's mom."

Skylar watched as Seth invented an answer. He smiled like a man who'd forgotten he was human.

"We're going to start our own republic."

"In that case," Floyd said. "Maybe we'll come by later and see how it's going. 'Cause maybe we want to start our own as well."

They climbed out of the pickup truck. Seth, Thomas, and Larry shouldered bags, and the group began walking northward. Fifteen minutes later, as the sun dipped below the horizon, they knocked on the door to Tim's house. Larry recited the words Blaise had given them, and the door opened.

The scene ended.

Just in time for the flame of Skylar's faith to wink out completely.

THIRTY-SIX

My Diary: Natalie Black
May 20, 202-

S omething is wrong with me.

For a while, I thought this ringing sound was my imagination. Then I decided it was a temporary thing induced by stress. Don't people get that? Tinitus? Is that how you even spell it?

But once we started walking, the ringing got a lot worse. Maybe it's the heat. Maybe it's exhaustion. All I know is I can't ignore it any longer. I have to face the reality that I could be sick. And in this new world, there are no hospitals, no doctors to call, no searching for your symptoms on Google. All you can do is wait and hope for the best.

Seth will have to take care of the boys if something happens to me, but what exactly will he do in a world where men like that awful Floyd are willing to eat humans? It hasn't even been a full week since the pulse. It shouldn't be like this yet, but it is because there are so many people who have nothing. So many people forced out of their homes by fire or hunger or pure desperation. I realize now Thomas could never have protected his supplies, not indefinitely. There are just too many people. Too many people.

I was afraid Tim wouldn't let us in, but Blaise's trick worked after all. Tim is a small man with silvery hair and a spooky smile. He showed us to his living room, where we all collapsed to the floor. He brought us peanuts and beef jerky and water. Normally I would never eat beef jerky, but a girl can't help it when she's as hungry as I was.

While we were eating, Seth explained what happened to Blaise, but it turned out Tim already knew about the cancer. It's part of the reason they wanted to recruit help, in case Blaise couldn't make it all the way. You can tell Tim is impressed by the way Seth took charge, and especially how he was man enough to give Blaise relief at the end. So far, no one has said anything about Floyd and his cannibal friends. What's the point?

I'm proud of Seth for rising to the occasion again, like on the day of the pulse, when he took us to buy groceries. But I'm afraid it won't last. I've come to understand there's something inside that won't let him stay the course. In times of stress he is as good as they come, but Seth doesn't know what to do when everything is quiet. He's partial to noise.

Like this noise in my ears. Sometimes it hurts and sometimes it makes me feel alive. Focused. Like I could run a four-minute mile or solve a complex algebra problem or see the look on someone's face from ten miles away. I know that sounds crazy, but I don't know how else to describe it. Or maybe I feel this way because, for the first time in my life, I know who I am.

After we ate, I asked Tim if I could put the boys down somewhere. He showed me to a room with a double bed, and when I checked on them a few minutes later, they were both out cold. Poor things.

Afterward, Tim explained how his group had visited the warehouse three times to scout its defense. Most of the guards, they believe, are out front where the crowd of hungry people is gathered. The back side of the property is surrounded by trees, and yesterday, during a shift change, they realized a sniper was posted on the warehouse roof. I can hardly believe that. It's like we're at war over a Walmart. And Tim says our best chance to get into the warehouse is from the back. Which is where the sniper is. Which scares me to death.

It was several hours past dark when someone knocked hard on the door. I had fallen asleep on the couch and nearly jumped out of my skin. It turned out these were Tim's friends, Billy and Miguel, who had been scouting the warehouse again. They were so nervous and excited they could barely talk. Apparently, while prowling behind the building, they heard someone talking and then a gunshot. A little while later they found bodies, three that had been dead for a while and one guy who had just been shot. They don't know if it was a fight between the guards or if someone else is also scouting the warehouse.

I'll tell you what I know. I'm terrified. People are dying. My husband put a man down like a dog, a man Floyd and his friends are probably eating right now. Just awful.

I've been trying to put all this out of my mind, pretend like it isn't happening. The whole reason we came here is to survive, but so far the warehouse seems like nothing but death. This is a place I'm supposed to take my children?

In the morning, Billy and Miguel and Tim want to fire at the sniper to provide cover for a second, stealth group. Seth and Thomas prefer to make contact with the sniper first, like try to negotiate a peaceful approach. Neither of these options sound very good to me. I don't think there's any way we'll get inside the warehouse alive.

Larry spent much of this discussion rubbing his ears, or staring at the ceiling, which is strange because typically he can't take his eyes off Skylar. I'm beginning to wonder if something is wrong with him. What if I'm not alone? What if Larry hears it too, this ringing? I would ask him about it if he weren't so creepy, and if I weren't so frightened.

I never heard any ringing before all this, which makes me wonder if the pulse affected my mind somehow. Don't our bodies use electricity to send signals to and from the brain? Since the pulse broke all the electrical things, does that mean it broke me, too?

As the night wore on, I wondered if these men couldn't agree on a plan because none of them wanted to put themselves in harm's way. And men are like that. All talk talk talk. You brag about your guns, about how tough you are, but unless you're a soldier with field expertise, you don't know what real battle is like. It makes you sound ridiculous. And if you're reading this, and you're one of those Second Amendment wackos, then yes, I'm talking to you.

I haven't bathed in a week. I'm grimy and sweaty and I'm sure I smell like a wild animal. I'm sure we all do, but no one seems to notice anymore.

Eventually a plan was agreed upon: In the morning, Billy will approach the building from the front, where the crowd is, and attempt to reason with the guards. He believes they'll relent if faced with a real threat.

"Let's give them one chance to back down," Billy told us. "If he declines, we regroup behind the warehouse and mount an assault."

Even though no one asked my opinion, I explained the boys would go nowhere near the warehouse until we know for sure it's safe. To my relief, the men agreed. They plan to leave the boys with Skylar and me deep in the trees until the situation is stable.

I'm so happy when the boys are asleep, because I can't bear for them to endure this suffering. I'm afraid they are going to be scarred for life.

But if tomorrow isn't the end, maybe those scars are what they'll need to survive.

THIRTY-SEVEN

The sun was still hidden by housetops when they stepped out Tim's front door. The smoke in the sky was thicker than Thomas had ever seen it and the air carried an awful chemical odor. Twelve hours of walking in the heat had taken a toll on him, on all of them, but after a few hours of sleep his body felt halfway normal again.

His mind did not.

The warehouse, Tim explained, was about two miles away. They walked past empty farmland and then turned south onto a narrow, two-lane blacktop that took them along a lone row of houses. Ahead, a dark black cloud climbed toward the sky. To Thomas it looked like a massive, approaching tornado.

"What happened there?" he asked.

"Tire chipping plant," said Miguel. "My friend who works there told me to take the family and run if the place ever caught fire."

"I have a feeling we'll be on the move soon," Billy said ominously. "Warehouse or no warehouse."

As they approached the last house in the row, Thomas saw someone had scrawled a message with black spray paint on the broken and crooked garage door:

DONT HORD YOURE
FOOD MOTHERFUCKER

Then they turned northeast, where a loose and continuous group of walkers seemed to be headed for the warehouse. The building was so tall Thomas could already see the white shape of it above the tree line. A few minutes later they departed the highway and turned north, except for Billy, who went on toward the warehouse entrance. After another quarter mile or so, a grove of trees rose up beside the road.

"This is where we're going in," said Tim. "We'll stay well back until we figure out where the sniper is today. He's difficult to spot."

Eventually Tim stopped in a small clearing, shaped like an oval, smoldering with smoke-dimmed sunlight.

"We'll wait here for Billy," he said and stood next to Miguel.

Which sounded like an innocent and simple task, but soon the twins' eyes looked feral and they shifted restlessly on their feet. Natalie bit her nails. Larry seemed captivated by the rolling clouds of smoke. Skylar looked lost, as if she had disconnected from reality. Seth watched the warehouse with the precision of a military veteran.

The murmuring of the crowd floated toward them. Thomas found himself wondering, if real life was a script, how he might write these final few scenes. Because after everything that had happened, like traveling to Tulsa and back, like the theft of his food supplies, after yesterday's journey to Melissa, it was obvious the end was near. They would gain access to the warehouse or they wouldn't. There would be food and water or there wouldn't. But whatever happened over the next couple of scenes would probably decide the outcome. And in this case there was no studio executive ready to impose a happy ending. No profit to be made or stakeholders to please. Which meant this story was free to reach the conclusion it deserved. Every film, after all, was a question answered by its ending. If you wanted to write something important, something true, you were obligated to deliver honesty . . .even if the truth left moviegoers feeling devastated. Even if your most endearing characters didn't survive.

Even if you were the kind of writer who could never be honest with himself.

"Dad," Brandon eventually said. "I don't feel so good."

"Me, either," said Ben. "My stomach is yucky and I'm kinda dizzy."

"Hold on," Natalie whispered. "I think someone may be coming."

"You're right," Tim said. "There may be a patrol in the trees."

Tim was looking in exactly the opposite direction from where they had parted ways with Billy, which meant it probably wasn't him.

Eventually, Thomas heard what sounded like steps crunching through leaves and twigs. Was it a warehouse guard? Would he fire at them? How would a bullet feel when it tore into you? As a screenwriter Thomas had never written the interior suffering of his characters. Those details were left to a director and his actors.

The unknown person wasn't trying to be quiet, and soon they realized he was a lone refugee. Tim put up his hand and called out to him.

"You there!" he said. "What's your business here?"

"Help me," said the man. "I need help."

Tim crept forward with his weapon at the ready and motioned for the rest of them to stay back.

"If you need help," Tim said, "come this way with your hands in the air."

"Please," said the man. "I was supposed to be back days ago, but there was trouble at Marie's. Anthony knows me. I'm Jimmy."

Eventually the man was close enough that Thomas could see he'd been beaten and his arms haphazardly bandaged.

"What do you mean?" Tim asked. "Why were you supposed to come back here?"

"Do you guys not work in the warehouse?"

"No," said Tim. "We're here to get inside. Where the food is."

"We did the same thing you're doing," Jimmy croaked, obviously in pain. "We came here with guns and fought our way in."

"Why the hell did you leave?" asked Tim.

"To bring food back to the others. We didn't plan to stay in the warehouse forever."

"And you think the guards will let you back inside?"

"Of course. We left men behind."

The next tactical move was obvious. The only question was who would approach the warehouse and who would remain behind. And while they stood there, deciding how to proceed, Thomas heard someone else approach. This turned out to be Billy.

After a brief discussion, Billy announced a plan that did not go over well with Seth.

"I think we put together a small team and approach the warehouse at their mercy. Jimmy out front and the women behind him. Me and Seth and Thomas will each follow one of you."

"Are you out of your mind?" Seth said. "I am not sending my wife out in front of me."

"Finding this guy is a stroke of luck," said Billy. "They aren't going to shoot him, and they aren't going to shoot women, either. Especially not her."

He thumbed in the direction of Skylar.

"What if he's lying?" said Seth. "Using us somehow?"

But Thomas knew Jimmy wasn't lying. That sort of unearned plot twist would be a cheat.

"If he's lying," said Billy, "he's the first one down. We'll jump in front of the women before the sniper can shoot again and pull them back to safety. But that's not gonna happen. I just spoke to their leader and he's about to bring food to the crowd. They're giving up."

"Then why don't we go out front with the rest of them?" asked Seth. "Instead of this chickenshit approach?"

"Because as soon as that idiot wheels supplies out the front door, he'll have a riot on his hands. Those hungry people ain't gonna wait in line. If we want any chance at the food, we have to do this now."

Seth glared at him. Larry looked relieved, like he was happy to sit back while others put themselves in harm's way.

"I think Billy is right," Natalie said. "I don't think they'll shoot unarmed women. And anyway, I'm ready to help. So far I've barely done anything."

"Same here," said Skylar. "I'm happy to be out front."

"But someone will need to stay with the boys," Natalie said.

"Miguel and I will make sure they're safe," said Tim.

"Me, too," said Larry.

In *The Pulse*, a character like Natalie would never have left her children behind, let alone put herself in harm's way. This was where Thomas had gone wrong, and why Skylar had flown here to correct him. Just because women were less physically strong than men didn't mean they wanted their safety gift-wrapped for them. Most healthy humans longed to be valued, to be needed by someone else. Whether you were a man or a woman didn't matter. You contributed where you could, even if it meant putting your own safety at risk.

A minute later they marched out of the woods in the order prescribed by Billy. Jimmy first, the women next, Thomas, Seth, and Billy in the rear. As they marched, Billy yelled their demands in a loud and commanding voice.

"We are not here to fight! But we deserve a right to eat the same as you! We are not here to fight, but we must protect our families! I repeat: We are not here to fight!"

Thomas was so nervous he could barely put one foot in front of the other. He watched the roof of the warehouse and eventually saw movement. There appeared to be two snipers. One scrambled toward the side of the building while the other held a gun trained on the approaching group.

Ahead, Thomas saw at least twenty docks where semi-trucks had parked trailers to be loaded or unloaded. And, tucked in a corner, there appeared to be an employee access door. Billy also saw this door and led them toward it.

"We are not here to fight!" he yelled as they reached the building. "We were in the woods behind the warehouse and discovered this man approaching from the east. He says he's been here before. He says you supplied him with food and water. Why shouldn't we be treated the same?"

"Where are your other men?" someone yelled back.

"Watching from the trees. They have orders to attack if this doesn't go well. We are well-armed. I advise you to help us."

Thomas couldn't see who they were speaking to because of a long semi-trailer that stood between them. That meant the guards couldn't see them, either.

"Approach slowly," the man said. "Make any sudden moves and my sharpshooter will be forced to take you down."

"We are aware of your sniper," said Billy. "We are not here to fight."

When Billy pushed Jimmy around the corner of the truck, Thomas cringed. But no one shot him. Soon all six of them, with Skylar and Natalie now in the back, were standing in front of two men and one woman. The woman held her rifle in a near-ready position.

"I am Anthony Williams," said one of the two men. He was thin and composed amid all this chaos. "Manager of this facility. Paige and Aiden have been helping protect our interests."

"Billy Pate," said Billy. "This here is Thomas Phillips and Seth Black."

Jimmy, who until then had appeared semi-conscious, jerked his neck to look backward at Seth.

"So your name is Seth Black?"

Thomas wasn't sure why this mattered, but he could sense it coming, the big reveal, the unexpected twist that would propel the story into its final act. Did he believe it now, finally? That none of this was happening, that somehow he was living in a reality that wasn't real?

"So what if it is?" Seth said.

"You here from Tulsa? Have a wife named Natalie?"

"I'm Natalie," said Natalie.

"How do you know us?" Seth asked.

Jimmy turned directly toward Seth and smiled. There was blood in his teeth.

"I'm Jimmy Jameson," he said. "You owe me $213,000."

The look on Seth's face, upon hearing this news, was something close to horror. Whereas Thomas was forced to suppress a smile. Because the twist was even more obvious than he might have imagined, this incongruous meeting of two men separated by geography and sheer population. What was easier to believe? That Seth and Jimmy had somehow found each other by pure chance? Or that it had been the guiding hand of an author determined to confer meaning to a random celestial event that had ended the world?

Life without order, without a narrative, was pointless. To desire order was to be human.

To believe you could alter that order was foolhardy. Hubris.

But Thomas planned to try, anyway.

HARD EIGHT ⊢

THIRTY-EIGHT

H i, there. It's Aiden again. Shit is getting real, don't you think? You probably remember Anthony and me speaking to one of the heavily armed men in the crowd, who you now know as Billy. When he told us about the soldiers in the helicopter taking pictures, Anthony decided to send food outside. I went back to the roof just in time for Paige to spot Billy and the others walking out of the trees. My mind had become a universe of chaotic, screaming nonsense, and even as we met the new people, I was working out how to get back to the roof. Without Paige.

269 rounds, remember?

After introductions, during which a strange exchange passed between Jimmy and a man named Seth, Anthony led everyone into the warehouse.

"I need to go back to the roof," Paige said as we walked toward the common area. "And Aiden should probably come with me. I could use another pair of eyes. Something is different this morning."

"I'll send him up shortly," said Anthony. "For now, I'd like Aiden to stay here while we get to know our new guests."

Paige looked at me carefully as she turned to leave. I wondered if she could sense what I planned to do.

"We still have three men in the trees," said Billy. "And a pair of young boys. You're running out of time here."

It was easy to see who the boys' parents were, especially the mother, who kept looking over her shoulder toward the door.

"And your sniper is right," Billy added. "With that awful smoke, the crowd ain't gonna wait much longer. There are starving babies out there. Pregnant mothers."

"But I already promised to—"

"Too little, too late. As soon as they see food, it'll be pandemonium."

"It's pandemonium everywhere now," Jimmy croaked. "We fought a group of assholes who wanted to take Keri and Chelsea away. Marie died trying to save her daughter."

Keri was such a distant memory it was like I had known her in a different life. And anyway, she was probably happy to be a sex slave if it meant she could eat.

By then we'd almost reached the common area. Billy was on high alert, his gun drawn. Seth and Jimmy kept looking at each other in an awkward way, as if neither believed the other was really there. The woman who wasn't the mother was small and beautiful and strangely familiar. I felt a sense of destiny, as if every person present had been summoned for a purpose.

While my mind spun and my ears rang, someone cried out behind us. I whirled around and saw a couple of young boys running in our direction, their faces frightened and relieved and hopeful. But Seth and Natalie looked horrified and lurched forward to intercept the boys' approach. Behind them marched three more men.

"I told you to wait in the trees," Billy said.

"They wouldn't wait," growled one of the new men.

Two of these guys were carrying military rifles and looked ready for anything, but the other seemed more like a college professor. His eyes were wild and uncertain. Afraid.

Seth pushed the boys toward their mother and said this to Jimmy:

"I don't understand what's going on. How in the hell are you here?"

"I live ten miles away," answered Jimmy. "You live in Oklahoma. What the hell are *you* doing here?"

Seth nodded at Thomas.

"We came with him. It's a long story."

"I assume you brought the money you owe me?"

"Not exactly. We came *after* the pulse."

"Bullshit," said Jimmy.

"Thomas has a running car. An old Mustang. The day of the pulse, he drove to Tulsa and brought us back."

Billy didn't seem to believe this.

"You have access to a working vehicle, and you *walked* all this way with Blaise?"

"There wasn't enough fuel," Thomas said. "There wasn't enough room. And the car would have attracted too much attention."

The entire scene felt unreal. Not only did Seth and Jimmy know each other, not only did Seth owe Jimmy a king's ransom, but he lived hours away . . .by car. The odds of them accidentally crossing paths would have been astronomical in the old world, but after the EMP it should have been impossible. The only way to explain this meeting was that it was no accident.

But who could have arranged it?

* * *

"This is all his doing," said Larry, pointing at Thomas.

During yesterday's journey, as the sun beat on his bald head, as the ringing in his ears intensified, Larry devised a brilliant plan. He would, upon arrival at the warehouse, reveal to everyone how this awful world had been created by Thomas. Had been *wrought* by him. And maybe on its face the notion sounded absurd. But Larry was convinced, when people saw Skylar Stover, they would be compelled to believe. Her appearance would legitimize his claim, especially if she publicly agreed with him.

The ironic thing was, until now, Larry himself had not been convinced. Until now his primary goal had been to strike blindly at Thomas. But this exchange between Seth and the wounded man raised the possibility that Skylar was right, that the pulse and everything after might be a dream, a story designed by the hand of an invisible writer, an external Thomas. How else to explain this unstable scene?

"Don't you get it?" Larry said to Seth and the wounded man. "All of this is a story Thomas wrote and now we're trapped in it. How else would you two have crossed paths?"

"Larry," Skylar said. "I was lying to myself when I said that. I didn't want to accept reality because I was afraid to die."

"But you were right," Larry said. "This whole scene proves it. And so does this awful ringing in my ears."

"My ears are ringing, too," said one of the men. "It's like a bell trying to beat itself out of my brain."

"This is what I'm talking about!" shouted Larry. "Thomas writes movies for Hollywood. His new screenplay is about a pulse, and this is that story come to life."

He moved his arms upward in an exaggerated way to emphasize the magnitude of his claim.

"Larry," said Thomas, as if to a child. "If you and Aiden both hear the same ringing sound, maybe it's something to do with the pulse. Like a physical problem in the brain."

"I hear it, too," Natalie blurted. "I've been hearing it since the first day."

And that's when Larry remembered reading, months or years ago, an article about the discovery and mapping of magnetic particles in human brains. Possibly they were genetic remnants of some long-lost navigation system, similar to that of birds. Could the pulse have damaged these particles? Reoriented them? Reversed their polarity?

The problem was this explanation did not line up with the story he wanted to believe. Larry had always considered himself a victim. Ever since he was a little boy, ever since those awful nights in the shadows, when his father's hand had reached—

And that's when he felt it, the cognitive split, as if his sanity were a branch broken in two. His mind went blank as he reached for Skylar. His arm found its way around her neck. He pushed his pistol against her temple.

Skylar screamed and thrashed. The boys screamed. Natalie grabbed her sons and ran into the darkness of warehouse shelving.

"Larry," Thomas said. "Aiden and Natalie hear it, too. It's not your fault. It's the pulse. It's done something to you. Put the down the gun."

Before Larry could answer, he heard an odd sound on his right. Something like a laugh or a cough or a cry. He turned his head in the direction of the noise and saw Aiden, eyes open wide, smiling like someone who'd also lost his bearings.

He was cradling a military rifle. A machine gun. He raised it perceptibly. He fired.

* * *

The rifle kicked in my arms. The sound of it was enormous, echoing around the DC for what seemed like forever. Billy and his tough-looking friend went sprawling. Both of them hit the concrete floor and smeared blood like a couple of sponges.

Outside, the sound of the crowd swelled in response to the gunshots. If I didn't head for the roof now, I never would.

"Put down your weapons!" I yelled. "Every one of you, put your guns on the ground or I will open fire."

Larry looked at me defiantly.

"I'm taking Thomas and Skylar outside," he said. "I want to show those people why they're here. I want Thomas to pay for doing this to us."

I could have shot him. With my automatic weapon, I could have shot them all in seconds. But Larry's charade, I realized, might delay the crowd long enough for me to reach the roof. And I'm not going to lie: It intrigued me to consider all this a film scene, the climactic conclusion of my extraordinary life. I was a special man meant for special things, even if no one else had ever acknowledged as much.

"Remove the clip from your weapon," I said to Billy's remaining friend. "Then remove their clips as well."

I pointed to the dead bodies.

"Toss the clips out that door. Throw them as far as you can. Seth, pick up your gun and throw it out the door. Throw Thomas' out the door. I don't want complications. I have work to do."

When I was confident I wouldn't be shot, at least not right away, I backed away from them, toward the warehouse door. As soon as I fell into shadows, I turn and ran.

The noise of the crowd continued to swell. Near the exit, from my hidden stash of weapons and ammunition, I grabbed two extra clips and stuffed them into my pants. It was all I could carry for the moment.

As I climbed the stairs, I devised a story to tell Paige. She was already approaching when I reached the roof, holding a handgun at waist level that looked ready to fire.

"What the hell happened down there?"

"There was an argument among the new people. Two men are down. The crowd is coming. Anthony wants everyone to leave and needs you inside the warehouse to provide cover. I'm supposed to fire warning shots from up here."

"What good will it do to fire warning shots?"

"To stop the crowd long enough for you guys to get away."

"What about you?" she said. "Will you leave or just go full Alamo?"

"I'll be fine. I like to go it alone."

"I can't put my finger on it," she said, "but something is off about you. Like you have no empathy. Like you're not even human."

These words were meant to provoke a response, but I didn't take the bait. I kept my eye on the prize.

Eventually Paige backed away and lowered herself onto the ladder. She watched me carefully, but she needn't have worried. I respected Paige too much to shoot her.

When she was on the ground, I scrambled toward the front of the roof and peered over the edge. The crowd had grown more belligerent. They were reacting to something near the fence line. Something I couldn't see.

Then it hit me. The woman who looked so familiar was a famous actress. The blonde chick in *Darkest Energy*. Skylar Stover.

Larry had taken her outside to prove his claim that all this was a film. And maybe he was right. Maybe my imminent scene was the climax.

I surveyed the crowd until I found the woman from before, the fat one in red. The one whose shirt read I'M A LUCKY DEVIL.

I shouldered my weapon.

Placed my finger on the trigger.

* * *

Natalie kept seeing the image of Billy and Miguel going down in a heap. She kept hearing the machine gun, the staccato roar of it, which was an evil sound, like industrial human death. But clutching each of her legs was a seven-year-old boy even more terrified than her, and love for Ben and Brandon had focused her mind. She had to get them out of this warehouse. It was the only thing that mattered. The problem was Aiden, the man with the awful eyes, who had run by only moments before. She didn't know where he was.

Seth and Tim were still in the open area of the warehouse. Larry had taken Skylar and Thomas hostage. Natalie didn't want to leave the others behind, but if forced to pick, her allegiance was to her sons. What she needed was a sign or sound to know if Aiden was nearby or long gone.

She would have expected the ringing in her ears to hinder her ability to hear, but instead it seemed to isolate actual sounds. Because now she could hear soft footsteps. Like someone creeping forward on the balls of her feet, trying to mask the sound of her approach. Natalie realized she could almost *smell* the person coming. It was the woman from the roof. The sniper.

"Paige!" Natalie whispered loudly. "Is that you?"

The footsteps stopped.

"Paige, it's me, Natalie. My sons are here."

Now the footsteps crept forward and turned into the row where Natalie and the boys stood. Paige was a silhouette. Her heartbeat was fast but not frantic. She was a woman in control of her emotions. A woman of unusual strength. She held her gun as if it were a part of her body.

"What happened?" asked Paige. "Are you guys okay?"

"For now we are. But I'm afraid to take my boys outside unless I know that awful man is gone."

"Aiden is on the roof," Paige said. "You should run for the trees. He's watching the crowd out front and probably won't see you."

Natalie felt a rush of relief, but also guilt. Now that Paige was here, maybe there was something to be done about Seth. About Skylar and Thomas.

"Larry took my friends out front," Natalie explained. "He thinks the pulse is Thomas' fault."

"Why?"

"It's a long story. But we walked all day under the sun to get here. I can't just leave them behind."

As Natalie said this, the crowd grew suddenly quiet, as if taking a breath.

"Listen," said Paige. "Give me two minutes. I might be able to help. If I see your husband, I'll tell him where you are. He can help you get away."

"Thank you," Natalie said. "Thank you so much."

"But if one of us doesn't return in two minutes, run out of here and head for the trees. Understand?"

"I understand. Please be careful."

It was too dark to tell, but Natalie thought maybe Paige had smiled.

"I can take care of myself," she said.

* * *

Larry stood at the fence with Thomas and Skylar. He felt like a king. All eyes in the crowd were on him.

He had walked across the lawn with his arm around Skylar's neck, her back to the crowd all the way, her identity a secret. Her skin was like silk. Her hair tickled his cheek. His hands wanted to roam across her chest, fondle her heavy breasts, but Larry was afraid Skylar would fight back if he broke concentration. She was a formidable kickboxer, after all. Anyone who followed her on Instagram knew that. Larry himself had downloaded every one of her videos, had fiddled with their brightness and contrast to add dimension to the contours of her Lululemon ass. How he longed to please her. To own her.

"By the way," he whispered to Thomas. "I'm the one who sent Matt to your house. You should have let me have some of that curry."

"You hate yourself," said Thomas. "So of course you hate everyone else."

"I should never have gone outside," Skylar lamented.

"It's not your fault," Thomas said. "It's my fault. I never took any of this seriously enough."

Rather than listen to the lovebirds coo in each other's ears, Larry puffed out his chest and motioned to the crowd.

"Are you people ready to eat?"

The crowd roared, an organism poised to pounce. Larry absorbed their power, exalted.

"Before I let you in," he said, "I want to know how you think the world came to be this way. Who here knows what happened?"

"An alien attack!"

"It's God's retribution for all our sin!"

"The Federal government did this to us! Oppressors!"

"No!" yelled Larry. "It's all this man's fault! This rich and famous screenwriter! He wrote this world and now you're stuck in his movie!"

Larry waited for the crowd to cheer louder, or at the very least jeer and boo Thomas. But they didn't.

"Come on, sir!" yelled a woman. "Just let us in! My baby is starving!"

"We don't even know who that guy is!" shouted someone else.

"But you know this woman!" bellowed Larry. He twisted Skylar around to face the crowd, the gun now pressed against the back of her neck. "Why would she be here except to make a movie?"

Surely, when these anonymous nobodies identified his dazzling princess, they would finally be convinced. Larry would accept the recognition he deserved after languishing in obscurity for so many years.

"Oh, my God!" yelled a woman. "That's Skylar Stover! What are you doing to her?"

"Yeah, man," said another. "What is this shit? Let the lady go!"

"Why are we even listening to this?" yelled a beautiful mother of three children standing not thirty feet away. "Who the hell are you?"

And that's when Larry decided Skylar had been right, even if she no longer believed it. There was no way this scene could be real, not when he was forced to listen while a lovely young woman hurled insults at him. Larry wondered how long this temptress had been there, though it seemed as though she had always been there, that he would forever see her face, those big, lovely eyes and that tiny nose and those perfect pink lips. Of course a woman like this loathed him. She had always loathed him. She would always be there with him, waiting to cut him at the knees with her haughty smile and biting wit, her note handwritten in beautiful script, *My boyfriend says you are a FUCKFACE*, and suddenly the ringing in Larry's ears rose up and clobbered him in the head. He seemed to fall to his knees, or the world turned sideways, and still the woman was there, hating him, looking at him as if he weren't human, as if he were a bug she could squash with the step of her foot.

P.S. Don't write back!

* * *

You probably didn't know human screams sound just like the screeching in my ears. Until then, I didn't either. It made me wonder if the sound

I'd been hearing all this time had been a literary device meant to fore-shadow my defining moment.

Dirty humans in the crowd went down by the row. It would have been nice to savor each kill, like the bittersweet flavor of lemonade, but the mass of them lost density as they fled from their fallen comrades. They spread in all directions the way a drop of liquid soap repels a film of greasy water.

The gun was a live thing in my arms, growing warm, punishing me. In moments I was through the first clip and was forced to replace it with another.

My targets were children, mothers, teenagers in football jerseys. A man in a flannel shirt and jeans was pointing a rifle at me when he fell backward, two beautiful maroon blooms spreading into the brown pattern across his chest. No good guy with a gun was going to stop me! And I get it, most of you think I'm a monster, but that's only because you accept the idea of meaning in the world, that our puny decisions matter. They don't matter. Nothing does. Whether or not this world is a movie is irrelevant. The important thing is I am not simply *allowed* to behave in absurd ways. I am *obligated* to.

Something whisked by me. A whip crack of a sound. A bullet.

As much as I enjoyed the carnage, the last thing I wanted was to be killed by one of my targets. By then the mass of them had pushed down the fence, and they were streaming toward the building, which meant my retreat would have to be careful.

When I reached the ladder, my path to freedom was still clear. But in the distance, running for the trees, I saw a woman and two children. The clip was nearly empty, so I switched the rifle to single-fire and allowed myself three shots. One for each of them.

Remember my dance in the rain, days ago, as I dodged bullets fired by Paige? This was the same scene except *I* had become the sniper.

I shouldered my weapon and fired. Fired again. And a third time. Finally, the woman went sprawling and dragged the children with her.

I climbed quickly down the ladder. On the ground, I crept toward the employee entrance and listened carefully. I could hear screaming. Gunshots. I darted away from the open door just in time for a bullet to scream past me.

My spare clips and weapons were inside, only yards away, but if it was Paige who'd shot at me, I wouldn't get another chance. The moment she saw my silhouette in the doorway, I would be dead.

There was no option but abandon the other guns and remaining rounds.

I ran.

* * *

When Seth saw Billy and Miguel knocked to the ground by gunshots, a moment passed where his mind went completely blank, like an email someone had been writing but quickly deleted. After walking so far, having overcome so much to get here, he couldn't believe it would all end like this.

"Put down your weapons!" Aiden yelled at them. "Every one of you, put your guns on the ground or I will open fire."

The darkness was closer than it had ever been. All his life Seth had known it would come to this. All his life he'd been waiting for the end.

"I'm taking Thomas and Skylar outside," Larry said inconceivably. "I want to show those people why they're here. I want Thomas to pay for doing this to us."

Seth understood how Larry felt. A couple of days ago, while he was drunk on whiskey, Skylar had convinced him to believe all this was Thomas' fault. But in the sober light of day that reasoning seemed desperate and futile. This was no movie and there would be no happy ending. It was reality, and it was always going to end poorly.

"Seth," said Aiden, "pick up your gun and throw it out the door. Throw Thomas' out the door. I don't want complications. I have work to do."

Seth could barely make himself move. His family was in danger and these weapons were the only means to protect them. But at the moment his options were limited, so he carried out the orders as instructed.

Soon Aiden was swallowed by shadows, and the sound of his retreat faded in the distance.

"We need our weapons back," Tim said. "Larry has lost his mind. He'll drive the crowd inside before we secure supplies."

"I'll get the weapons," Seth heard himself say. "The rest of you grab whatever you can."

He approached the open door of the warehouse, the place where a truck would back its trailer to be loaded or unloaded. The floor was about four feet above the ground outside. He jumped to the concrete below and retrieved a military rifle and two handguns, including his own. He could hear someone in the crowd yelling. Or maybe Larry yelling.

Anthony took the weapons from Seth and helped him up, back into the warehouse. Outside, the sound of the crowd grew quiet. After so much noise, the silence felt ominous.

"My wife and children are back there somewhere," Seth said to Anthony, pointing over his shoulder. "I need to find them."

"We should all go," said Anthony. "Now."

Seth nodded. But when he turned around, toward the darkness, he saw Jimmy doubled over on the concrete floor. His face was tinted green and his eyes were closed. Seth approached and knelt next to him.

"Jimmy," he said. "You want me to drag you out of here? I don't think I can carry you."

"Nah. My goose is cooked. Live fast and die young, right?"

"Just so you know," Seth said. "I was going to pay. If it weren't for all this, you would have gotten what was coming to you."

"I had a nice life. I got what I deserved. Now, go get your wife and kids."

"All right, Jimmy. Take care, man."

Seth stood. Tim had emerged from warehouse depths carrying a small box labeled PETER PAN CRUNCHY. Anthony held his rifle at waist level.

"We need to—"

The sound of running footsteps interrupted him. It was a teenage girl followed by a woman who might have been her mother. The two of them ran into the darkness, toward the warehouse exit. A few others followed, nodding at Anthony as they ran past. These were other warehouse employees, Seth guessed. Everyone was leaving.

Everyone except an imposing figure that emerged from the darkness, coming quickly this way. Seth raised his weapon, afraid Aiden had returned to kill them.

But it wasn't Aiden. It was Paige.

"Your wife and kids are safe," she said as she roared past. "They're waiting on you. I'm going outside to take care of Larry."

"Thomas and Skylar are still out front," Seth said to Anthony and Tim. "I can't leave them. I should help Paige."

"She doesn't need your help," Anthony replied. "You should go to your family."

While Seth stood there, deliberating, a gunshot erupted. It was barely yards away, just outside the warehouse door. Then Paige appeared near the dock. She was gesturing to someone, imploring them to run. The roar of the crowd swelled enormously.

And then from above, on the roof, more gunshots.

Bitter bursts of gunshots.

People began to scream. Everyone began to scream. And still the industrial battering of gunfire, like something Seth would expect to hear on a battlefield. So many shots. So much screaming.

Coming this way.

"Natalie!" he yelled into the darkness. "Take the kids and go. Run back to Tim's house as fast as you can! Go now!"

He hoped she could hear him. He hoped she was already headed for the exit.

While he stood there, watching for the silhouettes of his family, Seth heard Paige climb into the warehouse from the dock. Anthony hurried over and reached for Skylar. Seth helped Thomas inside.

"You guys need to run," Paige said. "I'll hold them off as long as I can."

But Seth knew now what he was meant to do. This was how he would save his family. Not by crawling into a car and going to sleep. Not by deserting them.

No, he would stand here and fight for them.

"Please take care of my boys," Seth said to Paige. "Help Natalie get them away from here. That's all I ask."

Thomas and Skylar were already running toward the rear of the warehouse. Tim followed, struggling with his case of peanut butter.

"Many people are coming," Anthony said. "I will stay and try to negotiate with them."

"Please," said Seth to Paige. In her smoky blue eyes he saw empathy. Ferocity. Admiration.

"Natalie will know what you did for them," she finally said. "I'll make sure of it."

Then she turned and sprinted away. Seth watched her go, running past Tim and into the darkness of the DC, where Thomas and Skylar had already disappeared.

The shooting above them stopped. Seth remembered Aiden's declaration, how he had "work" to do. The nature of that work seemed clear now. Seth imagined Aiden climbing to the roof with all the ammunition he could carry, standing above the crowd, firing into them, another mass murderer, only this time there would be no television coverage, no breaking news banner, no active shooter alerts.

Just a man with a ruined mind killing innocent, starving people for no reason other than he could. A crowd fleeing in fear, hungry, desperate to survive.

Now, the first faces of the crowd reached the docks. Hands appeared, reaching for purchase on the warehouse floor. Seth pointed his weapon toward the door, but there was no reason to kill anyone who didn't deserve it. These people were hungry and wanted to eat, just as Seth and his family had wanted to eat.

The first man finally hauled himself up and stood in front of the dock door. He held a handgun. Now another man with a shotgun. They crept forward with their weapons ready to fire, and Seth wondered what the impact of a bullet might feel like. The worst injury he'd ever sustained was a broken finger. There hadn't even been pain at first. Just an anxious sense of something terribly wrong.

More people on the dock were climbing up.

"You're the one who wouldn't feed us," said the man with the shotgun, looking at Anthony. "We stood out there for three days. Then you ordered your man on the roof to open fire on us. Why?"

"That man on the roof acted alone."

Anthony held a weapon. He could have pulled the trigger at any time.

"I was just doing my job," he explained.

"And I'm just doing mine," said the man with the shotgun as he fired.

The image of Anthony being hit at close range was something Seth refused to see. He looked down at his leg. Something had stung him in the thigh, the ankle. Something like a bee or a wasp. He reached down to swat his leg, to scare the bug away, and fell over.

Something was terribly wrong. He was on the ground. Fireworks were going off above him. Blood was spilling out of him.

That couldn't be right. Blood was supposed to be on the inside. He wanted to scoop it up and save it because there was no way to get it back. But he couldn't move his arms. They were bound to his sides.

Someone maybe stepped on him, crushing his bones together. He was rolling the bones. Standing at the head of a crowded craps table. A suited man on his right swallowed the rest of his whiskey and dropped $500 on hard eight. An Asian kid barely out of college explained to his three buddies how to bet. The boxman was bulky but observant, nothing distracted him, not even the famous actress who stood at the far end of the table holding Seth captive with her sea green eyes. She was speaking to him. The sound of her words was swallowed by cheers but he knew what she wanted. He threw bones at her. Tossed them against the interior wall of the craps table, little red cubes spinning in slow motion before settling near each other, four white eyes on each surface staring upward, and the suited man roared, the college friends cheered, and Natalie's words finally resolved themselves as if they'd traveled a great distance across post-apocalyptic plains to reach him.

Thank you, Seth.

HOUSE OF THE RISING SUN ⊢

HOUSE OF THE RISING SUN

THIRTY-NINE

Though she couldn't see any reason to live, Skylar was nonetheless afraid of death. It was all she could think about now, the moment when she would stop being aware of the world around her, when Skylar Stover would cease to be while the universe cruelly continued to exist. What a spiteful joke to be given something as lovely as life when the only point of the gift was to take it away.

In her mind the Walmart warehouse had always been more fantasy than reality, and during the journey she had bobbed like a fishing cork, sometimes floating on the allure of an alternate film reality and other times submerged into the dark truth of her imminent demise.

But watching two men be killed in front of her—first Blaise and then Larry—had condensed these possibilities into one. She wasn't going to survive this, none of them were, so now she was adrift.

As they wandered through the woods, as Tim told pointless stories about Billy and Miguel, Skylar thought she saw a moving form in the trees. She considered telling Thomas but didn't. If someone was hunting them, why bother to fight? Why not just get it over with?

When they were back at Tim's, a long discussion ensued about whether it made sense to go back to the warehouse. Even if every person in the crowd had grabbed an armful of food, Tim argued, there would still be more. But Thomas didn't believe it was safe, especially not for Skylar and him. Everyone had seen them. They would forever be associated with Aiden, who had opened fire on innocent people. The mood of the survivors would be dark. Savage. Power struggles were sure to develop, and eventually someone would seize control of the warehouse. Probably someone awful.

Eventually Thomas led Skylar into one of the empty bedrooms and announced his final plan to carry on with the charade.

"There's a lake east of here where I almost bought a cabin. It will take us a day or two to walk that far, but maybe one of those cabins will be empty. Maybe the air will be cleaner and we can, I don't know, hunt and fish."

Skylar laughed. She imagined a million people could be walking in that direction.

"You still think we can survive all this?" she asked.

"Don't we have to try?"

Not knowing what else to do, Skylar agreed to go with him. They probably wouldn't get far.

The roads headed east were less crowded than she imagined, and when they encountered other people, these interactions were brief and guarded. It was frightening to discover how little was understood about what had happened. The farther they walked from the city, the more terms like "EMP" and "pulse" were replaced by "aliens" and "God." Some believed the United States had been attacked by Russia or North Korea or both and expected military allies to eventually save them. One creative fellow explained, using disparate Bible verses, how the pulse had begun the Lord's tribulation period. The destruction of technology was meant to cast divine confusion on the Arab enemies of Israel as a way to stop them from attacking the Jewish state. All this, of course, was a convoluted prelude to the Rapture.

With every step she took, Skylar's mood sunk lower. So what if they found a place to stay? So what if Thomas could use his handgun to hunt for food? He would eventually run out of ammunition, and she didn't care to eat game, anyway. She preferred her steaks wrapped in butcher paper or sizzling on a plate topped by a pat of butter. Except she would probably never eat butter again. She would never see her family again. She would never ride in a plane or visit Paris or sit on her deck and watch the sun set over the Pacific. She would never win an Oscar. She would never buy another pair of shoes or put on makeup or stand under a curtain of hot water in the shower.

She would never feel safe again.

They walked and walked and eventually Skylar realized it was easier to breathe and the sky looked almost blue. When Thomas tried to talk to her, she answered him with silence. She didn't want him to believe, even for one minute, that she was happy to be here. She wanted him to be miserable the way she was. And if that meant she was an ungrateful, spoiled bitch, then so be it.

But when more hours had gone by, when the industrious look on his face refused to evaporate, Skylar ended the silent treatment and lit into Thomas.

"Why are we bothering with all this?" she said. "Why prolong the inevitable?"

"Skylar," he answered patiently, as if to a disobedient child. "I know you're frightened. You have every reason to be. All *I'm* trying to do is give us a chance to survive. I am not the enemy here."

"What I'm saying is why bother? Maybe I don't want to live with you in a little house on the prairie. Did you ever think of that?"

He turned and looked at her.

"I know you think you have a death wish, but if that's the choice you wanted to make, you could have done it already."

"I'm too afraid," she said. "Will you do it for me?"

He refused to answer.

* * *

They walked until dark, when Thomas suggested they stop and make camp. He directed her well off the road and eventually found a spot under an oak tree. A little while later she leaned into him, his arms around her, against the tree.

"I'm sorry," Skylar said.

"Me, too."

"I keep thinking what a waste this is. All we had to do was plan ahead a little. It's not like people didn't know this could happen."

"We gambled," said Thomas. "We gambled with our future and lost. I guess it's how we're wired. We never plan for problems, even when we know they're coming. We wait until the problem is already here, and this time that was too late."

* * *

Skylar awoke to a violet sky and the sound of birds singing in the tree above. Thomas' arms were wrapped around her and he was still asleep. Her mind wandered to her parents and her brother and what they might be doing . . .if they were still alive. She thought about babies born since the pulse, how so many of them would die senseless, blameless deaths. And what about the ones who didn't? What would those fierce children think of the old world, that place of magic and privilege and unparalleled luxury they might never know except through oral history? Would they believe unhappiness could exist in such a world? Would they understand why people with such easy lives were determined to fight over the most trivial differences?

What new superstitions would these post-pulse cultures develop? What belief systems would emerge from the melted copper apocalypse?

Would mankind ever regain its old glory?

* * *

After they shared twenty-one peanuts and half a bottle of water, the two of them set out eastward again. They walked for a while and eventually reached a town called Greenville.

"I think we should go around," Thomas suggested. "There's no telling what it's like. We're strangers. They may not take kindly to us."

"But maybe they have supplies. Maybe they would help us."

"And maybe they would shoot me and take you hostage. Are you willing to risk that?"

That Skylar didn't immediately answer this question annoyed Thomas so badly that for a while he walked well ahead of her. They curved around Greenville on its western and southern edges and saw walkers here and there. At one intersection, a man and his wife were huddled over a beat-up stroller in the parking lot of a Phillips 66. The couple watched with frightened and wary eyes as Skylar and Thomas went by. When she raised a hand to them, neither the wife nor her husband returned the gesture.

At the southern edge of Greenville, they passed an Hispanic man who took one look at the gun Thomas was carrying and offered a wide berth.

"Morning," Thomas said.

"Hungry," the man replied.

Not long after, they reached a junction in the road, and Thomas stopped.

"This is Highway 69," he said. "The lake is straight down that way. I'm surprised more people haven't come this direction, but maybe that means we'll have a real chance when we reach the lake."

"Or maybe the lake is crawling with refugees."

"Maybe. But we need water. I don't know how much longer I can go on like this."

She couldn't believe Thomas would admit he was suffering.

"Even if we stumble across an empty cabin," she asked, "what then?"

"Maybe we'll find a fishing pole. It's a pretty big lake."

"Fish?"

She waited for him to stammer through an optimistic lie about how he could catch enough food from the lake to feed them, but instead Thomas looked away and walked on silently.

There was a serenity about this new world she might have embraced if the serenity hadn't been a lie. They were out of water and food, and from this point forward every waking minute would be wasted trying not to die.

By now Skylar should have been willing to concede that the things she previously believed to be important were in fact worthless. Like expensive clothes and her precise body fat percentage and whether her next film project would be her last. But instead, she pictured a Ralph's just up the road. She imagined large trays of oranges and apples, potatoes arranged in towering pyramids, and chicken breasts laid out in rows, they didn't even have to be organic. That was the high-definition world she longed for. Not this low-fi, hardscrabble deathscape left behind by shortsighted men more concerned with today's profit than tomorrow's planet.

She didn't want this world, but she was also afraid to do anything about it.

* * *

Eventually they reached the northern tip of the lake and worked their way south until they found a clear shoreline. After mouthfuls of raw lake water, Thomas was reenergized, and to Skylar's chagrin his optimistic mood returned.

Against all odds, they managed to find an empty cabin at the end of a long and narrow path that had once been a road. Many of the houses near the lake were occupied, or concentrated in clusters, but this cabin was set well back from the water. It didn't appear to have been visited for some time.

Nevertheless, the pantry was stocked with dry goods that were old and stale but still edible, like rice and potato flakes and cans of beans and corn and soup. In a storage closet they discovered a couple of fishing poles and a tackle box full of lures. But the most important find, as far as Thomas was concerned, was the .410 shotgun and six boxes of birdshot. This discovery convinced him there was a real chance to survive. But for Skylar these meager resources only served to prolong her misery.

Thomas wanted to talk through her feelings. His unfailing support and optimism caused resentment to swell inside her until there was no room for anything else. She ignored him or hurled obscenities at him. But instead of retaliating, he absorbed these attacks and emerged more resolute than ever.

The first time she felt sick, Skylar's mood improved. She'd been wondering how safe it was to consume canned vegetables whose expiration dates were three and four years in the past. But Thomas seemed unaffected after eating the same meals, which meant her nausea was probably due to a stomach virus. Or stress.

But the very next morning she was ill again, and that's when Skylar began to panic.

Until then she had ignored the spotting and cramps, probably because conscious denial was the only way to insulate herself from true madness.

But once the veil had been lifted, the was no denying a very real and terrible possibility: She could be pregnant. She could be carrying Thomas' child.

By then only twenty-seven days had elapsed since their romantic encounter (assuming her painstaking count was correct), but there was no question when this potential fetus had been conceived.

The possibility of pregnancy left Skylar with an ugly truth: If she let herself die, she might take a fetus with her. And even though she believed in a woman's right to choose, even though she had campaigned politically to support reproductive rights, the idea of ending a possible new life in this dying world made her cringe. Paradoxically, though she hated this new world, she also felt a reluctant obligation to it.

But Skylar wasn't happy about the idea of a new life growing inside her, and she took her frustrations out on the man responsible for it.

"We can't stay here," she told him one morning a week or so later. To make their food stores last longer, they had agreed on a conservation schedule that left them hungry most of their waking hours. And she was no doubt hungrier than Thomas.

"What's the problem now?" he asked. "Is the rice too sticky for you? The water too flat-tasting?"

"I think I'm pregnant."

"That's funny. You're funny."

"It's not funny. It's awful. I need more food or else it's going to die."

"You can't be serious. How would you even know without a test?"

"A woman can tell," Skylar said. "Believe me."

"That's—"

All at once his icy stare melted. Thomas examined her as if hoping to find truth in her eyes. Finally, he reached across the table and grabbed her hand.

"Skylar, if you're really pregnant . . .I will eat less. I'll get us more food. We have to take care of the baby."

"It's not a baby," she said. "Not yet. But you're right, if I don't miscarry, we'll have to find a way to provide for it. Like more food and hopefully a doctor."

"So you think we should walk back to Greenville? Or find another town? I think there's one a bit farther down the lake."

"Let's look for another town."

That evening, while they ate small, messy chunks of fish alongside instant mashed potatoes, Thomas told her about his mother.

"It sounds like she was pretty upset with your dad," Skylar pointed out.

"I'm sure that made her angrier, but even before he cheated, she wasn't very nice. I wonder if she really wanted to be a mother."

"Some women don't. And then they're forced to defend their feelings, because everyone assumes something is wrong with them."

"But why have me, then?"

"Maybe your dad persuaded her. Or maybe she gave into the guilt."

"Maybe so," said Thomas. He looked out the window as if answers might be found in the approaching darkness.

"I think I understand your stories a little better now," Skylar said.

"How so?"

"In *Thomas World* you were searching for a woman who could save you. In *The Pulse* you were the savior. Probably because money made you feel more confident."

"I didn't consciously intend that."

"Even so, you need to understand something: Women don't want to be saved. They don't want to save you, either. They want to be respected. And if they find the right guy, maybe fall in love."

"It's not like I don't know that," Thomas said. "But I guess no matter how old you get, or how strong you feel, pain from childhood sticks with you."

"So use those feelings to power your art. Don't make some other woman carry that burden."

The next day they walked back to the highway. When they turned south, Skylar immediately saw a road sign announcing two towns ahead: KIOWA VILLAGE and EAST TAWAKONI. Less than an hour later, they came upon three men with rifles standing in front of a golf cart. One of the men was shorter than the rest, clean-shaven, wearing a ballcap and jeans and a green T-shirt. He addressed Thomas while the other men stole glances at Skylar.

"Can we help you folks?"

"We're looking for a town," Thomas said. "We saw signs for Kiowa Village and East—"

"This here is Kiowa Village," said one of the other men, a tall and skinny fellow who didn't sport much hair on his head but had grown plenty on his face. He looked at Skylar even as he answered Thomas. "We don't accept strangers."

"Will you let us pass through and try East Tawakoni?"

"Not sure you want to do that," said the bearded man. "They had a ration plan until some teenagers broke in and stole most of the food. You can find them four boys hanging from power poles off 276. The rest are starving and desperate."

By Skylar's count the pulse had occurred thirty-four days prior. As bad as things were now, what would they be like in a year? Why subject a newborn to such an awful world?

"Unlike East Tawakoni," said the shorter man, "we run an organized community. By God's good grace and our proximity to the lake, we are poised to survive this apocalypse. We have adequate supplies of food and there is plenty of water. But like Daryl said, we don't accept new citizens."

Now he looked at Skylar.

"But we do make exceptions for women. We need babies."

Skylar felt like she had fallen into the opening scene of a country-fried horror film.

But Thomas inexplicably said, "What guarantee would I have that she would be treated fairly?"

"You have my word," said the leader. "That's the only guarantee I have to give."

"Sorry we bothered you," Skylar said. She tried to turn Thomas around. "We'll be on our way."

"That's your choice," the leader told them, "but you might want to think twice before a famous actress like yourself walks around these parts looking for help. You might get more than you bargained for."

"Then we'll go back to where we came from. I'm not leaving my husband."

Thomas looked at her while the short man looked at Thomas.

"Are you a doctor? A carpenter? What was your trade before all this happened?"

"Nothing that would benefit you," said Thomas.

"Let's go," Skylar said.

"She ain't your wife," Daryl said. "Is she?"

"No, she isn't," said the leader. "If she was, you wouldn't give her up so easily."

Thomas wouldn't budge. He stood there like an oak tree, as if her fate was in his hands.

"Do you have a doctor in your town?" Thomas asked.

"We have a veterinarian and a kid who aimed to start medical school. Why?"

"I wanted to know if we could come back here for medical help."

"For her, yes. I'm sorry to be so tough about it, but we can't take every person who comes along. Ain't enough food. We expect more hungry folks coming down from Greenville and we'll fight them the way we fought off the first batch."

"All right," Thomas said. "Thanks for your help."

He finally relented and turned to leave.

"We'll figure out something else," Skylar said to them.

She wanted to rebuke Thomas for his casual condescension, but by now what was the point?

* * *

Every morning Thomas took the shotgun and disappeared into the woods looking for game: rabbits, birds, deer, anything. The first problem he faced was that local wildlife had fled to regions even more distant. But the bigger complication was the constant influx of hunters, almost all of whom were desperate fathers chasing game with handguns or pellet guns or knives. These men stomped through the woods, cursing to themselves, as if noise was the secret to attracting prey. Most of them, Thomas reasoned, would be dead by August. And so would their families.

In the afternoon Thomas rested on the shaded porch of the cabin. In the evening he prowled along the lake shore, tossing lures at the water and reeling them in. When he was a boy, Thomas told her, he would catch largemouth bass with spinner bait and plastic worms. But that teenage experience didn't seem to help now. And though he offered Skylar most of the fish he caught and cleaned, taking it made her feel guilty. He was barely producing enough food for one person, let alone two adults and a growing fetus.

The first time she picked up the pistol, she was impressed with its smoothness, with its heft. Here was a weapon built for one purpose—to extinguish a human life—and its solid mass and elegant design seemed to honor the gravity of such a crime. Still, wasn't it worse to curse a new-born baby to a lifetime of misery? By now she'd missed her period and there was no doubt she was pregnant.

One afternoon while Thomas napped on the porch, sweat beading on his upper lip, Skylar tiptoed to the bedroom they shared and retrieved the pistol from the nightstand drawer. She sat on the bed and hoped her parents were dead. She didn't want to think about them hungry and struggling against the humid urban heat.

If she'd been recording the days correctly, the date was June 30, six weeks and four days since the pulse. The fetus would be forty-one days old.

She picked up the pistol and pointed it at her nose. The interior of the barrel was a tiny black hole of oblivion. Of infinity. It was a singularity where nothing, not even life, could escape.

She raised the gun to her forehead and pressed it there. The barrel wasn't cool the way she expected. It was warm and felt almost wet, as if it were sweating the same as she. She slid her thumb over the trigger. She wondered about her brother. She wondered about Roark. If anyone could survive this, Roark could. He was a man who never went quietly. She remembered the drunken night when he lowered her to the carpet of the Wynn hotel, in the hallway outside their suite, when he hiked up her dress and shoved himself into her and she liked it. She liked it. A tenant in a nearby room had opened her door. Had seen them fucking like animals on the hotel carpet. The tenant calmly placed her dinner tray on the floor not three feet from Skylar's head and went back into her room. The click of the door lock had sent Skylar over the edge, had sent her tumbling down the waterfall. And while Roark grunted and shuddered, she thought to herself *If I die tomorrow, at least I lived today.*

Thomas had been different. He held her and caressed her and coaxed her to orgasm twice before he took anything for himself. Maybe he was truly tender or maybe he always submitted to the memory of his mother. Either way, the outcome was the same: He had given her a child and now the only thing left in the world was a choice.

Death? Or life?

She lowered the gun and stared again into the barrel, into the round and infinite darkness. She imagined she could see swirls of color in that warm emptiness, swirls that eventually morphed into the smiling, drunken faces of Beth and Deidre and Molly. She remembered how her drama friends had been blissfully miserable as mothers, and despite her reluctance to admit as much, Skylar understood now why she'd felt so empty around them. Because the cliché was true—you couldn't understand the biological suction of motherhood until your body was preparing to bear a child. And you couldn't know if you would end a pregnancy until that pregnancy was yours.

She returned the gun to the nightstand drawer and went outside to talk to Thomas.

* * *

The next morning he walked her to the city limits of Kiowa Village, where the redneck color guard stood waiting. She cried when she turned away from Thomas and was led into town. Even as she was met by a group of concerned women, who marveled at her celebrity and offered food like bread and fried catfish, she cried.

Every day brought another single man who offered to protect her, who hoped to become her husband. There was a playground in town, and in the center of it stood a roundabout painted in alternating colors of red and white and blue, six pie-shaped pieces. She watched children spin in circles, laughing and squealing and cajoling each other. She stole glances at the mothers and fathers and marveled at how unmoved they seemed by external forces of danger that were all around them. She was struck by a feeling of togetherness, of social connection, and in certain moments she could detect a congruity with the world that previously had been unknown to her. The roundabout spun in a circle, sort of how life was a circle, and she could sense—only barely, but it was there—that the meaning of this terrible event wasn't what had been lost, but what had been gained. That maybe the frenetic life she had lived, the things she had acquired, the glittery recognition by the world at large, had distracted her from a fundamental truth. The only point of life, as she previously believed, was not eventual death.

When you were poised to bring someone new into the world, the only point of life was life.

FORTY

My Diary: Natalie Black
July 202-

I first realized something was wrong with Brandon when he refused the Mounds bar. The boy won't touch an Almond Joy, but he'll eat six packages of Mounds if you don't watch him.

We had been walking for eight weeks and two days (I think). None of the rest of us were sick, so I assumed Brandon had eaten something we didn't notice. The boys get hungrier than we do, and they always bring stuff to us and say, Can I eat this? Can I eat that? It's so sad. I try to feed them as much as I can, but if Paige and I don't eat, we can't take care of them.

After the warehouse, and after we regrouped at Tim's place, Paige took us to her house to gather supplies. Like the rest of the food in her pantry. A mess kit. A tent. Matches and a lighter. Extra weapons and bullets. Jugs to store water in and tablets to purify it. We stop on the regular to refill, because water is so heavy, and we can't carry much of it.

Then, even though I begged her not to, Paige took us back to the warehouse. She promised to maintain a safe distance, and approach only if it looked safe, but all I could think about were those bullets whizzing past my head as that awful man tried to kill us. When I tripped, I thought for sure we were dead. But instead, for a reason I'll never understand, he stopped shooting and let us go.

We approached from the rear of the property, the same way we left it. By then two days had passed, and we assumed the building had been emptied or that a new group had taken control. Paige wouldn't say much about what she hoped to see or do. Maybe she wanted to look for something of her father's. Or maybe, one last time, walk where he walked.

But what we found was nothing like what we expected. It hurts to remember how excited she was.

"That's a chopper," Paige said as we peered through the trees. "A Chinook. Look!"

Until then, I'd never known what to call those helicopters with two sets of horizontal blades. I always thought of them as lovebugs, because that's what they look like, two choppers mating in midair.

"There are two of them," she whispered, her voice hopeful. "The Army is finally here."

But Paige was careful as always, and soon we saw soldiers in defensive positions around the aircraft. Others were arranged in a line, relaying food out of the warehouse and into the helicopters. Beyond this operation, a group of civilians had gathered. It was smaller than the original crowd, but I bet there were at least 100 people. Maybe 200. Occasionally, we could hear the sound of someone yelling at the soldiers, as if in anger.

"They're taking the food," Paige said. "But for what? To whom?"

I explained to her about Blaise, how he believed there was a haven somewhere protected from all this, like maybe an island in the tropics. Paige seemed skeptical, but whatever the soldiers were doing was not meant to help anyone nearby. They didn't take any food to the crowd, and when one man rushed the helicopter, the soldiers pinned him down and pushed a rifle into the back of his neck. I thought for sure they would kill the guy, but eventually they let him up, and he hobbled away.

Just before we left, Paige and I saw two more Chinooks approaching from the south. We heard them land on the lawn of the warehouse as we marched through the trees and away from there forever.

At first, as we walked northward, the sky remained a chalky sketch of blacks and greys and yellows. The heat was awful, and the smoke was so dense the air seemed to carry texture. There was ash on the road and in the grass and sprinkled over trees like snow. We rationed our water and refused to drink from ponds or streams, even though these were always surrounded by refugees. Later, we saw a lot of people on the sides of the road, collapsed or vomiting or just sitting there with glassy eyes. You don't want to drink unpurified water, especially when there's ash in it, so it's a good thing we had our own supply until we were clear of the city.

Gradually, the skies cleared, we left the ash behind, and it was difficult to tell the pulse had even happened. I wanted to walk in the direction of Tulsa, to see if my house was still intact, but Paige vetoed the idea. It was starting to piss me off that she treated me like a child. But then, as we approached I-40, we saw a huge cloud of smoke on the western horizon, like a looming cold front. If Oklahoma City was still on fire, it meant Tulsa probably was, also. That taught me a lesson about making good decisions.

We've supplemented our food supplies with small game. At first it was Paige who did all the work, like killing rabbits and possums, cleaning them, cooking them. I couldn't even watch. But tough times make tough women, as Paige likes to say, and now I help her with the food. My hands look like a man's hands.

Originally, Paige wanted to take us in the direction of Minnesota or Wisconsin, but the day after we crossed into Kansas, we saw another cloud of smoke to our east. We were past Wichita, but not close enough to see Kansas City burning, so we didn't know why there would be so much smoke . . . at least not until we ran into this awful-looking walker who had come from that direction. His face was red and shiny, and one of his eyes was nearly swollen shut. His bald head bubbled with blisters.

"What happened to you?" Paige asked him.

"Wolf Creek," he croaked. "Nuclear hell."

"Do you need help?" I asked him, shielding the boys behind me. "Where are you going?"

"Cibola," he said, and walked on.

After that we veered westward, even though the ground became drier and the air hotter. The idea was to find a place far away from a nuclear plant, in the plains or in the mountains, but there's no way to know for sure where all of them are.

I can't believe we've been walking so long. Paige thinks we're almost to Nebraska. I remember telling Skylar how a woman would never be able to make it alone in a world like this, and just look at us now: Paige and I have walked something like 500 miles together, taking care of two boys, and we're still alive. Also, the supernova seems brighter than ever, especially at night. But after it sets, there are so many stars in the sky it feels like we're in space.

I guess I should also put this in here: Paige has killed two people so far, both men.

The first was a nasty fellow who snuck into our camp and tried to steal our backpacks. Paige doesn't sleep the way you think of normal sleep . . . any sound wakes her up. Like sometimes the wind wakes her up. Anyway, she walked the man away from our camp so the boys didn't have to watch.

The second guy was perched above us on a small hill just east of Enid. I'm the one who spotted him. I think he was trying to steal supplies from people who passed by, and maybe this worked with others, but Paige drew her handgun so quickly the man never saw it coming. The sound of his body hitting the ground was awful and the impact left his head pointing away from his body in a direction that wasn't natural.

I think I'm in love with Paige, especially for the way she has taken care of the boys (and let's be honest, the way she has taken care of me). The first time we kissed, it wasn't even her idea. We were sitting together beside the glowing embers of a fire, after our first hot meal in three days, and the sleeping boys looked so peaceful. I couldn't help myself. I leaned forward and pressed my lips to hers.

And when I did, the entire world opened up, a reality so powerful I couldn't understand why I hadn't seen it sooner. Never in my life, not with Seth or Dan or the three boys I slept with in college, have I enjoyed the body-shaking desire I feel for Paige. It seems impossible, in a world where true love is a luxury, to have found her. But I did. And what I feel is more fundamental than lust. Paige is the engine that gets me from one day to the next. Every morning, I wonder what new challenge or reward we'll encounter. Maybe that sounds earnest, like the end to a cheesy movie, but I know my feelings are authentic because I let her read my entire journal. I never imagined I would open myself like that to anyone.

I miss Seth a lot. We were married for many years, and you don't disconnect such a profound experience from your life overnight. But I know he's in a better place. Seth was not a happy man, not even on his best days.

He suffered through terrible darkness that he didn't share until it was too late, and I think that's why he was willing to sacrifice himself for us.

During our big talk, the day of the pulse, he made it clear he had never cheated on me. But just because there was no woman doesn't mean he was faithful. He lived every single day with someone who wasn't me, treated her to lavish trips, to glamorous dinners and free drinks and fancy hotel suites. He drained our shared bank account and stole money from his father. Maybe the depression wasn't his fault, but Seth still shouldn't have hidden it from me.

If you're wondering, I still hear the ringing in my ears. I was as surprised as anyone to find out it wasn't just me, but knowing that made it easier to adjust. It's always there. I can hear it if I pay attention. Most of the time, though, I don't even notice.

And I don't know if it makes me see better or hear better or think better, but I'll tell you this much: I can shoot almost as well as Paige now, and she's been practicing her whole life.

We're camped off the road a bit, just north of a town called Phillipsburg, and I'm writing this by the fading sunlight. Paige is napping next to me. Brandon's sleep has been restless, and I was about to check on him, but he just sat up and looked at me. You can't imagine my relief.

"Mom," he said. "Where are we?"

I told him we would be in Nebraska tomorrow.

"That's cool," he said.

Now he's smiling. Watching me write this. My heart is so warm and full.

"Where will we go after that?" he just asked.

I haven't felt this much hope in probably my whole life.

FORTY-ONE

t was easier to feed himself after Thomas left Skylar with the men in Kiowa Village.

But it wasn't easy to live with the idea that he was somehow broken, that years of emotional abuse from his mother had turned him into an unworthy romantic partner.

It was true that the best place for any baby to survive this awful new world was in the protective embrace of a community, but not being involved at all left Thomas feeling impotent and worthless. The right thing to do wasn't always the best thing for you personally.

He killed the occasional rabbit or squirrel and caught just enough fish to keep his hunger in check. If he could avoid digging into his stores of rice until winter, there was a decent chance he could survive indefinitely in this new world.

In the bed at night, Thomas imagined Skylar beside him, her form cupped into his. He imagined waking up next to her, basking in the glow of her beaming smile. And even if Thomas wasn't earnest enough to believe he loved her, he was sure with time he could. If nothing else he wanted to provide for her, protect her, to be a father to their unborn child.

A week ago one of the desperate hunters had wandered to the cabin and tried to get in. Thomas had been lying on the couch, half asleep, when he heard the front door rattling. At first he'd been seized with hope, with the idea that Skylar had come back, and he scrambled to the window to see who was there. Instead he found a bulky man in a pink golf shirt and plaid shorts. The man's hands were trembling. He reached again for the doorknob and tried turning it. He threw his weight against the door and turned the knob again. That's when Thomas knocked on the window with his pistol and pointed it at the man's head.

After that, no one else came by. At least not until now. Not until you.

* * *

"You know what's funny?" I say to Thomas while he pours dried potato flakes into boiling water.

"What could possibly be funny about this, Aiden?"

"I've been watching the lake for more than a week now and refugees are crawling all over the place. Up and down the shoreline, every cabin has had to fight off multiple break-in attempts. Several of these intruders have been wounded or killed. But you sit here and make powdered mashed potatoes and don't have to worry about a thing."

Thomas carves a spoonful of those potatoes and tosses it onto a plate. He makes a second plate and offers one of them to me.

"My pick?" I ask.

"Of course."

By now I've been on the run for many days, and even though I've snuck into two cabins (and killed six people in the process), I'm still hungry. I wolf down the potatoes in seconds and desperately need a drink. You know how it gets when you eat a bunch of sticky stuff and can't swallow.

Thomas is stirring two glasses of lemonade mixed from individual sugar-free packets. When he hands me one, I drink it in four large gulps, desperate to wash down the potatoes.

"So how do you do it?" I eventually ask him. "How do you keep refugees away from your cabin? Did you use your screenwriting skills to build some kind of force field around this place?"

Thomas smiles like he knows something I don't. I hate that fucking look. Only a person who thinks he's better than you smiles like that.

"If you really have so much power, why not fix all this shit? Put the world back to the way it was?"

"What makes you think it's me who keeps people away from the cabin?" he asks. "How do you know it isn't you?"

I blink. This is something I hadn't considered.

"In my first film," Thomas says, "the main character, who was me, always managed to avoid danger when it grew too close. He never got a speeding ticket. He never showed up on security cameras. Since the whole film was told from his point of view, the story wouldn't work if he got into impossible trouble. Plus, I didn't want those things to happen to me."

"Makes sense."

"An ensemble, omniscient piece leaves room for characters to die or otherwise meet their end. A first-person story only works when the protagonist makes it to the last scene."

"Enough with the artsy-fartsy philosophical crap. Just tell me if you wrote all this."

"I'm not completely sure, but I think this might be *your* story."

"That sounds like a politician's answer to me. And I don't like politicians."

"Let me put it another way: Since the pulse, have you run into any barrier that couldn't be overcome?"

It's a fair question. I rewind my memory, back to the carnage at the warehouse, to the journey to get there, back to the miraculous appearance of Ed's pickup, to the evening when I killed not just Mitch but his lover, back to when I convinced Jimmy we should look for a warehouse in the first place, back to Keri's loft, where I drank lemon vodka and ravaged her like a porn star might, back all the way to that night at Cinnamon when Jimmy paid twenty thousand dollars for a night of debauchery most men will never know . . .after reviewing all this, I realize I've walked through this fantastical story almost unimpeded. Which is ironic, since before the pulse I hadn't caught a single break my entire life.

"You're saying you wrote all this for me?"

"I don't know," Thomas says. "I don't think we'll ever know."

"But if what you just said is true, I should be able to do anything I want. Like, I could kill you right now and everything would be A-OK."

"Maybe, but even a first-person story ends eventually. And if the writer is any good, the ending you receive is the one you deserve."

"Even after I murdered a hundred people on the lawn of the DC?"

"If the writer is any good," Thomas says again.

That fucking smile is still on his face, that look of arrogance. He takes a bite of mashed potatoes and watches me carefully. He drinks a swallow of lemonade. Mine is mostly gone, but I pick it up and suck down what's left.

Except now I notice it doesn't taste right. It's too bitter. It smells like almonds.

"What the fuck did you put in my drink?"

"It's crazy what you can find in a cabin like this," he says. "Fishing rods. Dry goods. Propane. It's almost unbelievable."

As I wait for him to go on, a strange sensation threads into my arms and legs, as if the muscles in them have turned to stone. I look at my hands. They don't feel like mine. My fingers won't move. My arms and legs and my whole body suddenly gasps for air.

"Even sodium cyanide," Thomas says.

"But how did you—"

A thick tube of molten goo rises in my throat. I can't speak. My body begins to shudder violently. My insides seem to crumple, as if my entire being has become a human windpipe being choked. I can't breathe, I can't think, I can't kill him.

I can't fucking BREATHE . . .

"You murdered a bunch of hungry kids and parents on the lawn of the DC, you sick bastard. The world has had enough of your kind making the rest of us suffer."

So maybe Thomas isn't a good writer after all. Maybe he's a talentless hack who only ever writes his deepest desires hoping to make them come true.

"And even if it's not your fault, even if you can't help the way you are, we certainly shouldn't give you the tools to hurt anyone else."

Or maybe this is the ending I truly deserve. Really, at this point, the decision is yours.

Whichever way you lean, it won't change the outcome for me. I've reached the end of the road, the last step, the most electrifying moment of my miserable life.

* * *

Every day the sun rose and the supernova rose and Thomas ate rabbits and birds and fish. He sat on the back porch and watched the sun set. He watched the supernova set. There was a row of bookshelves between the kitchen and the den, and one afternoon he took down a novel and tried to read it. The first character in the story was a fellow named Tawakoni Jim, which made him chuckle, since Tawakoni was the name of the lake keeping him alive. But when, in the first chapter, a town was obliterated by a giant tornado, Thomas returned the book to its shelf. He saw no point in reading about death when death was no longer an abstract, faraway concept but a reality he lived with every day.

Instead, to pass the time, he took naps in the living room or maybe the back porch. Sometimes he dreamed half his body was standing on a rocky shoreline, while the rest of him stood on a dinghy tied to the shore by a rope. Invariably he would take out a knife and cut the rope, which left part of him floating away on a small and unstable watercraft while the rest of him watched from the solid mass of dry land. The floating part of him knew the dinghy could capsize at any moment, so he reached for the shore, hoping to be saved. But the version of him on stable ground was afraid to help. Was afraid of drowning in the water. So Thomas was left with a choice: risk safety to bring the halves together again, or stand there and watch as he was ripped apart forever.

Had Aiden really shown up here? Had Thomas murdered him with cyanide? Had he buried the body in a shallow grave behind the cabin? The answer was there if he wanted it—all he had to do was grab the shovel and dig. But Thomas couldn't decide which discovery would be worse: a rotting corpse or smooth, unbroken ground.

The details of Aiden's surprise visit were still fresh in his mind. It didn't seem like an incident he would have imagined. But Thomas was desperately lonely, hungry all the time, and couldn't ignore the possibility that he had hallucinated the entire episode. For that matter he could still be dreaming. Maybe he'd run out of food weeks ago and was lying in bed while his body consumed itself, suffering through the last, surreal moments of this incomprehensible life.

He thought about his mother. He thought about his high school crush on Natalie. Had he liked Natalie for who she was, or had he invented a version of her to counterbalance his mother's anger? Had it been the same with Sophia? Was Skylar a real person or manifestation of biological need?

Probably it didn't matter. If you could accept the past, if you could recognize the person you had become, you could arm yourself with tools to make new and better decisions now and in the future. Whatever had driven his mother's anger, whether she had created those circumstances or inherited them, Thomas was not obligated to perpetuate the cycle.

Today, he could decide to remain in this unchanging daily grind, this lonely march toward death. He could try to put the world back to the way it was. Or he could boldly point his life in a completely new direction.

One day when both suns had set, when he went inside to lie down, Thomas noticed in the shadows of flickering candlelight a black shape sitting atop the row of bookshelves. At first he thought it was a small safe, or a toolbox, but when he used a stepladder to get a better look, he realized the shape was not a safe or a box at all.

It was a manual typewriter. A black Underwood typewriter that weighed a ton and might have been a century old.

A little more searching revealed half a ream of blank white paper, and when he loaded a sheet, and typed his own name, he discovered an ink strip in working order.

You could never know if what you believed to be real actually was. What mattered was what you did with the reality you had been granted.

Thomas rolled the paper to the middle of the page, centered the text, and lay his fingers on the keys.

Even if there would be no more films for a while, that didn't mean he couldn't write. Stories had been told on stage centuries before the camera was invented. This made Thomas remember a novel he read once, where a troupe of actors, twenty years after a global flu pandemic, traveled from town to town, performing, hoping to keep art alive. Hoping to inject a little humanity into a world that had lost so much of it.

He typed HOUSE OF THE RISING SUN.

He typed SETTING - AIRPORT, MORNING

He wrote until candlelight was overcome by pink sunshine streaming through the windows.

He wrote until the sun had risen high into the sky, until he could feel its heat beating on the roof.

When he was done, when he was staring at a short stack of typed pages, Thomas knew there was something he could offer the town of Kiowa Village after all.

He put on shoes and grabbed his gun and hid his stores of rice and canned goods in the spot where the floorboards were loose (so his supplies wouldn't walk away a second time). He tucked the script under his arm and headed for the door.

That's when he heard footfalls on the porch. Someone was outside.

Thomas watched and waited. He imagined he could hear seconds ticking by, each one like the sound of a typebar striking a sheet of paper.

And then he heard it, finally, a sound so friendly and out of place that Thomas could hardly believe it had happened: Someone had knocked on the door.

He approached slowly, his hand on the butt of his gun. He turned the knob and stood behind the door as it opened.

"Where are you going?" asked Skylar, who was wearing a blue shirt Thomas had never seen, and who was visibly pregnant.

"To see you," he said.

"I'm glad to hear that. Because I've been waiting."

"You have?"

She nodded. She was trying to hold back tears and failing miserably.

"I choose life," Skylar said, and stepped into his waiting arms.

AUTHOR'S NOTE

Nearby supernovae are extraordinarily rare, and the electromagnetic effects one might have on the Earth are far from certain. But the danger of losing electrical power and devices is real. An EMP attack or coronal mass ejection (CME) from the sun could disable large swaths of the electrical grid, and many electronic devices would likely be damaged or destroyed. Earth narrowly avoided a direct hit by a CME in July 2012, and some scientists estimate a twelve percent chance of it happening for real in the next ten years.

In *House of the Rising Sun*, I leaned on dramatic license to upend the lives of my characters. An actual event might be less severe. And certainly the aftermath of an EMP would unfold more gradually than in this novel. I intentionally compressed the timeline to maintain narrative momentum.

Still, you don't have to be a hardcore prepper to give yourself a chance to survive. A little planning can go a long way, even if you don't want to buy a bunch of name-brand gear.

Some housekeeping notes: The Food Pyramid at 81st and Yale no longer exists, at least not in this timeline. There is no Walmart DC in the location described, but the layout of my fictional one is based on real facilities and mostly accurate. I don't know what's on the 53rd floor of the Empire State Building, where Skylar's dad works, and Google was not very helpful there. Lakewood Village was selected as a setting for its location and is not the enclave of *nouveau riche* mansions it seems to be in the novel. Cinnamon, where Keri works, is completely invented.

Most other geographical errors you may find are intentional or immaterial to the story.

Blaise, who directs Thomas and his group to the Walmart DC, was inspired by the second track on Godspeed You! Black Emperor's EP *Slow Riot for New Zero Kanada*. This song is built around the audio interview of a real man in Providence, Rhode Island who called himself Blaise Bailey Finnegan III, an apparent alias inspired by Blaze Bayley, former singer for the band Iron Maiden. The quote at the beginning of this novel is part of a long interview (basically a rant) about a looming apocalypse not unlike the one that occurs in the pages of this book. A few lines of dialogue on pages 294 - 295 resemble bits of this rant as well.

Finally, if this is the sort of thing that interests you: I conceived this story in 2010 as a way to write a post-apocalyptic novel that didn't feature zombies or viruses (imagine that!) or an imminent asteroid impact. It became *House of the Rising Sun* when I realized a supernova could become my story's inciting incident. But the manuscript did not become a novel until 2016, in the months leading up to U.S. Presidential election. Though I expected one candidate to win, I built the world of this novel with the other outcome in mind, and I'd love to know how you feel about it. Please visit www.richardcox.net/HOTRS to share your thoughts.

Richard Cox is the author of five novels. He lives in Tulsa, Oklahoma with his wife and two daughters. In his spare time he likes to hit bombs.